BECKER'S RING

Also by Steven Martin Cohen

Seven Shades of Black

BECKER'S
RING

Steven Martin Cohen

CROWN PUBLISHERS, INC.   NEW YORK

Published by Crown Publishers, Inc., 201 East 50th Street, New York,
New York 10022. Member of the Crown Publishing Group.

Random House, Inc. New York, Toronto, London, Sydney, Auckland

CROWN is a trademark of Crown Publishers, Inc.

Manufactured in the United States of America

Design by June Bennett-Tantillo

Library of Congress Cataloging-in-Publication Data
Cohen, Steven Martin
Becker's ring / Steven Martin Cohen.—1st ed.
p.   cm.
I. Title.
PS3553.04334B4   1996
813'.54—dc20   95-30282
                                          CIP
ISBN 0-517-70077-8

10   9   8   7   6   5   4   3   2   1

First Edition

This book is dedicated to Barry Greene,
who, in fact, does weird things to plants.

Acknowledgments

I would like to thank the following people, who freely provided technical assistance, guidance, advice, insight, anecdotes, trivia, moral support, their ears or other body parts, or simply their time: Steffie Brooks, Barry Greene, Dr. Marc Bodow, Dr. Jay Fogelman, David Jacobs, Diana Gietl, Joe Tumang, Deirdre Donnaly, D.V.M., Larry Segan, Holgar Gruenert, Dr. Paul P. Calle, Dr. James Grimes, Nina Jachnowitz, Dr. Frank Chiarulli, David Ernst, Lynn Rhatigan, Lieutenant James Tuminaro Jr., Barbara Jaye Wilson, Bob Zimmerman, Bob Moore, Jane Prendergast, Peter Stathatos, Bob (the Guru) Cohen, VON LMO, Jeff Virgo, Dawn Lamb, Lori Shields, Marc Segan, Dr. Francine Segan, Detective Michael Houlihan, Detective Richard Quelch, John Chan, Rondal R. Bridgemon Jr., Stephen Wilkowski, Blanche Cohen, Carmine DeSena, Neil Patterson, Ed Brown, Joel Runes, Marc Rubin, Jon Walas, Joan Teshima, Anne Teshima (my fiancée, who listened to all my ravings and still decided to marry me), my agent, Barbara-J Zitwer (who listened to all my ravings, and still decided to represent me). Some people were quite helpful but wisely chose to remain anonymous—thanks for lending a hand.

I can't begin to offer the necessary thanks to Ann Patty (aka Aunt Patty), my editor, who guided me through the necessary revisions as this book solidified into a fully error-corrected stream of ones and zeros. Thanks a million.

Your ill child,
Steve

The characters and situations in this book are solely a product of the author's imagination, and if there is any similarity between these characters and situations and any characters and situations in real life, it is purely coincidental, and too damn bad.

Pounding Drumsticks

At four o'clock in the morning, just as the bars were closing, a car drove north on Manhattan's West Side Highway. The traffic was light on this particular spring Thursday, and the potholes were kind to the aging suspension of this rusting '77 Chevy Nova wearing New York plates. A cool breeze blew off the Hudson River into the open driver's side window, carrying with it the scent of fresh marine air lightly seasoned with diesel oil fumes. The clicking of the engine valves slowed as the car decelerated onto the Ninety-sixth Street exit ramp. Not a soul could be seen on this landscape of late-night urban desolation. The car slowly idled eastward, past a burned-out wreck that had been in the same charred spot on the grass since summer the year before.

The old two-door sedan came to rest inside the tunnel of an overpass. The shift lever was delicately worked out of the drive position and into the park position on the loose steering column. The amplified engine noise reverberated in the semicircular cross section of the fifty-foot-long crumbling cement and steel-girder cavity. The passenger door opened, and the body was kicked out onto the broken glass and litter covering the urine-soaked sidewalk. As the car rolled away, the body lay there lifelessly, slumped over a curb on its back, arms outstretched, legs spread wide.

Moments later, the arms moved, because this white male body was not dead. The anesthetic was simply beginning to wear off. While he didn't know it yet, the man had been unconscious for the past two weeks. The outside stimuli of the world slowly crept into his heavily medicated brain, which fought its way back to consciousness. His legs moved. His left arm slid through the shards of glass. He emitted a squeaky noise through his nose. He was beginning to exit the dream state, which was the closest to consciousness he'd been since he last walked about on the streets, almost like a normal person, doing the things normal people do, almost.

Ramon and his younger brother Julio were both pushing .4 percent blood-alcohol level. Julio's divorce had just gone through, and Ramon had taken him out to celebrate his freedom from the bitch by poisoning him with cheap whiskey. Like real men, they downed their shots after last call while laughing themselves nearly to the point of tears. They still had some energy, so they decided to mosey on down to the river and blow a joint before calling it a night. They stumbled west on Ninety-sixth Street, laughing and slurring their speech. As they told and retold the same stories, they approached the overpass and saw the silhouette of a figure moving in the tunnel.

"Dat dude drunker den we are, man," Ramon told his brother while still laughing. "Look at dat dude."

The figure in the tunnel began flailing its arms wildly. It smashed down on a hubcap, and the loud metallic noise startled the approaching brothers, and they froze in their tracks while watching from the other side of the street.

"Shit," Julio said. "He *all* fucked up. Look at dem arms. . . ."

The man was now fully conscious, but still on his back. He held his arms up in front of his face, and what he saw horrified him beyond anything he'd ever imagined could be possible. He screamed maniacally through his nose. With every exhaled breath, he screamed the screams of gurgling panic mixed with the frantic sobbing of horror—the horror of acknowledging something radically different about his body. He violently shook his head from side to side. He screamed as if his mouth had been taped shut. He banged the back of his head on the broken glass of the pavement—up and down, up and down—pulverizing shards into slivers. He spasmodically rolled into the street as if he were being electrocuted from within. His screaming terrified the two drunk brothers, who watched helplessly from twenty feet away. The man rolled onto his stomach and rose to his knees, shaking his arms in the air like a grizzly bear. His face puffed out like Dizzy Gillespie and his eyes bulged as he emitted as much noise through his nose as he could.

"Shit man!" Ramon yelled. "He ain' got no mouth! Julio! Get da fuck outta here!"

The mouthless man rose to his feet, became dizzy, then fell back to the ground. He was still heavily sedated, and would be for quite some time. He crawled in circles, howling like a wounded beast. Then he instinctively crawled eastward, toward civilization, whimpering in his own personal nightmare.

The usual number of belligerent homeless people had to be thrown out of the all-night deli on Broadway, just south of Ninety-sixth Street. Other than that, things had actually been calmer than average until something very strange stumbled through the doors. Mr. Barsto had seen a lot of strange things stumble through those doors over the years, but he'd never seen anything quite like this. He watched curiously, because he'd never seen such a facial deformity. The man had both a wild and glazed look in his eyes, and chilling, bloodcurdling noises radiated from his head. Mr. Barsto moved closer to the telephone because it looked like trouble. It sounded like trouble. It was trouble.

The man raved and gurgled, out of control. Mucus dribbled from a hole on the left side of his cheek. It oozed through his short beard, down his chin, and onto the floor. The crazy man pounded his arms on the counter as spit and viscous fluids sprayed from the hole in his face. His jaw moved up and down as if he were chewing something, and it produced an unnatural, disgusting sucking sound. Then he pounded the counter more violently and raved unintelligible, horrible, panicky sounds.

Mr. Barsto now knew it was time to dial 911. He tried to stay outside the direct line of sight as he whispered to have the police please hurry. He hoped this monster would leave his store without seeing his face. The crazy man waved his arms in the air and pounded the merchandise displays, sending things flying to the floor.

"Get out of here!" Barsto yelled. "Get the fuck out of here! I just called the cops! Now go! GO!!! GET THE FUCK OUTTA HERE!!!"

The man with the dripping hole on the side of his face became even more frantic. He trumpeted, spit, sucked, and pounded the counter until the glass broke. And then he continued to pound the shattered counter with his bleeding partially healed stumps—the stumps where only two weeks earlier his hands used to be.

A car merged from Rock Hall Road onto Doughty Boulevard, heading toward the Atlantic Beach Bridge at 5:30 in the morning. Instead of continuing straight, to the bridge, it slowed to a crawl, then, without signaling, turned left just before the Seagirt Avenue overpass, onto a dirt road.

And that dirt road led through the tall weeds to the brackish water of Bannister Creek, where the Inwood and Far Rockaway blacks would catch their porgies and undersized fluke by day, and it was a spot where one could quietly park by night—a perfect time-share arrangement until the town would decide someday to award a gratuitous contract and put up a fence.

The car stopped next to a pile of sand, and the headlights were extinguished. The driver got out and began emptying box after box of sand onto a dirt pile—boxes on the front seat, boxes on the backseat, and boxes in the trunk. With each unloaded box of soil, the suspension springs pushed the sedan farther away from the ground, until the entire payload was emptied.

For the past seven months, this had been a regular routine. It was funny how the pile grew quickly at first, then after a while, it grew much more slowly as it took on professional-looking girth, just like the piles the men with hydraulic machinery leave.

With all the boxes of soil emptied, the driver got back into the car and drove away. Exactly twenty-one minutes later, the same car reappeared and emptied another carload of dirt.

In a basement workshop in a private home somewhere, a table saw screamed as the blade ripped through a two-by-six, the long way, to clean up the edge a bit, and to develop a good perpendicular surface. This piece of wood was part of a project, a project to build a unique tool, the likes of which had never been seen by human eyes.

The lights burned bright, into the wee hours of the morning, as pencil marks, combination squares, power tools, and human ingenuity brought an idea from concept to existence through the magic of hard work and single-minded determination.

A six-foot length of wire mesh was uncoiled from a four-foot-wide roll and cut with a pair of tinner's snips. The mesh was flattened out and pressed up against a vertical dirt wall which had been sculpted and smoothed to a precise shape. The rectangle of mesh overlapped an adjacent piece of similar mesh by one foot and was held in place using one-foot-long lengths of rigid wire with a loop bent into the end, similar to the shape of tent pegs, only these pegs were pushed into the wall, horizontally, rather than into the ground, vertically. Several gallons of ferro-cement were mixed and slathered onto the wire mesh, till all the metal was covered. After this first coat, the wall looked like stucco, and was left to dry. When dry, another coat of ferro-cement would be applied, then another, and then another, till the wall was good and strong, forming a shell—a growing shell which slowly encompassed an internal volume as the pages of the calendar turned.

3   Roosevelt Hospital

"Dr. Spellman, please report to the ER immediately," the announcement over the intercom squawked. "Dr. Spellman, please report to the ER immediately."

"I think Spellman's sleeping," an orderly told Dr. Aboonda. "He just got off a forty-hour shift. He may not answer the page."

"Please get him, now!"

"I'm on my way, Doctor." The orderly jogged off to Spellman's secret hiding place.

Back in the emergency room, another street crazy had been strapped to a table by a gaggle of big strong men dressed in white. His arms were restrained. His legs were restrained. His chest was restrained. And a pillow had been placed under his head so he would not sustain further injuries to the back of his skull, which was caked with layers of dried blood, pebbles, and glass in his hair and skin.

The monitoring sensors were being pasted to his skin as he squirmed and wiggled like a bluefish flopping about on the deck of a party boat.

Nothing had prepared the staff for what they saw there on the restraint slab. One nurse had to leave the ER to regain her composure. She'd seen all types of carved-up, bullet-riddled emergencies in her six months in the ER, but for some reason, this particular medical specimen touched a raw nerve.

Dr. Aboonda wore a mask so he would not inadvertently breathe the airborne spray that spurted aperiodically, like Old Faithful in menopause, from the stomalike hole that, he surmised, had been surgically placed there, deliberately. He'd never seen anything like it. He wanted Dr. Spellman's opinion before he medicated this gentleman whose heart was about to explode from the excitement. His blood pressure was somewhere in the stratosphere, and his heart rate was topping two hundred. He possessed all the outward signs of a dust-crazed psychotic, but Dr. Aboonda knew something was different about this one, something beyond the obvious.

Dr. Spellman entered to witness a geyserlike fit of spraying, muscular contractions, and pleas for help that almost solidified into moaning words. He slipped the mask on his face and walked closer. He examined the stumps where the man's hands used to be. The patient violently shook his arms within the limited confines of the restraints. Spellman looked at the area of the lips as squeaky, muffled screams and moans bellowed from clogged nostrils and the spurting blowhole. The fine suture scars were still clearly visible. This had been a professional job of surgery. . . .

Dr. Spellman patted the blowhole in the cheek with a large wad of gauze to absorb the mucus and fluids so he could get a closer look at the craftsmanship. The patient's tongue jammed into the man-made circular mouth, trying to penetrate or enlarge the three-quarter-inch sucking and blowing hole. There was still scar tissue at the two bleeding amputation sites on the arms, and on the lips, and at the little blowhole.

Dr. Spellman turned to Dr. Aboonda and said, "I've never seen anything like it before. Looks like all this happened two or three weeks ago. Jesus! Whoever did this knew what he was doing. Look at that suturing! Welp, use standard psychotic-reaction procedures. Also, call the police—I'd like them to have a look-see. Some rogue physician's clearly gone over the edge. I'm going back to bed now. Any problems, you know where I'll be—"

"No," Dr. Aboonda interrupted, "I don't know where you'll be. I—"

As Dr. Spellman was leaving the room, he raised his hands because he'd heard and seen enough for one night. "I knew I should have taken the train back tonight. Jesus H . . ."

An IV drip was started, and the vital signs of the handless man with the blowhole in his head slowly moved into more normal territory. Once again, this mysterious man was sedated, and under a doctor's care.

4   Another Late Night

Lt. Brenton Kramer entered the hospital and dangled his gold shield in front of the security guard, who was half-asleep at his second job. Brent walked to the elevators with the slightest hint of a limp. He felt a little stiffer than usual; perhaps it was the weather; perhaps it was a sympathetic reaction to being inside a hospital elevator again —the smell of the place, the ambience, the long hallways of late-night low-level activity humming in the dull, flickering dazzle of endless fluorescent fixtures—that smell again, only stronger this time, and that middle-of-the-night state of mind that slows even the most active brain to a hypnotic meandering.

Thoughts of Tammy drifted in and out of focus, and he knew he would have to make up with her, sooner or later. It might as well be sooner. As he walked past a dried smear of human shit on the wall, he figured he would call her up and offer to take her someplace special for dinner. Marriage was a great institution, as long as Tammy was in a good mood.

Brent automatically stopped in front of a door, ran his fingers through his slightly graying hair, then entered the observation room, where he was met by Dr. Aboonda. "Over here, Lieutenant," Dr. Aboonda said. "This is what I was talking about."

With squinting eyes, the lieutenant examined the curious thing before him. The patient was wheezing through his blowhole. In with the good air; out with the bad; in with the good air; out with the bad—every breath an effort. Brent watched the cheeks puff out when this pathetic thing exhaled, and compress hard against the teeth when he inhaled.

"He is much calmer than he was when he first arrived in the ER."

Lieutenant Kramer lifted the limp arm with his hand, looking closely at the end of the stump, as if he could see through the bandages straight to the bones. He reached across the patient's body to examine the other stump. The man twisted and fought the restraining straps in a halfhearted, drug-subdued thrust, and the lieutenant let go. Even in sleep, the patient moaned in the pain of emotional torment. Lieutenant Kramer looked at the area of the lips. He quickly counted about sixty suture holes, thirty above where the top lip used to be and thirty below where the bottom lip used to be. He looked at the hole drilled in the man's cheek. Brent was clinically composed but speechless.

Lieutenant Kramer turned and was about to speak when the doctor said, "We found this note in his pocket," and handed a piece of paper to the lieutenant, who instinctively took it by the edges.

The typewritten note said:

INSTRUCTIONS FOR CARE AND
MAINTENANCE OF FREDDY LOPEZ

(1) He can no longer hold a knife or a
gun, and this is good. He can no longer
hold a fork or a toothbrush either, but
this is a small price to pay. Please
chop up Freddy's food into pieces small
enough to place in his mouth through the
feeding and respiration stoma. He can
drink his fluids through a straw.

(2) To prevent mouth infection and tooth
decay, please brush his teeth after
meals by inserting the toothbrush
through the stoma.

```
Other than (1) and (2), he is a
perfectly normal human being, and he
should live a perfectly normal life
span. He may have a little difficulty
getting dressed and undressed, but he
will adapt to his new life in time.
He is stable and will not hurt society
anymore.
```

Lieutenant Kramer lifted his eyes from the paper and gazed at the sedated creation before him. His eyes returned to the note, then he slipped the note into a Ziploc plastic bag. He glanced over to Dr. Aboonda and said, "How many people touched this note?"

"Only the nurse who checked his pockets. She gave the note to me, and I held it for you. You are thinking about the fingerprints, right?"

"Right," Kramer said. He then removed a large folded plastic bag from his pocket. "Dr. Aboonda, I want all his personal effects and his clothes placed in this bag."

"He is wearing his clothes, and there was nothing else in his pockets."

"He's sedated, right?"

"Yes, but—"

"Call some orderlies. I want his clothes for analysis. He won't be missing them."

Brent looked at the man's face while he waited for the muscle men to arrive. He glanced back at the note and said softly, "Freddy Lopez . . . who would want to do this to you?"

The patient's clothes were replaced with a hospital gown, and with that, Lieutenant Kramer turned to leave with his bags and his thoughts. He stopped for a moment at the door and said, "I'm going to have a police photographer here inside of three hours. Can you move him to the secure room?"

"Okay. We'll have him there before your photographer gets here," Dr. Aboonda replied.

"Good. By the way," Brent said as he glanced at the expanding and contracting facial tissue of Mr. Lopez, "his cheek is acting like a valve. He might inhale more easily if you put a spacer or some kind of bite plate in his mouth to keep his teeth apart. Even a piece of surgical tubing would work."

Dr. Aboonda's eyes opened wide at that thought. "That's a . . . very good idea, Lieutenant."

"Good. I'll send you my bill in the morning. One more thing. How soon will I be able to speak with him?"

"I would give him at least eight hours."

"I'll be here at fourteen hundred hours."

"What?"

"Two o'clock."

5   The Ninety-fourth Freddy

Chemistry is an analytical science when viewed from the theoretical textbooks spouting qualitative and quantitative analysis, stoichiometric relationships, transport phenomena, quantum mechanics, probability, and the like. But any practical chemistry is still an art, its roots extending way beyond the alchemist and the first ape ever to burn his furry little fingers on a hot rock.

Lieutenant Kramer knew he could have a microchemical sample analyzed by ten different labs and get ten different results. Of course, any lab could tell you the difference between a gram of coke and a gram of dog shit, but telling you the difference between a microgram of coke and a microgram of dog shit was quite a different matter. It was for this reason that Brent Kramer almost exclusively had his micro evidence analyzed at Riverview Research Labs, a private lab over on the West Side of Manhattan.

They had some of the most sensitive machinery in the country, and the chief engineer there was an artist, with a sixth sense for seeking out where the relevant molecules to a complex puzzle were hiding. Nigel Atkerson, the chief engineer at Riverview, was also a consultant to the police Crime Scene Unit, and he happened to be a close personal friend of Brent's. If a case was important enough, or interesting enough, or weird enough, Brent could have samples analyzed in hours rather than weeks—weeks being the norm with many of the overworked police labs. The chief engineer at Riverview was also a lunatic, but Brent resisted this personal diagnosis as often as he could, choosing instead to use the word *eccentric*. In any event, this case clearly fell into the weird category, and he knew Nigel would find it an irresistible diversion from the deepest caverns of central Mexico, where he'd been for the past three weeks on vacation.

Brent called his friend at his home and reached the answering machine. "Nigel, my calendar says you should have returned from Mexico two days ago. If you're back, I've got a little job for you. You're gonna *love* this one. I . . . never mind. Just call me when you get in. In fact, why don't you meet me at the security desk of Roosevelt Hospital at fourteen hundred sharp today. . . . But you have to promise me that you won't laugh."

Brent shook his head as he sifted through printouts of the police reports extracted from the massive databases of both the City of New York Police Department and the FBI. There were presently ninety-three people by the name of Fred, Freddy, or Frederick Lopez incarcerated in the United States. As of three weeks previous, there had been ninety-four. Brent was as sure as Sherlock Holmes that the ninety-forth Freddy Lopez, aka *Zippy,* was restrained and under heavy sedation on a nice comfortable bed in Roosevelt Hospital, compliments of the city of New York.

The photo and fingerprints of Freddy Lopez were silently extruding from the rollers of Midtown North's brand-new plain-paper fax machine. With the new millennium just on the horizon, the lieutenant was pleased that some residual technology from the second half of the twentieth century was finally seeping into his precinct via the miracle of trickle-down economics and deficit spending.

Mr. Lopez had spent the last ten years and nine months at the Mt. McGregor facility, where he was sentenced to live for a period of between eleven and twenty years. He had shot two people, killing one in cold blood, although the charge had been reduced to involuntary manslaughter.

And the survivor was never really the same, plagued with paralysis and numerous medical problems as a result of a .38-caliber slug buried inoperatively inside the base of his brain. His life subsequently alternated between church and the bottle. The fact that he bore no malice toward the man who had killed his girlfriend and medically ruined his own life not only helped Mr. Lopez earn his release from prison, but was unequivocal proof that the bullet had, in fact, caused irreversible brain damage. In Brent's mind, it was still an open question as to which had done more damage: the bullet or the staggering effects of Christianity and alcohol.

According to the parole report, Freddy wasn't really such a bad guy, anyway. His advocates persuasively argued that since Freddy was on drugs when he shot the couple who stupidly refused to surrender their car to him, he wasn't responsible for his actions, and the hard-assed judge gave him a bum rap; he simply didn't belong in prison and posed no real threat to society.

Zippy, as they called Freddy in prison, worked hard in the prison laundry, probably because that was how drugs were smuggled into the facility. He studied karate and kick boxing. And he even learned to read, too. He'd only been in three major fights, and one of those fights had resulted in a dislocated shoulder of a guy who refused to be butt-fucked by *Zippy,* who was only in the mood for a little love after getting high. With prison space as competitive as admission to a four-year tuition-free university, other people needed Freddy's correctional slot more than he. Added to the four-odd months he had spent in jail awaiting his speedy trial, it was time to let him go.

The recommendation for his release went unchallenged, oddly enough, and Mr. Lopez was released after paying his debt to society. And that debt to society was precisely worth 3,925 days of Mr. Lopez's time, at a total cost of incarceration to the taxpayer of $341,312.48—slightly more expensive than one Ivy League education and a simple house in the suburbs!

Lieutenant Kramer often wondered why he was a cop at all. It was situations like this that crystalized the futility of it. He secretly knew that law enforcement was a catastrophic farce in its present form, but he enjoyed playing the game of cat and mouse. This was his own private secret, which he shared not even with his wife or his closest friends. He loved the challenge of tracking down people. Once he'd caught his man, though, he expected nothing from the courts. Brent, the man, knew that Mr. Lopez deserved a good old-fashioned biblical execution for committing murder, but Lt. Brent Kramer, the New York City detective, was now obligated to find Freddy's surgeon/stylist. But it went much deeper than obligation. This was an open invitation to engage in the only form of enterprise worth living for——other than sex and spelunking: to find a mentally disturbed needle in a mentally disturbed haystack.

He glanced up at the clock above his door and noticed the second hand quivering spasmodically somewhere between the eight and nine position, unable to make its way over the top. The position of the other hands were irrelevant; it was that damn second hand he wanted. He reached over to the pile of pink erasers by the phone on his desk, and threw one at the glass faceplate. As always, the second hand took the vibrational hint and continued on its circular journey, as it had been doing since before he was born, forty years earlier.

Brent smiled as he placed Mr. Lopez's fingerprints into a brand-new manila file folder. "We won't be needing these anymore," he said out loud to himself. He was attempting to see the picture in his sleep-deprived mind. He looked into the words of the note and knew someone had done his homework carefully—perhaps a vigilante, perhaps a do-it-your-selfer who had it out for Freddy Lopez personally, perhaps a relative of the victim he murdered, perhaps even the person who *bore him no malice*. All leads would have to be checked. This person must have had his eye on Freddy specifically, because it all seemed too coincidental to Brent. He smelled the sickness of the note, and he knew he was looking for a highly intelligent and determined madman—a madman with a dry sense of humor. Yes, it could prove to be a very interesting challenge, and Brent loved a good challenge.

Brent wanted to begin the analysis of the clothing and the note, but he was exhausted. It would have to wait till later in the day. He lay down on the couch in his office, with thoughts of his wife, Tammy, and within moments, he was asleep.

It was two minutes to two in the afternoon, and a short, stout woman in her early fifties, wearing a blue gown, attentively eavesdropped on a slim five-foot-eight-inch-tall man with jet black hair talking to the security guard in the front lobby of Roosevelt Hospital. The guard found Nigel Atkerson to be the most amusing thing to arrive in the more than thirty shifts on this boring job since he'd been released from prison for another parole violation.

". . . So this guy asks me why I always keep a pencil in my right ear," Nigel said. "I can tell the man's an idiot before he even opens his mouth. So I tell him that my penis normally points to the left. If I didn't counterbalance it with a weight on the right, I'd spend my entire fucking life walking in left-handed circles. . . ."

"Yeah, I got dat same problem myself," the guard replied.

"Perhaps you should move to the southern hemisphere. Left-handed circles up here sometimes become right-handed circles down there."

Nigel saw his friend Brent entering the lobby and so he quickly excused himself from the laughing security guard and followed Brent to the elevators. "So what's this about, Brent?"

"You have to promise me that you won't laugh," Brent said with a falsely serious face as he grabbed Nigel by the arm. "You look great."

"I feel great. I really needed to get away."

The woman who'd been watching Nigel talking to the guard followed the two men into the elevator just as the doors were closing. She looked the two men up and down carefully, as if she were checking them for insects. Then, as Nigel was about to speak, she said, "What time is it, mister?"

Without skipping a beat, Nigel replied, "One-fifty-nine."

"How do you know what time it is without looking at your watch?"

"It's a talent I have."

"Do you masturbate?" she then asked, as if it were the most natural utterance in the world to say to a pair of complete and total strangers.

Brent slowly placed his hand over his face and forced himself to look at the ceiling, because he knew if he saw any part of Nigel's face, he would burst out laughing.

Nigel, while inwardly imploding with a million independent potential sarcastic responses, managed to keep a straight face long enough to say, *"Aaaa . . .* what do you want me to promise I won't laugh at? Not that there isn't plenty around this nuthouse to laugh at. By the way, what did they do, clone a duplicate of Dr. Ruth here out of an old Pap smear?"

Brent continued to stare at the ceiling. "I'm going to show you a medical anomaly." Then he leaned over to Nigel so the psycho lady wouldn't overhear him. "It's a man-made anomaly."

"This is not another Rorschach test, is it?"

"Well, almost."

"You didn't answer my question!" the lady insisted with her nasal voice.

Nigel looked at her and said, "Lady, yesterday, I had sex with a backhoe. And the day before that, I got off with a John Deere model JD-four-ten front-loading tractor; know what I mean?" Then he winked at her, as if they were both on the same channel.

The doors opened, and the two men quickly departed as the psycho lady said, "I thought so. You know," and then she screamed, "I CAN SPOT 'EM A MILE AWAY. YA HEAR THAT, A MILE AWAY!!!"

Nigel said to Brent, "I think that lady ought to be on some kind of medication—like potassium chloride."

"I thought the four-ten was the backhoe, not the front-loader."

"You're right. I better tell her I got the models mixed up or she won't sleep a winky-poo tonight. So are you gonna keep this a secret, or what?"

"Just follow me, and read this." He handed Nigel the police report of the Mr. Lopez he believed the handless man to be, then explained what he had learned about the criminal career of Freddy Lopez, aka Zippy!

"Zippy?" Nigel said. "His name is Zippy, like Zippy the Pinhead?"

"That's what the report says. Here." Brent handed Nigel a transcribed copy of the "care and maintenance" note.

"He is stable?" Nigel said. "Interesting nomenclature." Then his eyes suddenly lit up. "Say, how'd ya like to climb the George Washington Bridge tonight?"

"Nigel, I'm *not* climbing up the George Washington Bridge, at least not tonight!"

"The Verrazano?"

"No bridges. No caves. No sewers or abandoned subway tunnels. How about some of that soda bread you love so much?"

"Ehhhh . . ."

"I'm buying."

"Sold to the man with deep pockets. Soda bread it is. . . . You sure you wouldn't—"

"Nigel!" Brent sighed. "What do you know about deliberate mutilation?"

"Mutilation? Interesting question." Nigel became theatrical and overanimated with his hands. "Mutilation has played a *splendid* role in history. Now take your Catholics, for instance. The Catholics are big on religious mutilation. Saint Origen castrated himself. I personally think the man had a serious family problem, probably his mother, but you never know; it might have been those choirboys. Now Moses, on the other hand, he *almost* castrated himself. Personally, I just don't think he had the balls. But I think Moses figured there'd be big money in circumcision someday. You do see the fundamental difference between Catholics and Jews? I think Moses was just trying to set a good example, but he probably had a problem with his mother, too, 'cause nobody can convince me the whole thing boils down to a little smegma."

Brent was mildly amused. "Do you know anything a bit more contemporary, and maybe a little more secular?"

"All right. There's a disease called tricatillomania. It's a self-mutilation disease. People who rip and tear their skin off because it feels good, or they rip their own hair out—sometimes strand by strand, sometimes a wad at a time—or they deliberately puncture their skin with sharp objects. People who suffer from borderline personality disorder often indulge themselves in self-mutilation—like some of my ex-girlfriends. . . ."

"Yeah, they went out with you!"

"Some people like to purposely put their hands into rotating machinery because of some irresistible urge to know what would happen if they touched big meshing gears or blades or anything that can pinch or crush. It's just like modern democracy. Why?"

Lieutenant Kramer waved to a nurse behind a desk who pressed the button allowing access to the high-security private room with the door that could be opened only from the outside. "The gentleman in this room was brought here early this morning. . . ."

The patient was still restrained, and sleeping restlessly. His stumps were by his sides, secured in place, and his vital signs were still being electronically monitored. Nigel walked up to the strapped-up freak and stared at the suturing of the mouth. He carefully observed the stoma on the man's cheek and the surgical rubber tube taped in place to keep the teeth apart. He curiously looked at the endless coils of gauze terminating ten inches below the patient's elbows.

They stepped away from the bed. Nigel faced Brent and pressed his lips tightly together with his fingers, trying to imitate the way a man with his lips sewn shut might talk, and said, "Guess the note is correct. He *can't* lift a knife or a gun." Nigel continued normally, but with growing inflammation: "And if that motherfucker was still in prison, where he belongs, or dead, where he more belongs, *we* wouldn't be here examining a . . . a goddamn art project. That's what this is—somebody's goddamned senior project! I think what we have here is an example of the crowning achievement of the criminal justice system. You wanted me to promise not to laugh at him. Well Brent, I think he *is* funny; I think he's an example of exactly how far we've come as a culture. Not only do I want to laugh at him; I want the world to laugh at him. Maybe he could do his very own show—introducing, tonight, *The Freddy Lopez Show,* live from New York. Here's Zzzzzzippy!—with a rim shot— bing! He should be doing speaking tours. Dress 'im up in a lobster bib. Jam a pair of puppets on ol' stumpy there—I'll bet we could teach him ventriloquism. Maybe he could do stand-up. He could tour with Shari Lewis and Lamb Crop. Can't you just see *that* lovable face on the cover of *Time?* I personally think his left side shows his true character, don't you? I can see it now—the man who should have been executed by the state but was deliberately released to be deliberately modified by some clear-thinking person for the benefit of society at large." Nigel continued in a whisper, "Brent, they did us a favor. Why don't we just pack our bags and quietly ignore this one?"

Brent was quite used to Nigel's histrionic ravings and his intense anger at the system. He knew it was Nigel's way of letting off steam. "You think the person who did this was clear-thinking?"

"Crystal clear! The type of clarity that inspires concise, pre-meditated, deliberate action. The type of clarity that inspires *all* great work. Look at those stitches. Yes, the type of clarity that exists only in the mind of a madman—an artist! I like him already!"

"I'd like to keep the publicity on this one to a minimum if possible," Brent sighed.

"Why? Because it might be a royal embarrassment to your system? Brent, why are you still a cop? Weren't you having more fun when you were—"

"Please don't start this again with me. Look, he's moving. You woke him."

The patient began doing more than moving; he began moaning and spitting through the blowhole. His heart rate rose, but still within spec. His eyes opened and he began to cry as he rubbed his arms against the mattress to convince himself that his hands were still really gone, and that last night was not a nightmare. In the recently severed nerve endings of his wrists, he could still feel his fingers wiggling freely about, but no other input from reality could confirm these phantom sensations. He tried to open his mouth, and his sewn-up lips stretched like a drumhead. *"He yeeee* [Help me]," were the first coherently incoherent words he'd cried since his metamorphosis. It was a chilling, muffled, unarticulated sound. Nigel glanced at Brent, nonverbally communicating his intentions, then attempted to leave the room to get a nurse, but he found the door locked. Brent said, "Dial six-four to—" Nigel raised his index finger, indicating that he got the procedure.

Lieutenant Kramer looked down at the whimpering man and said, "Can you understand me?"

"Yeeee," the man sobbed while nodding. *"Wa wa wi weee* [What wrong with me]?" Mr. Lopez's words were muffled; all the sound of his speech radiated from his nose and the hole in his cheek. He was not quite used to speaking without a mouth or lips to articulate his words.

"Is your name Freddy Lopez?"

"Yeee. Wa wa wi weee [What wrong with me]??!!"

"I don't know," Brent said.

"Aye yie yeee," Freddy sobbed.

"Did you say, 'Untie me'?"

"Yeee."

"I'm afraid I can't do that yet, but we're getting someone who can. Look, Freddy, we're going to do everything we can to help you. My name is Lieutenant Kramer, and I'm a police officer. I would like to ask you some questions so we can find out what happened to you. Is that all right with you?"

"Yeee," Freddy cried as he looked into the lieutenant's eyes for comfort.

"Can you tell me anything about how this happened to you?"

"I don yo a ha-ya a eeee [I don't know what happened to me]." The *m*'s and *p*'s were impossible for him to pronounce, and clear liquid dripped from his nose and down his cheeks.

"Do you remember anything at all?"

"Yoooo [No]." He sounded like a cat mewing.

"What was the last thing that you *do* remember?"

"Aye yo yooooooow [I don't know] . . . *aaaaaaahhhhhhhhhhh-hoooooooooohhhhhhhh!"* Freddy began shaking his arms up and down within the confines of the straps. He thrust his tongue into the hole in his cheek. In his mind, he squeezed his hands into fists. And in his mind, he could feel a facsimile of such a neurological simulation being executed. But no confirmation in reality existed, or would ever exist, ever again. The disparity between the desire of his mind and reality was overwhelming, incomprehensible, and irrefutable. *"Eeeeeeeeeeeeeessssse! Heeeelll yeeee* [Help me]. *Aye yie yeee* [Untie me]!"*

Dr. Wally Spellman entered the room with Nigel and a nurse as Freddy was struggling with the restraints. Brent put his hand on Freddy's arm and sternly said into his ear, "Freddy, you've got to calm down or they're not going to let you out. Freddy, please take it easy." These words had an immediate calming effect on Mr. Lopez, more than any sedative could have had. "Hello, Wally," Brent said with a smile. Do you think we could remove the restraints on Mr. Lopez?" Freddy was now as much the model patient as he'd become the model prisoner during his appearance before the parole board.

Dr. Spellman hesitated for a moment, shrugged his shoulders, and said, "Sure, Lieutenant. Why not?" He wanted to be accommodating to the lieutenant, and he secretly calculated that if the patient became too unruly, the three men could probably overpower him, while not getting bitten by the patient's conveniently sealed-up mouth. A doctor in the Bronx had been bitten by an HIV-infected street crazy, and he subsequently became infected. It was more than a legitimate concern. Patient/doctor interactive protocol in questionable situations was now routine procedure.

The straps came off, and Mr. Lopez sat up in bed as Dr. Spellman cleaned up his face and began to examine him.

"Did he tell you anything?" Nigel asked Brent.

"Not yet. But his memory is probably still a bit foggy."

After Dr. Spellman's cursory exam, Brent and Nigel were left alone with Freddy Lopez, who was beginning to gain his composure.

"Freddy, we want to find the person or persons who did this to you. What was the last thing that you remember before this happened?"

Freddy's speech was nearly impossible to decipher, and he had to repeat his tormented noises dozens of times with different choices of words so he could be understood. Nigel taped a pencil to Freddy's right arm, but his exaggerated drunklike swirls on paper were even less coherent than his speech. Visually or verbally, he remembered nothing at first. But the lieutenant jogged his memory with question after question.

After Freddy Lopez had left prison, he took the bus to New York. He went to his friend Jimmy Sergeant's apartment on Fifth Street between avenues A and B, where he was to stay while he "got his shit together." He remembered getting high with Jimmy, which is about as close as he came to getting his shit together.

Nigel silently watched and listened to the almost-humorous interchange between Freddy and the lieutenant. Nigel felt a perverted excitement provoked by Freddy's medically altered condition, while simultaneously overcome with a conflicting compassion he found difficult to justify, especially in light of his expressed hatred for revolving-door justice, which had now been routinely extended to the crime of murder. The world was surely going mad. Nigel hated everything Freddy represented, up until the moment the suffering thing in straps began to act like a man rather than a restrained lump of flesh.

"What did you do after you got to Jimmy's house?" Brent asked.

He remembered hanging out. He remembered watching a little TV. And he remembered seeing his friend Louie. He and Louie had gone out to a bar to get drunk and try to pick up some punk rocker chicks. He remembered Louie going home, and he remembered walking home to Jimmy's place. He remembered it to be about two or three in the morning. . . .

. . . Yeah! I was walkin' home a Jimmy's, an' I felt like I was stab. I was stab in a back. Yeah, it was late. I was walkin', and thinkin'. Yeah. Then I feel like a stabbing pain in my back, like a ice pick or somethin'. That's it! Someone sneak up on me an' stab me in a back wit a knife. . . .

7   *Pfffffffft*

A dark figure sat quietly and patiently in a car parked under a broken streetlamp. Most of the streetlamps on the block were burned out. The Brownsville section of Brooklyn was not exactly high on the city's beautification or maintenance priority lists, and the decaying neighborhood proved this fact in a thousand different ways. Burned-out building after burned-out building made this place look more like Warsaw after World War II than just another neighborhood in just another borough. Arson was not only a regional industry here, but a way of life.

A man walked along the street with a bounce in his step and anger in his heart. He had every reason to be angry, though. All his old connections from before he went away were either dead, or in prison, too. And he'd just been ripped off by the new dudes, who sold him a gram of lidocaine instead of cocaine. It cost him a hundred bucks and he was pissed. He would get even with them. Nobody ripped off Jerome Lewis and got away with it! He would make those fuckers pay—one way or another. He rehearsed in his mind what he might do to them. He would probably just kill them as soon as he could manage to get hold of a gun. But all his old firearms contacts were either dead or doing time. How the neighborhood had changed in the past fifteen and one-half years.

Jerome was absorbed in his rage, with thoughts of revenge in his heart, as he crossed the bridge over the railroad tracks and continued down the deserted street. He heard sirens off in the distance, echoing between the abandoned buildings. He walked, staring at his feet. Rage!

Inside the car, the driver could see up and down the entire street. The squeaks of old compressing springs under the driver's shifting weight accented the sound of a long brass zipper being peeled down the length of a slender leather case on the car seat. Something long and metallic with a telescopic sight was carefully removed from the leather case. A moment later, a bolt was cocked as the window was cranked fully down.

Jerome Lewis was unaware that someone was watching his every move as he was preparing to cross the street. He was unaware that at that precise moment, from only thirty-five yards away, a rifle was pointed at his back.

Pfffffffft.

"Ugh!" Jerome reflexively grunted. "Fuck, man! Fuck! Ahhhh fuck! Shit, man!" He felt as if he'd been punched in the back with something sharp. He ran toward the sidewalk, then back into the street. He frantically reached to his back from above and below to try and touch the spot where he was hurting, the spot a little to the right of his spine. He thought he'd been shot, but it didn't feel as bad as he'd always imagined being shot in the back would feel. He could barely touch it, and ran over to the wall of a building. He rubbed up against the bricks, but he couldn't force the thing out of his back. He hyperextended his arm as far back as it would go, then he felt it—something like a . . . like a . . . He ran back out into the street, grew dizzy, and fell to his knees. . . . like a . . . his head grew heavy and clogged, as if his cranium were filled with hardening epoxy. . . . like a . . . round thing . . . like a pencil . . . or a battery . . . but . . . fatter . . . He collapsed into a pothole, facedown, in the middle of the street.

An engine started and a car pulled up to Jerome Lewis, who was almost unconscious, with his face in a crumbling road crater. The driver slid across the seat and the passenger door opened. The dark figure exited the car and knelt next to Jerome Lewis. The dart was pulled from his back and his pulse was taken. He was then lifted and placed into the trunk of the car. The dark night shadow removed a hypodermic needle from a folded napkin. The needle was pointed upward and tapped to dislodge the air bubbles, which rose toward the tip of this twenty-five-gauge stainless steel hollow shaft. The plunger was squeezed until the clear liquid sprayed from the pointy tip.

Jerome Lewis was going to get his shot after all.

8   Soda Bread

Being a New York City cop never managed to curtail Brent's eccentric behavior, and if he had any tendencies to mellow, Nigel was certainly no help. Nigel was a natural enabler of odd or screwball behavior, and he could talk people into doing things they would never dream of doing on their own, and he could make it seem like the most rational thing on earth to do. If it could physically be done, Nigel reasoned, and if there was any chance you could sociologically get away with it, he would rise to the challenge, without the inhibitions that normally constrain the behavior of average people. On a one-to-ten scale of strangeness, if Nigel could get you to do a four, it then became possible to get you to do a five, then a six. And Brent was not immune to the peculiar effects of Nigel on the human nervous system. They instantly became friends the day they'd met fifteen years earlier during a monthly meeting of the Northern New Jersey Chapter of the National Speleological Society. They began exploring and mapping caves together in the United States and Mexico, and when they weren't underground crawling through stream passages and mud, they often engaged in more urban aboveground activities, like bridging and tunneling. Often, Brent rationalized, he accompanied Nigel's madness just to keep him out of trouble, but trouble is always best when shared with a friend, and in some sense, Brent and Nigel were soul mates.

Tonight, however, Brent was pleased with himself not only because he'd prevailed over Nigel, but also because he was right where he and his aching bones wanted to be—munching on a piece of warm raisin soda bread and sipping a creamy Guinness stout on tap. He continued amusing himself with the printouts from the Pattern Crime Unit's database. Pattern crimes had been Brent's speciality, up until the time of the accident—a terrorist's bomb had exploded a year earlier, landing him in the hospital for twenty-one days.

Brent's recovery had been quick, up to a point. Chronic back, leg, and joint pain still plagued him, though, and he suffered residual headaches from the concussion. It was also around this time that the forty-year-old police lieutenant began to sprout a garden of silver follicles from the scalp that measured five feet eleven inches off the floor, and that sat above his chronically aching, magnificent brain with its genius IQ.

Brent stretched, rubbed his hip, then felt a hand touch his shoulder. He looked up at Nigel and said, *"Why* do you insist on sneaking up on people?"

"How's the leg?" Nigel asked, ignoring the question and instantly focusing his Pavlovian attentions on a piece of warm soda bread.

"Jim Thorp," Brent replied, which was his way of telling Nigel that with enough exercise, eventually he'd be better than new.

Nigel's pint of stout appeared on the dimly lit table as he devoured a fist-sized piece of soda bread. Knowing it would irritate Brent, Nigel said, "So whadda ya have on your vacuum-tube computer printout there? I *love* this soda bread."

"You know, about ten years ago, some guy tried to take out his own appendix?" Nigel coughed some Guinness out of his nose as he began pounding the table while convulsing in laughter. Brent continued: "Apparently, according to the report here, he had his *Gray's Anatomy* and some other medical books spread out all over his kitchen table with the tools he boiled, and after he managed to remove six whole feet of his small intestine, he realized he didn't know what the fuck he was doing, and finally called for an ambulance. . . ."

Nigel blew his nose and said, "So he tried to save a couple a bucks and . . . Great reason for nationalized health . . . I can just see him standing there with his guts draped over his shoulder to keep 'em from dragging on the floor . . . or maybe he just coiled 'em neatly on a tray and carried 'em around like a cigarette girl. . . ."

They laughed it up until Brent caught the waitress's eye. "So tell me," Brent said, after he ordered his chicken potpie, "you guys are really splitting up for good?"

"Looks that way. Pam decided to stay in California with her daughters." Nigel ordered a Reuben. "She just bought a place out in Frisco."

"Is she gonna make you give up the loft?"

"No. She said I could stay as long as I wanted, as long as I keep paying the maintenance." This was clearly an emotional topic for Nigel. "In her own words, 'I still love you. I just can't continue the relationship any longer.' Two years! Two fuckin' years, Brent! I'll be getting the divorce papers next week, or next month, or whenever the hell she gets around to it. You know women; they can't tell the difference between inches and time. . . ."

"Does Pamela want anything from you?"

"No! Not a thing! We're on perfect terms. No broken dishes. No temper tantrums. No lawyers—well, one lawyer; we both have the same lawyer. Can ya believe it? The lawyer said it'll be the cleanest divorce he's ever seen. Yeah, she's gonna be the perfect ex-wife. At least I didn't drop dead like her last husband did. Brent, I just *can't* break the two-year barrier. It's like the speed of light for me. I don't know what it is. I think women are nuts. I *love* you, and that is why I must leave you. . . . Nuts! They're all nuts!" While chewing frantically on another piece of soda bread, Nigel broke into verse:

> *I love you, and you love me, and therefore I must leave you.*
> *I love you, you don't love me, and therefore I must marry you,*
> *And when I do, when you love me, then I'm free to leave you.*
> *I leave you when you love me, because I am a WOMAN!!!*
> *Ahhhh ha ha, ha ha, ha ha . . . Ahhhh ha ha, ha haaaaaa—*

"If you choke on that bread," Brent interrupted, "you can do the Heimlich on yourself."

"Yeah, yeah. Maybe I'll remove my own intestines with a butter knife. So how's life with Tammy?"

"Pretty good, actually. Not to rub it in or anything, but she's the perfect mate, except that she's mad at me at the moment. In fact, I spent last night at the office. I figured we just needed a day or two to cool off."

"You can always stay at my place."

"I might if you'd clean it up a bit, but we made up, and we're going to dinner tomorrow after she's through with classes. She's finishing up at FIT soon, and—"

"And to think I gave her up for Pamela," Nigel interrupted. "Stupidest thing I ever did! Once again, I made the wrong dumb decision. Last time *I* ever choose age and wisdom before youth and libido. I thought an older woman would be stable. Stupid me! So you got the stable one and I got the nut—again!"

"What makes you think Tammy is so stable?"

"She's just upset because you're a cop."

"It's more than that. She's riding the same hormone roller coaster every woman rides."

"Yeah, hormones! Some roller coasters are small, and some are so big, they make you pay to get off—at least emotionally. Hormones! I think I'm gonna have all my glands surgically removed; maybe I'll do it myself. I think my next ex-girlfriend is gonna be Asian—an Asian with red hair! You wouldn't know any, would you?"

"Nigel . . . there *are* no red-haired Asians!"

"That's my point. I'm fed up. Through! If I ever get involved in another relationship . . . I hope my *dick* falls off!"

"I'll be sure to remind you," Brent said as another basket of steaming soda bread arrived. "You know," Brent said as he took a swig, "Pamela thinks you're crazy."

"Oh! She thinks *I'm* crazy! I got news for her. I have physics on my side. She has fizzies! There's only so much astrology and crystals and spooky little spirits a sane person can take."

"She told Tammy she thought you'd lost your mind the day your crossbow booby trap shot that robber."

"Yeah, in Saudi Arabia they'd have cut his hand off. Here they just—"

Brent laughed. "You're some piece a work, Nigel." The food came, and another round of stouts. Then Brent said, "Say, speaking about cutting off people's hands—"

"Someone finally administered a little bit of old-fashioned justice," Nigel interrupted. "Someone got sick of them getting away with murder—literally!" Nigel held his lips shut and tried to say, *"And I love the mouth."* Both men looked at each other, then began laughing, only a little at first, but it grew, till the two of them were practically in tears, unable to catch their breath, laughing, trying to outdo each other simulating the speech of Freddy Lopez.

"Heeeeelll yeeeeee."

"Eeeeeeeeyaaaa."

"Yaaaa yaaaa yaaaa yaaaa yeeeee."

Nigel breathed in and out, simulating air passing through the blowhole, and they roared with laughter until people turned to watch them. Then they quieted down, and Brent said, "Did your analysis turn anything up so far?"

"Ehh, we found some glass. We found dog hair. We found cat hair. We found rodent hair. We found fragments of pigeon feathers. We found synthetic and natural fibers. We found several varieties of pollen and loads of spores. We found nonaromatic hydrocarbons. We found blood, Freddy's blood—yeah, lots of Freddy's blood. We found some plant material. We found some soil. It's still gonna take some time to sift through the rest of the material we pulled out of Freddy's clothing, but from what we *can* determine so far, there don't seem to be any remnants of another human being on him— except for one of the cops who took him to the hospital."

"Then that leaves us with his blood." Brent groaned as he felt a mild shooting pain grip his back. "Our own serum-analysis group found Thorazine, morphine, and Valium, all commercially available. We found some other chemical—similar to curare, but not curare. Whoever did this knew exactly what he was doing and had all the right stuff. We found the IV feed hole in both his subclavian vein and his right arm, along with remnants of the tape that held it in place. We also—"

"I'd like to run his blood past our serology group as soon as they're all set up in the new lab."

"Good idea. We still have some keeping cool for you, but you'd better hurry. The concentration—"

"Brent, you know what strikes me odd?"

"A tuna fish sandwich could strike you odd."

"Only if it came from that mold-spore deli down the street

from your precinct. This soda bread is delicious. Thanks for suggesting this place. What strikes me odd is that ol' Freddy boy here doesn't remember one single thing between the time he *felt like he was stabbed* and the moment he just *appeared* on the Upper West Side...."

"Well, we also found traces of what we believe is midazolam, also known as Versed. It produces a form of hypnotic amnesia."

"I've heard of Versed," Nigel said, jogging his memory. "Isn't it supposed to be safer than Valium?"

"Yes. Valium can cause respiratory problems."

"Those drugs had to be continuously administered somehow to keep him under that long. Could he have been unconscious the whole time?"

"Possibly," Brent said. "It was only two or three weeks though, but we have lots of medical questions we need answered."

"And, is it medically possible even to *keep* someone unconscious for that long and still not affect their immune system?"

"I'll have to check. We have a lot of medical questions we need answered."

"...Because he seemed pretty well healed, except for the injuries he inflicted on himself. Yes, and we need to know what's the minimum equipment necessary to perform such an operation."

"You mean, provided this was done in someone's kitchen, as opposed to an operating room?"

"Yes...or a private *office?*" Nigel sang.

"A private office. Yes. That would make a hell of a lot of sense."

"You have your homework cut out for you, Brent. Do you know how many private offices there must be within a hundred miles of the Upper West Side? Don't forget your dentists, either."

"We don't have the resources even to consider such a search."

"What about the note?"

"It came from an IBM Selectric. Possible nick in the lower-right-hand corner of the lowercase z, but the z was only used once in the note, so we can't be sure. Paper is standard twenty-pound white copy paper. No watermark. No fingerprints. Maybe Mr. Lopez will have something more to tell us soon. He'll be a lot easier to talk to after Spellman opens up his mouth."

"You mean you're gonna let them ruin a perfectly good piece of modern art?"

"Please. Spare me."

"Ar-right, ar-right. So when do they cut *Zippy* a new mouth?"

"Tomorrow, at eight hundred."

"Oh, that reminds me," Nigel said, "thinking of stumpy boy there, I got a joke to tell you. . . .

"This pirate with a hook for a hand and an eye patch over his eye is sitting at a pirate bar, drinking. The bartender asks him how he lost his hand. 'I lost it in a sword fight on the high seas,' the pirate says. Then the bartender asks him how he lost his eye. The pirate says, 'Aye, a bird shit in it.' The bartender is confused and says, 'That shouldn't cause you to lose your eye, though.' The pirate says, 'Well, laddie, it was me first day with me new hook.' "

9   Externally Normal

A two-car garage door automatically opened to admit a '77 Chevy Nova, which pulled within inches of the gray-painted cement wall before the engine was switched off. The electric garage door motor hummed as the door slid along the guiding tracks, then hit the pavement with a metallic crash. The driver exited the car and opened the basement door, gaining entry to the house.

Externally, this was just your average home in your average affluent Long Island neighborhood. The house was set far back, on a picture-postcard hill, surrounded by a well-groomed lawn on two acres, with tall trees and thick bushes along the corner property perimeter. Islands of flower beds dotted the lawn between the walkway to the front door and the driveway, which sunk into the hill, disappearing into the garage below basement level. An ornate antique gas lantern hung from the hand of a nineteenth-century cast-iron coach house Negro at the base of the walkway near the street. Dense foliage, small trees, and bushes lined the first forty feet of the driveway, and all the land to the right of the driveway was wooded, like a forest. Externally, this was just your average affluent house.

Internally, this was far from an average house. The unconscious body of Jerome Lewis was removed from the trunk of the car and carried fireman-style up some stairs to the main level of the basement, into a bathroom, where he was plopped onto a toilet seat that was completely covered by a large plastic tarp. All Mr. Lewis's clothing was quickly removed and stuffed into a plastic-lined metal hamper to be burned, later, in a faraway place. A fifteen-minute break was then taken to administer a little self-sterilization. Then the unconscious man's naked body was carefully placed into the bathtub and completely scrubbed, then rubbed down with antiseptic chemicals. He was dried with paper towels and carried into a room. He was placed faceup onto a specially constructed padded table.

A strap was tightened around his right arm, halfway between the wrist and the elbow. His hand and lower arm hung off the end of the table; his left arm was fastened in a similar manner, and it, too, hung off the end of the table. A pair of padded wooden stops were clamped into position to prevent forward motion of the arms. A strap was tightened around the right leg—between the knee-cap and the pelvis, and another strap was tightened halfway between the knee and the ankle. The left leg was then secured in a similar manner. A strap was fastened across his pelvis and one across his chest. A strap was fastened across his forehead, and another custom-built clamp was adjusted to prevent sideways motion of the head. Mr. Lewis was now completely secure in this otherwise perfectly normal-looking Long Island house.

A hundred-watt droplight hung from a nail in a ten-foot-long vertical, square piece of wood and illuminated a single person shoveling sand from a loose pile into thirty individual one-cubic-foot duct tape–reinforced corrugated boxes. Each box was filled to the two-thirds mark, making them lighter and less messy to carry. Fifteen boxes were taken to the garage and placed into the front seat, backseat, and trunk of the car for disposal at the Bannister Creek pile. Nineteen minutes later, the car returned to pick up fifteen more boxes, which were on deck, stacked, and ready to be quickly exchanged with the empties. This procedure had been worked out to the minute, choreographed to the footstep, and rehearsed to perfection throughout the years, and it had become second nature. Thirty boxes of sand, or 2,400 pounds' worth, could be removed, loaded, and dumped in exactly one hour and twenty-nine and one-half minutes, including the five minutes it took to clean up.

10   Two Scheduled Surgeries

A pulse oxymeter, which measures oxygenated and deoxygenated hemoglobin, an EKG for monitoring the heart rate, and a Dynamapp for automatically monitoring blood pressure were all wheeled up to the operating table in this temporary space. IV bottles were suspended from hooks above Jerome Lewis. Several bags of plasma stood ready and had already assumed ambient temperature. A stainless steel tray full of sharp tools was placed on a table. The shiny tools were still warm from the autoclave and were laid out in the order of their expected usage. Sutures were spread out like insect specimens at a museum. A portable cabinet was rolled up and a flat drawer was opened; it contained a number of stainless steel brackets, small stainless steel plates, and a number of fine stainless steel bolts and nuts. A specially designed fixture was removed from a plastic bag—a complex tool that resembled a miter box, with lots of preset angles that could be independently swiveled into position. It was conveniently placed next to the patient. The intensity lamps were switched on. The tourniquets were ready. Another tray of tools, much larger tools, was wheeled into position. One of those tools was a stainless steel hacksaw.

Freddy Lopez was groggy as he lay in a hospital bed at Roosevelt Hospital. It was noon, and the plastic surgeon had just stopped by for the second time to check up on his reconstructive handiwork. Freddy was barely aware of the doctor's presence as he was examined.

Freddy opened his mouth for the first time in nearly three weeks. While he no longer possessed a pair of lips in the conventional sense, it still felt good to open his mouth, painful as it was. His tongue rubbed the flesh-colored shields covering each lip. The stinging amplified as he probed the internal perimeter of his brand-new mouth.

His tongue slid over to the side of his mouth. The little hole in his cheek was now gone—sewn shut, in what was only the first of what would be a series of reconstructive operations to fix his face. All that remained was something that resembled a puckered-up little anus in the middle of the left side of his face.

His tongue returned to his mouth. The raw tissue in the center of each lip was numb. He could taste each tiny stitch as his tongue explored the new landscape of the canoe-shaped opening. It wiggled about with horrified curiosity. As he looked at the pair of stumps, tears accumulated in his eyes and ran down the side of his face as he acknowledged the fact that his surgery was limited only to the region above his neck and that he would never touch his dick with his fingers ever again.

11   The Last Dirt

A car pulled back into the garage after yet another run to the creek with a carload of dirt, but there was something very different about this run: It was the last. All the dirt was now gone, and the light was very bright at the end of the tunnel.

After cleaning up a bit, the patient was examined. Respiration normal. Blood pressure, well, consistent with what it had been for the past four weeks, so probably normal. No infection. Good spirits. Restrained and under control. A bit smelly at times, but that was to be expected.

A few IV solutions were changed, and so was the cassette

tape filling the room with Ravel's Trio in A Minor, hour after hour. Too much of anything was no good. But all and all, everything was going so well.

And the days passed.

The dust was vacuumed from the freshly cured cement floor of a room, and bucket after bucket of epoxy paint was carried in so that the final waterproofing coat could be applied to the walls and floor. The ventilation fan was switched on, and a person began diligently mixing gallons of liquid into a large tray. Completion was only twenty-four hours away. It was an exciting time.

12   The Egg Room

$$\frac{x^2}{a^2} + \frac{y^2}{b^2} + \frac{z^2}{c^2} = 1$$

Today was the day of the great unveiling, and everything moved ahead of schedule, as usual. The new recreation room had taken more than eight years to build—the culmination of thousands of hours of dedicated work, unyielding commitment, discipline, and the knowledge that some great light lay at the end of the tunnel. And it did, almost literally.

The room was elliptical in shape, with an east-west-oriented minor diameter of sixteen feet and a north-south-oriented major diameter of thirty-five feet. The wall was seven feet high along the elliptical perimeter of the room and ten feet high at the highest point in the center of the domed ceiling. Nobody knew of the existence of this underground egg. Nobody except the one person who had painstakingly created it—the person who had dug it out from the earth, cubic foot of sand by cubic foot of sand. This elliptical bubble in the earth was a homemade exoskeleton of steel-wire mesh, rebar, and ferro-cement. Built on the principle of an arch, it supported the thousands of pounds of earth above it, along with the weight of the eastern solarium, whose floor lay only inches above the very top of the dome's apex.

Eight years is a long time. But time goes faster when infused with a burning sense of purpose. When the sun rises, the day is structured with a routine and with a daily goal in mind. Progress is measured against that goal, one cubic foot at a time. And all those cubic feet began their wondrous march from the ground with the first pounding of a $2.49 chisel into the eastern wall of the basement on a Wednesday. No municipal building permit had been applied for. Except for one human being's secret, this plan was strictly off the books. A four-foot-wide-by-five-foot-high rectangular hole was chiseled out, and a downward-sloping ten-foot-long passageway grew into the earth. The walls were cemented into place only one or two feet behind the exposure of each new slab of removed soil. And so it progressed, into the volume of space that would become the main chamber, and the slender egg slowly took form, supporting itself as it grew throughout the years. Each cross section had been carefully planned, and carefully gauged and contoured with precise lengths of timber, positioned at exact floor coordinates all scientifically laid out, with the dimensions transferred from the three-dimensional model of the room that had been constructed from balsa wood.

First, the cross section along the sixteen-foot minor axis of the egg was sculpted into the soil. Then the room grew perpendicularly outward from the center line, toward the ends. On average, fifty cubic feet of soil were removed each week. Some weekends, as many as a hundred cubic feet disappeared from the basement, carload by carload, to be dumped at construction sites (an opportunistic windfall, where the appearance of a few extra yards of dirt would never be questioned), on public land, off the pier and into the water at Woodmere Docks, and by the railroad tracks in a few mysterious but unquestioned piles of light orange Long Island soil which imperceptibly grew in size as the years passed. And even several thousand cubic feet raised the height of the back end of the yard without raising suspicion. One point eighty-three million pounds of soil later, and the job neared completion. Eight years can be a very long time. But time goes faster when infused with a burning sense of purpose.

Fluorescent lights illuminated the windowless egg room. The floor dipped a half a degree toward the north, terminating in a one-foot-diameter funnel at the wall. In spite of the epoxy waterproofing, in the event of a flood, a sump pump would clear this collection basin in the floor; no chances could be taken with water. And a symmetrically placed pair of ventilation ducts in the curved ceiling, each ten feet off center, twenty feet apart, led straight up through two feet of earth and into the floor of the room upstairs. A variable-speed fan mounted in the north vent could force the exchange of air between the upstairs and the egg below. But these ventilation ducts were slightly different from normal ventilation ducts. Each was equipped with a ten-micron filter, replaceable from below. Today was to be the first test of the complete system.

The manufacturer of this ellipsoid walked down the stairs to the basement, then visited the captive audience in what would soon become the old OR. Jerome Lewis was awake, but in a dissociative form of anesthesia, both there and not there, mouth drooped with the control and occasional drool of a stroke victim, plastered into communion with the dull passage of hypesthesia time, cloistered away behind the black opaque cloth covering his eyes, comfortably zonked out on maintenance cocktail #5, a blend of 85% Valium and 15% Versed, with a pinch of curare.

This was the time of night when it was best to work. There were no interruptions—no phone calls, no chance of unwanted guests in the house—a time when a person could concentrate, unencumbered, on the task at hand.

The plywood board was moved, exposing the steeply inclined hallway to the egg room. It was a triumphant moment—to march into the body of this room. The dimmer switch was turned and the exhaust fan began to rev. Warm air from the solar-heated space upstairs exchanged with the cooler air from the egg room. The perimeter of the egg room was inspected, and each and every attachment bolt—the three-inch-long, half-inch-diameter stainless steel threaded bolts that protruded from the ferro-cement walls at frequent intervals—was caressed. The room was lovingly admired, the walls touched and rubbed with outstretched palms, as if a pulse were to be found. The sculpting of the walls was finally complete. The electric installation was finally complete. The air system was finally complete, and it was all working perfectly—everything.

Then began the arduous task of moving all the medical equipment from the old OR to the egg room. There was a plan. The operating area was to be the south end of the egg. The preoperative, postoperative, feeding, and exercise area was to be at the north end. Bulky item after bulky item was muscled into its new home—the operating table, the clamps and custom fixtures that had been so lovingly designed and built throughout the months, the cabinets and tools, the monitoring equipment, the refrigerators, the autoclave, the hardware, the high-intensity lamps, and all the little things that completed the new environment.

Yes, Jerome Lewis was the last person to have been transformed in the old OR. From now on, things would be very different. There would be no risk of operating on patients in the basement OR anymore. All that would now take place in the seclusion of the egg room, a room that no one could ever discover—the room designed for this purpose alone. But Jerome would make it to the egg room after all. He might not know it, but he would make it there, because he was a very special person. He was number one, and everything was working out so well.

The egg is one of the many evolutionary miracles of the universe. With a minimum of material, the egg derives the great mechanical strength it possesses to withstand many times its weight in externally applied force. But an egg is so much more than a geometric and structural object. It is also an embryonic home where great biological transformations occur, powered only by the warmth of a good mother.

A cherry picker wearing the light blue logo of Con Edison crept up a deserted street. Two things made this an extraordinary fact: first, the neighborhood. Nothing short of a total blackout or a transformer explosion could waste a precious work-order sheet for a repair crew; it would be an unthinkable misallocation of resources to repair a measly streetlamp at a place like Wallabout Street in Brooklyn. Second, it was 3:30 in the morning; nobody works at 3:30 in the morning, even people who are paid to do so.

But there it was, rolling down this desolate street and coming to rest beside a dark and slender streetlamp. The workman stepped out of the cab and jogged to the side of the vehicle to read the hydraulic pressure indicator. Nine hundred psi gauge pressure. Satisfied, the workman climbed into the rear, up onto the boom, and into the basket. The joints of the linkage flexed as the hydraulic controls guided the basket up into the air, all the way to the sodium-vapor globe which had not emitted one single photon of visible light for over thirteen months.

An object lay on the floor of the ascending basket, an object wrapped in several layers of burlap. This object lashed in burlap was toroidal in nature, and heavy, perhaps 150 pounds. From the center of the burlap emerged a locking carabiner like the ones used in rock climbing and mountaineering. A loop of nine-millimeter dynamic climbing rope was placed over the lamp, onto the flange supporting the useless globe.

The workman raised the basket another eighteen inches, so the floor was level with the center line of the globe. The circular burlap object was inserted over the streetlamp, the way one would thread a needle. Then the carabiner was clipped to the loop of rope to support the weight of the burlap-clad object that was to be lowered around the lamppost, all the way to the street. A piece of one-inch tubular webbing was clipped from the loop of rope over to the safety railing of the cherry picker's basket, so the burlap payload would not accidently slide down the curved steel shaft of the streetlamp if control was lost.

The hydraulic controls were then delicately manipulated,

slowly lowering the object, carefully, with attention to every detail of the shifting weight. Down the object went, closer to the ground.

The basket could only be lowered to within twelve feet above street level. At that height, the burlap load was transferred to another rope, and the object was hand-lowered the rest of the way to the sidewalk. The workman energetically hopped out of the basket and removed all the ropes and the carabiner from the burlap object.

Then the cherry picker disappeared into the slum's nighttime darkness, back to the never-ending construction site located under the overpass of the Brooklyn Queens Expressway. This was the precise location from which this piece of equipment had been borrowed —only slightly more than an hour earlier. The electrical clip lead was removed from the ignition system, and the motor instantly died. The workman exited the cab and hopped into a nearby car. Ten minutes later, that car appeared next to the streetlamp and the burlap object that had been left there.

The workman observed the street, the apartment buildings, and the factories, then left the vehicle and quickly cut away all the burlap and rope and carefully placed them in a plastic bag, along with the gardening gloves and coveralls worn during this entire exercise. What remained on the lamppost would make history in only a few short hours.

"... This late-breaking story just in," the CBS morning newscaster said. "As bizarre as it seems, a naked man has been found attached somehow to a lamppost on Wallabout Street in Brooklyn early this morning. We *are* expecting live coverage momentarily. Apparently..." The newscaster hesitated as he listened to the earphone prompter. His face contorted as he faced the camera. "Apparently, I am told, the man's hands have been amputated and his arms *were surgically* joined to each other, to make a ... sort of a loop, or a hoop. I know this sounds fantastic ... and ... hold on, please. Our cameras are setting up right now as I speak. I am told the images you are about to see are *very* graphic, so if there are any children or sensitive people watching, you might want to have them leave the room...."

At the lamppost on Wallabout Street in Brooklyn, all was pandemonium. Police were baffled, their function degenerated to controlling the accumulating crowd of bewildered bystanders. Nobody knew what to do with the freak, and his presence was making some people confused, angry, and unruly. Many did not think what they were looking at was even a human.

"...Kill dat fuckin' thing, man!" one man yelled at the police.

"...Izz a alien," a woman kept repeating over and over. "Izz a alien from outta space come here ta take ova 'n shit."

"That thing da *devil!*" another man yelled. "Kill da devil!"

A crazed Puerto Rican man ran up to the naked prisoner of the lamppost and began kicking him in the ribs. The attacker was tackled, cuffed, and arrested.

"We need backup here," a policeman said into his radio as pump shotguns were distributed to some of the officers from the trunk of a squad car.

This was the first week on the job for one of the police officers, and he quietly excused himself from his partner as he walked to a nearby parking lot and threw up between two stolen cars. The Police Academy had never trained him for such a contingency, and he could not believe that what he had just seen was real. Looking into that man's terrified eyes had produced an incomprehensible revulsion he would not forget for the rest of his life.

News crews were falling over themselves to stake their gold rush–style claim close enough to capture this medical phenomenon on videotape. The microwave uplinks were being established. Bystanders were clicking their point-and-shoot cameras like newsmen at a presidential press conference. A cameraman tripped and crashed to the pavement, with his $25,000 camera buffering his fall. Another cameraman took his place to get into position, and another, and another. New technical crews arrived every few minutes.

"Kill da pig!" people began chanting.

"ALL RIGHT! BACK UP, PEOPLE," a police officer yelled into a bullhorn, followed by the shrill whistle of feedback. "BACK UP. GIVE US ROOM. PLEASE BACK UP." Grumbling bystanders reluctantly complied.

Other police cars arrived on the scene with sirens screaming, and police burst out, wearing riot gear, armed with rifles.

And then the televised images everyone had been waiting for. They were dramatic, as promised, but not nearly as dramatic as they might have been. Some coats now covered the naked body of the black man with his arms looped around the cool morning's lamp-post in a big, friendly, surgically induced bear hug. Those coats covered the words that had been burned onto his back with a fifty-watt wood-burning tool:

I AM A
MURDERER
AND I AM
LEGALLY
FREE.
I AM NOW
STABLE.

Millions of viewers preparing to leave for work were treated to a close-up of this man's surgically joined arms. On this particular morning, the best part of waking up was not Folgers in their cups. Many would follow the lead of the policeman who had thrown up. The image would be played and replayed throughout the days and weeks to come. The public had gotten what they wanted. The professional news hunter-gatherers also captured the unforgettable image of the man's face and mouth, which had been sewn shut, just as another man's had been sewn shut only seven weeks before, but with no publicity. And the dribbling hole in the side of this one's face provided a vivid focal point on which to center the crosshairs of a Steadicam.

Brent Kramer's telephone rang in his New Jersey home, where he was fast asleep in bed with his wife. It was already early afternoon and this was supposed to be his day off; as he emerged from the dream state, his subconscious whispered to him that this was not to be the case. He reached for the receiver and placed it to the side of his head without yet opening his eyes. He grunted, then listened. Brent's eyes opened wide as he blurted, "His arms, too?!! *Why* did I know we hadn't seen the last of this?" Brent looked at Tammy's head on the pillow, then continued: "I'll check it out, Al. In fact, I can be at the Holland Tunnel in a half hour. Why don't you cab it down to Canal and Church and I'll pick you up on the southeast corner...." In a brief glance, Brent could see that his wife was disappointed. "...Okay, Al, see you soon." He hung up the phone and bounced out of bed.

"What's wrong, honey?" Tammy asked with a wake-up yawn.

"We'll see in a minute," Brent said as he threw on his pants. "This isn't gonna be pretty, sweetheart."

"Oh, you mean the news?"

Brent grabbed the TV remote control and clicked on CBS. And there on the screen was the mind-blowing image of a black man without a mouth hugging the lamppost while spitting and spraying through a blowhole in the side of his left cheek.

"This is the grossest thing I ever saw in my life," Tammy said, with disgust plastered on every square inch of her otherwise-beautiful red-freckled face. "It's just like something Nigel would think of doing."

Brent pondered this thought for a moment. "Nah! Nigel wouldn't waste his time ... probably."

The crowd on Wallabout Street was reaching circus proportions. Traffic was backed up everywhere. Helicopters circled above. It was nearly two o'clock in the afternoon, and only now was the proper machinery requisitioned to extricate the center-ring attraction from his metallic hitching post. Thousands of people hung out on the street, drinking beer, smoking dope, and taking pictures. Parents walked their baby carriages and children as close as they could get. Most saw nothing except the backs of the people in front of them, but a few could catch a real glimpse—the ones pressed up against the police barricade. A three-year-old boy was screaming, "But I wanna see, Mommy! I wanna see!" She yelled at him in Spanish and he began to cry.

People listened to portable radios and watched portable TVs to catch any developing news from the spot where that news was developing only two hundred feet away. It was already an international story. Television shows were being interrupted all day to give updates. Millions of people were talking about it all day at work, with televisions and radios blasting nonstop on this special occasion. Speculation was already running wild, with panels of doctors and psychiatrists and retired police officials giving their slant on the situa-

41

tion. The front page of almost every major newspaper in the country was put on hold until the last piece of film peeled off the drying drums of the automatic developing machines so only the most revealing images could be chosen to go to press. On Wall Street, surgical supply stocks had risen unexplainably, and the market exhibited anomalous volatility across the board. Artists at *Mad* magazine were already working on the next month's theme for Alfred E. Newman, and the late-night talk-show joke writers were taxing their skills to make their bosses look good onstage. And an overweight black activist with a flamboyant hairstyle had even called a news conference where he would declare that this was clearly the beginning of a new wave of antiblack racism, and that black people would no longer tolerate the attitudes of white racist America. ONLY A WHITE MAN WOULD DO SUCH A THING would be the quote and front-page headline of a Black Muslim newspaper.

A group of boys were break-dancing and hip-hopping on Wallabout Street. The Jehovah's Witnesses were out in force, preaching the good word and the evils of Satan. A line thirty people long accumulated at a portable hot dog stand. Other vendors sold ice cream, soda, sugared nuts, shish kebab, and some kind of tropical fruit–colored drink with vodka and rum. A vendor was selling pinwheels, flashlights, and plastic hammers that made a squeaky noise when you hit something hard with them. This was Wallabout Street's very first block party.

The news teams clearly had the visual advantage in this gathering, with their telephoto lenses focused on the action from their suspended perches high above the roofs of the news trucks. The surgically altered man alternated between screaming and sobbing and spitting out the blowhole on the side of his face. He could not believe where he was, or what was going on, or why all these people were here; and his brain was still dense with the anesthetic. His arms hurt where they had been joined, and phantom sensations bombarded his mind with impossibly conflicting signals.

A police psychologist had just arrived and knelt next to him. "Hello," he said with parrotlike inflection. With a sickened disgust transparently radiating through his professional, sweet, quivering voice, he continued: "My name is Doctor Arkindablotta, and I am a therapist, and I'm very happy to make your acquaintance. . . ."

A heaving viscous projectile burst from the drooling blowhole on the side of the man's face and hit Dr. Arkindablotta squarely on the nose, dripping onto his upper lip.

"Eccccch!" the doctor squawked, recoiling in horror, then wiped his face with the arm of his ill-fitting suit jacket.

In the interim, newsmen shamelessly fired questions at the freak as the knobs on the control-room soundboards were frantically twiddled to find some optimal gain and filter settings to make some sense of the garbled, incomprehensible moans and noises emanating from the head of this primo news story—the kind all journalists dream of.

Sgt. Alfonce Perato (rhymes with *potato*) steadied himself as Lt. Brent Kramer drove up onto the sloping, cracked sidewalk and parked alongside an abandoned factory. Sergeant Perato opened the passenger's side door, then grunted as he pulled himself out of the car against gravity. Gravity had been plotting against him for quite some time now. The more he ate, the more gravity maliciously schemed. Alfonce knew it was time to lose a little weight. For years, he'd been promising his wife he would trim the belly. And at that moment, he decided it was time to spend a little time at the gym, but he hated the gym and the type of people that went there.

Brent popped a shield on his dashboard and said, "Come on, Al, out of the car."

"Yeah, yeah . . . Ohhh," Al grunted as he finally stood on his two feet, "I *gotta* lose some weight."

The two Midtown North detectives quickened their pace as they approached a gaggle of cops and nonverbally introduced themselves by dangling their badges. The police led them through the barriers to the internal perimeter of gawking spectators surrounding the imprisoned man. Brent and Al rolled their eyes as they saw the psychologist sitting on a towel on the sidewalk, with his legs folded in a lotus position. His presence seemed to be antagonizing the man hooped around the lamp, rather then calming him. The detectives approached a thick-necked little bull of a man wearing a blue suit, with a radio stuck to the side of his head. "Are you the officer in charge?" Brent asked.

"Yeah, I yam. Lieutenant Salinella," he barked with that unchallengeable authority Brent hated in men of low intellectual stature and high seniority and rank. From his accent, it was obvious that this cop's country of origin was Brooklyn. "Who a you?" he asked.

"I'm Lieutenant Kramer, and this is Sergeant Perato, of Midtown North. I'm glad to—"

"This ain't your jurisdiction, Lieutenant. Wadda ya doin' here?"

Brent Kramer had already discussed the jurisdiction problem with the police commissioner, and he was not about to get into a pissing contest—yet. He sized up this little man with the radio firmly grasped in his hand. "Can I speak with you for a moment, Lieutenant Salinella?" The three men walked to the side of an ambulance, and Lieutenant Kramer watched news cameras and parabolic microphones tracking them from a distance with the expectation of a newsworthy conversation. "I have a low tolerance for publicity. Can we step inside so we can keep this off the news?"

"Lieutenant, I really ain't got time for your paranoias," Salinella said. "There's a situation here, *if* ya haven't noticed."

"Very well," Brent said. "Al, can I borrow your radio for a moment, please?" Sergeant Perato removed the walkie-talkie from his belt and handed it to Brent, who turned the squelch control all the way down and the volume all the way up. Loud, scratchy static blast from the box, which he held up near his shoulder, pointed toward the wheeled towers of news gatherers. He then saw several technicians rip their overdriven headphones from their heads while groping for their control knobs.

Perato smiled; he was always learning useful tricks from Brent. Then Brent said to Lieutenant Salinella, "Look, what I'm about to tell you, we don't want to get out. You see, this is part of an ongoing investigation. . . ." Brent explained to the lieutenant that the gentleman before them was not the first mutilation victim. And then Lieutenant Salinella got a radio call telling him that the case was being transferred to Midtown North by order of the police commissioner himself, and that he should extend any help to the detectives from Manhattan.

Lieutenant Salinella was noticeably pissed off, and he felt that these troublemakers from Manhattan were somehow responsible for it. "Lieutenant," Brent continued, "one more thing. Do you think it's possible to get some partitions or sheets or something so we can make this a little more private?"

"What do you want us to do, build a fuckin' house around 'im? In a couple a hours, we'll have 'im off that fuckin' pole, anyway. What the fuck difference does it make?"

"Please, the man's on public display here, and we need to find some things out from him if possible."

"Yeah, we weren't able to get shit outta him. He sounds like a fuckin' retard. Good luck!"

Brent sighed to his sergeant, "You tell 'im, Al."

Sergeant Perato looked at Lieutenant Salinella and said, "We're all on the same side, Lieutenant. Do you remember when your precinct needed the Hell's Kitchen car-theft file we'd spent twelve years accumulating? We just handed the file over to you, in less than an hour, I believe, no questions asked, along with three full-time detectives who cumulatively spent almost two hundred hours we never bothered to bill you for. Please. Do you think you can help us out?"

Lieutenant Salinella was already losing valuable camera time, screaming into his radio for the benefit of his friends and relatives and even the six-figure book deal he imagined in his future when it came time for him to find the ghostwriter and reveal the brilliant police career he'd lived in his mind. He and Sergeant Perato were able to scoff up something from the ambulances to isolate the lamp-post from the probing public eyes. In the meantime, Brent Kramer watched the police shrink playing verbal patty-cake with the tormented soul on the streetlamp, the undulating crowd, the news trucks, the cameras, the police in their riot gear, the people leaning way out of the windows in their apartment buildings, the vendors, and the helicopter cutting across the blinding sun up above—all rather surrealistic. Finally, some metal stands were erected and curtains were lashed between them. Only then did Brent Kramer and Al Perato approach the sorrowful sight before them.

"—Please sir, you've *got* to try and calm down," the psychologist pleaded. "I know you must have *many* negative feelings associated with this awful situation—"

"Excuse me," Brent interrupted, "could we be alone with him for a while? We'd like to speak to him."

"The patient is *highly* agitated, as you can see," the police shrink blathered. "I'm not sure that would be advisable at this time."

"Why not?"

"I don't believe we've met yet," the doctor patronized. "I'm Dr. Arkindablotta, and I'm a psychologist employed by the department precisely to deal—"

"Yes, that's obvious. But I'm afraid that doesn't change anything. This won't take long, Doctor."

"I'm really not sure that—"

"Look, Doc, I don't wanna have to shoot you in the nuts, but I will if I have to." Brent and Al both smiled shit-eating grins at the doctor, and in unison they both flicked their jackets open to reveal the black leather straps of their shoulder holsters.

Dr. Arkindablotta could not believe that he'd been threatened by these two flatfoots. "Your behavior is *completely* unprofessional. You have usurped my authority in front of my patient, and it makes me feel diminished. . . ."

"First, could you vanish before you diminish, Doc?" Brent said.

"I shall return!"

Al pointed at the shrink with his thumb and said, "Yeah, *he's* no MacArthur" as the good doctor threw the green curtain aside and stormed off in a huff to complain to Lieutenant Salinella and his radio, who at the moment were doing a slightly higher-tech imitation of Napoléon.

Brent and Al were now alone with the man. They both knelt down next to the lamppost and tried to avoid staring at the man's arms, or his mouth, or the hole in the side of his face. The man's eyes naturally drifted toward the highest-ranking officer, and Brent said, "My name is Brent Kramer, and this is Alfonce Perato. We're cops. I'm not gonna feed you a bunch a bullshit about how rosy the future is for you. I know you're too intelligent for all that shit. I am gonna ask you to trust us, though. Some maniac did this to you, and we're gonna try to catch the person or persons responsible. Do you understand me?"

"Yeeeeeee yaaaa yaaaa," the man wheezed through the hole in the side of his face while shaking his head up and down.

"I'll take that to mean a yes." The lieutenant paused for a moment to collect his thoughts. He had just accomplished more in thirty seconds than the rest of the goons had accomplished since early in the morning, when this awful discovery had been made.

"Can you tell me your name?"

"Jooooo ooooooo," it sounded like.

Lieutenant Kramer was perplexed, and he thought about the communication problem they faced. He thought about the famous line from *Cool Hand Luke:* "What we've got here is failure to communicate—a failure to communicate." "Okay, we're going to try something different. I'm going to go through the alphabet, one letter at a time. When I get to the first letter of your last name, I want you to make a noise and nod your head. Do you understand?"

"Eeeeeeee," the man said, shaking his head yes.

"Okay, then. We're going to start now. Is the first letter of your last name an *A?"* Lieutenant Kramer looked into his eyes and the man shook his head no. "Is it *B? . . . C? . . . D? . . . E? . . . F? . . . G? . . . H? . . . I? . . . J? . . . K? . . . L? . . ."*

"Eeeeeeee," he said, bobbing his head up and down.

"Good! Good! The first letter of your last name is *L?"*

"Eeeeeeee!"

At that moment, Dr. Arkindablotta burst through the curtain and said, "Will you stop upsetting the—"

With mystical swiftness, Lieutenant Kramer produced his nine-millimeter, cocked the hammer, and said, "One more interruption, Freud, and I'm gonna jam your nuts so far up your asshole, it's gonna take you a week to shit 'em back out!"

Dr. Arkindablotta scurried back outside the curtain to find someone to share his diminishment with.

"That man is such an asshole!" the lieutenant said as he holstered his weapon.

"Eeeeeeee!" the man said, bobbing his head up and down to register a big affirmative.

"Now where were we? Yes. The first letter of your last name is *L."*

"Eeeeeeee!"

"Good! Now the second letter of your last name. Is it *a? . . . b? . . . c? . . . d? . . . e? . . ."*

"Eeeeeeee! Eeeeeeee!"

"Good. Very good. The second letter of your last name is *e?"*

"Eeeeeee!"

"Now for the third letter. . . ." And so it went, yielding a *w*, then an *i*, then an *s*. "LEWIS! Your last name is LEWIS?"

"Eeeeeee! Eeeeeee!"

"Excellent. Now let's figure out what your first name is. . . ."

A half hour later, Kramer and Perato were on their way back to their precinct in Manhattan. Brent picked up the car phone and told Detective Bassett to run a computer check on the gentleman at the lamppost. ". . . Our man is named Jerome Lewis. No middle name. My hunch is that he was recently released from prison. Why don't you check the recent graduating class. . . ."

Lieutenant Salinella, who still had his two-way radio glued to the side of his face, directed the crane into position, making sure the cameras always caught his good side. The straps were lashed around the top of the streetlamp to support its weight as it was unbolted from its base.

The police shrink, still in possession of his nuts, had recovered his pride and held Mr. Lewis low and out of the way during the unbolting process. He was rewarded for his troubles with another spurting projectile of saliva-diluted mucus in his face.

With a hop and barley–carbonated belch left over from the pair of metabolizing lunchtime tall boys, the last nut was removed from the base of the streetlamp, and the crane raised it, finally separating it from the base. The wires were still attached, and they were cut after the 220-volt power had been disconnected. And then the mutant man was free at last, at least from the constraint of the lamppost, and he was ambulanced away, escorted by a procession of police cars and sirens.

Moments later, the crane operator lowered the streetlamp to the ground, where it would remain for the next two months, until scavengers torched it into small pieces and sold it to a scrap-metal dealer in the Bronx, proving once again, that every cloud has a silver lining for someone.

The new freak on the block was now on his way to Roosevelt Hospital, where covert experience had already been gained in the art of opening up a man's mouth.

As for the crime scene, there was no useful evidence even before the circus began, and all the useless evidence had been completely obliterated and scattered to the four winds, except for the videotaped memory of the day the circus came to town.

14   Another Glimpse at the Specimen

Lt. Brent Kramer walked with navigational single-mindedness through a protoplasmic blob of cops, security and medical personnel, newspeople, and political hacks from various levels of state and local government. Many of these people he recognized from the publicity he'd received during the Gulf War terrorism incident. And unfortunately, many of these same people recognized him immediately.

"Lieutenant Kramer," a newsman said loudly, drawing undue attention, "is there anything you can tell us at this time?" Now Brent was a marked man, and the crowd turned as if he were a bread ball tossed into a pond full of hungry fish.

"No."

"Surely you can tell us something."

"No, I can't. . . . Well, let me rephrase that. . . ." The hallway instantly grew quiet as Brent turned to face them. "I can see that you're all responsible, sensible journalists, and I know that you all understand the need for the utmost sensitivity and discretion in matters such as this. Roosevelt Hospital was named after a great man whom your forebears in journalism bore the professional respect and courtesy to photograph only from the waist up. Thank you very much, people." Brent made eye contact with the nurse at the desk and was buzzed into that same high-security hospital room where Freddy Lopez had been kept six weeks earlier. Only a handful of medical personnel, detectives, and law-enforcement consultants knew that both these victims shared the same surgeon/stylist.

Dr. Spellman sat with his stethoscope pressed against Jerome Lewis's chest, not listening to a thing he heard, because he was too busy staring in amazement at the loopy thing that began at one shoulder and ended at the other, or vice versa. Mr. Lewis's mouth had been sewn shut just like Mr. Lopez's had been, and the blowhole was identical, too—but in total, he was a more evolved creation. The doctor seemed to be tapping and poking the patient in all the right places when Lieutenant Kramer quickly slipped into the room and pushed the door closed tightly behind him to prevent the salesmanlike foot-in-the-door from the parade of newshounds eager for a glimpse or a tidbit. "It's a madhouse out there," a nurse said to Brent once he was safely inside the room.

"Yeah, but look what they do for a living," Brent said as he watched Dr. Spellman examining his patient.

Brent had read the report Sergeant Bassett had compiled for him. Jerome Lewis had just served fifteen and a half years in Attica State Penitentiary for two counts of manslaughter during a botched car jacking. He had been suspected of a dozen other car jackings, but none could be proved. It was Mr. Lewis's misfortune to get shot by an off-duty cop who heard gunshots and ran to the crime scene with his gun drawn.

Caught red-handed, Mr. Lewis was just another product of society, his attorneys argued. He was not responsible for his actions; someone else was. During the late seventies, the "society's fault" argument was in its heyday, and every jury heard it sung in one form or another, with a criminal defense attorney on one knee like Al Jolson in blackface singing "Mammy"—with arms outstretched, tearfully pleading every biological and sociological and psychological minutiae of mitigating circumstance. Everything from poverty to Pavarotti was society's fault. And all too many juries *were* liberated from their common sense by skillful manipulators of the human mind, convinced that what they saw in the photographs of the bloody corpse *was* really *their* fault, rather than that of the sweet lil' ol' defendant with the orbiting halo who sat before them. Reasonable doubt.

But it didn't work for Jerome Lewis. The prosecution argued that the someone else who *was* responsible for a double murder also happened to reside somewhere within the body of Jerome Lewis, and therefore, just to be on the safe side, all of him should be locked up.

So at least in that particular courtroom, on that particular day, Mr. Jerome Lewis was found guilty of involuntary manslaughter and given thirteen to twenty-five.

So he was eligible for parole after thirteen years. He failed his first parole hearing. But two was Jerome's lucky number, and at this next hearing, twenty-four months later, he was deemed to be completely rehabilitated and ready to be returned to society. And, in fact, he was ready; he had had fifteen and a half long years to analyze the mistake that had landed him in Attica. That mistake was not the attempted car jacking; it was car jacking while stoned. Even at the sentencing, Mr. Lewis had sworn to himself that he would never shoot up and drive someone else's car, ever again.

It was a peculiar twist of fate, but Mr. Lewis *would* never shoot up and attempt to drive someone else's car ever again. Someone else saw to that—the same someone else who had manicured *Zippy*.

At that very moment, a rather large man labored under a pair of high-intensity lamps that supplemented the light from the main source above. The smell of soil filled the room in which he worked. Potted plants were everywhere. The man reached for a glass of water and raised it to his lips. He pushed a gooseneck-mounted magnifying lens out of the way, then sipped the water. As the cool water sloshed about inside his mouth, he admired the work before him. The older splices seemed to be taking nicely, but it would take months to assess properly the success of the new ones. He sprayed a mixture of water, growth hormones, and plant food onto the soil of this surgically modified plant, then extinguished the high-intensity light sources. The rest of the nursery seemed to be doing well, and the time had come to call it a day.

The man then lumbered out of the laboratory and slammed the big metal door behind him. He walked up a flight of stairs and into the kitchen. He removed a container of mixed vegetables from the refrigerator and placed them in a microwave oven. Then he reached across the kitchen table and switched on an old ten-inch black-and-white television. At first the TV whistled; then a two-inch-wide horizontal bar of flickering light gradually appeared. The bar slowly grew in height as electrons boiled off the filament-heated barium oxide, and the vertical roll slowed, then locked into a folded, distorted, breathing image of a crowd of people. The bell on the microwave rang, and the man shook his head as he watched the arm loop of Mr. Jerome Lewis fill the screen of this ancient vacuum tube-powered television set.

"Wally?" Brent said, then motioned for Dr. Spellman to join him in the corner, where they could quietly talk. "Have you told anyone about Freddy Lopez yet?"

"No. I wanted to talk to you first."

"Thanks for the consideration. I think it might be best to keep it quiet until we learn as much as we can about this."

"My lips are sealed—no pun intended."

Brent laughed. "Look, I need some of his blood before he metabolizes away the good stuff. I'd also like to look at the X rays of that joint."

"Me, too. We'll order up a set, and we'll get you your blood."

At the bedside, Brent examined the healing skin at the connection line circumscribing the artificial joint as Jerome looked up into his familiar eyes. Brent touched the skin at the zone of attachment. He felt the subcutaneous contour of little plates and hardware inside this perverse man-made appendage.

And then Jerome Lewis said, *"Iyyyeea ciii a reee."*

"What?" Brent softly said.

"Ciii-a-reee! Ciii-a-reee!"

"I don't know what you're trying to tell me. I guess we can do what we did outside. Okay?"

"Eeeeeeee."

"How many words? One? . . ."

"Eeeeeeee." Jerome shook his head up and down.

"One word, then."

"Eeeeeeee."

"Okay. First letter: Is it *A* . . . *B* . . . *C* . . ."

"Eeeeeeee."

"First letter is a *C?*"

"Eeeeeeee." Dr. Spellman and the nurse watched this painful information-extraction process with bewildered amusement.

"Second letter," Brent said. "Is it a . . . b . . . c . . . d . . . e . . . f . . . g . . . h . . . i . . ."

"Eeeeeee. Eeeeeee! . . ."

"So we have a *C* followed by an i. . . ."

"Eeeeeee! Eeeeeee! Ciii-ga-ree! Ciii-ga-ree!!"

"You want a cigarette?!!"

"Eeeeeee! Eeeeeee!! Eeeeeee!!!" Jerome raised and lowered his arm loop and practically shook his head off his neck with excitement.

"Hmmmm. Six weeks without a cigarette, huh?"

"Eeeeeee."

"You wouldn't consider quitting? You've already gone six weeks." Jerome's eyes grew angry. "All right . . . just checking, just checking. We'll get you a cigarette."

"Nurse," Brent said, "do you think we could scrounge up a cigarette for Jerome?"

"I presume I could find one, Lieutenant." It was clear that she was not pleased with the prospect of copping tobacco for Jerome Lewis.

Aiming to please, Brent said, "Any particular brand, Jerome?"

"Aaaaoooo wooo wooo."

"I'll take that to mean: 'Anything you can find, nurse.' "

"Ohhhhhh . . ."

The nurse was buzzed out of the room in search of Jerome's cigarette, and Brent rejoined Dr. Spellman on the other side of the room. "Wally," Brent said, "why do you suppose Mr. Lewis is so impossible to understand, while Lopez was merely difficult to understand?"

"Possible the added trauma of having his arms connected. Maybe decreased blood flow to the speech centers of the brain? I really don't know. I suspect we'll find out more, though, once I open up that mouth."

Both men watched Jerome Lewis, and Jerome watched them, until the uncomfortable silence was broken by the nurse, who had succeeded in her mission, with three Marlboros and a pack of matches. The seamed drumhead where Jerome's mouth used to be stretched into what resembled a smile, and he wiggled his way to a more erect posture, and actually began drooling from his blowhole in anticipation of the smoke he was about to inhale. Jerome's eyes practically burned a hole in the nurse as he endured the agonizing delay of her putting on a pair of latex gloves. Then she patted the stoma dry with a tissue. She lit the match and held the cigarette up to the undulating blowhole. Jerome's eyes were rolling like slot-machine tumblers as he inhaled madly to achieve the necessary negative pressure to inhale smoke through the length of cigarette and into the artificial hole in his cheek. The nurse slowly comprehended the physics of this airflow system, and she converged on a method to hold the cigarette sealed against Jerome's cheek so he could take the appropriately concentrated drag, just like the good old days when he could poison himself unassisted. But nostalgia was not foremost in Jerome's field of concentration. Nicotine was the name of the game, and the sooner the better. Jerome was as desperate as any junkie could have been under the circumstances, and Brent and Dr. Spellman watched in amazement and pity as funnels of smoke were expelled sideways from Mr. Lewis's head. And the cigarette was reduced to ash, all the way to the filter.

"Wooooorrrrr! Wooooorrrrr!!!"

"I think he wants another one," Brent said.

The nurse nervously lit up another cigarette, and as Jerome smoked it, providing an occasional noisy cue that the nurse instinctively understood without actual linguistic comprehension, he took on the first signs of contentment since he first experienced consciousness, back on the lamppost early that morning.

15   Medical Review

A battery of light box–illuminated X rays hung on three walls surrounding the mahogany conference table at Roosevelt Hospital. The doctors passed around loose X rays as if they were glossy porno at a college frat-house beer bash. And all these X rays shared one thing in common; each piece of film had the name Jerome Lewis indelibly exposed in the lower-right-hand corner, and the myriad photographic angles provided all the coverage necessary to satisfy the most curious medical mind, with plenty left over to gawk at. The connection zone of the forearms mesmerized the doctors. The calcification at the connection site was normal for a five-to-six-week recovery period, and the hardware and screws were all plainly visible. Perfectly professional job.

Both Brent Kramer and Nigel Atkerson were present at this medical review of the bizarre off-the-books surgery that had been performed on Jerome Lewis. One did not have to be a doctor to understand the meaning of the X rays, and at times Nigel had the gleaming twinkle of Satan in his eye. He clearly saw the humor in this situation, and he made no attempt to hide it. In fact, Nigel's enthusiastic interest seemed to infect the room in some unexplainably darkened way.

Dr. Spellman raised his hands and the room fell silent once again in anticipation of the next little dribble of information. "So, as you can see from the film, a step-cut osteotomy had been performed on the radius and ulna bones, similar to the way we might shorten a limb. Only in this case, they connected both arms together—"

"Just like tree surgery," Nigel blurted.

"Tree surgery?" Dr. Spellman said.

"Yes. Look at the triangle pattern of the mating bones. It's just like the way branches are spliced together to produce seedless oranges, or macadamia nuts."

"Well, yes, I guess. I'm not really familiar with how they do it to trees and bushes in Hawaii, but in people medicine, we call it a step-cut osteotomy." Some of the doctors smiled. "It's actually called a Milch procedure. The diagonal cuts increase the contact surface area and make a stronger bond. Apparently, the person who did this is familiar with the Milch procedure. . . ."

"Why?"

"Because this is called a Milch procedure," Dr. Spellman said, pointing at an X ray. "Anyone who did this is familiar with the Milch procedure."

"Ah, 'a rose by any other name . . .' "

"You seem to like your botany, Mr. Atkerson."

Nigel shook his head. "It just doesn't seem all that profound to me. In fact, it seems rather obvious to anyone with an engineering background or some common sense—maybe even a little of both. Tell me, Doctor, is it also called a Milch procedure if they do it to a tree? Hell, one time I saw the branches of a tree grow together in the

Bronx Botanical Gardens. In fact, there were several examples of it. . . ."

"What's your point?" Spellman challenged, now slightly insulted because a medical procedure could be so flagrantly trivialized by this nonprofessional. "Do you think his arms grew together because he slept in a funny position?" Some of the doctors chuckled.

"No. I hadn't made that leap yet, but isn't it possible that someone could have reinvented the wheel?"

"Well, I guess so. But isn't it as good a starting point as any to first look for someone *familiar* with the procedure?"

"Yes. I absolutely agree. But it would also seem to me that any osteopath familiar with this Milch procedure would be very high up on our list of suspects, and only the most naïve or arrogant person would do such a thing and think he could get away with it for any length of time."

"We're talking about an insane person. Probably an insane doctor, I'm sorry to say."

Nigel added, "Or a nurse, or a dentist, or an anesthesiologist, or a medical student, or a medical student who flunked out, or a motivated experimenter—you know, a hobbyist or a handyman with too much spare time on his hands. . . ."

"Or an insane osteopath," Spellman insisted.

"Or any ol' psychopath will do."

Throughout this exchange, Brent listened carefully, fully amused, but enough was enough, and he could see that Spellman was reaching his limit. Brent poked Nigel in the ribs lightly and said, "Let him finish now."

"Thank you, Lieutenant," Dr. Spellman said, then continued. "So the bones were connected using a Milch procedure. Perverted, but medically intriguing nonetheless. The radius veins and arteries were cross-connected, as were the ulna veins and arteries, forming a pair of AV shunts. You can see it a little bit on the X rays, but the angiogram shows it best. The decreased pulmonary resistance is no doubt depriving the rest of the body of its normal blood flow, resulting in mild tachycardia. However, we've scheduled the reversal surgery for this Thursday. Yesterday, incidentally, I opened up the lip scar tissue and closed the stoma."

"Dr. Spellman," Brent said, "what trade publications are specific to osteopathy?"

"The *Journal of Bone and Joint Surgery.*"

"I need to borrow a year or two's worth of past issues."

"I keep those in my office," Dr. Spellman said. "I'll get them for you later today, after the review meeting."

"Good. I need to call them and get a circulation list."

"I hope you have plenty of manpower, Lieutenant, to locate our mystery doctor. . . ."

"Dr. Y," one of the other doctors in the room said.

Spellman turned to face him, and said, "Now, why wouldn't you call him Dr. X?"

"Well, Dr. Y is as good as Dr. X." He and Spellman had been having a personality conflict for some time.

"Call him Dr. Who!" Nigel blurted.

"Why?"

"Dr. X! . . ."

"Why not Who?" Nigel said, pretending to be hurt.

Brent said, "Dr. Who is already taken."

"Huh?" some doctors said in unison, not being familiar with the TV series *Dr. Who.*

Spellman said, *"X* always stands for the unknown."

"In a one-variable universe," Nigel fired off, wanting to keep the doctors going as long as he could; then he turned to Brent and said like a whining child, "Call him Dr. Smegma."

"Smegma?" Brent said.

"What's wrong with Dr. Y?"

"Y is stupid!" Dr. Spellman said with increasing frustration. "Everyone knows *x* stands for the unknown, and we *don't* know who we're looking for."

"Smegma," Nigel whispered in Brent's ear.

"SIGMA!" Brent said. "We'll call him Dr. Smeg—Sigma!"

Nigel burst out laughing and Brent hit him in the ribs with his elbow and said, "Enough of this," then looked at Dr. Spellman. "Let's assume for a moment, that our Dr. Sigma is an orthopedic surgeon, as you say. How many are there, approximately, in the New York/Long Island/Westchester/New Jersey area?"

"Oh, maybe . . . about five or six hundred. There's a lot a broken bones out there."

"And malpractice," Nigel said.

"Shhhhh!" Brent said to Nigel. "Back to our patient for a

moment, though. Could Mr. Lewis have been unconscious through-out the whole time when he was . . . wherever he was, during the healing period?"

"It's unlikely. When a person is in bed for a prolonged period of time, he develops bedsores or skin ulcers. With bedridden patients and the elderly, we have to turn them frequently to prevent exactly this from happening."

Nigel laughed out loud at the thought of turning "them" frequently, and he envisioned Dr. Spellman, dressed like a witch doctor, turning Jerome Lewis by the crank of a flaming rotisserie. Spellman's eyes peered at Nigel, and he wondered what this man must have thought to provoke such a curious outburst.

Brent said, "So then either he was awake or someone was paying very close attention to him?"

"Well, the patient seems to have healed along a normal recovery curve. Had he been unconscious during the period in question, not only would his healing have been retarded but I believe his muscles would have atrophied somewhat. So he probably was walking around and getting *some* exercise. There were no signs of atrophy, except in the arms, which is to be expected, considering . . . How do we feel about that?" Dr. Spellman asked his colleagues.

Several nods and grunts confirmed how "we" felt.

Brent continued, "So then it's safe to assume that he was probably conscious some of the time?"

"Yes, we believe so."

Nigel leaned over to Brent and whispered into his ear, "Notice the way they always say 'we' when they speculate, and then they never hesitate to say 'I' when it comes time to take the credit for some personal achievement, no matter how trivial."

"Nigel, sometimes you act like you were born yesterday," Brent whispered back.

"Do you have a question, Lieutenant?" The doctor added, "Or you?" looking disapprovingly at Nigel.

"Many questions," Brent said, "and some of them might possibly be answered by Jerome Lewis when he comes around. Dr. Spellman, how would you feed a man without a mouth for five or six weeks?"

"Hyperalimentation at first. IV solutions of vitamins, fat solutions, protein solutions, glucose, et cetera. All standard stuff. But you have to get him off IV and any hyperosmolar solutions as soon as possible to avoid burning the blood vessels. After he's off IV, you'd go to enternal alimentation." Brent seemed confused. "That's when we place a rubber tube through the patient's nose and down the esophagus. You then pump feeding solutions directly into his stomach."

"Can we detect any of that in his blood?"

"Probably not. It's just food. Any normal food thrown into a blender and made soft and pumpable will work. He might have been fed Sustacal, too."

"What's that?"

"It's like a milk shake. They feed it to old people. It's commonly available."

"What about the hyperalimentation?"

"You probably won't detect that anymore. It metabolizes pretty quickly. And whoever did this seems to know what he's doing, so he probably went enternal al shortly after the abduction."

"But we still have some of his blood from the day he . . . checked in. If we knew what we were looking for, couldn't we detect the difference among the different suppliers of those feeding solutions you mentioned?"

Dr. Spellman looked at the table for help. Blank stares. "That's a little esoteric for us, Lieutenant. You'd have to check with the organic chemists at the drug companies."

"Could you do that for me?"

"Lieutenant, I'm not exactly a research assistant. . . ."

"Wally, you know all the right questions to ask. I want to know everything I can learn from that man's blood. Maybe you could at least find the right people and have them get back to Mr. Atkerson here. We need suppliers and customer lists."

"I can assure you, anything short of a court order won't produce a customer list from a drug company. And even if you could get customer lists, it's still like finding a needle in a haystack."

"That's what I do, Wally. I find needles in haystacks. . . ."

A lively discussion ensued, covering the subjects of chemistry, medicine, psychology, forensics, philosophy, Shakespeare, and even surgery. The plan was to separate Mr. Lewis's arms and remove all the plates, bolts, and hardware, which would then be turned over to the police for analysis.

"That's about it for us, then," Lieutenant Kramer said as he and Nigel Atkerson rose from the table. "I'm going up to visit Mr. Lewis now and see if I can jog his memory a bit. So you'll get back to me with that information on your punch list, Doctor?"

"I'll call you later today, say at four-thirty, quarter to five."

"Okay. And thanks for letting us sit in." Brent and Nigel left the room as the medical review continued.

"The next patient is Sylvia Berman. She's seventy-six years old and in reasonably good health. She fell in her kitchen and shattered her pelvis. This one, I think, is a good candidate for that new hip replacement they've been making all that noise about up at . . ."

Brent and Nigel walked down the hallway with renewed pessimism. Brent said, "I'm gonna see Jerome now. You wanna come?"

"I haven't got time. I've got more tests to run, and I'm giving an improvised munitions lecture at Picattiny tomorrow, and I've got to prepare for it. Keep me informed, though."

"You don't think too much of Spellman, do you?"

"Dr. Stillborn?"

"Spellman!"

"I don't know *what* to think. He's a little pompous and smug. Also, I don't think we're looking for an osteopath."

"I agree, by the way. But why?"

"I don't know. Gut instinct, I guess. Why don't *you* think we're looking for an orthopedic man?"

"I don't know, either," Brent said. "Same gut instinct, I guess."

"Great guts instinct alike."

"Yeah. And so do ours. In any event, I'm gonna call the bureau and get a list of any doctors who had their licenses revoked in the past ten years."

"Probably a good idea." Nigel smiled. "Brent, you *know* we haven't seen the last of this."

"I know."

"In fact, I rather think it's *just* beginning," Nigel said, with an evil grin from ear to ear.

Brent and Nigel stopped in front of a candy machine as a man approached. He stared at them, then said, "Aren't you Lieutenant Kramer?"

"Who are you, and why do you want to know?"

"I'm a reporter for the *Jersey Journal.*"

"I thought they were keeping all you journalists out of the building for a change," Brent challenged. "How did you get past security?"

"I'm not really on the clock at the moment. My mother is in for open-heart surgery, and I was visiting her before the operation. I saw your face on the news the other day, and I thought I recognized you here in the hall. Damn shame about that poor boy."

"Yes. Damn shame," Brent said.

"Hey, wait a minute, guys," Nigel exploded, "what is this— a liberal convention?!! You know this guy you're both 'damn shaming' over is a goddamn murderer. That's the damn shame. People are *dead* because of him! Don't forget that, kids! Christ! This is the *only* fuckin' country in the world where you're innocent *after* proven guilty! Far as I'm concerned, that punk got off easy!"

"Who are *you?*" the reporter asked as Nigel worked a pair of latex gloves onto his hands.

"I'm Dr. Atkerson," he said, almost in the voice of Peter Lorre, while sinuously flexing his fingers like the cilia of a one-celled animal. Brent rolled his eyes.

"That's some attitude you have for a doctor," the reporter said.

"Well, you've heard of new math, right? Well, this is *new medicine.*"

"What is your connection to the patient?"

"Oh, you mean the hooper?"

"That's what you call him?!" the reporter said in disbelief.

"Well, I could bore you with a bunch of medical terminology in Latin, but here in real medicine land, we simply call him a hooper. Excuse me, son, but the lieutenant and I were discussing something very important. Could you excuse us for a moment?" Nigel sinuously flexed his fingers again, almost as if he were going to strangle the reporter.

As the reporter walked away, Brent said, "You know, Nige, one day you're gonna get yourself murdered."

"I'm not gonna run around in fear of every life-form that happens to scurry past my visual field. By the way, you said that both these guys were just recently released from temporary storage, right?"

"Yes, both abducted within days of being released, and they both committed car jackings."

"Coincidence?"

"Can't assume that it is. I've already sent memoranda to all the parole offices in New York State."

"What about Jersey and Connecticut?"

"First things first. New York has plenty of offices as it is, and both these boys were incarcerated in New York. We'll eventually expand our radius, though. And *will* you take those stupid gloves off? . . ."

16   Memories, Mattituck, and More Memories

Lt. Brent Kramer entered the hospital room of Jerome Lewis. It was the first day after his reconstructive lip surgery, and Brent knew Jerome would be in no mood to idly shoot the breeze. Mr. Lewis delicately pressed his raw, rubbery lips together as he watched the cop slowly approach him. Brent sat on the edge of the bed and waited for acknowledgment from Jerome, which came in the form of a pair of drooping eyebrows and a frown. "It's me again," Brent softly said. "How you doing today?"

"Okay, I guess. Iss good ta talk again."

"I know it must be painful for you to speak, but I need you to tell me what you remember about the past six weeks, before you forget any valuable details that might lead us to the maniac who did this to you. By the way, I took care of the outstanding warrant for your arrest. They thought you absconded. I explained the extenuating circumstance when I spoke with your parole officer. He's very relieved—well, let me rephrase that. He's relieved that you didn't intentionally stand him up. In fact, he'll be here to see you later today —I think around three or three-thirty."

"I ain' goin' noplace," Jerome Lewis said slowly and painfully. Another stalactite of drool formed on the side of his mouth. His lips were numb, and his face had developed a slight pull to the left due to the disappearance of a three-quarter-inch hole in his cheek. "What gonna happen ta me?"

"Well, I suppose you'll be here for a while. Doc Spellman knows a good surgeon who will separate your arms, and I think they plan to fit you with a pair of artificial hands. You'll never be as good as new, but they'll do the best they can. As far as your future is concerned, you're going to have to start concentrating on your brain, not your hands. As hard as it may seem right now, you're going to have to look toward the future, not the past."

"You sound like all dem pep-talk dudes down at da prison," Jerome said with a pained smile.

Brent returned the smile and put his hand on Jerome's shoulder. "Except for one thing; your situation now is a lot different than it was then. Jerome, do you mind if I tape-record our conversation?"

"Go on," he said, with an upward thrust of his surgically joined arm loop. "Do what you gotta do, man."

Brent removed a small recorder from his breast pocket and placed it on a table next to the bed. He pressed the record button and sat up on the edge of the bed. "I'll try to avoid asking you questions that require answers that use letters like *p* or *b*." Jerome thought about what the lieutenant had just said, then began to laugh. Brent smiled, then said, "I'm glad you still have a sense of humor. I think you're gonna need it."

"I'll try not ta lose it, man."

"Good. All right, let's get started. You were released from Attica on Friday, April sixteenth. Is that correct?"

"Yeah."

"Where did you go after that?"

"When I got to the city, I went to the police station ta let 'em know I was here. Den I seen ma parole officer in 'n afternoon. I fill out some forms 'n shit."

"Where did you go then?"

"I wen' home ta Joey's place. Dat's where I was stayin'."

"When were you abducted?"

"I doan know, maybe three, four days later."

"Tell me about it."

"I was out, walkin' on 'n street 'n shit."

"What street were you on when it happened?"

"I was walkin' up . . . aaaa. I doan know da name a da street,
It was like . . . near Sutter—da street dat go across the train track."

"What time was it?"

"It was pretty late, man. Maybe four o'clock inna mo'nin'."

"What were you doing out that late over there?"

Jerome paused momentarily. "I was hangin' out 'n shit?"

"Hanging out doing what?"

There was now an uncomfortably long pause. "Checkin' out
da neighborhood 'n shit. I doan remember."

"You *don't* remember what you were doing before you were
abducted?" Jerome shrugged his shoulders, and he was embarrassed.
Brent switched off the tape recorder. "Jerome, this is now off the
record, and between you and me only. You see, I believe that someone was watching you, stalking you, and they didn't make their move
till they were damn sure of your habits—your routine. Your parole
officer isn't gonna hear a word you say to me, and I'm really good
at keeping secrets. Now tell me, were you trying to cop some
drugs?"

After another long pause, he meekly said, "I guess so."

"You copping blow?"

"Hell yeah. Been so fuckin' long, I forgot what iss like. Could
you blame me, man?"

"No. And thanks for being honest with me. I'm gonna switch
this thing back on now." And Brent clicked on the recorder. "Did
someone jump you from behind? How were you overpowered?"

"I felt like I was shot, or stab or somethin'."

"Stabbed?" This was the exact word Freddy Lopez had used.

"Yeah. Stab in ma back—like real hard!"

"Almost like being stabbed with . . . maybe a pin or an ice
pick?" Brent asked.

"Yeah." Jerome shook his head up and down. "An dat was
da last thing I rememba . . . until . . ."

A car turned left, north, onto a nameless dirt road off Route 25A in the little town of Mattituck in Suffolk County. The dirt road ran alongside a huge sand quarry off to the left a little beyond the dump, with dense woods to the right. Three-tenths of a mile in, the dirt road took a lazy right into the woods, terminating at a clearing near a field of low bushes and several mosquito-breeding swamps protected by thickets of sticker bushes. The car parked on a bed of moss next to a fat oak and a large fallen maple. The hunter, dressed in full camouflage military fatigues, locked the car door and hiked off along one of the many trails lacing these woods.

The sound of a dirt bike reverberated through the forest. Its straining fifteen-horsepower two-cycle engine screamed a different note every time it climbed or dropped the hills while kicking up dirt and leaves in its skidding wake. It had just completed the second pass through the loop and headed back toward the quarry.

The hunter sweated profusely while hiking, and periodically wiped beads of moisture from under the bridge of a pair of aviator sunglasses. A quarter of a mile later, the paramilitary figure adjusted a sun visor, and took up a position of high vantage, overlooking the sloping faces of the quarry and the garbage dump off in the distance.

A plume of dust drifted into the crosswind, perpendicular to the wheels of the motorcycle, which clawed its treads up toward the flappy layer of root-knotted topsoil overhanging the exposed golden quarry sand. The angle steepened, and the bike fought for hard-earned inches of height while gouging its way deeper into the rain-hardened sand. Thick purple-gray smoke belched and puffed from the exhaust pipe and pitted muffler. Losing purchase, the front wheel tipped up like a wild, bucking mechanical horse, and the bike and rider banked to the left, heading back to the trail again. The back wheel fishtailed as the machine and driver accelerated over the edge of the sand pit, back toward the woods.

The motorcycle slowed as it approached the edge of the forest. A small freshly cut white pine lay on its side, blocking the trail. The motorcyclist shifted to neutral as he analyzed the situation, a situation that had not existed a mere half hour ago. His mind plotted a course through the woods, around the obstruction. He revved the engine several times, then raised his left boot to kick into first.

Pfffffffft!

A sudden sharp pain in the right shoulder. A heart attack? No. The feeling of being punched hard, punched hard with pinpointed pain. The cyclist's left hand reached over to the impacted area. There was an object of some kind—something cylindrical. It had punctured his flannel shirt and his undershirt, pinning them to his skin like a message to a corkboard. He pulled this small spear from his body and curiously examined its unfamiliar shape, taking particular notice of the blood—his blood—on the end of the thick, hollow steel pin. But by then, it was too late. The liquid contents of the hypo dart were entering the bloodstream from a higher concentration pooled one inch within his freshly punctured muscle tissue, and the tranquilizing effects were quickly taking command of his metabolism and consciousness, and he collapsed to the ground while still straddling the seat of his motorcycle, with the engine still idling out of gear.

"... Yeah! I rememba dat voice," Jerome Lewis said. "He use some kin'a 'lectronic thing—ya know, ta fuck up da voice so I couldn't re-ca-nize it. It sounded all fucked up 'n shit. Dat mothafucka sound like a horror movie shit."

"So the voice was disguised electronically?"

"Yeah."

"Did you ever see this person? Can you tell me what he looks like?"

"No! Whole time, I was blindfolded! Mothafucka kept me in 'n dark da whole fuckin' time."

"Could you tell if this was a man or a woman?"

"I think it was a man. But da only thing I had ta go on was dat one fucked-up voice. It sounded like two or three people talkin' at once—like *Satan* shit. He grab me real tight on ma arms 'n shit—like ta lead me round da place. I was all fucked up—like on drugs 'n shit. I neva had no drugs like those. He walk me around 'n put me on dat exercise bicycle. He say, 'Pedal hard now. You got ta get yo' exercise. You got ta ride fo a half hour in na mo'nin an a half hour in 'n afternoon.' Dat's what dat mothafucka say ta me." Jerome Lewis was now in tears as he relived his foggy, half-anesthetized experience. "I did'n' even know he sew ma lips shut. Dat mothafucka! He had some kin'a thing he put aroun' ma head to keep me from openin' my mouth—some kin'a box thing—wit screws 'n shit. I rememba now. All I could feel wit ma tongue was ma teeth onna inside a ma mouth. I thought dare was tape or somethin' on ma mouth. I knew ma lips hurt, but I did'n know he done all dat shit ta me. I knew he done somethin' real bad ta da side a ma face. Like I could feel dare was dis cold spot on my left cheek. An ma arms was inside dis, like, machine ta hold 'em in place . . . so I couldn't move 'em 'n shit. I knew somethin' was wrong after like . . . several weeks . . . like when I started ta realize dat dey was growin' together. I still couldn't believe dat shit . . ." Jerome was agitated, tormented, tangled in the hazy, fragmented memories of his first confrontation with authentic madness—his first confrontation with the cognitive dissonance exploding in his own conscious mind, which struggled in earnest to reject that which was incomprehensible, that which was unfathomable by any familiar logic, by any standard of normal sensations in his body. How could what happened actually have happened in the real world? What could do this? What could cause this? It was a challenge for any standard of sanity. "My arms were clamped in some kin 'a thing," he sobbed, ". . . 'n da next thing I know . . . I'm around dat fuckin' lamppost 'n people are kickin' me 'n yellin' shit at me—'n people wit cameras 'n shit askin' me questions about all kin'a shit . . . I didn't know *what* dem fuckin' people were talkin' 'bout—"

"Let's backtrack a minute," Brent interrupted. "Were you able to smell anything—like perfume or cologne or deodorant or anything that would help identify this person?"

"Not dat I could think a. Whole place smell like a docta's office. Ya know, dat docta's office smell?"

"What were you able to hear?"

"Oh! Dat's da other thing. Dare was music playin' the whole time. All I ever heard was music."

"What kind of music?"

"It was dat classical shit."

"Did you recognize any of it?"

"No. I neva listen ta dat shit."

"Were you listening to the radio or to tapes? Was there a station identification or commercials?"

"No. Juss music. Muss a been tapes."

"Were you able to hear anything above the sound of the

music—you know, like children playing out on the street, or cars passing by, or car horns, or anything—you know, sounds from the outside?"

"No. All I heard was da music. Whenever I was awake ... Dat same fuckin' music ..."

"Could you tell if you were in the city, or the suburbs, or the country?"

"No. Only da music ... Wait a minute! I did hear ... Wait! Wait a minute! I did hear somethin' from da outside. I heard airplanes! One day I heard lots a airplanes. Like dey kept comin' every like ... five minutes ... for like a hour or two. Maybe more. I rememba now. Dem fuckin' airplanes. Yeah!"

"How loud were the airplanes?" Brent knew that this was a subjective question. It was a question that required a qualitative answer. An experiment would have to be performed, and he knew who the only person was who could perform such an experiment properly.

17   The Dotted Line

Marshall Stanley strutted out of the elevator at Roosevelt Hospital, radiating the confidence of a six-foot-tall man who knew exactly where he was and what he was doing. He wore the same green pants and shirt the surgeons wear, and a green cap covered all the curly light brown hair on his head. A stethoscope was draped around his neck and he held a clipboard in the same hand that displayed his Rolex. He adjusted his glasses as he approached the door to the room where he knew Mr. Lewis was kept. He sized up the bored policeman who stood about ten feet from the door, guarding Mr. Lewis.

Marshall Stanley walked up to the nurse with the door buzzer control somewhere below the desk, smiled, and said, "Hi, I'm Dr. Stanley, and I'm from Reconstructive Orthopedics over at Lenox Hill. Dr. Spellman asked me if I would have a look at Mr. Lewis here and then I could make some recommendations. Did he tell you to be expecting me?"

The nurse was taken completely off guard, and she said, "No. As a matter of fact, he didn't. I thought Dr. Christy was—"

"Darn!" Marshall Stanley looked at his watch, then said, "I've got to be back at Lenox in less than an hour."

"He's in a meeting right now. Perhaps you should join him there. As a matter of fact, I think they're discussing the case."

With a troubled look, he pointed at his watch and said, "I was just trying to save time."

"Mr. Lewis is next-door. Let me buzz you in."

"Thank you very much. I appreciate it."

"You're welcome, Dr. Stanley. Please dial six-four when you want to leave the room."

"Okay." With a big friendly smile, Marshall Stanley waved to the nurse, then smiled at the policeman as the door surrendered to the buzzing solenoid lock.

He closed the door behind him and quickly walked to the bed of Mr. Lewis and sat down next to him. He pulled the blankets down and looked at the man's arms. "Oh, this is great," he said out loud, then began shaking Mr. Lewis out of his dreamy, drugged-up sleep.

"Wuz goin' on?" Jerome said, with sleepy dust in his eyes.

"Jerome, your ship has finally landed."

"Wus you talkin' 'bout? Dey got so many doctas at diz fuckin' place."

"*Jerome,*" Stanley sang. "I ain't no doctor."

"You dressed like a docta. Who da hell are you, man?"

"I'm your fairy godmother. I'm sort of a financial navigator, you might say."

"Den why don you juss navigate yo ass outta here?"

"Do you want to know how you can make a *lot of money?* More money than you've *ever* made in your life?"

"What chu talkin' 'bout?"

"Now look, no amount of money is gonna bring back your hands. But I believe it's possible for us to make the most out of your . . . unfortunate situation here. I'm telling you that you should wait a while before you have those arms separated. I mean, hell, if you could wait three or four months before you get the operation, what difference does it really make to you, especially if you can make a couple a hundred thou—maybe even a *cool mil!* Who knows?"

"You sayin' I could make all dis money if I waits fo dem ta gimme my operation?"

"That's exactly what I'm saying. And I know exactly how to make us both rich—very rich."

"Wait! *How* you know I'z gettin' a operation to cut dis apart?"

"You don't watch the TV and the news in here. Jerome, you're a bit of a celebrity, ma boy. And as I was saying, I know how we can make big bucks off it."

"Yeah? What I gotta do?" Jerome had apprehension in his voice.

Marshall laughed. "You misunderstand. It's perfectly legal. And you'll be famous, too. But more important, you'll be rich."

"Who da *fuck* are you?"

"I'm your new agent and manager, Jerome." Marshall Stanley held a business card in front of the eyes of Jerome Lewis. The card said:

MARSHALL R. STANLEY
Agent/Manager/Promoter

PHONE (212) 555-2101   1266 Avenue of the Americas
FAX (212) 555-2102   Suite 2114
New York, NY

He then produced a contract from his clipboard. "Are you afraid of being in front of large audiences?"

"I ain' afraid a *nothin'!*"

"That's the spirit, ma boy. I think we're gonna get along fine, you and me. All you have to do, Mr. Lewis, is sign right here. . . ."

"You outta you fuckin' mind? I can't sign shit!"

"We'll just put the pen in your mouth and you can make an X right over here on the dotted line. . . ."

"What do you mean, you *don't* want the surgery, Jerome?!!!" Dr. Spellman could not believe what he was hearing. "You wanna *stay* like this?!!"

"Fo da time bein' I do." Jerome Lewis was sitting up in his bed, with his stubborn spine against the backrest. His arm loop rested on a pillow, almost giving the appearance that his hands were in a hand warmer.

"Are you afraid of the outcome of the operation?"

"I ain' afraid a nothin'."

"You'll be much more comfortable when your arms are separated."

"Maybe I will. Maybe I won't. Whose ta say?"

"Then you *are* afraid of the operation."

"I toll you, I ain' afraid a nothin'!"

"It's nothing to be ashamed of. It's very frightening, this whole thing. I understand."

"No, you don' una'stan' nothin'! I got to start thinkin' 'bout ma future 'n all. Mista Stanley, he explain the whole thing ta me crystal clear."

"Who is Mr. Stanley?"

"Ma agent!" Jerome proudly said.

Dr. Spellman hesitated, gazing off into space. "I'm not following this line of logic. You have an agent?"

"Yeah! An' he gonna take good care a me." Jerome lifted his loopy appendage into the air and rocked it side to side like a hinged parallelogram. "You see, he say, what I got here, iss a *asset.*"

"Oh God, I don't believe this. I really don't believe what I'm hearing here. You don't *want* the operation, because—let me see if I have this correct—because your agent is going to exploit this tragedy commercially?"

"Dat's *a-zactly* what I'z sayin'! We gonna make a fortune outta dis here tragedy, as you call it."

"This is perverted. This is sicker than sick. I don't believe this. Wait a minute! When did all this transpire?"

"Say wha?"

"When did you meet this individual, this Mr. Stanley?"

"He come in here just a hour or two ago."

"How did he get in here? That door is locked twenty-four hours a day. There's a security system."

"Security, ma ass! He juss walk his ass right through that door dress like a docta. I even sign a contract wit a *X*—my *X!* You see, my hands a little tied up at da moment. Security!"

"Excuse me one moment—I have to cheek something." Dr. Spellman dialed sixty-four. "Could you buzz me outta here, please?" Dr. Spellman left Jerome Lewis to his budding career as a human zoo specimen and approached the nurse. "Did you let anyone in Jerome's room in the past few hours?"

"No, but I've only been on duty for a half hour. Karen was on, and she'll be back at one o'clock. She's at lunch, Doctor."

Dr. Spellman then asked the policeman on duty what he knew, and he told the doctor that another doctor, about six feet tall, had entered the room at about eleven o'clock and that he had remained in the room with Mr. Lewis for roughly ten minutes.

"Reconstructive Orthopedics at Lenox Hill!!! I never heard such bullshit! Karen, do you know what the hell you let into that room? A theatrical agent! A personal manager! Some bloodsucker that's gonna . . . charge people money to see 'im! Is this for real? No, this is *not* for real! This is some kind of demented . . . mercenary . . . cartoon fishbowl we're living in! I can't *believe* this!"

"He mentioned *you* by name," Karen said meekly. "I thought he was legit. I'm terribly sorry. I breached procedure. I don't know what to say, Doctor. . . ."

Dr. Spellman looked at the nurse, who was almost at the point of tears. "I'm sorry, Karen. I didn't mean to rail at you like that. I . . . Wait a minute! I'll bet this Dr. Stanley is the one who did this, so he could . . . I can't believe this! He purposely . . . I need an outside line right away. I need to call Lieutenant Kramer this second!"

Rusty Blake was three days overdue for his appointment with his parole officer, who now had decided to track Rusty down at his job. It was a no-brainer job—loading bags of fertilizer and seeds onto and off of trucks, but at least it was a real job. And Rusty seemed to have a good attitude—that is, for the six days that he'd been there. On the seventh day, he just didn't show up. This behavior didn't surprise the owner of Eastern Long Island Farm & Garden. He'd employed ex-cons before, and they often just stopped showing up, same as Rusty Blake. He just rolled his eyes when Rusty failed to show, and slapped the HELP WANTED sign back in the window. And that was the last he gave it any mind, until Officer Vinny Pollo of the regional Division of Parole in the town of Happauge called and asked about Rusty's whereabouts.

"Doesn't surprise me in the least," Rusty's former employer said. "They often seem real enthusiastic at first. Then they skip town. Can't half blame 'em, can ya? Who wants to load bags a shit all day?" Then he thought about Ken, the forty-five-year-old retardate who'd worked for him for more than four years, till he got pancreatic cancer and died in no time flat—best employee he'd ever had.

"Well, if he shows up," Officer Pollo said, "please have him call us here at the Division of Parole." Officer Pollo then read that memo on his desk for the second time. The memo requested that all cases of parole violation in New York State be reported to a Lt. Brenton Kramer, of the City of New York Police Department, Midtown Precinct North. It was part of an investigation, so Officer Pollo called the lieutenant in New York. "You wanted to be informed about parole violations?" he half-asked and half-told the lieutenant.

"Yes, I do. Tell me about it." Brent was surprised that someone was actually being cooperative without it being forced out of him.

Officer Pollo told Brent Kramer about Mr. Blake's failure to keep his parole appointment and his failure to report to work.

"What was Mr. Blake's crime?" Brent asked.

"He shot a man eight or so years back during a robbery attempt. Paralyzed him from the waist down."

"What kind of a robbery was it?"

"He was trying to steal the man's car outside a movie theater."

"His car, you say?!"

"Yes. Is that significant?"

"It sure is. Is the paralyzed man available for questioning?"

"I'm afraid not, Lieutenant. He died last year."

"I see. I need all the case data you have. How soon can you fax it to me?"

Rusty Blake's unconscious body had already been washed, prepped, and clamped to a table in numerous places. A series of electronic monitors had been hooked up and were actively beeping, blipping, and doing the things they do. A tourniquet was tied just below the elbow joint of both arms, which hung off the sides of the custom-designed operating table.

The surgeon reached for a razor-sharp scalpel, looked at the clock on the wall, and touched the halogen-illuminated target line inked onto the skin, five inches above each wrist. A deep incision was made, circumscribing the skin of the forearm a full 360 degrees. The blood vessels were severed and drained by squeezing the arm and hand with a massaging action. Four parallel incisions, ninety degrees apart, were then made in the skin, perpendicular to the circumscribing incision and in line with the axis of the arm. The four flaps of skin created by these cuts were each peeled back and separated from the subcutaneous muscle tissue. The muscle tissue, veins, arteries, and nerves were severed to the bone, cut and peeled away, and pinned back with safety pins, so that they were temporarily inside out, and out of the way, completely exposing the radius and ulna bones.

By this time, bleeding was minimal. The miter box clamp was then attached to the radius and ulna bone, and tightened into place with a pair of C-clamp–type screws. The stainless steel saw was placed against the zigzag form of the miter box's guiding reference surface, which resembled the teeth of a bear trap. And then the reciprocating motion of the saw—up and down, penetrating its way into the radius bone until hitting the angular stop of the first triangular tooth of the miter box. The accumulation of abraded bone tissue and marrow formed a pink gritty paste that accumulated at the contact zone of the bone and saw blade, and it stuck to the slimy blade, which penetrated the human bones with moderate speed, not quite like a hot knife through butter, but with no difficulty, either. The saw was removed, and the second cut was begun, sixty degrees to the first cut, following the precise form of the tool, and then another cut, sixty degrees to that, and finally a fourth; and the radius was completely separated the same way one might cut out cross sections of a model airplane wing.

And this same process was repeated with the ulna bone. As the final cut was made, the right hand and connecting bones simply fell away, limp and lifeless, completely amputated, never to be commanded by human nerve tissue again. Total time to hand drop-off— eight minutes and forty-three seconds. Then the exposed tissue and bone was temporarily wrapped in sterile plastic wrap, so it would remain moist during the surgeon's amputation of the left hand.

Eight minutes and fifty-eight seconds later, the amputated left hand was placed alongside the right, inside a stainless steel tray. These hands were now right where they belonged.

The triangular cuts in both bones of both arms were mated together perfectly and held into position with a homemade fixture specially designed for the final assembly. A pair of small stainless steel plates (a top plate and a bottom plate) with four predrilled holes was clamped into position over the mated ulna bones, and a similar pair of plates was clamped into position over the mated radius bones. An ordinary variable-speed Black & Decker drill was still warm from its bath in the autoclave, and it was used to drill the eight through holes in the four mated bones. Four fine-thread stainless steel bolts were installed in the holes of the radius plates, and then four bolts and nuts were installed in the ulna plates. All eight nuts were tightened, and the ends of the bolts were hacksawed off flush with the ends of the nuts. The joints were cleaned to remove any extraneous metal particles, and the muscle tissue from both arms was trimmed away so left and right tissue mated flush and cleanly. The tissue was then sutured together.

The ulna veins and arteries were cut to length and cross-connected to form the AV shunt. Tiny sutures artfully joined vein to artery and artery to vein. And this same procedure was performed on the radial veins and arteries. The tourniquets were removed from both arms, and the collapsed and drained blood vessels filled themselves with life-giving blood, swelling to their rated dimensions under the influence of an anesthetized heart still pumping slowly but reliably, beep after pacing beep.

Next, the skin from both arms was mated and cut to form. Tiny, skillful, regular sutures joined the skin closed, and the osteotomy was complete—the second of its kind ever to be performed in the world of medicine—noteworthy as it was; and Milch had never realized the full implications of the procedure that bore his name.

A stopcock was opened, and a small volume of diluted curare was metered into the subclavian vein of the patient. The stopcock was closed, and the patient was monitored during the transient response of the vital signs, till the new equilibrium state was stable. A spreading clamp cranked open the patient's mouth. A dental-type suction vacuum was placed in the mouth to remove any unwanted fluids during the impending procedure; there would be much unwanted fluid, the majority of which would be the color red.

The nonmoving arm of a modified C-clamp was placed into the open mouth. A sharp cylinder of red-hot steel was removed from an RF induction furnace. The cylinder was three-quarters of an inch in diameter, one inch long, and it glowed cherry red when inserted into the movable end of the tool. The tool was manually held into position over the left cheek, and the handle was turned. The tool was cranked closed, similar to the way one might fully close a C-clamp, except when this tool closed, the red-hot cylinder of sharp steel sizzled as it bored a hole in the left cheek. With each turn of the handle, the sharp blade penetrated another sixteenth-inch into the cheek tissue. Smoke and sizzling steam rose from the razor-sharp cylinder of steel as it gouged out a self-cauterizing core sample of human cheek flesh. And finally the tool was tightened as far as it would go, with the end of the fully advanced cylinder compressing firmly into the base plate inside the mouth. The handle was loosened and the tool was removed from the mouth. The cylinder of cooked cheek tissue still hung in place by a few strands of skin and flesh. The little plug of skin was gripped with a pair of needle nose pliers, and the remainder of the stubborn tissue was cut away with a scalpel.

There was still some bleeding, and an ordinary twenty-five-watt soldering iron fitted with a stainless tip was touched to the leaky spots along the inside diameter of the fresh new hole. Each hissing sound was sweet, satisfying music to the discriminating ears of the surgeon, who delighted in nearing the conclusion of the day's surgical activities. Then the inside of the hole was sutured up, and the spreading clamp was removed from the patient's mouth.

The surgeon watched and listened to the monitors. All the high-intensity lamps had been shut off. All the tools had been cleaned and placed into the autoclave. Everything was clean and ready for another day. All that was left to do was monitor the patient's recovery.

It had been a day of no small achievement, and the time had come for that hard-earned glass of wine.

A pair of amputated hands sat in a stainless steel tray on a table, next to a glass of wine. And, as a very special patient recovered from his unique surgery, the only sounds other than the scratchy voice of Caruso to be heard in the OR were an occasional glass of wine being poured, and the steady sound of the heart rate monitor:

beep ... beep ... beep ... beep ... beep ...

20   Fun with Decibels

Brent Kramer sifted through copies of the *Journal of Bone and Joint Surgery* to get a feel for the magazine and the mind of the person who reads it. Federal Express had just dropped off the half-inch-thick circulation list for that magazine when the new computer programmer knocked on the broken glass of his office door. She was a gorgeous, well-dressed thirty-two-year-old Asian policewoman named Sally Chu. Every eye in the room was glued to her ass as she entered Brent's office.

Nearly a year earlier, well before the origins of this case,

Brent had put in a requisition for the full-time services of a programmer because he proposed to design a cross-referencing database program that would overlay a map of the metropolitan area.

For years Brent had wanted such a database program. Astonishing as it was, police work was still in the dark ages when it came to applying standard computer methods used in every walk of industrial life. It made Brent crazy just to think about it. One would think the police might lead the country, rather than so pathetically trail it. Oh, they'd gotten pretty good at checking license plates and Social Security numbers, and even fingerprints if you went through the FBI, but that was all direct comparison to an active list. That wasn't what modern police work was all about.

Twenty years ago, the patent office database was more sophisticated. You could search through all the abstracts of all the patents using key words, such as all patent abstracts possessing the words *digital, magnetic, multiplexing,* and *integrator;* then you could get a printout of all such patent abstracts; and that was available two decades ago! Brent wanted a similar system to log all the cases, the MOs, the offenders, the victims, the relatives, where they live, what they do, whom they know, and anything else relevant. It was *still* all done manually, just like they did it before the biplane and the barbershop quartet. Insurance investigators could cross-reference twenty-four different databases; why not the police? But there was *never* any money for it. Money for parades, they had. Money for the mayor's goddamn bedposts, they had. Money for rebuilding Grand Central Station, they had. Money to solve real crimes? The answer was always *no.* The President visiting the city for one day costs more than the entire system would cost a hundred times over. Why couldn't the damn President go visit Chicago next time?!

Brent called it Big Brother Phobia syndrome. He felt that even the police themselves somehow feared that if it became too easy to cross-reference too many lists and databases, it would somehow limit our freedom. Well, they were right. It would. But only for the crooks. And crooks seemed to be running the show. But it also meant something else—something even more revealing about government and all large organizations. If fewer cops could solve more crimes, they wouldn't need as many cops. And this was not politically sound. If they could get away with hiring autistic, blind cripples as cops, they would, but they can't, so they do the next best thing. They hire lots of double-digit-IQ cops and legally tie their hands in the name of freedom and human rights for the bad guys, while the rest of us must play the role of good little sheep being led to the slaughter. It was all part of the grand cosmic inside joke.

It's considered good visible police work if you round up a gaggle of prostitutes every so often, and it's good visible police work if you bust a couple of kids smoking dope to clog the courts occasionally; after all, clogged courts are good for getting more money. But other than roundup-style police work, the big boys aren't really interested in solving real crime. They talk about it at press conferences and during campaigns. And whenever they get the money, they measure their success by how many warm bodies they can hire, because it gets votes. It is measurable, and easy to say on the news: "We hired eight hundred more police officers." That means we must be taking that bite out of crime. But the real function of the police is to draw the chalk mark *after* you're killed, and to write parking tickets because it generates nonconfrontational revenue—hell, they don't even ticket the people who jump red lights and cause gridlock, because they won't confront someone face-to-face without a court order. The whole police department was all for show in the reasoning of Brent's darker moments.

But the mutilation of Jerome Lewis was an embarrassment to the government. Political opponents were taking full advantage of the situation. There were open cases a hundred times more important than Jerome Lewis could ever be. But the media had gone crazy with this one. It was so visual and easy for the average person to understand in a fifteen-second sound bite. Twenty-eight thousand murders per year was just a silly statistic. But one look at the scar across that man's surgically joined arms and those gorgeous sealed-up lips and you knew we were all in serious trouble. No question about it. King Kong himself could be the mayor, and he'd still have to answer for that one.

So when Brent said he needed some fancy computer stuff, the boys upstairs said, "Is that all?" One must be prepared to take full advantage of a situation when it comes along.

Brent hired Sally because, of the two hundred applicants, she had the best credentials; she had a physics degree from MIT, she was fluent in Pascal and C + +, she was mathematically literate, she had done a lot of work with computer graphics, she understood databases, and she'd written a compiler as a high school senior. And she was a policewoman from San Diego County. She was just what Brent was looking for, and he had a feeling she was just what Nigel was looking for, too. The reason: Sally's hair. The most striking physical attribute about Sally Chu was her long red hair, dyed of course, but red. Nigel had always sworn that if he'd ever met an Asian woman with red hair, his marriage would be in serious jeopardy. Well, Nigel's marriage had managed to destroy itself, without the aid of any outside influence. Brent smiled as she closed the door behind her.

"Hello, Miss Chu. Glad to have you aboard."

"Thank you," Sally said with a mild accent she'd never quite lost since she and her family had come to California from Hong Kong when she was fourteen years old. "I hope I could be of service to you and the department."

"I'm sure you will be. I haven't got a whole lot of time to talk right now, but most of the hardware should be arriving this afternoon, and I have the Hagstrom maps and the topo quads for the city and surrounding areas. I guess the first thing we ought to do is work out a plan. Have you read all those technical papers from the Computational Sciences group at the FBI?"

"Yes, I have. I also have a few ideas of my own I would like to discuss with you when you have time. In the meantime, I found some bugs last week in the network software I could fix right away."

Brent smiled from ear to ear. He hated the existing network software at the precinct. Sometimes the network behaved as if it were possessed by evil spirits. Often, the same commands had completely different results, depending on how many users were on the system, which files were being accessed, whether or not someone in another part of the building was printing something out, and it even seemed to matter who was using the system and what time of day it was. The E-mail was unreliable, depending on the length of message and the time of day. Brent hated the software house that designed the screwball package. He could never get through to them on the telephone. "They should all be killed," the lieutenant muttered under his breath as he contemplated his new system.

"Excuse me?" Sally said.

"Nothing. Go right ahead and do whatever you can to improve things."

Sergeant Perato could not resist an excuse to get a better look at the new policewoman. He tapped on the door and Brent waved him in. The sergeant smiled at Sally, and Brent introduced them. Brent said to Al, "Miss Chu is going to write Nigel's program."

"Yes, that's related to what I wanted to tell you," Al said. "I'm on my way over to Roosevelt Hospital to pick up Jerome Lewis and take him to Nigel's loft on Greene Street for the acoustics test."

Brent knew Al was just looking for any excuse to get a better look at Sally, and he said, "Good, call me when you're through with the test."

"Glad to meet you," Al said to Sally, then left.

"Where were we?" Brent said. "Yeah. Do anything you can do to improve the system. Just don't tell anyone—especially Captain Percella. It should just mysteriously improve without any explanation."

"Okay. We could reboot the system late at night, when network activity goes down." Sally grabbed her maps and went to her new office with her Macintosh PowerBook.

Brent flung an eraser at the clock, then picked up the phone to call Marshall Stanley, Jerome Lewis's supposed agent. "Another one that should be killed." He left the following message: "Mr. Stanley. This is Lieutenant Brent Kramer of the Midtown North Precinct. I'd like to have a little chat with you regarding Jerome Lewis. I'd like you to call me at your earliest convenience. My number here is five-five-five-eighty-eight-hundred. If I'm not in, please leave a message telling me where you can be reached. Thank you."

Nigel set up the omnidirectional microphone six inches above the head of Jerome Lewis, who sat in a chair facing a pair of run-of-the-mill high-quality speakers. WQXR was playing the typical gambit of classical music, and a string quartet happened to be gracing their eardrums at the moment. Jerome said that the music he'd heard in the mysterious medical facility was more like a full orchestra, with "horns 'n drums 'n stuff." Dvořák or Stravinsky was more what Nigel had in mind for the actual test he would perform, but he figured Jerome should catch up on his classical-music exposure in the event that he would randomly hear the office music that Dr. Sigma liked subjecting his patients to.

Nigel tipped the hand truck back and wheeled the second

five-foot-high Voice of the Theater bass reflex speaker to the middle of the loft, some fifty feet away. He pointed it and its mate back-to-back so only reflected bass sound would be heard at the listening point where Jerome Lewis sat. He then placed the high-frequency horns on top of the bass reflex boxes and connected them to the biamp, which was fed by an old reel-to-reel tape recorder. This separate sound system was where the airplane sounds would radiate from. The more conventional sound system was where the music came from.

Sergeant Perato walked around the loft, looking at all the interesting things Nigel owned. It seemed that Nigel had been a shit collector from his early childhood on, and the only thing that kept him from overrunning the loft was the resisting effects of his now-defunct marriage. It seemed that Pamela, who was an artist, had been doing a good job of controlling Nigel's expansion, considering that she had her own shit collection to compete with his. The contrast between the two competing messes seemed comical to the sergeant, who had never been to Nigel's house before. Knowing Nigel, though, nothing he saw surprised him. The mess boundaries almost seemed like a war being fought on several fronts, with some forces advancing and others retreating. But Nigel's mess was overrunning his ex-wife's, because she'd run back to California. The sergeant correlated the personality of each mess with the mind responsible for it. All in all, there seemed to be at least a hundred little projects in varying stages of completion, projects ranging from art to science to home improvement, nested in every conceivable location, occupying every available square inch of surface area in this three-thousand-square-foot loft.

The library was a fascinating contrast of personalities as well, with books on art history adjacent to speleological literature; jazz, blues, and general music next to munitions; science bordering archaeology, forensics, and criminalistics next to literature; and architecture next to computers and electrical engineering. Chemistry and physics occupied an entire ceiling-high bookshelf by itself. And then there was the bookshelf of trashy novels and science fiction.

Jerome said, "You could throw some cool parties in dis place if you clean all dis shit up, man."

"I'll keep it in mind if I decide to open a disco," Nigel said. "Okay. We're ready to begin now. I'd like you to put this blindfold on, so you can judge the sound levels accurately, without visual influence."

"You wan *me* ta put it on?" Jerome said, raising his loop to accentuate his medical condition to Nigel. And the thought of a blindfold did not please Jerome much. It reminded him of an execution. And worse, it reminded him of the six weeks he'd spent blindfolded.

Nigel looked at Jerome and said, "I'm having a rhetorical conversation with myself. What I meant to say was, I'm gonna put this blindfold on you, *smart-ass,* so you can judge the sound levels accurately, without any visual influence!" Then Nigel placed the blindfold over Jerome's eyes and loudly snapped the elastic band on the back of his head.

"Ouch!" Jerome said, then turned his head to look at Nigel through the darkness of the blindfold.

The classical radio station was replaced with a tape of Stravinsky's *The Rite of Spring,* played by the New York Philharmonic. Jerome sat in the little wooden chair, with his loop in his lap. Nigel increased the volume a tad, then looked at the fluctuating needle of the decibel meter, hovering at the 35–40 db level. "About how loud would you say the music was playing, Jerome?"

"Louder!" Jerome said. "It was much louder den dis." Nigel upped the gain. "Louder." Nigel continued turning the knob. "A little louder. . . . Yeah! Dat's about right."

75–85 decibels.

Sergeant Perato found this curious. "He played the music this loud, nonstop?"

"Yeah. Every minute I was awake."

Both Nigel and the sergeant looked at each other and shrugged. "Okay," Nigel said. "Here come the planes." He switched on the reel-to-reel machine, and the huge speakers rumbled with the sound of a Boeing 707 Nigel had recorded when he was back in high school. The loudness was about equal to the loudness of the music. "How was that?" Nigel asked Jerome.

"Dem planes was louder den dat."

The next plane was due for arrival in a few seconds, and Nigel upped the gain. The room thundered with the sound of the jet, and Jerome twisted as his mind slipped back to the unpleasant memories of two, three, and maybe four weeks before, when he was clamped up in a mechanical healing apparatus, wearing a blindfold; the only difference was that this blindfold was held on with elastic; the other one had been taped on his face. "No. Dem planes was even louder." Nigel increased the volume further. Both he and the sergeant knew that the louder the planes were, the smaller their search area would be.

The next plane screamed, with higher frequency components than the other two. "Yeah! Dat's about right!"

130–140 db.

"That's pretty loud," Sergeant Perato said.

"Yeah . . . well, dem planes was pretty loud."

"**I'll bet they were,**" Nigel said, passing his voice through a rack-mounted harmonizer.

"*AAAAhhhhhhhhh!!!*" Jerome screamed. He turned quickly, tangling his legs in the legs of the chair. Then, as he reflexively stood, he tripped, being off balance due to his weird appendage, and fell to the floor, kicking the chair up into the air and over his head.

"**Please, Mr. Lewis, don't wreck the place,**" Nigel said, increasing the pitch offset of his voice slightly. "**See why you should get your operation? You can't even stand without *fucking up!*"**

"Dat like da sound a dat voice! You scare da shit outta me, man. Do dat shit ta me, man! You tryin' ta *fuck* wit ma head!"

"**It sounded like *this?*"** Nigel switched in another harmonizer channel, so that there were two pitch-shifted voices instead of only one. The mere sound of the harmonizer freaked Jerome out. He rubbed the blindfold off of his face with his arm loop as another jet came in for a landing. "**Does it bring back memories, *Jerome?*"** Nigel said with a slightly gleeful element in his voice.

"Please cut dat shit out, man," Jerome pleaded.

Sergeant Perato shook his head for Nigel to stop processing his voice through the effects generator.

"But Brent told me I could have fun," Nigel said to the sergeant, pretending to be disappointed.

"No, he told you you *would* have fun. There's a big difference, Nige."

Closing up a mouth is not like sewing up a simple laceration in the skin and underlying tissue. It requires planning and care, like anything else. But skin is still a very versatile living material. When you slice it up, it wants to heal again. It wants to reconnect to itself, and this wins 90 percent of the battle for both patient and doctor alike. But skin is still very stupid. It does not know when it is doing something it is not supposed to do, and it can therefore be outsmarted without great difficulty. Skin grafting works so well because skin wants to heal—no matter what. It wants to attach itself to any other compatible skin it touches. A billion years of evolution has seen to this, and it's amazing just how well skin does its job, even if it is the wrong job that it is doing. With the help and immobilizing effects of a needle and some thread, you can connect almost anything to anything else, and with a few simple tools, most of which are sharp, the possibilities are limited only by the artist's imagination.

And the skin of Rusty Blake was healing on two separate fronts on this second day after his surgery. He was groggy. He was horizontal. And he was restrained, with straps on his legs, his waist, his chest, his neck, and his head. His arms were securely clamped in the healing fixture, and a heavy black piece of cloth was taped across his eyes to protect him from any unnecessary light that might indiscreetly reveal the image of his agent of modification. And office recovery music was in the air, loud and without end. In his foggy state of mind, he did not know what had been done to his hands, and he could not possibly have anticipated that he was soon to be unconscious again, and under the knife. But Rusty was a man with a destiny, a destiny that would make speaking and eating difficult in the very near future. But he would receive his nourishment and care. Somebody would see to that.

And that special somebody was walking down a flight of stairs at that very moment, unaware that Dr. Sigma was the name the police detectives had coined for the person they searched for—that special somebody approaching the restless body of Rusty Blake.

An IV drip tube led from a stopcock down to a needle taped over the subclavian vein at the intersection of the neck and shoulder.

A hand slowly raised to the horizontal, and the stopcock valve was rotated sixty degrees. A clear fluid began to flow, drip by drip, disappearing into the body of a man. Rusty thought he heard the presence of someone. "Who's there?" he said into his blindfolded darkness. There was no response. Only the music—loud music. "Come on! Who's there? Take this thing off a me. I know you're there, damn it! Show . . ." He paused, sensing that he had slurred his speech, and still not believing that his consciousness was slipping away, ". . . show yourself!" Rusty grew groggier. He could feel himself disappearing in stages under the influence of a mixture of sodium Pentothal, succinylcholine, and Valium. Thoughts no longer took the form of phrases. Images in his mind became fragmented and discontinuous. The last word he muttered through his lips was, "Fuck . . ." and as the heart rate slowed, the music was temporarily turned down so a highly motivated person could concentrate on the important task ahead.

Lips bleed profusely when cut. Lip and nose blood always seems a little different from blood from other parts of the body. It is not logical, and certainly not chemically or biologically true, but blood from the mouth area always seems a bit thicker, a bit stickier, a bit more viscous, even, perhaps, a bit redder. Perhaps it is only psychological, having something to do with the visceral memories of tasting our own salty blood after a mouth injury, swallowing it, then waiting for it to accumulate again, and again, and again. And whether cut unintentionally or intentionally, the thick red stuff oozes freely from hundreds of engorged, traumatized capillaries.

Necessity is the mother of invention, so a procedure had been theorized, tested, and implemented, one that minimized the mess. The top and bottom lips were placed into a homemade clamp, sort of like a rectangular tourniquet. A pair of screws compressed a pair of parallel plates, forcing the lips to squeeze out, while maintaining the pressure that would minimize the flow of blood when the vermillion borders of both lips were sliced off with a scalpel that was sharper than sharp.

First, a curved suturing needle pierced the lip and was held tightly with a pair of hemostats, to act as a handle to apply a constant pull on the lip to be removed. Then the knife separated the vermilion border from the facial tissue as the lip was pulled away, maintaining tension where the cutting edge of the scalpel touched the flesh. The tissue under tension enabled the blade to pass through membrane with very little sawing action. The rounded vermillion borders of the top and bottom lips were completely removed and discarded like wads of slippery fat from a cheap dinner steak.

Both Freddy Lopez's lips and Jerome Lewis's lips had been removed using this very same technique. As the surgeon worked, the thought occurred more than once that it was a shame that this simple technique would never find its way into the *New England Journal of Medicine*. Anonymity has its price.

The vacuum suction gurgled as it removed bubbles of excess blood beading up and sweating away from the thousands of severed little capillaries as the sutures were fastidiously applied to the raw sirloinlike tissue, one at a time, evenly and professionally spaced, one row along the inside of the mouth and one row along the outside.

After the last knot was tied in the last stitch, the clamp was removed, and the excess blood was absorbed by a piece of gauze that had been placed between the teeth and the inside of the lips before the jaw-securing clamp was applied. Direct pressure was applied to the lips by an Ace bandage wrapped around the face. The flow of drugs was terminated and a saline drip was begun.

Within twenty minutes, Rusty Blake began recovering from his anesthetized fog, and by then, a clamp was securely around his head and jaw to prevent him from opening his mouth, and classical music filled the air with culture and emotion from another era.

22   Real Science

A key switch was rotated, and a shutter instantly closed, extinguishing the optical pumping beam which fed the ultraviolet dye laser. The UV output beam energy dropped to zero, and a half-second later, the organic dye circulation pump automatically shut itself off. The six-foot-six-inch-tall man in the lab coat slipped the laser safety goggles off the top of his head and removed the fluorescing electrophoresis samples from the homemade UV exposure chamber he had built. He switched off the DC power supply, then watched the needle of an analog electrical voltmeter drift all the way to the left, from 300 volts to zero. One by one, he removed each of the sixteen samples from the quarter-inch of ionic migration-field solution, and placed them on a sterile napkin in another tray to dry. He opened a small refrigerator, removed a bottle labeled "Stain # 11C−6%," and held it to the light to check for optical homogeneity and chemical breakdown. A small exhaust fan was switched on and an eyedropper was removed from a drawer. The man took a deep breath, then placed one drop of the reddish brown chemical onto each of the sixteen microscope slides. He positioned the tray of staining samples so it was directly under the exhaust, then walked away from the immediate area for three minutes. With a child's anticipation, he returned to rinse each of the samples with distilled water, which he squirted from a plastic squeeze bottle. Next, he carefully placed a thin glass coverslip on top of each sample of the mutated cambium specimens.

The man in the white lab coat carried the tray over to another workstation and carefully placed it on the surface. He delicately removed a plastic dustcover from a stout Bausch & Lomb stereoscopic microscope—an old top-of-the-line model from back in the fifties. He tilted the microscope arm, then adjusted a pair of high-intensity lamps for maximum illumination. One by one, each of the slides was examined, and with every turn of the focusing knob, the man smiled a slightly bigger grin. He rotated the X-Y stage controls, surfing his way around the perimeter of each sample. The mutations were finally all positive, and reproducible. "Ex-cell-ent," he softly said, overenunciating each syllable. "Ex-cell-ent."

The large man in the white lab coat glanced at his watch, then began the laboratory shutdown procedure, realizing that it was now time to watch a little TV. "The en-tro-py," he said. "Must keep out the en-tro-py. . . ."

"Five . . . four . . . three . . . two . . . one . . ."

"On Tuesday, May twenty-fifth, the world was shocked when a horrible discovery was made on Wallabout Street in Brooklyn," Jane Whitney said on a very rare live televised show, standing before the backdrop of a roomful of seated people. "As many of you recall, early in the morning of that strange day, a man was found imprisoned in the most bizarre fashion imaginable, with his arms wrapped around a lamppost. His hands had been brutally amputated, and then his arms had been connected together in a crazy surgical procedure that can only be likened to a modernistic version of a medieval torture. For almost nine grueling hours, that man was a public spectacle, until he was removed from the lamppost by police and workmen. In addition to the amputation and connection of his arms, his mouth had been sewn shut, and a feeding and breathing hole had been placed in his cheek." A close-up photograph of the sewn-up mouth and blowhole filled the screen momentarily, then the picture switched back to Jane. "We have with us today the victim of that insane torture and mutilation. I would like to introduce you to Mr. Jerome Lewis. . . ."

The applause was deafening as Jerome Lewis pathetically sat there in a chair, by himself, drooling, before the audience of the *Jane Whitney Show*. His loop was in his lap, a position he'd grown accustomed to while sitting. And right there, in the front row of the audience, sat Marshall Stanley, Jerome's agent and promoter, with the biggest smile he'd worn in years, because he felt as if he'd discovered the very next Beatles, at least for as long as he could ride the wave of gruesome public curiosity at Jerome's expense, all the way to the bank.

Jerome seemed a bit nervous as he looked to Marshall for a cue of some kind. And Marshall gave him one. He flapped his hands, indicating that he wanted his client to raise the loop, but Jerome just stared, paralyzed with stage fright. The audience was out of control, and the applause sounded like a hailstorm on an aluminum toolshed. Marshall overlapped his arms, with his hands on his elbows, to mimic Jerome's loop. He raised his simulated appendage while whispering with exaggerated lip motion to Jerome, "Flash the cheesecake! Flash the cheesecake!" They'd rehearsed what Jerome would do in the greenroom, and a hundred times before. But under the heat of the blinding stage lights, and staring at all those pairs of ghoulish eyeballs, and the cameras, and the woman with the microphone, Jerome's tongue was frozen to the roof of his mouth, and his mind turned into a wet sponge. But Jerome finally did get the hint.

Following Marshall's cue, he raised his loop, and the clapping, hooting, and whistling instantly subsided, replaced with gasping open mouths. Jerome wore a custom-made white T-shirt, with a slit from one sleeve to the other. This slit was buttoned horizontally across his chest.

"...Camera two, stay with those arms. Come in closer. Closer. Closer..."

The connection zone of Jerome's arms filled the TV screens in millions of homes across America. This had been the most publicized *Jane Whitney Show* ever. The bidding war for first public display had driven today's take well into six figures, with the promise of much more to come. Jane had even outbid Geraldo, Oprah, and Donahue, and the producers felt they were really out on a limb with this one—no pun intended.

The room was dead silent. For a moment, even Jane was at a loss for words. With all her professional experience, she'd never seen an audience respond like this one. Her grip tightened around the shaft of the microphone. "I almost don't know where to begin," she softly said as Jerome lowered the loop back to his lap. "Jerome, what was the first thing that went through your mind when you found yourself out there on the street, attached to the lamppost that awful morning?"

With all the rehearsing Jerome and Marshall had done for the live debut, this question had never been considered. Jerome said nothing. His mind was blank. Marshall tried to communicate an answer telepathically to his young prodigy in the chair up there under the lights, but telepathy never works on TV, even for the pros.

"Jerome, I know you must be a little nervous," she said, then walked out from the audience and sat down next to her guest in another chair that had been placed onstage during the full-face camera shot of Jane during her last statement, followed by a series of horrified expressions of disbelief from a random sampling of the audience. She put her hand on Jerome's shoulder and soothingly said, "I know this must be very difficult for you." Jerome snapped out of his debilitating fright and looked into Jane Whitney's understanding eyes. "What was the first thing that went through your mind that day, on the lamppost, Jerome?"

"I . . . I don' know," Jerome said in a barely audible voice. Jane's face was less than a foot from her guest's, and she looked directly into his eyes. "First of all, everything I seen was like . . . upside down. So I think I was goin' out a ma mind."

"And that was the result of being blindfolded for six weeks?"

"Yeah. Dat's what dem experts tell me. I ain' seen nothin' for six whole weeks, and yo' brain suppose to make da image you see go upside down or somethin'."

"How sensitive were your eyes after not being able to see all that time?"

"I could barely keep 'em open. Dey was tearin' 'n' "— *beeeeeeeep.* "Dis clamp was on ma head all da time. I thought dey did somethin' ta ma brain 'n'—*beeeeeeeep.* The people in the control room kept a tight rein on Jerome Lewis's language on the video digital delay, and while the surgery was not considered too obscene for national television, the word *shit* definitely was.

"Jerome, do you have any idea who would want to do this to you? Someone in your past? An old enemy? Someone who wanted to get even with you for something?"

"I don' got no idea. One minute, I'm on da street; da next minute, I'm on dat lamppost wit all dem people laughin' at me, 'n yellin' at me, 'n tryin' ta hurt me 'n'"—*beeeeeeeep.*

"We have some videotaped footage of you that we're going to play from that morning. . . ."

"I can't believe this," Lieutenant Kramer sighed, shaking his head in disgust. "I just can't believe this." He turned the volume up on the television in his office as he, Sergeant Perato, and Sally Chu watched in disbelief.

Captain Percella entered Brent's office to watch the show also. Brent called him the "String Bean," because he was very tall and very thin. He was an excellent cop and an excellent administrator, but he rarely got involved in any of Brent's police investigations unless they went off the deep end, as this case was in danger of doing due to the publicity. Since Brent had the best TV in the precinct, the captain couldn't resist the invitation to watch the show.

"So this is wealth creation in America," the captain said. "They oughta all have their heads examined."

Then Sally said, "Ten to twelve million people are supposed to be watching this today."

"Gee, that's all?" Brent said as he threw an eraser at the clock.

At that moment, the phone rang, and Brent snatched it up almost immediately. "Lieutenant Kramer here."

"Brent, turn on channel—"

"I'm watching it, Nigel!"

"Oh God, this is so great!" Nigel said. "Did you see that close-up? This is TV at its best! What did I tell you? Remember what I told you about the *Freddy Lopez Show*. Well, this is the *Jerome Lewis Show*. What did I tell you? Am I a genius or what?"

"You're *what* all right! I think there's something wrong with you, *and* that Marshall Stanley."

"Come on, Brent! Lighten up. It doesn't *get* any better than this! I think you're getting old. Look! Look! Look at his mouth!"

"I'm watching. I'm watching." In the file footage, there was a beautiful close-up of the sealed-up mouth of Jerome Lewis, and he looked like an old man with his dentures removed, chewing his gums. And then his head turned, and the viscous, drooling blowhole revealed itself.

Nigel continued: "I have to say, though, that nothing beats seeing it firsthand. How much do you think he's getting for doing the show?"

"I don't know. I *do* know there was a bidding war over him, though. Dr. Spellman says that they . . . wait a second . . ."

Back on television, Jane Whitney said in her softest voice, "Jerome, what was it like trying to speak without a mouth?"

Nigel laughed into the phone, then said, "Stoma do, and stoma don't, and Jerry Lewis here does it through a blowhole!"

Jerome answered Jane. "It was all"—*beeeeeeeeeeeeeeeeeep.* "I couldn't make no words come outta my mouth, proper like. Da police tried ta get me ta tell 'em what happen 'n"—*beeeeeep*—"but it was real hard just ta tell 'em ma name, let alone give 'em mo details."

"Brent," Nigel said, "how much did they offer you?"

"Five thousand. By the way, are you taping this?"

"Yeah. You wouldn't do it for five grand? You crazy?"

"This isn't right, what they're doing, and Marshall Stanley— unbelievable! They don't get any lower. As for me, I won't sit up there like some trained seal and give answers on command so they can sell ... vaginal moisture-replenishment chemicals." Sally looked over at Brent when she heard the *v* word.

"Hey," Nigel said, "when you need vaginal moisture, you need vaginal moisture. What do you have against vaginal moisture? Where would the world be without vaginal moisture?"

"I haven't got *anything* against vaginal moisture. I just don't think this is what people should be doing for a Christmas bonus." Sergeant Perato and the captain also looked at Brent curiously when they heard the *v* word.

"Speaking of vaginal moisture, is Sally there?"

"Yeah. Wanna talk to her?" Sally looked at Brent.

"Not at the moment," Nigel said. "Wait. What's she wearing?"

"You need to be slammed on the head with a two-by-four— possibly several times."

"I know. As far as the other thing is concerned, who cares if Jerome picks up a little extra cash on the side? What's he gonna do otherwise, go back to poverty with honor? And as for you, my friend, why are *you* even bothering to watch the show if it's so distasteful?"

"It happens to be part of this case ... and it's interesting."

"Right! And it's so much more. This is what America's *all* about. People, sensitive beautiful people, socially relevant beautiful people like Jerome Lewis here, willing to share their misfortunes publicly with each other for a small sum of money. And they haven't mentioned a damn thing about his police record yet. They're making him out to be a victim. What about *his* victims? You could have set the record straight! You were crazy to turn down the five grand. Shithead!"

"I don't want to discuss it with you anymore. Do you have the decibel map for the metropolitan area?"

"Yes, I do. I stayed up all night working on it. Your FAA contact was real helpful with the traffic patterns."

"You're the only one I know who could do it."

"Don't patronize me. Wait till you get my bill. By the way, I think Sally was wearing a garter belt the last time I saw her. Is she . . ."

A man in a white lab coat impatiently paced back and forth in his kitchen as the vertical syncing bar on his black-and-white TV rolled more slowly, then locked into a distorted but stable frame of squashed and partially folded guests sitting in chairs in the front of a roomful of people. Then he sat at the kitchen table and began to fiddle with the linearity and vertical-hold controls to obtain the least distorted image during the extended warm-up period of this dinosaur of an appliance. He watched the television for a moment, then began adjusting the brightness and contrast controls to sharpen up the picture of the black loop of flesh before him.

". . . And now we have with us the plastic surgeon who separated the lips of Jerome Lewis, Dr. Wallace Spellman." Any applause seemed feeble in comparison to the applause for Jerome Lewis at the beginning of the show. "Dr. Spellman, when Mr. Lewis first came to the hospital, what was your reaction?"

"Well, Jane, due to all the publicity, I already knew the nature of the problem. When he arrived at the hospital, as you can imagine, there was a great deal of commotion associated with his presence. When I first saw him, though, I was shocked, not as a doctor, but as a man. As a doctor, Jane, you see a lot of strange things, but I never saw anything like this before." Marshall and Jerome were not the only people who had been rehearsing their lines for the show.

"We have some X rays you provided for us. Could you briefly explain what was done to the arms of Mr. Lewis?"

"Sure, Jane. . . ." And Dr. Spellman gave the watered-down explanation of Mr. Lewis's surgery as Jerome sat there like a prize fruit at a county fair. "I was against Mr. Lewis's postponement of the operation to separate his arms, because there is an increased risk of tachycardia, because of decreased circulation in the rest of Mr. Lewis's body due to the decreased resistance to the flow of blood in his arms."

"I'm not sure anyone understands exactly what you've just said, Doctor."

"Well it's really quite simple, Jane. All the capillaries in the hand represent a certain pulmonary resistance to the flow of blood, and when Mr. Lewis's veins and arteries were cross-connected—"

"Wait, Dr. Spellman. Before you get into a complex scientific explanation, we have to break for commercial. Please hold that thought. . . ."

"Hey, Brent," Nigel blurted over the phone, "I thought you said ol' Doc Stillborn thought it was disgraceful for the hooper to go on national television, too."

"He changed his mind."

"*Hmmmmm.* Interesting. How much did *he* get? I'll bet they offered *him* more than five grand."

"They did. He's getting ten."

After the commercial, Dr. Spellman did finish his thought.

Then Jane Whitney asked, "For you, Doctor, what was the most difficult challenge that Mr. Lewis presented?"

"This had never been done before," Dr. Spellman said. "It's not that it's all that difficult to do. It was simply a brand-new procedure to reverse. The vermilion border of both top and bottom lips— that's the rounded portion of the lips here"—he pointed to his own lips to demonstrate—"had been completely removed, and the raw tissue sewn together." As Dr. Spellman spoke, half the people in the audience held their heads in horror, and the camera danced like a drunk leprechaun from face to face.

The man in the lab coat attentively watched his television, just as millions of other Americans were doing at that exact moment, and he began nervously twirling his hair with his finger. He looked up to his telephone on the wall, then back to the TV screen. Then he impulsively grabbed the phone and dialed 1–212–555–1212.

"...So we did the best we could do to separate and reconstruct Mr. Lewis's lip tissue. He still requires at least two more operations, but considering what we learned from Mr. Lopez's lip reconstruction—"

"Mr. Lopez? Excuse me, Dr. Spellman, are you saying this happened to someone else before?"

Brent slapped his forehead. "Jesus Christ, Wally!" Brent hissed at the television set.

Dr. Spellman was squirming in his seat, and he said, "I misspoke myself...."

"Son of a bitch," Marshall Stanley said under his breath as he smacked his thigh, already putting two and two together in his mind as he scribbled the name Mr. Lopez on a piece of paper.

Dr. Spellman's face grew tomato red. He knew he just fucked up big-time, but only in front of 4 percent of the entire country.

24   Hooper Madness

Marshall Stanley's eyes were still tearing from cigar smoke as he marched into the elevator on the eighth floor at the Toy Building on Fifth Avenue. His eyes were tearing for another reason, though; he felt he had just had another splendid meeting to push his new high-concept toy and doll line: Hoopers. He looked with pride at his portfolio case filled with airbrushed drawings of Hooper Toss; Hoop It; Hoop It Up; Hoop It Up Now; Hoop It Up Now, Baby; Make-a-Hooper; Hooper House; I'm a Hooper; I Dream of Hoopers; The Hooper Family; Those *Crazy* Hoopers; I Love a Hooper; Hooper Time; Hooper Madness; and The Hoola-Hooper; but Sigmond Toys,

Ltd., of Hong Kong thought they might have a little trouble with that last one because they were always getting sued for knocking off names, products, lines, and anything else they could lay their hands on. But Marshall had a good feeling about Sigmond Toys. He knew they spoke the same language as he—the language of opportunity from anywhere it came. And they even loved the hooper coffee mug and hooper sweater—both high-concept items, too.

The elevator doors opened in the lobby and Marshall walked to the pay phones to retrieve his messages before his next meeting with Mr. Holidays, the trim-a-tree company, to hawk a line of hooper Christmas tree decorations. Then he heard the following message: "Lieutenant Kramer here, once again. Mr. Stanley, this is now the fourth time I've called you. If you don't return my call this time, I'm gonna simply have you picked up. Once again, my number here is five-five-five-eighty-eight-hundred."

Marshall hung up the phone and muttered to himself, "I wonder what the fuck *he* wants?"

On the day after the airing of the *Jane Whitney Show,* Midtown North was hopping with peripheral activity that had nothing to do with police work. It was a hot June afternoon, and the air-conditioning system was out again, which only compounded the annoyance of the reporters hanging around, all the strange phone calls overloading the switchboard, and the tedious but often hysterical hooper jokes circulating around the precinct like the swirls of hot air from the overhead fans.

Brent leaned behind him to turn his personal window air conditioner down a notch, then grimaced at the malfunctioning computer screen as he tightened his grip on the receiver of the telephone. "Look," he said, "I know how much publicity this thing is getting, but you have to put it in perspective. I have homicides I'm working on. You know what a homicide is, don't you? Manslaughter? Murder? . . . Oh, *come* on now, I *didn't* say I was ignoring it. I simply said we have to put it in perspective. It's not the only case on my plate. . . . Of course it's horrible—deliberate mutilation. But there *are* other things that are more important out there. . . ."

At that moment, Nigel burst into Brent's office and was immediately overcome by the cool air. He floated over to the couch and collapsed, spreading out to maximize the contact surface area between his body and the cool leather object. As far as Nigel could surmise from Brent's tone of voice, it seemed that his patience was shrinking in proportion to the rate at which the piles of paper on his desk were growing.

And Brent continued making faces at the phone. ". . . I think that's more political than practical, but I do understand your position. Look, someone just walked into my office about the case right now, so I have to go. I'll keep you informed as to our general progress, but no press leaks, okay? . . . Okay. Bye." Brent hung up the phone, looked at Nigel, and stuck his tongue out at him.

"Are you losing your mind, or have you already lost it?" Nigel asked.

"Politics! Say, I got this really strange call an hour ago, and it's from some botanist up in the Bronx. Since you made such a stink about botany during that medical review, I figured this was right up your alley." Brent glanced at the piece of paper. "This Dr. . . . Inst-lokk-ronn . . ." Brent laughed as he stared at the piece of paper, then theatrically turned it upside down. "I'm not even gonna begin to try to pronounce this gibberish. He says he does to plants what our Dr. Sigma here does to people. He seemed very distant, perhaps even a little cop-phobic. Why don't *you* go check it out? You might find it interesting." Brent crumpled up the piece of paper and tossed it over to Nigel.

"Hmmmm," Nigel said with a smile, "a botanist. I'm gonna make myself scarce at one of the desks out there and find out who he is before I actually call him, okay?"

"Good thinking. Wait! No two-hour calls to fuckin' California, okay? I had to explain that shit to someone."

"Yeah." Nigel got up to leave, then turned in the doorway and said, "By the way, how does a hooper pick his nose?"

Brent had been hearing hooper jokes all morning, and this was about the last one he had any budget left for. "How?" He sighed.

Nigel shrugged his shoulders and said, "I dunno," then walked out as Brent's phone rang. Nigel heard Brent laugh out loud as he closed the door.

"... Mr. Stanley," Brent said, "how did you manage to stumble on Jerome Lewis?"

"I don't have to have this conversation," Marshall Stanley said in a low monotone.

Brent perceived a familiar brand of professionally robotic detachment in Mr. Stanley's voice. He'd dealt with these types before. "During your EST training they might have taught you that you don't have to have any conversation you don't want to have, but I think you might consider having *this* one. In fact, I strongly recommend it."

Mr. Stanley was a bit perplexed. Not only did he feel that EST had changed his life for the better, but he wondered how the police lieutenant knew he'd been involved with EST in the first place, and that was several years ago, anyway. "What does EST have to do with it?"

"You're a very creative fellow, Mr. Stanley, so *creative*, in fact, that you must have taken the creativity workshop they offered."

"What of it?"

"How did you find Jerome Lewis?"

"Don't you need a search warrant or something to question me?"

Brent struggled to contain his laughter. "I'm not searching your apartment at Three Seventy-five East Sixty-eighth Street. I'm searching your mind."

"You've been checking up on me, I see." Marshall was swollen with flattery.

"I try to keep abreast of current events. For instance, did you know that your EST guru is a fugitive?"

"No, I hadn't heard, and I'm not connected with them anymore."

"That wouldn't be because they're out of business, at least in this country?"

"No, it wouldn't. I was just ready to move on. How much do you know about me?" Marshall said, almost half-flattered.

"How much do you know about Jerome Lewis?"

"I don't have to answer these questions."

"Yes you do."

"I know my rights."

"No you don't."

"You can't intimidate me."

"Yes I can. And I will, because, Mr. Stanley, you're dangerously close to obstruction of justice, in my opinion, and in this *ahhh* conversation, as you call it, my opinion is all that matters. You see, Marshall, honey—you don't mind if I call you honey, do you? 'Cause that's what they're gonna call you down at Rikers, and you'll be the twinkle in somebody's eye, I promise you. Marshall, honey, knowingly or unknowingly, you're a prime suspect in Jerome's mutilation because you're *directly* benefiting from it. You *do* see my point? I urge you to reconsider your obstinate position. Let's not be too difficult, *huh?* By the way, did they offer any seminars in obstinateness?"

"No!" Marshall was beginning to get pissed, but he thought about the lieutenant's words for a moment. "When I first saw Jerome on the television, it occurred to me that this minor setback for Mr. Lewis could be transformed into an opportunity."

"You call having your mouth sewn shut and both your hands amputated a *minor* setback? . . . So you sought out Mr. Lewis for purely humanitarian reasons?"

"Well . . . yes. I made a commitment to turn the negative into positive."

"Is that what you learned in EST?"

"Will you leave EST out of this conversation?! EST empowered me, and made me everything I am today. Ten years ago, I made a *commitment,* and a *promise* to myself to—"

"How did you find Jerome?"

"I followed the ambulance to Roosevelt Hospital—same as lawyers do. Then I chose the right moment to go to his room."

"How did you find out which room they were keeping him in?"

"I'd rather not say."

"Why?"

"It would get an innocent person in trouble."

"Innocent? No, it won't get any *innocent* person in trouble."

"I don't believe you."

"Marshall, honey, remember, obstruction of justice is subject to a very broad interpretation. . . ."

"I tipped a security guard, all right? I told him I was a newsman."

"It's called bribery, not tipping." Brent thought, He must have taken the Fink Workshop, too. "Then what?"

"I dressed up like a doctor and told the nurse that I was the doctor from Reconstructive Orthopedics at Lenox Hill, and she bought it. She let me see him—just like that. Jerome *wanted* to make a deal. I didn't twist the man's . . . whatever that thing is. Then I showed him the contract . . . *ba-da-bing, ba-da-boom* . . . the rest is history."

"Don't you know that the longer Jerome Lewis waits to have his arms separated, the greater the medical danger he's in?"

"He's in no immediate danger."

"Yes he is."

"No he isn't. I had him checked out by my *very own* physician."

Marshall gave Brent the name of the physician who had checked out Jerome Lewis, along with a host of irrelevant information about himself and how EST had changed his life for the better. He almost sounded as if he was trying to recruit Brent into an organization that was out of business, or at least on its way to the former Soviet Union to fleece the Russians this time.

But Brent was reasonably certain that Marshall Stanley had never heard of Jerome Lewis before the story hit the news. Brent knew that Marshall was in the clear, but Brent had also been curious to know exactly what kind of person Marshall Stanley really was. All Brent's preconceived notions were correct.

"Mr. Stanley, I don't approve of what you're doing. I want you to know that I'm gonna have my eye on you."

"Look, Lieutenant, I didn't break any laws. . . ."

"You most certainly did, mister! In your . . . effort to turn negative into positive, you were trespassing on city hospital property; you misrepresented yourself as a physician, and while you didn't actually practice medicine, said misrepresentation gained you access to a restricted area; and let's not forget . . . tippery. So don't be handing me that 'I didn't break any laws' bullshit. I could get the hospital to press charges against you. Stanley, I think you're a weasel, and I think you already know that by now. And if *anything* should happen to Jerome Lewis's health while under your magnanimous tutelage, the list of charges against you might just suddenly grow to felonious proportions. That should give you something to think about when you go empowering yourself into situations where you don't belong, Mr. Stanley. The next commitment you make should be my words to your memory!"

"In your opinion, Lieutenant."

"Yes, in my opinion. And my opinion throws an awful lot of weight in this town. Don't you forget it, honey!" Brent gently placed the phone into its cradle. "I *detest* that man," he said out loud, then clicked off the tape recorder.

25   No Ice Water in Hell

"Oh God!" Nigel said to Sally as he tried to avoid fixing his eyes too obviously on the boundary between her skirt and her legs. "You weren't actually planning on entering the entire map into the computer street corner by street corner, were you?"

"Of course I was. How else you get the coordinates of where all the people live?"

She was definitely wearing stockings and a garter belt again. No doubt about it now. When she unfolded her legs, Nigel saw the clip, and he tried to remain focused on two very important things at once. "There are lists you can get. They've already done most of the work for you. You just have to know where to look.

"The Census Bureau has something called a census tract map, and it's available on CD-ROM; you can call 'em up and order one. The tract map is where you extract the longitude-latitude coordinates for any given address, which you get from the various databases. Then there are commercial lists you can get that break the areas down into zip codes, and you have to overlay the zip code map on top of the topo map. Now the trick is to make all the different formats compatible." Nigel's eyes drifted to the garter clip and the concentric circles at the top band of her stocking; then he looked back up to her face. "A typical search would work like this:

"Say that Dr. John Doe lives at Eighty-eight University Place, New York, New York, one-triple-0-three. Now you check to see if any part of the boundary of zip code one-triple-0-three intersects the mathematical curve of interest from my file, or any area file, for that matter. If it doesn't, go to next name on the list. If it does, extract the latitude and longitude data from the census tract map, and then you do the test to see if those coordinates are inside or outside the contour line. If they're inside, there you go." To bed, Nigel thought as the perversion centers of his brain outlined and enhanced the contour of Sally's nipples.

"I get the procedure. You are right. If I do it my way, I could spend the next six months like a high-tech coolie—tapping on keys till I am old maid—reinvent the wheel."

Then Sally smiled, and giggled. Nigel watched her legs and skirt, all hiked up, exposing the tops of both stockings. And when she made the squeaky noise, Nigel's brain stem had a core meltdown and dripped to the center of the earth, halfway to the part of the planet where this bombshell originated from. Sally began to look embarrassed when she realized the edge of her skirt was about six inches north of where it was supposed to be. She looked at Nigel, who was pretending not to know that she was embarrassed, then said, "I do not wear panty hose that often." Nigel gazed at her in disbelief, trying hard to produce no facial reaction to this statement. "My grandmother did not let me wear panty hose when I was little. She said it would cause me to get an infection, so I wore the garter belt instead." Then Sally wiggled her skirt back to where it was supposed to be. "I guess old habits are hard to break."

Nigel tilted his head, then thought, Thank you, God . . . and Granny, while contemplating the virtues of family values. Momentarily shifting his focus, he said, "I have an appointment this afternoon, so I'm outta here, but I'll stop by later."

"Okay, Nigel. I will find out about the CD-ROM from the Census Bureau, and then I will order the ROM drive unit and do the interface."

"Good. By the way, that was great work you did with the system here."

"Oh, it was nothing. There were just a few simple bugs in that part of the utility package. At first, I called the company who wrote the package. All those people *really, really* stupid! I never heard such a ridiculous name for a company in all my life—even back in Hong Kong! The name of company is Advanced Data Software

Solutions and Neural Network Information Transfer Systems, Inc. That is one big oxymoron, especially after I speak with them. They do not know their ass from a hole in the ground." Nigel burst out laughing, not only because of what she'd said but also the way she'd said it; her Cantonese accent always seemed to grow with her level of agitation, and certainly with her level of embarrassment. "What is so funny. Is it true? Don't you think?"

"It's true, every word. In any event, Brent was *very* pleased. The E-mail and communications software still need some work, but he said he hasn't had one faulty printout in two days, which for this place is like a quantum anomaly."

"Lieutenant Kramer tells me you went to MIT also. What was your major?"

"Electrical Engineering, with a minor in physics and a masters in chemistry." And oral sex, Nigel thought. His brain was now refocused, and completely out of control.

"That is a strange combination of disciplines."

"I'm a strange guy," Nigel said, mesmerized by the waist-length dyed red hair protruding from the scalp of this devil woman with the undergarments from hell. "Say, what are you doing for dinner, Sally?" Going to hell, Nigel thought. Going to hell . . . Going to hell . . . Going to hell . . . Going to hell . . . Brent always said there ain't no ice water in hell. . . .

26   Becker

Dr. Becker Instlokrownctjz was a name highly regarded in the field of experimental botany, and as a horticulturist he was renowned for stem and trunk grafting and controlled growth techniques. It was universally agreed he was an original genius, but in the opinion of everyone Nigel had contacted, the most noteworthy attribute of Dr. Instlokrownctjz was the unique brand of strangeness the man exuded. He was jokingly referred to as a man who lived up to his name.

His house sat on the inside edge of a sharp turn, actually molded into the smooth granite rocks of a fifty-foot embankment located in a hilly area in one of the few remaining high-class sections left in the Bronx that had not crumbled into memories or mayhem.

Nigel pulled into the IR sensor-lined driveway of this weird structure, which existed on at least six levels above the driveway; the top two levels actually appeared to overlap the top of the cliff. The topography was breathtaking. Nigel observed the IR Fresnel lens of a ten- to fifty-micron sensor array, along with the blinking LED adjacent to the lens assembly just under a window above the garage door. And then he observed not one, but five tracking video cameras —one above the garage; one at the top floor, looking down at the surface of the driveway; one above the front door he was cautiously approaching; one on the far right side of the house; and another poking its lens assembly out from the thick ivy which circumscribed an oak tree on what could be considered to be a front lawn of sorts. Nigel remembered the words of Ms. Bremelstein at the Brooklyn Botanical Gardens: "Don't be alarmed at anything Becker says or does. He's really harmless, and he's very sweet." And Dr. Instlokrownctjz didn't really seem as bad on the telephone as she implied people thought he could be in person.

Nigel climbed the spiral cement steps leading to the walkway and the front door, which seemed to be somewhere between the second and the third levels of this abnormal piece of non-Euclidean real estate that somehow had eluded the city codes. Nigel repeated the man's name under his breath so he could greet him properly: "Inst-low-krownct-ja-zzzza, Inst-low-krownct-ja-zzzza, Inst-low-krownct-ja-zzzza . . ." As he approached the front door, a zoo's worth of mechanical objects suddenly erected and sprang to life from both sides of the walkway, nearly scaring the shit out of Nigel. He reflexively rotated in a full circle as these multijointed mechanical creatures began pecking and nipping at his feet as if this were a Disneyland audio-animatronic enactment of the Pillsbury Doughboy walking through a herd of hungry ducks. And they made noises, too! "This place must be a *blast* during Halloween," Nigel said out loud, then looked up at the front door before him, which had opened sometime during his disgraceful pirouette. And there, in the interior shadows, stood the imposing figure of Becker Instlokrownctjz, smiling like a large, clean-shaven, 280-pound happy child with a pituitary disorder, all six foot six of him.

"I assure you, Mr. At-ker-son, it *is* a blast during Hal-lo-ween, and the rest of the year, too. I'm so glad you like it. Come in. Come in."

"Like it? I love it," Nigel said as he entered. They shook hands in the doorway. "This place you have here is *very* cool, Mr. . . . Inst-low-krownct-ja-zzzza?"

"You are one of the few people who . . . sort of got it right. Little less exaggeration on the *z*. Just a subtle *za* will do."

"Interesting name. Where do you hail from?"

"Slovakia, originally."

"No Czech?"

"I never met a check I wouldn't *sign*."

This seemed a painfully corny reach for a man of fiftyish, bordering perhaps on adolescence. He must have been saying that for so many years, he didn't even know he was still saying it. "Very interesting name."

"It kinda shorts out your mouth, doesn't it?" Dr. Instlo-krownctjz said.

"I guess you have your father to thank for that."

Dr. Instlokrownctjz hesitated for an uncomfortably long moment, and Nigel suddenly felt as if he had not only met his match but that he might be brutally killed any second in an uncontrolled maniacal outburst of superhuman strength. Dr. Instlokrownctjz's head tilted in reptilian little jerks, as if being twisted by a slow, sputtering, underpowered stepper motor; then his face contorted as if a massive stroke sat perched on the horizon of the very next tick of any one of the millions of second hands on any one of the millions of mechanical clocks inside Dr. Instlokrownctjz's living room. Nigel took another casual step back toward the front door just in case. While Nigel smiled on the outside, he felt very apprehensive on the inside, as if perhaps he sat on that same precarious perch with Dr. Instlokrownctjz.

"You know, in all my years on this planet, nobody has ever made such a statement to me in response to me saying what I just said to you."

Nigel breathed a sigh of relief, realizing this man, whose

house he was completely inside of, was, at least for the time being, not completely and totally insane. "Well, in the next few minutes you're likely to hear a lot of things nobody on the planet has ever said to you—in *all* your years on this planet, that is."

"Mr. At-ker-son, I think you might *just* be right. Yes"—Dr. Instlokrownctjz shook his head *yes* repeatedly, as if he'd just solved one of the great mathematical proofs of the century—"you might just be right."

"They tell me you're quite a botanist."

"Who tells you, if you don't mind me asking? I just like to know who my admirers are."

"Well, the people down at the Botanical Gardens, and the *American Horticultural Journal.*"

"Them?"

"Well, them, and others. Dr. Instlokrownctjz"—Nigel's pronunciation was better than last time—"apparently you are very highly respected in your field."

"That is very kind of everyone, whoever *they* are. By the way, do you mind if I show you around?"

"No, not at all." In fact, Nigel did mind a little bit, because he still wasn't 100 percent convinced that Dr. Instlokrownctjz wasn't a jovial old psycho with a sharp knife in his pants, simply wearing a smile while waiting for the right moment to amputate his arms. "Dr. Instlokrownctjz . . ."

"Please, you can call me Becker."

"Good. I believe in conservation of syllables in the universe."

Becker exploded into laughter. "I like you, Mr. At-ker-son."

"Good. Then you can call me Nigel. Only my enemies call me Mr. Atkerson, and the IRS, which keeps telling me they're my friend, incidentally."

"In that case, you're Nigel to me."

"The formalities dissolve. Good! Excellent!" As they climbed the stairs, Nigel absorbed himself in the staggering myriad masks and spears on the walls of this strange man's house. "Becker, among other things, I'm a forensic-science consultant, as I told you on the phone earlier, and I do a lot of work with police departments. As you can probably imagine, we've been getting hundreds of wacky calls, and since I myself originally thought this case had strong parallels with tree grafting, Lieutenant Kramer asked me to follow up on you. What I find particularly interesting is that you called *us* about the case."

"Yes, I've taken a special interest in this case myself, because whoever is doing all this to people is doing exactly what *I* do to plants."

Nigel stopped dead in his tracks, looked at Becker, and said, "You just said, 'people.' "

"Yes."

"But this was only done to one person, Jerome Lewis."

Becker smiled. "Not according to that talk show that aired yesterday. I normally don't watch a lot of tel-e-vision, but that was a show I couldn't miss. And the surgeon mentioned another person, and then they mentioned the surgeon's blunder on the news, too."

Momentarily satisfied, Nigel continued, "You know, one time, must have been several years ago, I was in the Bronx Botanical Gardens, and I noticed an abnormally large number of trees with branches that grew back together, making loops. Naturally, I thought about it when I saw the X rays of Jerome Lewis, and—" Becker began to smirk, and then he started chuckling. "What's so funny?"

"Who do *you* think was responsible for all those grafts you saw at the Botanical Gardens?"

"You?"

"Who else!"

"Say, do you know what a Milch procedure is?"

"A what?"

"I thought so. Well, anyway, it seemed awfully strange that a tree-grafting expert decides to call out of the clear blue sky. This is why—"

"You're here," Dr. Instlokrownctjz interrupted.

"Yes, this is why I'm here—perhaps, also, because you called us. . . ."

"No. *You're here.* I mean, we're here."

Becker opened a big metal freezer door, and inside was the strangest array of plants Nigel had ever seen in his life. Nigel also observed something odd about the geometry and placement of the room, which was about fifty feet long and thirty feet wide, with an eight-foot-diameter rock pillar in the center. This room was not under the frame of the building! It was inside the mountain. The exposed rock walls circumscribed the perimeter of the room, except for the occasional patch of ferro-cement to cover and plug the sand-filled interstitial cavities between the gneiss conglomerate strata.

"A great example of room and pillar construction," Nigel casually said. "I hadn't suspected any of this was going on in the Bronx, however."

"Well, new real estate is so expensive nowadays," Becker said with a smirk. "So I man-u-facture my own."

"This room is ... *ohhhhh*"—Nigel performed the calculation in his head—"about fifteen thousand cubic feet."

"Can't fool you." For the moment, Becker decided to hold off showing Nigel the other rooms he had mined into the earth.

"It's not a question of who's fooling who. It's just a calculation." Nigel was growing increasingly impressed as this new relationship progressed. "We're talking roughly ... *ehhhhhh*, two million pounds of rocks. Where did you put it all, if you don't mind me asking?"

"Oh, some is here, and some is there. Some of the more in-ter-es-ting specimens are in the rock garden upstairs. And the rest are lying around town."

"You didn't move two million pounds of rocks all by yourself ... did you?"

"Of course not. I beamed it out into space," Becker quite naturally said.

Nigel remained expressionless, waiting for the next utterance of elucidation.

"No. I haven't built my transporter yet. But I used the next best method. I had the students help me. And the local minorities just love to haul rocks in exchange for small quan-ti-ties of loose cash."

"I see," Nigel said, barely able to contain his laughter. He found this conversation's amusement value rising exponentially. "How did you make the big rocks into little rocks?"

"Have you ever heard of a rather cute substance called Tovex?" Nigel's face blossomed like a starving child in a candy store. "I take it you've heard of the stuff, then?"

Nigel could not resist telling Becker that he had done a little more than simply hear of the stuff, and that he was an improvised munitions expert and instructor and gave lectures on the subject. For the next five minutes as Nigel studied the plants, they exchanged stories about explosives they had known and loved. And Nigel approved of Becker's home-improvement methods, because it didn't seem that it had gotten too out of hand. Becker had certainly done his technical homework, and in the world, extra provisions *should* be made for certain people and their eccentricities. And Becker was a walking eccentricity if ever Nigel had seen one.

"It's odd that we haven't met till now," Nigel said. "I would have thought our paths might certainly have crossed by now. Ever done any caving? You seem the type."

"I used to do a little spe-lun-king in the sixties."

"That was a little before when I became interested," Nigel said.

"I'm more into mining than spe-lun-king. I'm a little large for the sport."

"I see." Nigel looked at all the artificial lights in the room, none of which were on at the moment. All the light seemed to be coming from one single very bright light piped through a tube pointing straight down through the rock ceiling. From there, the light was distributed to the various sections of the room via a set of front-surface mirrors and diffusers over each cluster of plants. "I take it that that's concentrated sunlight collected via a tracking mirror on the surface?"

"You're very astute, Nigel. But actually, the light comes from an *array* of tracking mirrors. All the light focuses on one big parabolic reflector which sends it down the tube at many times a single solar intensity. The rest is exactly as you say. You see, I like to control the quantity of sunlight in my experiments. I expose my plants to differing levels of what I call solar in-ten-sities. For instance, anything growing on the ground in the sun is equivalent to one solar in-ten-sity. But if I add another solar in-ten-sity, by reflecting the added light from a mirror, I can do anything from cook the plant, to control the sex, flower size, hormone production, or even impart . . . mu-ta-tions." Becker's face lit up. "Using different filters, I can expose my plants to varying wavelengths and mixtures of wavelengths. I also pump dye lasers to generate coherent sources. Ever heard of stilbene one?"

"Yes, as a matter of fact. It'll give you a line anywhere between four hundred and four-thirty. I've done a lot of work with R6G, myself."

"Ve-ry good. You are an in-ter-es-ting fellow, Nigel."

"An interesting fellow with a physics degree."

"In-ter-es-ting. So by controlling the wavelength and in-ten-sity, I gain all these in-ter-es-ting parameters to create . . . mu-ta-tions. And my mirrors track the sun throughout the entire year. It all runs off a computer. It really works quite well."

"Have you ever done any work with cannabis?"

"No comment."

"Hey, I only said I work *with* the police," Nigel assured Becker. "I never said I *was* the police! I'd be curious to—"

"No comment."

"Well, then, let's talk about this case for a moment."

"Okay, let's talk." Dr. Instlokrownctjz then wiggled his index finger up and down over his lips and made a babbling noise.

Without skipping a beat, Nigel said, "I like a man devoid of any conventions whatsoever." Then the two of them laughed. "I take it you're not married?"

"No, I haven't made the right one yet."

"You better hurry," Nigel said. "You're running out of time."

"Hey, I've only just started building my genetic-engineering lab. Give me a break, will ya?"

"I guess I should place an order now—for myself."

"Where do you want her leaves?"

"Just a fig leaf will do . . . in the conventional spot."

"Consider it done."

Nigel wasn't sure at this point whether Becker was being playful or serious, but it did give him more cause for thought. "Tell me, Becker, do you have any ideas about who might be doing this? By the way, I have to ask you, off the record, it's not *you* by any chance, is it?"

"If it was, do you really think I would just call up the police and tell them?" It was difficult for Becker to contain his smile.

"Probably not. But then again, you might just be proud enough of your work that you might want the recognition."

"I might be crazy, but I assure you, I am not insane."

"That's a good answer." For now, Nigel thought.

"The person who is doing this has to have access to lots of drugs. It's probably not happening in a hospital—more likely a private office . . . or a home. . . ."

Nigel had been through this entire line of reasoning with Brent, but he still let Becker mull it over in his brain, more to see what he would either come up with on his own or what he might omit on purpose. Becker went on, thinking out loud as he walked about in his lab, with his right hand supporting his chin. And he was rationally touching all the bases. "Look at this," Becker unexpectedly said. "These are two bonsai oak trees I've been nursing for quite a number of years. I grafted them together. I call this piece of art *Holding Hands.*" And it did look as if the two tiny trees were holding hands. "To my knowledge, nobody else is doing this sort of stuff."

"Who else knows you do this?"

"Lots of people. Like the ones you called to check me out. . . ."

"Have you ever given any lectures or published any papers on the subject?"

"Yes, I have."

"I'd like reprints of your stuff."

"I have all that upstairs."

"Good." Becker's presence seemed to drift in and out of focus, almost as if something was gnawing at him. "Becker," Nigel tested, "is something bothering you?"

Becker snapped back to planet Earth with a mildly startled response, and he said, "Yes . . . something is both-er-ing me."

Nigel instinctively took a step back. "What?"

"I have this awful feeling, that, somehow, I am *indirectly* responsible for everything that has happened to that young man. . . ."

"How so?"

"I have this un-com-for-ta-ble sen-sa-tion that whoever is doing this got the idea from me."

Nigel watched Becker's face carefully. "How do you support yourself?"

"Structurally, or financially?"

Nigel exploded with laughter. "Financially!"

"I'm a professor of botany at Columbia University"—Becker seemed to be speaking from a faraway place inside his mind—"and I'm also a visiting lecturer at a number of in-sti-tu-tions . . . but my parents left me with a tidy little sum when they passed on. I also sell in-ter-es-ting plants." Suddenly, Becker was 100 percent back. "For instance, I was offered fifty thousand dollars for the pair of plants I just showed you, *Holding Hands.* I didn't want to sell it because it is one of my personal favorites. My plants are very valuable. . . . So the question is, Who has both access to the necessary drugs, and the knowledge of how to do it, and, of course, the *willlllll* to do it . . . a motive . . . revenge . . . religion . . . artistic expression? That narrows it down to several thousand people, and it'll probably turn out to be none of the above."

"I think you're right," Nigel agreed. "I think this is coming from left field."

"They don't come much more left field than I. I need to think about this. By the way, would you like to see my armor collection?"

27   Division of Parole

". . . So anybody can just call up out of the clear blue sky and get status information on any parolee and you provide it without any record of whom you provided it to?" Brent asked his friend Mark Silverman, the public information officer at the New York State Division of Parole.

"Yes. Until they change the law, the public has the right to know what's going on with regard to the status of an incarcerated person."

"But you don't record the conversations or keep records?"

"Absolutely not."

"You don't know how many calls there were regarding any specific parolee?"

"No," the information officer said. "Unless it were an extraordinary case. But even then we don't take down actual numbers regarding any specific case."

"How many people from your office provide this information?"

"One. All the information goes through me."

"What kind of people typically call you for information?"

"Newspapers journalists, family and relatives, and concerned people."

"Concerned people, *huh*. How many calls do you get requesting information per week or month?"

"I get about a half-dozen calls each day."

Brent hesitated for a moment, then said, "Do you work from one desk and one phone?"

"No one's ever asked me that one before, Brent, and I've been doing this for fourteen years." Mark was becoming amused. "Yes, I usually talk to people from this phone. Why?"

"Would there be a problem if I were to set up a tape recorder on your line until we catch our man?"

"I don't think there would be a problem with that. I might need to get the authorization of the chairman of the Division of Parole, but—"

"I'd rather not do that," Brent interrupted. "I know you. I don't know him, and if this whole thing is gonna be effective, the fewer people who know, the better. I'd prefer it if you could just discreetly let my man into the building and let him quietly do his thing."

"I suppose . . . I could arrange it, Brent. Oh, and as far as the list of upcoming hearings for inmates meeting the profile you requested, I think that will still take me a few days to assemble. . . ."

28   Looking Toward the Future

Lt. Brent Kramer examined Nigel's takeoff- and landing-pattern acoustic maps of Kennedy, La Guardia, Newark, and Teterboro airports, and the surrounding areas. It seemed an almost-impossible area to cover, but then again, the entire metropolitan area was an even greater area to cover. And what if Jerome Lewis's overmedicated mind had only imagined that he'd heard jets at five-minute intervals? What if it was all for naught? Then Dr. Sigma, whoever he was, could be anywhere, and they would be right back to square one. But what if Dr. Sigma really was somewhere within the curved loudness boundaries that Nigel billed the NYPD $2,400 to draw? At least Brent had a pretty picture to show for it. And then again, he was getting the computer power to correlate addresses on a map.

Nigel's map represented a complex series of teardrop-shaped blips radiating from the runways, not unlike the relief lines one might see on a topographic map of an egg-shaped mountain lying on its side, cut in half the long way. While simple in theory, the generation of the actual lines representing any statistical decibel boundary is a computation-rich combination of several superimposed effects, even ignoring for the moment the unknown effects of the wind.

As a landing plane approaches the edge of a runway, it naturally gets closer to the ground, which means the source of the sound also gets closer to the ground, and the acoustic inverse square law does its thing. But sound radiates from the exhaust of a jet engine in a complex three-dimensional pattern, with the perceived loudness depending on the listener's angle to the sound source. To further complicate matters, different jet engines produce different patterns, with individual spectral signatures at various angles. Both General Electric and Pratt & Whitney provided spectral-lobe data to Nigel for a variety of commercial and military engines, while the FAA provided the landing and takeoff patterns. One fancy computer program and a tragic quantity of coffee later, a unique map was produced—perhaps the only one of its kind since the noise abatement hearings in the sixties, seventies, and early eighties, and nobody had those maps or the raw anecdotal data that produced them.

There were many potential starting points, and many databases to cross-reference—medical, surgical, anesthesiology, and dental journals. There were four domestic manufacturers of tranquilizer guns: Telinject, Capchun Guns, Pneudart, and Ballistivet. Brent was securing customer lists from each, which was not an easy thing to do. Private companies don't want to give up their customer lists, even to the police, and the drug companies were the most difficult to deal with of all—agonizingly self-righteous, gratuitously secretive, and evasive to the point where they behaved as if they were doing something illegal. And perhaps they were. These people lived in a world of their own, with their own rules and inbred attitudes, and if they'd managed to slug their way through the FDA, their insurance premiums, and the legislative process that legally permitted them to avoid the payment of federal taxes by allowing them to move most of their operations to Puerto Rico, they felt they had rightly earned a special position somewhere between God and government—these dispensers of legal potions, lotions, and elixirs. Their attitude was: Over our dead bodies, asshole!

And Brent was just about ready to oblige. He picked up the phone.

". . . Lots of physical therapy. Every day I try to do a little exercise," Brent told Special Agent Carl Spatts of the FBI in New York.

"Is it doing any good?" Carl asked.

"Eeeeeh, hard to say. I get better in stages. There's no improvement for a month, then all of a sudden I'm a notch healthier. The headaches are the worst thing to deal with, but even they're coming less frequently, and the severity is less."

"Well, we're rooting for you here."

"Thanks, Carl. By the way, congratulations on your promotion."

"Thank you very much, Brent. I'll be up in Albany soon. So what's on you mind?"

"I need a little favor. . . ."

"Kramer, you never need *little* favors. If they were *little* favors, you wouldn't call us."

"Look, you've got lots of friends in the pharmaceutical companies, right?"

"I know a few people. Why?"

"I need some customer lists, and I don't want to serve up paperwork for each and every one. I'd much rather go the nonadversarial route. I'd prefer if they would all just quietly cooperate with me, but I'm getting nowhere with these people. I need someone with a subtle touch."

"I can tell already that I'm not gonna like this. What do you need to know?" He sighed.

"Take down the following list." Brent rattled off the polysyllabic names of the drugs he needed customer lists for, and the companies that manufactured them.

"These are all used in anesthesiology," Carl said.

"Correct."

"This is for the hooper case, isn't it?"

"Yes, only it has a slightly different name on my file folder. . . ."

Brent watched Captain Percella and Sergeants Perato and Bassett enter his office and take up their usual positions—the sergeants on the couch and the captain standing over by the tall green filing cabinet, with his feet crossed and his chin touching his chest.

"Look, Carl, I gotta go now. Please get back to me ASAP, okay? . . . Well, I have full confidence in you. Bye." Brent looked up and said, "Looking a bit toward the future, we turn our attentions to the names over on the blackboard."

And on the blackboard were the following names, along with a few relevant upcoming dates in their lives.

	Alex Hall	Clayton George	Charles Ebel	Malcome Tobias, Jr.	Lamont Brown	Julio Clem
PAROLE HEARING	—	10/1/93	12/17/93	1/31/94	2/11/94	3/4/94
RELEASE IF PAROLE GRANTED	7/2/93	10/29/93	1/14/94	3/7/94	3/11/94	4/8/94

Brent continued, "We've done some preliminary research, and the following is a list of people presently incarcerated in New York State, in order of release, starting with Alex Hall, who is scheduled for release from Watertown State Penitentiary tomorrow morning. We're gonna keep an eye on him. I've requested that he be held an extra four days, till we can free up some manpower from the medical side of the investigation. By the way, Captain, are we any closer with those extra manpower requisitions?"

"I *knew* there must have been a good reason you wanted me here," Captain Percella said, cautiously shaking his finger at Brent. "So far, we *still* have to make do with what we have. You have your programmer and the nutty consultant. I'm doing the best I can. Maybe in a few weeks they'll free up some people from downtown."

"Yeah," Brent sighed. "Results without man-hours. In any

event, Spatts is gonna get me some pharmaceutical customer lists, and that warden up in Watertown hasn't returned any of my calls, or acknowledged the receipt of any of my communications in writing, but I'm gonna call him again after we're through. . . ."

29   It Ain't No Aerobics

An intravenous drip of Versed, Thorazine, and a gratuitous pinch of morphine kept the brain of Rusty Blake in a zonked-out, hypnotic but conscious state, hallucinating inside his very own private animated-cartoon world, comfortably distant from any unsettling neurological stimuli that might alarm a more sober mind. His true state remained buffered from the troubles of the world, which, for Rusty, lay only as far away as the severed axons of the nerve cells approximately two linear feet from his brain stem. His mouth was sealed shut and healing normally, with the chin clamp on his head to prevent him from opening his mouth. His arms were connected and healing normally, with a clamp holding them fixed tightly to prevent any extraneous mechanical stress that might prevent the traumatized bone tissue from knitting properly. And air freely passed through the blowhole in his left cheek, supplementing the air passing freely through his nose. Rusty Blake was an altered being, but not unique on the planet. He had an older soul brother in the fraternity of emerging medical art, and that upperclassman was at this moment taping *The Tonight Show*.

Jerome Lewis had transcended the horror of his own tragedy and was now a living caricature of himself—a cult figure, a comedian, and a clown, transformed into pixels and sound for the digestive machinery of the world. He was the Hooper Man—a unique marketing positional niche. The X-ray image of his joined bones appeared on T-shirts and posters. His face was on posters. The Hooper puppet toy license deal had already been negotiated. Every juicy image or spin-off that could be produced was exploited and pumped into a revenue-producing machine at a rate equal to or greater than its ability to cut checks. The Hooper Man was an industry, under the professional guidance of Marshall Stanley. This was the big break Marshall had been preparing for his entire life.

A basketball net had been woven around the arms of Jerome Lewis, and, to the tune of "Sweet Georgia Brown," a group of Harlem Globetrotter imitators were shooting hoops with a basketball-sized Nerf look-alike, and the Hooper Man's chest and face was the living backboard. With millions of folks at home watching, drinking beer, snacking at the refrigerator, making love, and sleeping themselves into the next day's drudgery in exchange for the paycheck, Jerome Lewis was a human basketball net, and the Hooper Man. And the studio audience loved it. He played the part better than any orange hoop of steel ever could, because Jerome was really alive. Jerome was a natural. At times, he became a little bit dizzy and had to stop playing for a moment or two, but this could only be expected, considering that his heart was sending a great percentage of his blood in senseless diversionary circles. The condition known as tachycardia was considered to be an acceptable risk for Marshall and Jerome, considering the money that was being made in the interim.

But Jerome was publicly getting *his* exercise, and it was now time for Rusty Blake to privately get his. Dr. Sigma slowly walked down the stairs leading to the recovery room, where Rusty lay strapped to a horizontal cushioned board. Music from *West Side Story* performed by the Boston Pops Orchestra filled the room with romance and merriment.

Dr. Sigma was wearing a headset similar to the ones worn by telephone operators. The headphones and the springy plastic band that joined them acted as a mechanical support for the little microphone gooseneck that protruded around from the right earphone. The wires from the microphone connected to a little box which clipped to a lanyard around the doctor's neck. On that box was a glowing red LED. This box was a toy known as a MegaMike—a digital harmonizer and voice-modification machine. While this toy enjoyed very little commercial success during its short-lived exposure to the marketplace, it served a very useful purpose down here, where its success was measured by how well it camouflaged the human voice.

"Hello, Rusty," came the tremolo-demented facsimile of a pitch-offset human voice from the speaker inside the little black-and-

119

yellow box. **"It's time for our exercise."** Rusty's head moved slightly in response to the unworldly sounds he was hearing over the Boston Pops Orchestra.

The clear plastic tube connecting the hypnotic, mind-bending drugs to the needle taped on Rusty's neck was about six feet long, giving him a small radius of mobility. The IV bottle was lifted off its hook near the front of the restraint board and placed onto another hook, closer to Rusty's feet. Rusty was unstrapped. **"I want you to sit up now,"** the synthesized voice said. Rusty was guided to a sitting position. His feet hung off the end of the horizontal surface he'd spent the night strapped to. The doctor kept him in this position for a few minutes to minimize the shock of standing.

Rusty Blake was then nudged to a standing position. An exercise bicycle was set up next to where he stood on his shaky legs. After the initial dizziness subsided, his rump was guided onto the seat of the bicycle. **"That's it. That's it. You're doing just fine."** Rusty's chest was strapped to a vertical backboard mounted behind the seat. This would prevent him from falling, as well as prevent any unwanted sudden motion, should Rusty become agitated and decide to take an unscheduled walk somewhere. At the moment, though, he was very pliable and in a very suggestible state of mind. The arm-healing fixture was also secured with straps to a pair of wooden supports that protruded perpendicular to the backboard. All the hardware was working splendidly, considering that most of the bugs had been corrected through experience gained with Jerome Lewis.

The day the Versed feed malfunctioned, Jerome had become most difficult. The Versed feed might have been down for two or three hours, possibly all afternoon. Jerome had actually come out of his trance. He almost needed to be tranquilized with the hypo dart the doctor always kept in the pocket of the lab coat, always within arm's reach.

Back in those days, separate IV bottles were hung for each drug. To adjust a mixture, the individual valve for the individual drug had to be turned, and they all mixed into a common feed line into the bloodstream. Things had evolved since then. Now there was the nighttime mixture, and there was the daytime mixture, and there was the exercise mixture. And if the proportions of the premixed cocktail had to change, the rack of bottles would replace or supplement the premix. Yes, a lot had been learned during Jerome Lewis's metamorphosis, and progress continued.

Rusty's IV bottle was then placed on a higher hook and the stopcock was adjusted to reduce the flow. **"All right now, Rusty. I want you to pedal with your feet."** The doctor grabbed Rusty's feet and rotated them in the desired direction to get him started. Rusty pedaled, halfheartedly at first, but he got the hang of it eventually, and there he sat, pedaling away, with a clear tube leading straight to the subclavian vein in his neck. The only thing missing was a little exercise leotard, the doctor thought. He was so cute. **"Pedal, Rusty. Pedal. That a boy. You're going to have company soon, so you get your exercise. You've got to get your exercise. Half hour in the morning. Half hour at night. Pedal, pedal, pedal, you naughty boy, you. . . ."**

30   You Know How It Is

A brown '77 Chevy Nova turned right on Cannon Place in the Bronx, then rolled down the hill. It parked on the left side of the street, opposite the retaining wall on the right. Internal combustion ceased, and the driver inside slumped to an observant reclining position within arm's reach of a long metallic object conveniently zipped up in a leather carrying case.

Today's target was Alex Hall. He was a short, thin man, perhaps 120 pounds. He would be easier than most to spot, because he had greasy, slicked-back black hair, a mustache, and a Fu Man-chu—style goatee. In theory, he would be checking in with the Fiftieth Precinct after his scheduled release from Watertown State Prison, where he had been a guest for the past seven years, compliments of the taxpayers of the state of New York. His crime: murder, which had been reduced to involuntary manslaughter, and this was only for the murder they'd caught him for. Alex had shot and killed a man in his car. He would have gotten away with it, too, except that fellow gang members ratted him out. And Alex had a score to settle, now that he was out.

Alex had quite a record, even before he got his gun. Back in grade school, he was a mean kid. He'd taken a liking to torturing cats and dogs. It was all there in the reports. All there in black and white. In high school, Alex was even meaner. He killed a dog by placing Drāno into a wad of steak. He got into trouble for that one, but not enough to make any difference. He electrocuted a cat by taping all four of its legs together, which was Alex's idea of a rodeo, wrapping it in a wet towel, and tossing it on the third rail of the downtown IRT number 1. Alex had stolen cars, raped a few bitches, who deserved it anyway, according to him, and committed several armed robberies as his confidence level rose. He was the kid who threw the cobblestone off an overpass of the FDR Drive, instantly killing a twenty-four-year-old woman, but nobody ever knew this fact; not even Alex knew, because he hadn't watched any television that week. He was a crazy kid who did whatever he wanted, whenever he wanted to. He'd set fire to a couch on a pile of garbage, and six cars subsequently caught on fire. He torched an abandoned building for kicks. He dealt drugs when the mood overtook him, and he generally had a good head for anything antisocial.

And Alex was now a free man, and would be walking up Cannon Place sooner or later. It was where he'd be staying, back at his mommy's house, just like when he was a little hoodlum.

And the daytime street activity was displaced by the nighttime street activity. Roaming gangs of punks displaced mothers with their baby carriages, just like back in the old days.

Except for one thing: Now there was a welcome committee.

"What?!!!" Brent belched in disbelief. Half the coffee in his mouth took the path on the wrong side of his epiglottis, sending it clear to his nostrils and eardrums after he began violently coughing.

"Yes. I *believe* he was released at nine-thirty this morning," the administrative assistant in Watertown told the lieutenant as coffee dribble from his nose. He sneezed three times in rapid succession. "Are you okay?"

"No! . . . I'm *not* okay. Don't you know whether you released him or not?"

"Well I'm not one hundred percent sure. . . ."

"You told me on the phone yesterday that Warden McFarland told you he would detain Alex Hall for the requested period of time. Is that true, or am I dreaming?" Brent wiped his tearing eyes.

"Yes, that's true."

"So what happened?"

"He changed his mind, I think."

"Why didn't someone call me, then, so we could change our plans on this end?"

"We're very busy, Lieutenant. This is no country club. We have our own problems to deal with."

"Yes, I'm sure you do. And that's why you released Alex Hall. . . . Look, I'm sorry. I don't mean to yell at you. May I speak with McFarland?"

"The warden is a very busy man, Lieutenant."

"However busy he might be, screwing up an ongoing police investigation . . . I can assure you that I'm busier. I need to know where Alex Hall is, and I need to know fast."

"Lieutenant, can I have your telephone number again? I'll have Mr. McFarland get back to you as soon as—"

"Look, Alex Hall might just come back as the next hooper. I don't care where McFarland is, who he's with, or what he's doing. Please get him right this minute. . . ."

Warden McFarland was simply nowhere to be found. Recriminations would have to wait. All questions would have to wait. Hall was just another glass of milk the system deliberately spilled, and it was time to find a napkin, quickly. After an interminably long punishment on hold, Brent told the administrative assistant, "Please have McFarland call me when he gets in. . . ."

Brent Kramer immediately called the Fiftieth Precinct in the Bronx. "Captain Garcia, please. . . ."

After the greatly abridged preliminary pleasantries, Captain Garcia told Brent that Alex Hall had not checked in, to his knowledge, but that he would have to check. Then Brent told the precinct captain about the problem. Captain Garcia said, "So you're asking me to have my men drop what they're doing and stake out Hall's mother's house?"

"Yes, don't we do that anymore, Captain?"

"Well, it's not that we don't do it anymore. We love nothing more than to sit on the street and watch some guy's mother's house in the event that he shows up after being released on parole."

"But Hall could be abducted as we speak. We'll relieve your people in, say, three or four hours. You're up there and I'm down here. Surely you could watch the house, maybe even the train station? I'm convinced the man's life's in danger."

"Lieutenant, everyone's life is in danger up here, and we're already overallocated as it is. *You know how it is.* We got men working two shifts."

"They wouldn't by any chance be men a year away from retirement, would they?"

"Lieutenant, I *resent* that remark! If you wanna stake out that house, use your own manpower to do it. We got our own caseload. Just don't get in our way up here or I'll step all over you. I gotta go now." Captain Garcia slammed down the phone.

Brent called Alfonce Perato into his office. "Al, drop what you're doing, grab a uniform, and get up to this address in a hurry. They're no help up there."

"I'm on my way," the sergeant said as he took the address and grabbed his hat.

Brent followed the sergeant to the stairwell. "Be careful, Al."

"Yeah."

"Wear your vest."

"Yeah. I hate that thing," Al said, then continued muttering, "I gotta lose some weight."

As it turned out, four of Captain Garcia's detectives and eight of his uniforms doing double shifts *were* only a year away from retirement, and Brent did know "how it is."

"Yes, Lieutenant," the deep voice of a slightly pickled and annoyed Warden McFarland said to Brent. "What can I do for you?"

"Mr. McFarland, did you read my communication directed to *you* personally, regarding the upcoming release of Alex Hall from your facility?"

"Let me *seeeeeee.* Was that the request to have Mr. Hall's

release from my facility postponed for four days *without* reasonable cause?"

"No. It was the request to have Mr. Hall's release from your facility postponed because he would be in imminent danger if he was to be released. You must be referring to a *different* directive. Could you read me the exact wording of the memo in your possession?"

"No, Lieutenant. I won't. Because we're referring to the same paperwork."

"Can you tell me why you released Mr. Hall without first contacting us? Was there something ambiguous or confusing about the concept or the wording?"

"Look, Lieutenant. We had no reason to detain him. He was scheduled for release. We *did* hold him an extra half hour longer than we should have, and I hope he doesn't take legal action against us for it," McFarland slurred, almost laughing. "You *know* how it is. In our opinion, we had no reason to detain him. . . ."

"Even if it means he'll be maimed or killed?"

"Lieutenant, don't you think you're blowing this whole thing *wayyyy* out of proportion?"

"Why did you tell your assistant to tell me you were going to hold him the extra time?"

"Lieutenant, I personally think you're overreacting. I've seen this type of thing before, and it rarely amounts to anything. Two or three years ago, some cop thought some parolee's friend was going to—"

"Warden, I could care less about some noteworthy experience in penal history! Fact of the matter is, you breached procedure, and your action *won't* go unnoticed."

"Don't threaten *me* there, sonny boy, 'cause I've been around the block a lot longer than you! Don't be tellin' *me* how to do my job, you two-bit cop!"

Brent glazed over. "Sorry to trouble you, Warden. Perhaps I'll learn the error of my youthful ways."

"Damn right, you *punk* you!"

"Good-bye, Warden. Sorry to have bothered you with trivialities." Brent hung up the phone as he glanced at his watch. "I'll have your head, you drunken pig," he softly said to himself as he pressed the stop button on his tape recorder and removed the gold-plated three-millimeter audio jack from the receiver of the telephone.

Sergeant Perato and P.O. Haskel sat in stalled northbound traffic on the West Side Highway. They exited at Seventy-ninth Street to try to save some time on Amsterdam Avenue or Riverside Drive. The siren blasted on their unmarked car as they cut between cars and through red lights, fighting their way for each hard-earned block of northbound progress on their way to the Bronx and the Major Deegan Expressway.

A man with a mustache and a Fu Manchu–style goatee walked up Cannon Place from the direction of Orloff Place. He stopped in front of a private house for a long, reflective moment, then opened the squeaky iron gate. He walked toward the house he hadn't seen in nearly eight years.

Pfffft.

Alex Hall struggled to reach the little dart lodged between his shoulder blades as a figure silently approached him from behind. A halothane-and-ether-soaked rag was jammed into Alex's astonished face and held firmly against his nose and mouth as he was rotated about the hip of this powerful assailant, keeping him off balance as he struggled, increasing his blood-circulation rate. It all happened so quickly that Alex had no idea what was happening; actually, he momentarily thought that this might be one of the old gang members getting him before he could get them. The lighter his head grew, the more uncoordinated and feeble his resistance became. And then his flailing spasms subsided to limpness.

Alex's body was carried fireman-style and dumped onto the front seat of the car. His shirtsleeve was rolled up and he was injected with a hypodermic needle.

Then a distracting muffled sound came from a few cars down. It was the sound of a hammer hitting the passenger's side window of a parked car next to the retaining wall. The car door opened, and what looked like a Hispanic male entered and slid over to the driver's side. He removed a can of electronic-component cooler from his bag and sprayed it onto the lock mechanism of the Club that locked the steering wheel. The lock grew white with frost as the temperature plunged more than 150°F over the next thirty seconds. Then the cold brittle lock was whacked once with a hammer, and it shattered. The Club, endorsed by police departments and saturation-advertised all over the country, limply collapsed off the steering wheel.

Then the car thief hammered a screwdriver into the ignition lock and tapped away with the professional touch of a man who knew exactly what he was doing.

As the car thief searched for the correct combination of ignition wires, a shadow blocked some of the light on the job site. He looked up to see the frightening figure of a person staring at him. All he saw was a pair of eyes through the horizontal layers of black cloth that covered the face. It looked like an Arab.

"What da fuck . . ."

Pfft.

Instant pain. The thief pulled the dart from his side. "What da *fuck* you do dat for, man?" He looked at the dart, then tossed it on the floor of the car. "Dis shit didn' hurt me none, man. You gotta stop playin' wit *toys,* Batman. If you wanna hurt someone, you gotta use *real* bullets."

The black-robed figure stood silently, pointing the rifle at the car thief's face, tracking his every movement. "Stop pointin' dat shit in ma face, man," he said while holding his hand up to protect his eyes from the large-bore barrel. "Well, you gonna choot me or what?" No response. "Dis *your* car, man?" No response. "I ain' got time for dis shit, man. I got work to do." And then he began to feel a little funny, perhaps even a little dizzy, perhaps . . . He opened the door, took a few steps, stumbled, then fell to the pavement.

The spent dart was retrieved from the floor of the car; then the unexpected booty was carried, fireman-style, to the car and plopped right next to Alex Hall. It was like manna from heaven. It was never expected that this reconnaissance mission would even yield Alex, let alone an extra specimen for free. Another hypo was filled with a clear fluid from a bottle and the car thief was injected.

The floppy bodies of Alex Hall and the mystery guest were seat-belted into position, and the three drove off into the Bronx night, past an unmarked police car bound for the same parking space the '77 Nova had just pulled away from.

"Hello, Brent?" Sergeant Perato said.

"Yes, what do you have for me?"

"I'm at Mrs. Hall's house having milk and cookies."

"Milk and cookies?"

"Yes, milk and cookies."

"What are you doing inside? He'll be abducted outside, not inside."

"Haskel is outside. Anyway, I don't think he's gonna show."

"So he just disappeared off the planet," Brent Kramer said. "Just like that. They released him. He took a ten-thirty-five Greyhound bus from Watertown, New York, arriving at the Port Authority at five-forty-five, and that's the last anyone saw of him. Period."

"Apparently so. Mrs. Hall is worried. The latest Alex was supposed to arrive was seven, seven-thirty the latest. Did the bus . . ."

"Yes, it arrived on time."

"Hmmm. Well we found something else interesting up here on the street, though, and I think it might be connected. There's a car across the street with the passenger window smashed. There's a Club on the floor with the lock shattered—you know, freeze-and-smash method. The ignition wires are all exposed. With minimal contamination to the scene, I started the car myself, with a quarter, so there's no reason in chop-shop heaven that that car should still be there. And there's some blood on the seat. I want that car impounded."

"I'm sending the tow truck immediately," Brent said. "Good work, Al. What's the plate number? We'll call the owner."

"Echo, Warsaw, Papa, eighty-eight, Victor."

"You towed my car?" one inflamed man screamed into the phone.

"Yes, Mr. Bernhart. We'll return it to you in a couple of days," Sergeant Perato said.

"You know, I need that car to get to work. What am I supposed to do in the meantime—fly to work?"

"You'll either have to rent a car or use public transportation.

I know it's gonna be inconvenient till you get your car back, but it can't be helped."

"How come you took my car?"

"All I can tell you is that someone broke the window and tried to steal your car, and some important evidence was left behind in the car that was pertinent to another case."

"What, stealing *my* car isn't pertinent enough? I had two cars stolen from this fuckin' shithole already, you know. And now they tried to steal *this* one, too! You know, it wasn't like this twenty years ago. Goddammit! Goddammit!! This *really* pisses me off. I work! I pay my taxes! Goddammit! What do I get for it? I get shit! I get shit for it! It costs me thousands of dollars. You know they stole the fuckin' tires off that car only four weeks after I bought it, after they stole the last fuckin' car! Goddamnit! Didn't that Club do any good? . . ."

"Positive ID on a Jesus Romero?" Brent said as he typed into his terminal to pull up some information.

"Yes, Lieutenant. We lifted five good prints with zero ambiguity."

"Excellent. . . . Yeah, he's coming up on my screen now." Brent examined Mr. Romero's police record. He was a professional car thief all right. His nickname was "Detroit," and it wasn't because he was a Tigers fan. He was practically an OEM supplier of wheels. He'd only been busted eight times for car theft, and he'd never spent any time in jail, because stealing cars—in actual practice, as opposed to theory—carries no enforceable penalty in New York City. The frequency of his busts were decreasing, though, which meant one of three things: He was stealing cars less frequently, or the cops weren't bothering to bust people for car theft anymore, or he was getting better at it. Two out of three ain't bad, Brent thought. "He's a car thief all right. Good work, Abdul."

"One more thing, Lieutenant—FYI, along with the prints of Mr. Bernhart, we found the prints of a Sheila Tucker. Her street name is "Benny." The prints were consistent with the positional configuration that might produce lipstick on the zipper of a pair of trousers."

Brent smiled. "I'm sure Mr. Bernhart would be pleased to know that."

"I'm sure he would. I got a few more things to do before I wrap things up here."

"Good. And now for my blood analysis."

"Say hi to Nigel for me," Abdul said.

Brent called Riverview Research Labs and asked for Nigel, who was at that moment twiddling the knobs on the mass spectrograph in the Serology Department. Nigel put him on the speaker phone while he looked at the screen of the machine.

"Ketamine, Brent. I had to look this one up. Ketamine. I never heard of it being used in humans before. We also found morphine, succinylcholine chloride, and Valium, which we had antigens for, but Ketamine? And the concentrations seemed to be a little high. These drugs weren't metabolized, either. They were simply mixed with the blood."

"So what are you telling me about this mixture?"

"This cocktail was designed to knock someone out. Dr. Solderwick said a mixture like this could have an induction time of less than a minute at three to six cc's for an agitated adult male. I think it's obvious what happened here. . . ."

"You can pick your car up now, Mr. Bernhart," Sergeant Perato said. "Just bring two forms of ID to show the officer on duty when you sign for your property. Then the car is yours."

"I'll be there in an hour. This has been such a goddamn inconvenience."

"To add to that inconvenience, you have to get your steering column fixed and a new window. Are you gonna bring it directly to a shop, or are you gonna leave it back on the street again?"

"I hadn't thought about it."

"You also might consider having a Lojack transmitter installed in your car. If your car is reported stolen, they think they can track the car. It's not foolproof, but it might improve the odds."

"It's so refreshing to hear a cop admit that," Mr. Bernhart sarcastically spewed. "A gun might improve the odds, too. Sometimes I think I'm the last law-abiding citizen left on the face of the earth."

Sergeant Perato said, "Can I ask you a personal question, Mr. Bernhart?"

130

"Well, yes, I guess so."

"Have you let anybody use your car lately?"

"No. Why?"

"Well, in that case . . . were you wearing a condom?" Brent overheard the sergeant's half of the conversation, and smiled.

"Was I wearing a condom . . . when?"

"Why, when you were with Benny."

32 Happy Birthday, America

Both Alex Hall and the car thief without a name lay side by side, blindfolded, secured to a pair of three-quarter-inch plywood boards, and bound with heavy Velcro straps. An IV bottle hung suspended above each patient's head, and the doctor pranced around the OR, wearing only a pair of white bikini underwear. George Gershwin's Second Rhapsody, performed by the London Symphony Orchestra, radiated from a pair of eight-inch speakers as drops of clear fluid nourished the veins of each sleeping man with a generous mixture of cocktail # 6, a popular solution of Valium, morphine, and sodium Pentothal.

The doctor removed a pair of amber bottles from a refrigerator. One bottle was labeled "Anti-A" and the other bottle was labeled "Anti-B." A vial of blood from each man had been drawn and now sat in a test-tube rack, still warm, along with the four empty sterile test tubes labeled "1A," "1B," "2A," and "2B." One cc of blood from Alex was dripped into test tube 1A and 1 cc was dripped into 1B. And blood from the mysterious car thief was dripped into 2A and 2B. Then a single drop of anti-A serum was squeezed into 1A and 2A with an eyedropper. And a single drop of anti-B serum was dropped into 1B and 2B. After thirty seconds, no agglutination was observed in any of the test tubes.

This was most fortunate. Both Alex and the car thief possessed type O blood, and in the general American population, the odds of this were 18.49 percent. The anti-A and anti-B amber bottles were returned to the refrigerator, and a few other choice things were removed.

And now the doctor's attention turned to Rusty Blake, who, throughout the past six weeks, had transformed—like an ugly caterpillar into a beautiful butterfly; like an undisciplined freshman with a head full of mush into a trained and educated senior with a purpose, a mission; like an empty canvas into an oiled and pigmented masterpiece, signed with a message burned into his back that said:

HOOPER
BLOOPER
POOPER
SCOOPER
I KILL
NO MORE

It wasn't that the doctor was running out of new things to brand onto the backs of the laboratory creations; the good doctor was simply growing a bit more confident and freer with word association.

In any event, Rusty Blake was ready to be released back to the world from which he had come. And he was dosed with his last intravenous taste of solution # 3, a custom blend designed to keep him out for at least six hours after that last cc disappeared down the long plastic tube on its way toward Rusty's overmedicated metabolizing machinery.

The fixture that kept his jaw immobilized was carefully removed from his head. The fixture that kept his arms immobilized was unscrewed at all its many points of attachment. The catheter was removed from his subclavian vein, and a small circular Band-aid was pressed over the tiny red spot. All the straps came off, and Rusty's unconscious naked body was carried out to the garage and plopped into the car.

It was a warm beautiful night, with a light breeze sifting through the rippling leaves of the willow trees. And while it was only three in the morning, today was a very special day, not only for Rusty Blake, but also for the country that had produced him. With full pomp and ceremony, today the country would add yet another proud birthday candle to its glorious cake. Today was Sunday, July Fourth.

At quarter past ten in the morning, the streets of midtown were already accumulating an abnormally large number of people—families in from New Jersey and the boroughs wandering leisurely from shop to shop, vendors selling trinkets, people on the go, mats of firecrackers and much larger noises reverberating between the buildings, laser-bright sun—a beautiful Manhattan summer day. It was a particularly busy morning at the corner of Fifth Avenue and Forty-second Street. Nobody really gave a second thought to the homeless person asleep under the large beach towel next to a lamppost—until the towel suddenly flew into the air, exposing the naked body of Rusty Blake. The towel hung from a string attached to the lamppost about ten or twelve feet above the street. People gasped when they saw the exposed naked man. Everyone knew immediately what he was. But he was not hugging the lamppost as Jerome Lewis, the first hooper, had been. This one was chained to the lamppost like a motorcycle. Four motorcycle locks imprisoned Rusty by his arm loop to four stout stainless steel chains. And he was beginning to awaken from his long, medicated slumber. A crowd gathered at an alarming rate.

"That's the Hooper Man, Daddy," a child said with wonder in his eyes.

"No," his older sister authoritatively corrected, "the Hooper Man is an African-American. This man is a Caucasian American."

A wake of sparks sprayed twenty feet out into the street as the cutting wheel of a gasoline-powered grinder slowly ate its way through the hardened chrome steel of the first motorcycle lock. Then a celebration blockbuster exploded down the street a ways, distracting the rescue worker just enough to twist the power tool. The cutting wheel bound up in the three-quarter-inch slot it had cut. It violently twisted, pulling Rusty backward; then the cutting wheel shattered into pieces. One of those pieces flew off at high speed, tearing a nineteen-inch gash in the leg of a bystander behind the police barrier. "Jesus, save me, Jesus! Sweet Jesus, save me. Save me," she screamed over and over again. The erupting wad of swollen, raw muscle tissue looked much worse than it actually was, but it was a hundred-stitch distraction that would ultimately result in a lawsuit worth a thousand dollars per stitch, in the future dollars when the out-of-court settlement would ultimately be reached, not including the cost of the ruined shiny gold stretch pants.

"Shit!" the workman said. He killed the ignition and placed the tool on the sidewalk. "Hey, Daryl," he yelled to one of the emergency vehicles clogging the intersection of Forty-second Street and Fifth Avenue along with a brigade of fire trucks, police cars, and an ambulance, "you got another K12 in the truck there?"

Rusty Blake was mildly terrified at the activity surrounding him. He produced unintelligible gurgling noises, and what his tearing oversensitive eyes were seeing translated in his brain to incomprehensible images of bright light, which made him nauseous, along with the confirmation that his arms were somewhat different than they used to be, some indeterminate time ago into the past.

Then a series of gastrointestinal spasms explosively propelled liquid vomit from Rusty's blowhole and nose. He began choking, and EMS workers rushed for the lavage suction pump in the truck. "Try to spit it out!" one paramedic yelled as Rusty was tipped like a teapot so the maximum amount of fluid would drain from his cheek. Then a paramedic threaded the catheter into the three-quarter-inch hole in his cheek and the vomit drained from his mouth with the same gurgling sound produced at the dentist, except with the slightly more viscous components of a thick milk shake. Rusty had aspirated some of his stomach contents and he violently coughed. The attending paramedic vacuumed out the last of the liquid while looking into the hole with a small, powerful flashlight. He was ready to perform a tracheotomy if the wheezing man had any further trouble breathing. It was a close call, but Rusty seemed to be recovering.

The EMS workers tried to keep him calm and stable as the Fujitsu blimp passed overhead, with the live-news camera looking down at the curious crowd of 2,500 people, with still more accumulating.

The steps of the New York Public Library afforded the best vantage point for viewing the activity within the perimeter of the blue barricades holding back the sea of people.

And then the first of several news vans arrived to create as well as to report the event. A pushy little bald man with a pencil in his ear and a radio in his hand slithered through the crowd and barked, "It's a story all right," qualifying to his crew that this was, in fact, a newsworthy event, and the van began setting up.

The second grinder failed to start because the pull-start cord would not retract back into the mechanism, so the retaining nut and washer were removed from the first cutting tool and the broken wheel was removed.

One of the EMS workers searched through the gang box for the extra cutting wheels for the K12. He knew those wheels had to be in there somewhere. And they were, right next to the "jaws of death," which was the name they'd given to the Jaws of Life. The cutting wheel was handed to the rescue worker, whose eyes at the moment were focused on the nipples of a shapely señorita throwing encouraging glances his way. Rusty Blake heaved a bubbly mass of viscous slime from his virgin blowhole, and, in the spasm of a wrist and the blink of an eye, the retaining nut was on its way down a ventilation grating. "Shit!" the rescue worker said.

Then he was struck by a bolt of blinding creativity, and he removed the nut from the K12 with the broken starter cord and placed it on the tool that would start. Now the police pushed the crowd as far back as they could, and the sparks began to fly once again.

The television screen showed bold white words on a blue background, which read:

BULLETIN: NEWS UPDATE

"Another bizarre mutilation victim has been discovered, this time in midtown Manhattan, at Forty-second Street and Fifth Avenue. A mutilated man was discovered chained to a lamppost just across the street from the New York Public Library. His mouth has been surgically closed and his hands have been amputated and surgically joined together. Police and emergency workers are on the scene at this moment, and we will bring you live up-to-the-minute coverage momentarily. This case is similar to what we reported back on May twenty-fifth, when Jerome Lewis shocked the world with . . ."

The phone rang at the Kramer residence in New Jersey, and Tammy said, "Shit!" as Brent stopped what he was doing. "Not now, honey," Tammy pleaded. Brent lifted his head from between her tensed legs. The phone rang again. "Please don't answer it, sweetheart." Brent was torn between duty and drive, between job and blow job. His head dropped an inch, and the phone rang a third time. Tammy's hands closed into fists, and Brent knew it was already too late—too late to salvage that which was lost, and he sensed that his day off had evaporated, as well. He continued what he was doing, but the rhythm was lost. The answering machine picked up, and the tape loop reproduced Tammy's words: "Please leave a brief message at the tone, and we'll get back to you as soon as we can."

"Lieutenant? . . . Are you there?" It was the voice of Sergeant Perato.

Tammy said, "What does that potato head want this time?"

Brent replied in a muffled voice, "He's a super potato head now."

Tammy had lost it. Brent knew Tammy had lost it. Tammy knew Brent knew she had lost it. And Brent knew Tammy knew he knew she'd lost it. But they pretended they didn't know what they knew they knew, because no one wanted an argument, least of all the super potato head, who hoped he hadn't done what he thought he might have done, which in actuality he did, but he pretended he didn't.

". . . Lieutenant," Sergeant Perato continued with uncertainty, "If you're there, which I assume you're not . . . I hope you're not . . . whatever . . . we got another hooper chained to a lamp—at Forty-second and Fifth. . . ."

Brent said in unison with the sergeant, "A little closer to home . . ."

"Jesus," Tammy said, "you guys are even starting to think alike."

"Turn on Channel Seven, Brent, if you're there. I'm on my way over to Forty-second and Fifth right now. Talk to you later."

Tammy said, "Well, I guess you want me to turn on the TV." Brent kept doing what he was doing, without saying a word. Tammy knew that this was Brent's way of saying yes, so she grabbed the TV remote control and flicked on the set. With a *boink,* the picture sprang to life, and there on the lamppost was the oversaturated image of bright sparks blooming across the screen. As soon as Tammy raised the volume, Brent did a quick about-face, using Tammy's pubic bone as a backrest for his head. He grabbed her kneecaps with his hands and watched the close-up picture.

"That's Rusty Blake, all right," Brent said in despair. "And the next one is gonna be Alex Hall, and maybe even this Jesus Romero."

"This is so disgusting," Tammy said as a close-up of Rusty's loop filled half the screen and the grinder did its thing.

"You have *no idea* how frustrating it is to deal with the rest of the police department," Brent said, "and *everyone,* for that matter. It's like we're not even on the same side. They each have their own little fiefdom, and they fight you *every* step of the way, and it's all because people are so goddamn stupid."

"Who do you think is doing this, Brent?"

"I don't know. Whoever's doing it is getting a lot of practice, though."

The camera angle widened up a bit so the size of the crowd could be seen."

"Look at that, honey," Tammy said as she pointed at the TV. "It looks like that big beach towel my mother has."

"You're talking about that towel hanging from the lamppost, right?"

"Yes. How do you suppose it got there?"

"That's a damn good question. What the hell *is* that thing?" The camera zoomed in on Rusty again. "It looked like a string or something holding it. . . ."

"Are you sure Nigel didn't do this?"

". . . This is the second case like this to be discovered in the city, and so far, the police are unwilling to comment on the *obvious* connection between these two events. Our own reporters have . . ."

The chain was finally cut through and Rusty Blake was whisked away on a stretcher and promptly disappeared into the back of an ambulance. A third and fourth news truck showed up, but only the first two snagged any noteworthy images. And then the trucks packed up with their footage, on to yet another assignment in the news-rich Big Apple on this Fourth of July.

And the beach towel that had covered Rusty waved like a flag in the warm breeze, and it went completely unnoticed—almost.

Marshall Stanley could not believe his eyes when he saw the images of yet another hooper on the screen of his television set. He paced back and forth like a caged animal, thought a moment longer, and then picked up the phone. "Bill, you remember when you said, 'If there's ever anything I ever needed...'? ... *Ummmm hummm....* Well, as it turns out, I do need a small favor.... I need to borrow a little something from your closet...."

The phone rang once again at the Kramer residence in New Jersey, and Tammy said, "Shit!" as Brent stopped what he was doing. "Not now, honey," Tammy pleaded again. Brent lifted his head from where it was. The phone rang again. "Please don't answer it, sweetheart." Once again, Brent was torn between two incompatible worlds. His head dropped an inch, and the phone rang a third time. Tammy's hands closed into fists, and Brent knew it was too late, once again. He *knew* he should have disconnected the phone, and he *knew* that two strikes against him would be difficult to undo in the days to come, and *come* was the operative word here, because it would probably have to be self-inflicted—for both of them. He continued what he was doing, but the rhythm was lost, once again. And then his beeper went off, too.

"Please leave a brief message at the tone, and we'll get back to you as soon as we can."

"Brent, this is Commissioner Brown, your boss. Remember me?" Brent's mouth suddenly went dry. "The mayor is one *angry* motherfuckin' nigger, and he's on my case about this hooper shit. I said we could handle it, but he's making all kin'a noises about bringing in the feds. You know how I feel when he pulls that shit on me. Please get back to me as soon as you can. Say hi to Tammy for me, okay? Brown out."

It was a madhouse at Roosevelt Hospital when the ambulance pulled up with all the security of a presidential procession. Rusty Blake was surrounded by a protoplasmic blob of EMS workers and police officers, and nobody noticed one extra six-foot-tall police officer who followed the patient to the emergency room for his preliminary examination. Several police officers remained outside the ER for over an hour, while still others kept the accumulating reporters at a safe distance.

And then Rusty threw up again, and a pureed grayish brown liquid sprayed from the blowhole on the side of his face and then oozed from his nose. He began choking and another suction catheter was jammed into the dripping blowhole and began vacuuming out his mouth. The electronic monitors were hooked up, and Dr. Spellman entered the emergency room and said, "Another one?"

"Bo-de-ga de-da?" the cabdriver said, looking at Nigel as if he were out of his mind or something.

"Oh Jesus Christ . . . can't ya just take me to Fifth Avenue? Just make a right on Forty-second Street." It seemed as if the cab had a mind of its own. And the driver seemed more like a malignant growth that popped out of the seat rather than a licensed life-form who worked the controls of an internal-combustion engine mounted on four licensed wheels. "STOP!!!" The car screeched to a halt, more out of spite than because it was going someplace that someone actually wanted to go. "GO THAT WAY!" Nigel pointed east, down Forty-second Street. "Can you please turn right?" he whispered with the intimidating hint of a growl.

The cabdriver was really getting pissed. He didn't like this customer one bit. It seemed that all these New Yorkers had a damn attitude problem of some kind, and he had been in such a good mood when he left his eleven children and wife for his forty-eight-hour shift, and that was twenty-nine hours ago. He angrily leaned back and said, *"Eesh-ta boosh-ga rah-na Woo!"* then screeched the tires, and the cab fishtailed into a more easterly heading.

Nigel glanced over at the man's hack license. Boskuy Mokinktajupue. That was the alpha-numeric handle this transporta-

139

tional guru went by, and he looked like one of the mental patients out of the movie *Midnight Express*. And clearly he didn't seem to know a thing about city navigation or a word of English, which was why, in fact, he was a New York City cabdriver. But this was not completely the case, because when Nigel said, "STOP!" then "STOP!!" again, and the driver actually came to rest a half block farther east than Nigel wanted to go, the driver plainly said, "Three dollars, fifty cents." And that is exactly what Nigel gave him.

Disgusted, Nigel burst out of the taxicab from Bangladesh and met Sergeant Perato, who was accompanied by a few uniformed police officers. Nigel looked up at the lamppost and said, "I need a twelve-foot ladder." At that very moment, a police utility vehicle pulled up, and out of the back, like magic, came a twelve-foot ladder.

A six-foot-tall policeman exited the elevator and walked down the hospital corridor. He walked up to the nursing station and said to the nurse, "I'm here to review the security of the room before the patient is brought here."

The nurse said, "Yeah, they told us to be expecting him. I can't believe this. It's getting so crazy out there."

"You're so right," the officer said, then shook his head in disgust. "It's sick, and it's getting sicker. But we're gonna do our best to catch the person or persons responsible. Could you buzz me in so I can check the room?"

"What's there to check?" the nurse asked.

"I need to check the windows and the door, just in case they try something."

"Okay."

The buzzer hummed, and the cop disappeared into the room as he removed a tube of Krazy Glue from his pocket.

"...Emergency surgery was just performed to open the mouth of the latest mutilation victim, who was found chained to a streetlamp in midtown Manhattan only hours ago. The victim almost expired in two medical emergencies when he regurgitated into his surgically closed mouth, almost choking to death, so hospital officials made the decision to go ahead with the operation to surgically open up his mouth, thus gaining free access to his airway. We will keep you informed with up-to-the-minute details as this strange story unfolds. Now . . ."

"So here's how it was done," Nigel said to Brent over the phone. "Two hose clamps were tightened around the lamppost, one at a height of about eighteen feet and one at a height of thirteen feet. Inside both clamps were tied loops of seven-millimeter nylon dynamic rope, to act as pulleys. Actually, it was really clever. What he did was this: There's a piece of fourteen-and-a-half-foot-long length of five-millimeter dynamic rope tied to the center of the towel, whose dimensions are six feet by four-and-a-half feet. Then he ties a length of three-eighth-inch surgical tubing to the rope, and this is stretched as tight as it'll go. He tied a four-inch length of rope to the junction of the surgical tubing and the rope, and this sort of fuse rope was attached to the lower pulley. Now, this fuze rope was treated with a one-twenty-fifth molar solution of sulfuric acid—as far as I can determine. When the rope—"

"I get it!" Brent interrupted. "When the acid eats through the fuze link, it breaks, and the bungee cord pulls the towel off Rusty faster than you can say, *bon appétit!*"

"Exactly."

"Wait, though. There are a few things that still don't make sense. Like, wait a minute . . . I'm sketching this thing out right now. . . . No. The lengths don't add up. . . ."

"Yes they do."

"Wait. You can't get enough stretch out of the bungee cord. . . ."

"He double-looped it. He started at the top, looped through the bottom, came back up through the top, and back to the fuze link and the rope."

"I see. I have another question, though. How did he know the knots wouldn't get caught in the loops of rope?"

"Oh. He thought of that, too. He taped the knots with masking tape so they were tapered and streamlined. This guy's no jerk. In fact, I'm kinda hoping we don't catch 'im. He does real good work. A real professional."

"Yeah, Tammy thinks it's you who's doing this."

"She might be right. By the way, there were no fingerprints on anything."

"There were no prints on the Band-aid on Rusty's neck, either."

"I'm sending all the stuff over to you so you can do your thing with it," Nigel said. "How's your map work coming?"

"Very slow. Your girlfriend is driving me crazy."

"She's not my girlfriend . . . yet."

"Well, every five minutes she has another question. She tampered with the communications software and now it's worse than ever. It's like her confidence is eroding the longer she's here. Why don't you come by and—"

"Do a little consulting?" Nigel finished Brent's sentence as the blood in his body began redistributing itself.

33   The Brotherhood of Officers

Rusty Blake opened his eyes in the recovery room after his operation. The news had been correct: The operation *was* considered an emergency procedure, because Rusty had this unfortunate puking tendency, and without frontal access to clear his airway, he could easily have choked to death from his own vomit, just like Jimi Hendrix, except that Jimi never had his mouth sewn shut.

Rusty lay in bed, nervously twitching, and then raised the arm loop and stared at it as if it were not actually connected to him. He fought against the tremendous pain in his face as he opened his mouth. For the first time in more than five weeks, he stuck his tongue out of his mouth. Then he began to sob, as the reality of his medical situation sank in, slowly, in waves of mental anguish. Again, Rusty stared at his arm loop in disbelief and horror.

Even though Rusty had been abducted the day after the world had discovered Jerome Lewis hooped around a lamppost in Brooklyn, he'd hadn't heard the interesting news because he didn't yet have a TV or a radio.

"What happened to me?" he pleaded in pain to a nurse who had come in to check up on his monitoring machinery. She seemed distant, and more interested in the things that connected to the wires attached to him than in him himself. Then she looked at him and smiled, almost as if she were distorted through a fish-eye lens; then she mechanically continued what she was doing.

"I see you're up," she said with a smile. Then she continued, as if she were bribing a child with a lollipop, "I'm going to take your *blood pressure* now. Please don't be alarmed." She placed the cuff around Rusty's right arm and pumped up the pressure bulb. Then she placed the stethoscope to his skin. The nurse did not realize it at the time, but this blood pressure reading would be less than meaning-ful, at least the way she was taking it, because Rusty was hydraulically a different circuit than he and 5 billion other humans on the planet were six weeks before, except, of course, for Jerome Lewis.

Rusty gazed at her as if she held the answers to all his questions. She had short black hair, medium to slightly above aver-age–sized breasts, and she was a little on the pudgy side, but to Rusty, she was salvation, and the most beautiful thing in the world, and besides, she was the first human thing he could comprehend in a sane state of mind. "Please, ma'am," Rusty said using the facial muscles that had partially atrophied, "what happened to me?"

Her first impulse was to say, Freelance surgery, but instead she said, "It's going to take some time for you to understand every-thing that's happened to you. I am going to get the doctor, and he'll explain it to you better than I ever could." The nurses were always bitching that most of the doctors were incompetent assholes, and that the nurses were underpaid, and that they did most of the work, but it was times like this that she was glad that she could defer to a higher, male authority. "Just hold on there a minute and the doctor will be right with you." She did a quick about-face and left the recovery room.

"Wait . . ." Rusty was all alone in a room with three other beds. He raised his loop of modified tissue till it was horizontal and directly in front of his eyes. Then he raised it over his head to try to look at the other side of it. He repeatedly placed his tongue into the blowhole on the left side of his cheek, without the faintest notion of how any of this had come to be.

And then Dr. Spellman came into the recovery room with

the clipboard the nurse had given him. "You had us worried there for a moment." He sat on the edge of the bed and put his hand on Rusty Blake's jaw, clinically examining his lips.

"What happened to me?"

"Try not to talk if you can help it. I'll try to answer your questions as best I can. Your name is Rusty Blake. Is that correct?"

"Yes," Rusty said, shaking his head up and down.

"Mr. Blake, you have been the victim of a cruel human experiment. I don't know how to soften this news for you. Somebody . . . some lunatic surgically closed up your mouth, and I just opened it up again when you were brought here to the hospital. You almost choked to death when you threw up. Do you remember throwing up?"

Rusty shook his head no.

"Do you remember being outside at all today?"

"A little? . . . My hands?"

"We are going to try and rehabilitate you to the best of our ability, but it's going to take a lot of physical and mental fortitude on your part. . . ."

Rusty Blake was no longer listening to the doctor. "Why?!"

"I don't know why. It just happened." And then Dr. Spellman saw Lieutenant Kramer standing in the doorway. "There is someone important here to speak with you." Brent walked closer to Rusty as he switched on the tape recorder in his breast pocket. "Rusty, this is Lieutenant Brent Kramer, and Lieutenant Kramer, this is Rusty Blake." Dr. Spellman was grateful to defer to a higher male authority.

"Rusty, I'm a police officer, and I wanna catch the guy who did this to you and cut his balls off with my bare hands. So I'm gonna need your help to tell me anything you can remember about the past six weeks—since you were abducted that day in the sand pit. That's where we found your motorcycle. Do you understand me?"

"Yes," Rusty said, as the lieutenant's statement had just reminded him of that day on the bike; then he jammed his tongue into the blowhole.

Brent spent over an hour with Rusty Blake in the recovery room. Rusty remembered very little about his abduction. The last thing he remembered was the motorcycle, and that stabbing pain in his shoulder. And the next thing he remembered was being chained to the lamppost, and even that was foggy. Brent walked out with two vials of Rusty's whole blood in addition to the three vials that had been drawn upon Rusty's arrival, and rushed it to the Serology Department of Riverview Research.

Then Rusty was moved upstairs under police escort to his new room, which was, in fact, the very same room where Jerome Lewis had stayed before him, and where Freddy Lopez had stayed before Jerome. And this room had also been carefully inspected by a six-foot-tall policeman.

It was 3:30 in the morning, and a policeman was guarding the room where Rusty Blake lay sleeping. The hallway was deserted, except for the policeman and the nurse at the desk thirty feet away. Then a six-foot-tall policeman with a big paper bag quietly walked down the hall from the other direction and up to the officer guarding the room. "How ya doin', guy?" he said to the officer.

"I'm doin' okay. Where are *you* from?"

"Oh, I'm sorry," the six-foot-tall cop said. "My name is Sarretti, Joe Sarretti. I work down at One P P, directly for the commissioner?"

"Oh. You're here to check up on me?"

"Well . . . yes. There ya have it. I ain't gonna feed you no bullshit like them other assholes might. That's where the hooper lives?" Sarretti said, pointing at the room with a head gesture and a smirk.

"Yep. He's right behind that door. Thanks for your frankness, by the way."

"Don't mention it. Yep, they sent me here to sort a . . . help keep an eye on things. I'm sort of a night person. I hope my presence isn't makin' ya nervous. Say, I brought some food. Wanna sandwich?" Sarretti removed a big bottle of V-8, some Snapple, a pair of Budweisers, and two big overstuffed ham, turkey, and salami sandwiches on sinfully fresh rye bread liberally smeared with Grey Poupon mustard. He took a big bite out of one of the sandwiches, then said with his mouth full, "Here. Why don't ya try one, compliments of the commissioner."

The officer on guard took the sandwich and began munching away. Sarretti popped open his Bud and began drinking with all the gusto of a cop without a worry in the world. The officer started out with a little V-8, but when he felt reasonably sure that Sarretti was a regular guy and wasn't trying to set him up, he broke down and had just one beer. Then Sarretti produced another pair of Buds from the magic bag, along with some Danish and high-class chocolates—the ones with liqueurs inside. And then the last third of the six-pack emerged from the bag, along with two cups of rich gourmet coffee.

And all this food and drink was having a predictable effect on the liquid and solid exhaust machinery of the officer on guard. "I'm gonna go visit the head," he said. "Will ya keep an eye on the hooper for me?"

"Sure," Sarretti said.

And with that, he took off down the hall, to the little porcelain room. When he was good and out of sight, Sarretti bounced up from the chair and turned the doorknob to the room, and sure enough, the solenoid-activated dead bolt was still securely Krazy Glued in an insecure position, and the doorknob was rotated fully clockwise. He entered and turned on the light. He walked up to Rusty Blake and pulled the covers off him. He looked at the goofy loop of arm tissue, but he had no time to waste. He shook Rusty, who looked up with surprise at the cop, who then said, "I'm no cop, Rusty. And I have a little money making proposition for you. . . ."

In less than eight minutes, Marshall Stanley exited the room with a contract in hand, and he sat down on the bench just as the officer returned from the bathroom. "Look, guy," Marshall Stanley said, "I have to get back downtown now. You look like you know exactly what you're doing, and I have only good news for my masters. I'll be seein' ya around."

"Wait," his fellow brother officer said, "ya better take one of the these." Then he handed Marshall Stanley a handful of mints for his breath.

Marshall thanked the officer for the mints, then moseyed on out of Roosevelt Hospital. A half a block down the street, Marshall took a long, satisfying piss between two parked cars as he laughed till he was almost at the point of tears. While he was pissing, he removed the contract with the X on it and took one more look at it, just to make sure it was really real, and not merely a figment of his imagination.

34   *Late Night with David Letterman*

Paul Shaffer and the *Late Night* band finished playing their intermission interlude as David Letterman tapped his cue cards on the edge of his desk. The audience recovered from something that had happened during the break, and when the applause sufficiently died, David said, "Have you heard the news today about the new hooper that just happened to turn up in the city, chained to a lamppost?" Applause followed, along with whistling mixed with catcalls and cheering from the audience. "Well, it seems that the hooper population has just doubled. Our crack mathematics staff tells me that at this rate, in only two years and four months, we'll have over a million hoopers wandering around the streets. What do you think of that, Paul?"

The camera shifted to Paul Shaffer and his flamboyant shirt and he stood surrounded by all his electronic keyboards and sound machines. "Well, David, I don't think the band and I have much to worry about on that count."

"How's that, Paul?"

"I doubt very many of them will be becoming musicians." A wave of delayed laughter crept through the audience amid whistling and hisses.

"Well, that's probably true. Ha, haaaa. That's probably true. But what do you think we can do with all those hoopers? I think we're going to have a bit of an unemployment problem, don't you?"

Paul jeered at David as some of the low-level laughter died down. "Maybe we can balance the trade deficit by exporting some of them to Japan." The audience exploded, and the camera flashed back to David, who was grinning from ear to ear.

"Paul, that wasn't in the script. . . . Ha, ha, ha . . ."

Paul appeared on screen and said, "I couldn't resist that one, Dave."

"No, I guess you couldn't, Paul. . . . I'll turn *you* into a hooper. . . ."

Paul hugged his arms, hand to elbow, simulating the shape of a hooper, and the audience roared. "But look at it this way, Dave, as of now, the U.S. is the only manufacturer of hoopers in the world. I just thought we could take advantage of that fact. I'm only trying to help our economy, Dave."

"Maybe we should tell the President about your suggestion."

"I don't know, David. When Japan decides to act on that one, that's just one more thing they'll take us to the cleaners with. . . ." The audience cheered, and then Paul went on to say, "But as of now, we did the research as always, and we lead the world in hooper production. . . ."

"Can hoopers be patented, Paul?" Audience laughter.

"Gee, I don't know, Dave. We'll have to get our legal people on that one."

"Maybe we could help pay off some of that national debt in hoopers," David said. Audience laughter. "Maybe they could become the next unit of currency. . . ." More laughter. ". . . Maybe they'd be listed on the stock exchange. . . ." Still more laughter. ". . . Who knows where it could go? . . ." Laughter. ". . . The yen slipped relative to the Krugerand and the hooper. . . ." Laughter. ". . . The hooper index is down four percent over last month. . . ." More laughter. ". . . But next month, they're expected to be coming around. . . ." Audience explosion and catcalls. ". . . Ha, ha, ha . . . They don't talk back, but they sure do spit a lot. . . ." Catcalls, hisses, screams and howls, laughter, and more laughter. ". . . No, but let's be serious now, folks. This *will* become a growing problem in society. I mean, with all those murderers and car thiefs out of circulation, unemployed and all, we're headed for an outbreak of civil rest and low crime. . . ." The audience went ballistic with applause, howling and whistling. ". . . What would we do with all those useless cops on the take? . . ." The audience flipped out. ". . . I mean, on the beat. . . ." They flipped out some more. ". . . Sorry, sorry, folks. . . . Little slip of the tongue . . ." Letterman sensed this was one of his better shows, and he held the audience in the palms of his waving hands. It took a full thirty seconds for them to quiet down, and shots of Dave, Paul, people in the control room, and the audience were interlaced as waves of rejuvenating applause filled the house. And there were rumblings among the writers that this might not be an appropriate topic to breach. "... But seriously now, folks ... ha, ha, haaaa ... seriously now, folks ..." It still wouldn't die. "... Can you believe this, Paul? ... Ha, ha, haaaa ..." Dave held his arms in the air above his head, hooper-style, and another wave of hysteria overtook the room as he and Paul held their heads in their hands, laughing themselves silly. In all their years together, they'd never experienced such a volatile audience. The guests in the greenroom were rolling on the floor, as well.

Dave sensed a moment when he thought he could get a word in edgewise, and said, "Well, to meet this growing problem in society, here on *Late Night,* our dedicated staff has compiled a list of ten things you can do with a hooper...." The audience went wild once more. "... Jeez, you think they're warmed up enough, Paul?"

"I think they're warmed up enough, Dave."

"Well, here we go, then ... our list of ten things you can do with a hooper." A drumroll accompanied David as the text rolled across the screen. "Number ten, something you can employ a hooper to do ... napkin holder at Windows on the World ..." Applause and laughter. "Number nine ... plastic bag holder on the supermarket checkout line ..." Applause and laughter. "... Number eight, things to employ a hooper to do, folks ... outfielder for the New York Mets ..." Explosive laughter and applause. "... Number seven ... scorekeeper for the New York Mets ..." Greater explosive laughter and applause. "Number six, something you can employ a hooper to do ... ha, ha, ha ... piano instructor ..." Applause and laughter. "... See, Paul, there still might be some competition for those valuable slots in the musician's union, ha, ha, ha ... Number five, things you can employ a hooper to do ... hairstylist..." On the screen appeared a three-shot of Yul Brynner, Telly Savalas, and Mr. Clean. Applause and laughter. "... Number four ... applause machine for the *Joe Franklin Show* ..." Explosive laughter and applause. "... Number three ... something you can employ a hooper to do ... life preserver on the SS *Titanic* ..." Explosive laughter and applause. "... Number two ... something useful you can employ a hooper to do ... municipal worker for the city of New York ..." Explosive

149

laughter and applause. "... And here we go, the number-one thing you can employ a hooper to do ..." A drumroll and a cymbal crash. "... Garbage receptacle for the city of New York ..." Explosive laughter, applause, catcalls, whistling, howling, and as they went to break, the band played "Take Me Out to the Ball Game."

Jerome Lewis just happened to be watching *Late Night with David Letterman,* and when the commercial came on, he sniffled, and wiped another tear from his eye with his already-wet shoulder.

35   Legwork

Lt. Brent Kramer drove up a hill on a beautiful tree-lined street in Montclair, New Jersey. He pulled to the curb across the street from the house of Dr. Stella Isman and sat for a moment with the window open, alternating glances between his file notes and the property, immersing himself in the scents of green summer foliage. It was a large house, much too large for two people. Dr. Isman had been married to international banker Normand Baker Dryfus, who was killed in a helicopter crash during whiteout conditions while skiing in the Rockies. He left to his beloved wife the house and a fully diversified midrange liquid fortune, which Stella promptly took the conservative reins of. She unceremoniously resumed the use of her maiden name, and soon thereafter her twin brother, Richard, came to live with her in the big lonely house with the swimming pool sunken into the smartly landscaped yard. Dr. Richard Isman was a professor of applied mathematics at Courant Institute, and Stella now functioned somewhere between a freelance anthropologist and a recluse. She had worked for the Leakey Institute up until her husband's untimely death at forty-nine, then began spending more of her time on-line as a cyberspace anthropologist. Both Stella and her brother, Richard, were cousins of Marc Isman, who had survived

150

his shooting at the whimsical hand of Freddy Lopez one spring afternoon.

Kramer approached the front door while noting in the driveway a pair of identical white Volvo station wagons with the vanity plates BROTHER and SISTER. He rang the bell, and a barefoot woman in hot-pink tights and a cobalt blue exercise leotard answered the door. "You must be . . . Lieutenant Kramer. Come in," she mechanically said with a neutral smile. "I just juiced up a quart of carrots. Like a cup?"

"Yes, that sounds like it might hit the spot," he said while absorbing her image like a freshly opened synthetic sponge drinking its first teaspoon of water.

"Good! Make yourself at home anywhere. I'll be right with you." Then she said, almost as an afterthought, "Why don't you visit my new moose in the living room."

Brent watched her shiny posterior gracefully float off to the kitchen. Stella Isman appeared to be about thirty-six or -seven, five six, 120 pounds—all three variables melding into a deliciously proportioned female-form factor perfectly packaged for the male brain stem. My new moose? Brent thought as he looked around at the myriad stuffed birds, mammals, and reptiles adorning the walls, table surfaces, and floors of this house. And in the living room stood a moose—a fully grown and stuffed moose! And it seemed to Brent that half the animals in Africa were keeping the moose company.

Dr. Isman returned from the kitchen with two tall glasses of carrot juice and a tray of grapes, cheese, celery, and crackers, which she placed on a table. She saw the lieutenant staring at the head of a giraffe, and said, "My husband would shoot 'em, and I would stuff 'em. It was a convenient arrangement . . . for a while. The moose came from Canada last month. He was my last project."

"I presume your husband didn't shoot the moose."

"No," Stella sighed. "My husband's been dead for . . . going on four years now. Friends of mine work with wildlife management up in the northern territories. That moose was lame, and eventually dropped dead in captivity. Do you know how hard it is to bring a moose carcass into the United States?"

"No. I'd never really thought about it, but I imagine it must be easier than shipping Cray computers out of the U.S."

"Crays don't carry microorganisms," Stella said as she placed the tray on the table and sat. "They only *simulate* them."

"I never met anyone into taxidermy."

"See that sparrow on the windowsill? My mother taught me how to mount it when I was nine years old. Poor thing died in the jaws of a neighborhood cat."

"I take it you don't favor predators."

"Predator ... prey," she sighed—"it's simply the natural order of things. Anyway, if it weren't for the predator, I'd never have learned to mount the prey."

"I see you've mounted quite a few predators, though," Brent said as he slowly took a step closer to Stella. "Your mother is a paleontologist, I understand."

"Yes. Mommy works at the Museum of Natural History, assembling her bones in bliss." She pointed to a skeleton. "That duck-billed platypus was Mommy's gift to me on my thirtieth.

"So, Lieutenant, on the telephone you told me you wanted to talk about Marc—what he was like, before the shooting—all about the family and such?"

Brent seated himself opposite Stella Isman and sympathetically said, "You and your brother must be *very* close."

"Yes, we are. Dick is the closest person to me in the world, and my best friend, too. I don't think I would make any major decision without his knowledge or approval."

"Does Richard have a girlfriend ... or a partner?"

Stella laughed and said, "Lieutenant, my brother is not seeing anyone, at the moment, and he *isn't* gay, either."

"I wasn't implying ... well ..." Brent also laughed as he touched the glass of foamy juice to his lips, *"Hmmm.* Tell me about Marc; were you and Dick close to your cousin?"

"We lived around the corner from them in Sheepshead Bay. We were either over at their house or they were at ours."

"They, being Marc and Ed, his older brother?"

"Yes. Dick and I were very close, even as kids, and we were so much smarter than Eddie and Marc, and we knew it, too. Thinking back, we must have been impossible children. It's not that *they* were stupid; it's just that *we* had ... less conventional interests. Dick and I would play Scrabble while they watched television. They collected baseball cards; Dick and I collected stamps and coins. I remember once, when Aunt Janice bought Mr. Machine for Marc. Do you remember that one, Lieutenant? It was a robot full of gears? Well, once we were over at their house right after Aunt Janice bought it, and Marc quickly lost interest in it, and Dick and I spent the rest of the afternoon taking it apart and putting it together. We sort of absorbed it away from Marc; I think we still have it somewhere. Another time they were over at our house, and they watched TV while I was mounting a box turtle and Dick was carving a deer head out of a block of wood . . . for a Boy Scout merit badge, I think."

"Is your brother very handy with tools?" Kramer asked as he stuffed a cracker in his mouth.

"He's still pretty good with a knife, but I think I got most of the tool-user genes in our family."

Brent glanced around the room. "I can tell that you're very artistic."

"Well, I was always torn between art, anthropology, and zoology. Mounting animals combines elements of all three."

Filled with curiosity, Brent walked over to the moose, touched its nose, and said, "I never realized how big a moose actually is."

"They get even bigger, Lieutenant."

"How do you stuff an animal this large? It must take an awful lot of space."

"It does—the whole basement, and some of the rooms up here." Dr. Isman bounced up. "Would you like the tour?"

Stella took Brent to the basement workshop and explained how the skin is removed from an animal and how mannequins of various sizes are made to stretch the skin over. She also told Brent about herself, her lifestyle, her brother, her husband, how he died, how he lived, how much she missed him, and a number of anecdotal confessions of the love they shared. "Have you ever gotten involved with anyone since your husband's death?" Brent asked.

"Well, at the moment, I *am* seeing a gentleman. . . ."

And then a man with a meticulously groomed red goatee slid the glass door open and entered from the patio, leaving a trail of wet footprints from the pool. A pair of red ovals were impressed on the skin above his eyebrows, where the swimming goggles had been moments earlier. His glass of juice took priority over the lieutenant, even though he saw both in his unassisted visual field. He placed his glasses on, and then Stella said, "Dick, this is Lieutenant Kramer, and Lieutenant, this is my brother, Richard."

Dick puckered his lips as if he smelled something bad, then held out his hand and said, "Glad to meet you, Lieutenant..." He hesitated, tilting his head slightly.

"Kramer," Brent said with a smile. "Glad to meet you. Stella tells me you're a professor of mathematics."

"Statistics."

"That's probably within a standard deviation of the definition of math," Brent said.

Dr. Richard Isman cackled out a short nervous laugh, then said while wiggling his index finger, "That's very good, Lieutenant. I'll have to remember that one the next time I extol the virtues of a statistical existence to my students. You seem to know a little math yourself, Lieutenant Kramer."

"Enough to get by. When Dirac functions replaced continuous functions, I began to lose interest. What branch of math do *you* hang your hat on, other than statistics, Dr. Isman?"

"Infinite series, little bit of chaos, and statistics and quantum. I dabble in a little a this and a little a that. Like everyone else, I play with computers a little, too."

"Oh!" Stella playfully scolded. "He does *more* than play with computers, Lieutenant. Tell the lieutenant what your thesis was, Dick."

"She's my greatest admirer," Richard said to Brent, a little embarrassed.

Answering for him, Stella said, "An adaptive multidimensional convolution generator."

"Digital vision?" Brent said.

"Very impressive, Lieutenant," Dr. Richard Isman said as he puckered his lips again, and deposited a foamy carrot-orange mustache on his top lip.

Brent drove along Barret Road, watching the golfers on the greens of the Lawrence Golf Club, to his right. This was an exclusive neighborhood, dripping with wealth from every one- and two-acre plot of land. Brent turned left onto Pond X'ing, drove about two hundred feet, then turned left again, onto the long paved driveway which passed through a jungle of thick suspended vines and foliage. Wide storybook weeping willows and tall oaks surrounded this house, effectively hiding it from the street and the unwanted eyes of the neighbors. The house was situated on a slight hill, making it one of the highest structures in the backwoods of Lawrence, down by the swamps, the creeks, and the channel. Nearer to the house, the right fork of the driveway entered the garage, which was closed, and the left fork made a wide circle passing by the front door, where Brent parked. He rang the bell and waited, knowing that Julia Belden was expecting him and that it would take her some time to get to the door because she was a wheelchair-bound invalid.

"Is that you, Lieutenant Kramer?" came the words from the surprisingly clear intercom.

"Yes, ma'am, it is."

"I'll be right there. Hold on." Julia slid off the bed and into her upstairs wheelchair. She rolled to the edge of the stairs, steadied herself on the sturdy handrail as she rose, then sat on the platform of the stair lift. She pressed the button, the motor hummed, and the seat smoothly followed the graceful curved contour of the stairs, all the way to the main level of the house. She sat in the downstairs wheelchair, then rolled to the front door, where the police lieutenant from New York City was patiently watching a pair of Spicebush Swallowtail butterflies revolving around each other above a lilac bush. "Hello, Lieutenant. Sorry to keep you waiting."

"That's quite all right, Mrs. Belden. So where can we talk?"

"How about the living room." Julia smiled. "You can wheel me."

"I certainly can do that." Brent took the handles and slowly pushed her. "By the way, when you answered the intercom, you used my name. I could have been anyone."

"We don't get many guests. I knew it was probably you, Lieutenant."

Brent sighed. "Maybe it's just the cop in me, but I'd feel better if you let your guests tell you who they are first, rather than leave them with a simple yes-or-no decision."

"I appreciate your concern."

Brent wheeled Julia into the living room as they exchanged pleasantries. It was a large, striking room, with a baby grand piano halfway between the two large sliding doors they passed through and a greenhouse solarium at the far end, beyond a pair of etched glass doors. An interesting mix of African statuettes and bonsai trees sat on pedestals and furniture on many different levels relative to the eye. On the walls hung woven tapestries and handmade musical instruments from Ethiopia and the Ivory Coast. Brent sat on an upholstered brown leather chair, probably because it seemed to be the most out-of-place object in the room. He observed an eight-inch pile of newspapers next to a glass table, and there was a pair of scissors on a drink coaster.

"Who plays the piano?" Brent asked.

"We all did, at one time. We were a very musical family. Now only Frieda plays, though."

"That wouldn't by any chance be the Frieda Marx who was with your son in the car . . . when it happened?"

"Yes. She was Arthur's fiancée before he died. Now she lives here with me."

"Mrs. Belden, it said in the police report that your son Arthur was a urologist."

"That is correct."

"Is anyone else in your family in the medical profession?"

"My husband was one of the leading bone specialists on Long Island."

"Was?"

"Yes, Lieutenant. Ben died about seven years ago, about a year after Arthur was shot."

"Benjamin was your husband's name?"

"Alexander. Alexander Benjamin Belden. I always called him Ben. . . ." Brent watched Julia for a moment while she silently reminisced.

"Where did Ben work?"

"Right here in Woodmere. On Broadway."

"Did he have any partners who continued the practice after he died?"

"Yes. Leo Kaplan. He's a fine man, and a competent doctor —a Yale man. *My* husband graduated from Columbia," she said as she subtly thrust her shoulders back with pride.

"Was Arthur ever married before he became engaged to Frieda?"

"No." Julia patted her tinted light blue hair with both her hands. "Arthur was always a little on the chubby side. Even though he was a well-to-do doctor, meeting women never came easily to him."

Brent perked up a bit. "How did they meet?"

"She was one of his patients."

"Really? What was her problem?"

Julia laughed. "You ask a lot of specific questions, Lieutenant Kramer."

"I'm a curious guy, in a specific kind a way. Besides, this sounds like a *fascinating* story. I hope I haven't touched on a raw nerve." Brent hesitated, glancing over his shoulder toward the piano and the greenhouse; then he looked at Julia again. "What does Frieda do for a living?"

"She's a veterinarian in Cedarhurst."

"A veterinarian?"

"Yes, Lieutenant. Right here in town."

"I'd love to speak with her."

"She usually comes home for lunch. You can speak with her then. That should be in about a half hour. She can tell you all about herself and Arthur, and how they met."

"Good. In the meantime, do you mind if I see your house? It's *very* interesting."

"Yes, it is. Why don't you wheel me around? Then I'll show you Frieda's greenhouse. She calls it a solarium. I call it a greenhouse. She built it herself. She's very handy, you know."

Brent wheeled Julia throughout the house, and she explained the various rooms and objects of art as if she were a museum curator.

"How did your husband die?" Brent asked as they approached the greenhouse.

"A massive heart attack."

Brent pushed Julia into the greenhouse and turned to the right, and south. The greenhouse was divided into two sections: the right, where the floor was paved and the rows were wide enough to accommodate the wheelchair; and the left, where the rows were thin and one could only walk on flat stones between the thick foliage.

While they were looking at the various hydroponic vegetables and bonsai plants, Julia spoke about her husband, what a good provider he was, what a good doctor he was, what a good personality he had, and what a good father he had been to Arthur and Andy—especially what a good father he'd been.

"Tell me about Andy, Mrs. Belden."

"Andy was a big disappointment to us."

"In what way?"

"He gave up everything we had to offer him—the best schools money can buy, a meaningful career, everything—so that he could join a *religious cult* in California. A restaurant! He works in a vegetarian restaurant! For the Hare Krishnas! He likes cooking *spinach!*" Julia Belden was growing more agitated with every thought she had about her only living son. "He wears a dress, though *he* calls it a robe, Lieutenant, and he walks around all day with a shaved head. This is what he calls 'living the spiritual existence'! He looks like Gandhi! Andy . . . What can I do?"

Brent left Julia at the southern end of the solarium. He walked along the thinner paths, weaving between the rows of hanging plants and trays of geminating seedlings. At the far end of the solarium, he stopped in front of a workstation where there were some tools for doing detailed work—needle-nose pliers, diagonal cutters, X-Acto knifes with curved and flat blades, all kinds of odds and ends, a large magnifying glass built into a high-intensity lamp, and spools of wire mounted on a homemade rack. Brent reached out his hand to touch a pair of long stainless steel tweezers when he was startled by the words, "Lieutenant Kramer?" He looked up, and through the foliage of a long-leafed bush, he saw the face of Frieda Marx.

"You move very quietly, Ms. Marx."

"I've been through this place a million times. I know every square inch of it. I guess it just comes naturally to me. Sorry if I surprised you."

Brent studied her face carefully, noticing that there was the slightest imperfection above her top lip, just left of center. "This is quite a collection of plants you have here," he said.

"I've always been interested in the botanical arts. What brings you here, Lieutenant?"

"I'm interested in learning more about Arthur Belden, your fiancé."

"How come? He was shot in 1985, and he died in '89. Why the sudden interest in a case that's been closed for so many years?"

Brent touched the wide dark green leaf that had been touching his face, and he examined the radial venation. "Just because a case is closed, it doesn't mean we necessarily lose interest in it."

"What made you regain interest in it?"

Brent looked up from the leaf and said, "You're a very curious woman."

"Yes, almost as curious as a man." Frieda watched the lieutenant's reaction to what she'd just said, then continued. "It seems only natural to me that a person should be interested in the appearance of a high-powered police investigator showing up at his door and asking about a closed case."

"*His* door?"

"Yes, *his* door. I don't buy into all that political correctness crap, Lieutenant. *His* is correct English, at least when *I* went to school it was."

"Where *did* you go to school, Ms. Marx?"

"Cornell University. Veterinary medicine, Middle Size Animal School. Lieutenant Kramer, why the sudden interest in a closed case?"

"Some cases never close, Ms. Marx."

"A very philosophical answer, Lieutenant. Well, if you *won't* tell me why you're interested in Arthur, then what is it specifically you want to know?"

"Julia tells me that you met Arthur in a doctor-patient relationship."

"You make it sound so clinical—almost unwholesome."

"I didn't mean it to come out that way." Brent was lying. He'd meant it to come out exactly as it came out.

"Come, Lieutenant, let's get Julia and talk in the living room."

Brent slipped around to Frieda's aisle, and he followed behind her as she retrieved Julia from the less dense part of the solarium. Brent watched her movements. She wore baggy beige slacks and a vertically striped blue, white, and gray short-sleeve blouse. She was five ten, weighed about 165, and she seemed muscular. *Feminine* was not an adjective Brent would have used to describe her, or the way she moved.

As Julia and Frieda emerged from the greenhouse, Julia began to wheel herself into the living room, bound for the den. Julia said to Brent, "Are you married, Lieutenant?"

Frieda blushed and said, "Mother!" Then she turned to Brent and apologetically said, "She's always trying to marry me off to any eligible bachelor she meets. She's afraid I'm going to die an old maid."

Brent looked at Frieda's unflattering, overcompressed chest, then thought about Julia's description of her son not exactly being God's gift to womankind. Coupled with Frieda not exactly being God's gift to mankind, he tried to imagine the two as a couple. Perhaps they were God's gift to each other.

"I don't think you'll be an old maid," Brent said for Julia's benefit. "Probably when you least expect it, the right man will just . . . pop out of the ground."

"Well," Julia said as she turned the corner, "I'll leave you two to talk."

Brent turned to Frieda and said, "This is some piece of work, this greenhouse. Julia tells me you built it yourself."

"That's true. I seemed to be accumulating plants more quickly than I could find places to keep them. So Julia let me build the solarium."

"Fine piece of work. Have you ever been to the topiary garden up in Newport?"

"Yes," Frieda sighed. "Those people are just simple gardeners. They cut bushes and plant corn. I'm not impressed."

Brent paused for a moment, then got down to business again. "When did you first meet Arthur?"

"In 1983."

"Tell me about it?"

"I went to see him as a patient, because I was having chronic bladder infections. This is all confidential, Lieutenant."

"Of course. I understand," Brent assured her. "What was it like, that day in the car?"

Frieda Marx told Brent about how she had gone to see Dr. Arthur Belden at the Beth Israel Medical Center, how they became romantically involved and then got engaged, and then about the day Arthur was shot in the car. She told Brent about how she thought Arthur was going to die in her arms, about how frightened she was when she saw the blood pouring from his neck and the meaty clumps of tissue oozing from the exit wound, and how she could feel the splinters of vertebra with her fingers as she compressed the entrance and exit holes with both her hands to keep him from bleeding to death right there in the car. She told Brent about the ride to the hospital in the ambulance and the look on the faces of the paramedics. She had known Arthur would never recover.

As Frieda spoke, she seemed remarkably composed, but Brent could still feel immense pain under the surface as she recounted the experience. "From that moment on, Lieutenant, life was never the same around here. In one evening, a ten-gram piece of lead transformed this household from heaven . . . into hell. I referred most of my patients—my animals—to other vets in the area so that I could spend more time here, caring for Arthur. Then, the day after the sentencing, Ben died. He had a bad heart, but I think he held on to life, determined to live for that one day. I thought Julia would die also. She stopped eating. She stopped sleeping. She lost weight. Arthur was on an iron lung. At times, I thought I was losing my mind, holding this place together. We've been through hell in this house, Lieutenant, hell." Frieda paused, then went on to say, "I've got to get back to the office soon. Did you learn what you came to learn, Lieutenant?" She looked emotionally drained.

"Maybe," Brent said as Frieda stood up. He followed her lead and stood up, too. Frieda slowly walked toward the front door to see the lieutenant out, but he unexpectedly veered toward the kitchen, where Julia was. Frieda followed behind Brent, then watched impatiently as he looked intently at the door to the basement. "I'd like to take a look in the cellar. Would you show me around?"

"Certainly." Brent was already on his way down the steps when Frieda said, "The light is to the left, Lieutenant Kramer."

Brent walked back around under the stairs. He looked at the electrical service box, noting the different circuits to the house. He walked away from the electrical panel and over to the laundry room, where he looked at the washer and dryer. Next, he examined the gas burner. Frieda said, "We converted to gas a couple of years ago."

"Yeah," Brent said, "they say it's cleaner."

"But more expensive," Frieda added. She stood perfectly still as Brent walked over to the door leading to the garage. He opened it, walked down the five steps, then looked at the Mercedes. Then the lieutenant peeked into the bathroom. He noted the toilet, the sink, and the bathtub.

He walked into another open room, opposite the bathroom, about twelve feet by fifteen feet, which was paneled. He looked at the blackened patterns of dirt on the floor, some outlining the shape of rectangles, some outlining the shape of squares, and little circles outlining the many points of support for heavy things that had obviously been in the same place for many years. Brent looked over to Frieda in the doorway and said, "What was this room used for in the past?"

"This used to be Ben's office, before he moved to Woodmere with Dr. Kaplan."

"Oh."

"The waiting room used to be over there," Frieda said as she pointed to the laundry room. "Some of the partitions have since been removed, but this was where the examination rooms used to be."

That answered the question of why one of the circuit fuse slots in the electrical panel was labeled "X ray" and ran off the B power phase. Brent walked to the largest open space in the basement and looked at the table saw and the band saw and the drill press and all the tools neatly hanging on a Peg-Board above a workbench. "Do you do woodworking?" Brent asked Frieda.

"Ben used to make furniture. I do a little work here and there."

"Recently, I imagine," Brent said as he wiped his hand on some sawdust from the metal surface.

Frieda smiled. "How can you tell, Lieutenant?"

"Dust. There's very little dust on this surface."

"That's very good. Are you always busy being a cop, Lieutenant Kramer?"

"I happen to be on the clock at the moment. Most veterinarians I know personally own animals. I haven't noticed any here."

"Julia is allergic to dogs and cats."

Brent walked toward a *Threepenny Opera* poster on a sliding door.

Frieda said, "Why are you *really* here, Lieutenant?"

"Because we suspect that you and Julia might be in danger. You may not be aware that Charles Ebel died in prison." This was not true. He had simply been moved to another facility for the remaining months before his upcoming parole hearing. "There are people who blamed you, Julia, and Ben for landing him in jail. What's in here?" Brent asked as he pulled open a large sliding door, thick with years' worth of sooty dirt on it.

The door hit the stop, and Brent looked inside as Frieda said, "It's where we keep the wine." And sure enough, there were racks of wine in a six-foot-deep alcove of wood and shelves.

"Come in, come in," Mona Sigmond told Brent. Mona was fifty-five years old, and the mother of Aaron Sigmond, who had been shot by Rusty Blake because he happened to be driving the car that Rusty wanted at that particular moment. Aaron had not been killed, only paralyzed, and for this reason, Rusty had not been charged with murder, even after Aaron died eight years later. "Here, give me your coat, Lieutenant Kramer."

The lieutenant and Mrs. Sigmond walked into the living room and sat. "I thought that case was all solved and taken care of. Why are you looking into it all these years later?"

"Well, there are certain pattern similarities between your son's case and other unsolved cases, and perhaps there are some details that never came out after ... well, after the shooting incident. Tell me Mrs. Sigmond, what do you do for a living?"

"I'm a dental assistant. I've been a dental assistant for the past thirty years, I would say."

"What does your husband do?"

"He and his brother own Sigmond Toys, here in the city."

"Sigmond Toys, *huh* ..." That name rang a bell in Brent's mind for some reason, and then he heard a raucous man and woman giggling as the side door swung open with a small crash. Mona Sigmond said to the lieutenant, "That's just my husband, Seth, and Glory."

"... Did you see the look on that zipper head's face when I told 'im we were gonna cancel that Bongo-ball shipment?" Seth slurred. "Glor, I tell ya, we got those schmucks eating outta the palm of our hands. ..."

Then Seth Sigmond and Glory, his brother's wife, entered the living room, each holding a case of twelve-year-old scotch, and

Glory said, "And I can tell Arty's shittin' in his pants, because he's got two containers a product sitting on the dock with no LC. . . ."

They placed the scotch on the coffee table, and Mona said, "Seth, this is Lieutenant Kramer. He's a detective in New York City. Apparently, they're reopening Aaron's case."

Seth turned to Glory and said in a barely audible voice, "Glor, could you put those in the kitchen?"

Brent nonchalantly said, "You don't have to bother. You can leave them right here." Seth's face looked like time-lapse photography of a tomato overripening on a vine, then falling off. The lieutenant tried to ignore the fact that Mona's husband didn't even have the decency to zip up his fly all the way before greeting his wife; then he turned to Mona, who was obviously distressed, and said, "Tell me, Mrs. Sigmond, does anyone else in your family work in medicine, or any field related to the medical profession?"

"Why yes, Lieutenant," Mona said with a proud but distracted smile. "My son Cal is a dentist. . . ."

Brent and six other detectives sat around a conference table littered with white containers of dripping Chinese food. The names Freddy Lopez, Jerome Lewis, Rusty Blake, and Alex Hall were written across the top of a blackboard, dividing the board in fourths; the name Jesus Romero in parentheses was written directly under Alex Hall's name. And under each name was a list of the known victims of the respective people:

Freddy Lopez	Jerome Lewis	Rusty Blake	Alex Hall (Jesus Romero)
Susan Goldman (murdered)	Joseph Benito, Jr. (murdered)	Aaron Sigmond (paralyzed; died 8 yrs. later)	Donald Benson (murdered)
Marc Isman (survived)	Martin Delvazzio (murdered)		

Further information was handed out, which included the families of each victim, including any brothers, sisters, parents, aunts, uncles, cousins, and any friends who could be scoffed up, along with everyone's corresponding occupation.

"Gentlemen," Brent said, "all these names have been entered

into the database, and we need to check out anyone we haven't already checked out. Obviously, the flag setters are people like Meg Goldman, the nurse; Lawrence Lampert, the chemist, who happens to be the boyfriend of Dr. Stella Isman, oddly enough; she's the anthropologist whose twin brother is Dr. Richard Isman, a math professor. I saw Stella and Richard today, and these are major weird people. There's something strange going on over there, and I don't know what it is. Mathematicians are always goin' nuts, and Stella stuffs animals for fun. Maybe she decided to expand her radius a bit—like to living people. As the manpower becomes available, I think we should put a tail on them, see what they do and where they go—and the boyfriend, too. This Mona Sigmond, the dental assistant, checks out okay, but her son, Cal Sigmond, the dentist—his brother was shot by Blake— is a sibling of one of the victims and is in the medical profession; we need to put a tail on him, and I also want a court order to tap his home and office phones. I wanna know who he knows, where he goes, what drugs he purchases, and in what quantities.

"This Sergei Cherenkov, the electrical engineer, also checks out clean. We need to check out this Dr. Herman Weiner, the shrink. He's got a script pad. Check his house. Check his office. Check his basement, and his attic. These shrinks are always goin' nuts, too. This John Benson is a podiatrist. Same deal with him. Frederick Benson's whole side of the family is very interesting, We've got pilots, engineering students. . . . Lois Benson's a CIA operative, and *not* the Culinary Institute of America. CIA—could be anything. CIA. . . . I never trusted them. Bennett Hutchinson is a crystallographer. Check out their backgrounds to see if they have any medical experience. Peter Carter is a chiropractor. Glassner, Edward, he's a pharmacist. Lot's of drugs. Check 'em all out."

Then Brent passed a file folder around the table, and each detective, in turn, studied its contents. "Again, looking a little bit toward the future," Brent said, "we have *these* people."

The following names were on this list:

Clayton George	Charles Ebel	Malcolm Tobias, Jr.	Lamont Brown	Julio Clem
Lawrence Lent (murdered)	Arthur Belden (paralyzed; died 1989)	Ethan Barnes (murdered)	Clair Mook-Balanio (paralyzed)	Lauri Ann Politano (paralyzed)

"These are the next five parolees to be reviewed in upcoming months. The information is sketchier on the families of these victims, but we're going to fill in *alllll* the missing holes. And we called it right with Alex Hall, so someone's clearly got it out for these boys in particular. I don't think it's coincidence. This is deliberate. Notice that Admiral Hammond, retired, is in the same profession as Colonel Philip Benson. Is there some connection, some secret ring, some pact between these two—or others? Demented old men who serve their country their entire lives, military officers, judges, ex-cops... they see the whole ball a wax turning to shit before their eyes; sometimes they lose it over a flask of scotch. They rise above the law, thinking they *are* the law. This thing could go anywhere. It could involve anyone, from an individual to a secret ring. Be creative. Think crazy. Think on a psycho wavelength. This Alexander Belden—he's an orthopedic surgeon—at least he was when he was alive. I checked out his partner, Leo Kaplan, also an orthopedic surgeon. I saw Belden's widow. The son, Arthur, was killed by Charles Ebel. I met Arthur's fiancée, Frieda Marx—at least she was his fiancée when Arthur was shot in '85. Now she lives with Julia, who's an invalid in a wheelchair. Marx is a veterinarian. There might be something weird goin' on there...."

"Wait a minute," Sergeant Perato said. "Is this Lawrence Lent related to the same Alvin Lent that flipped out and—"

"Yes, Al," Brent interrupted, "the same. His brother Lawrence was killed by Clayton George up in Inwood. All right, we have our work cut out for us for the next few days. We meet here tomorrow at four o'clock again. Okay. We've all got some legwork to do. Let's get out there and see what we can dig up...."

36   Amazing Likeness

Nigel Atkerson had just finished the last few connections to the relevant phone line at the Department of Corrections building in Albany, New York. The full-phone bandwidth, long-play, reel-to-reel tape recorder in the basement of the building was hooked to the line, with an added little circuit so that any audio energy on the phone line would automatically trigger the recording function. The tape recorder could be called by telephone at any time, and the elapsed time could be downloaded, or the tape could be rewound, erased, and recorded over, or disabled and shut off. The recorder could also digitize sixteen-second blocks of tape and modem the data over the phone lines without any fidelity loss.

The information officer was the only person in the Division of Parole who knew about the tape recorder.

It had been a busy day for Nigel, so far, because he'd already secretly tapped the information officer's home phone, along with a smaller version of the same type of tape recorder, sealed inside a NEMA 4 weatherproof industrial control box that he'd attached to the phone poles outside his home.

Nigel hoped to drop off the rental car and catch the shuttle flight back to New York, just in time for the four o'clock briefing in Brent's office; if he could catch the earlier shuttle, the plan was a late lunch with Sally Chu, and possibly the devil himself.

On the blackboard in the conference room at Midtown North were written the names Clayton George, Charles Ebel, Malcolm Tobias, Jr., Lamont Brown, and Julio Clem. Above the names was the title in big letters which read: FUTURES MARKET. And the somewhat-expanded data sheets on these gentlemen already sat before the detectives.

Nigel and Sally entered, after returning from a posh restaurant. All eyes in the room focused on Sally's hand subtly touching Nigel's as she went to her office to get her notes. Brent shook his head, knowing no good was going to come of what he suspected was going to happen sooner or later, if it hadn't happened already.

"Sorry we're late, guys," Nigel said, then sat at the table and removed a yellow lined legal pad from his briefcase. Then the Chinese food arrived, and the men began systematically attacking the boxload of white containers.

"I thought you just had Chinese food," Sergeant Bassett said to Nigel.

"Very funny!"

The room of detectives began to make the sounds men make when they think they know what goes on behind closed doors between consenting adults. The fact of the matter was that each of them dreamt about creeping into Sally's pants, or whatever she kept down there, but apparently Nigel was further along than any of them. Then Sally returned with some computer printouts and her portable computer.

Nigel couldn't resist the thought of more food, and grabbed a plastic fork and dug in. With his mouth full, he said, "I hooked up the two recorders, tested 'em, and they're online as we speak—or eat, or whatever the hell we're doing."

"And I called Mark Silverman," Brent said, "the information officer, and told him if he got *any* calls for *any* of the names on the board to call me immediately so we could have the call traced and download the tape."

"Good," Nigel said. "Bet he'd be pissed as hell if he knew his personal phone was tapped also."

"The people in this room are the only ones in the world who know what's really going on."

Nigel said, "It's a good thing we don't trust anybody."

And Brent replied, "Yeah, my wife still thinks *you're* Dr. Sigma."

"That's only 'cause she knows me."

"I think he's Dr. Sigma, too," Sally said.

"Okay, let's get down to business," Brent said. "I had Charles Ebel moved to a new facility, and as far as anyone knows, he died in prison. We're gonna see who's curious about Mr. Ebel in the weeks to come.

"We have photos and some additional information to add to the sketchy files on the futures market. Here, take a look at these." Brent passed photographs around the room, deliberately clockwise, so Nigel would see the photos last.

Sergeant Perato smiled and looked at Brent. He looked again at the photograph in his lap and said, "Amazing likeness." Then Sergeant Perato said to Nigel, "Here, *you* take a look at these," and handed him the file.

Nigel reviewed the files of the five men, and the room watched his eyes. When he saw one of the photographs, Nigel's eyebrows almost raised off the top of his forehead. "Well, well, well,

Clayton George, five foot nine, one hundred forty-five pounds—he seems to have a twin brother of sorts." Nigel looked at Brent and Al Perato, who watched him with devilish expressions. "This is very funny," Nigel went on to say. "Are we all thinking what I think we're all thinking?" And the heads nodded yes.

Nigel buried his head in his hands and began laughing. When he had almost composed himself, he said, "*I* don't think he'll *do* it. In fact, a hundred dollars says he won't."

37   James LeRoy Washington III

James LeRoy Washington III (formerly *Handy Hands, the Nigger,*) used to be part of the urban fauna working the Port Authority Bus Terminal and Penn Station, harvesting the goodies inside pockets of unsuspecting marks. Now reformed, he'd become a security consultant and had begun studying prelaw shortly after he'd earned his GED. He was one of the few examples of a person of no means who had completely turned his life around for the better. And his life continued to turn, especially when he returned from a lecture he'd just given to a retired Jewish women's group and switched his answering machine to the play position: "James. Lieutenant Brent Kramer here. Give me a call as soon as you can. There's something very important I want to discuss with you. By the way, congratulations on your engagement."

"Hmmmm," James said out loud, "I wonder what the lieutenant wants."

"So lemme see if I got this shit straight now?" With a full measure of indignation, James LeRoy Washington III shook one of the hooper photographs at Brent. "You want *me* . . . to pretend I'm this . . . Clayton George dude gettin' outta jail, 'cause we such interchangeable niggas 'n all . . . so I can be a target instead a him . . . so dey might do *dis* . . . to *me* instead?" Brent casually looked at the pair of flabbergasted little slits James was temporarily using to see through, and said, after raising his eyebrows, "Yes."

James was pissed now. Up until fifteen minutes ago, he'd been more concerned with his upcoming remedial college English final exam than becoming a decoy. His summer courses were going so well, and he was successfully changing his English speech patterns so he would sound like an educated human being rather than the street pickpocket he'd been up until the age of thirty-two. But old habits are hard to break. When his emotions took hold of him, especially in the flames of anger, his older, more familiar speech flamboyantly emerged.

"You *really* gotta be kiddin', Krama. I almost got myself killed for you once. Hell! You *still* walkin' funny from dat thing. My heart goes out fo you. Don' get me wrong. I think you one a the finest people alive. But I got me a brand-new life now. I'm in college. I'm engaged to Sharon. And now you want me to go riskin' all dat shit so I can help you catch some psycho *duuuude* with a knife in one hand and a anesthesiology gas mask in 'n other?"

"I never said it would be *without* risk."

"You always had a gift for understatement, Lieutenant. Risk! Suppose yo' radio fuck up. Won't be the first time dat shit ever happens, you know. Risk! Suppose yo' car stalls out 'n you lose me cause I get outta range a that transmitter thing. Won't be the first time *dat* shit ever happens, either. Hell! Risk! Suppose that dude just a *little bit* smarter 'n you, Lieutenant. Huh? He made hisself some hoopers out a *these* guys. Suppose he decide to make hisself a *pretzel* outta *me*? I'd be crazy to put myself in that kinna risk. You *do* see my point, don't you?"

"Of course I see your point, James. On the other hand, a lotta people are being hurt, and if you don't do it, well . . ."

"On da other hand, a lotta people missin' their hands. That's why dey *hoopers* an' I ain't! Hoopers! Who da fuck thought dat name up, anyway?"

"Nigel," Brent sighed.

"Dat shit figures!" James exploded, throwing his hands theatrically into the air. "And cut my fuckin' lips off so I can be on da fuckin' *teeee veeee* with a hole drill in the side a ma head? What kinna nuthouse you runnin' here, anyway? . . ."

The phone rang. Brent picked up, and raised his finger to

James to delay the blowing off of more steam. "What!" Brent whispered; then his mouth opened wide. "Where?" James looked at Brent, trying to telepathically extract whatever he was hearing on the phone. "I'm on my way."

"What is it?" James asked as Brent slammed down the phone. He'd seen that same look on the lieutenant's face before, and he knew whatever it was, it was serious.

"Come with me," Brent ordered as he grabbed James by the arm, coaxing him to a canter with urgency. Both men jogged to the stairs. "I'd like you to witness something firsthand."

"You ain't takin' me on no mothafuckin' car chase again? 'Cause I still recoverin' from that shit." James huffed and puffed as he followed behind the lieutenant two stairs at a time.

"No. Consider it more a visit to the zoo. . . ."

The normal city noise from Fourteenth Street south was pierced by the erratic reverberation of sirens emanating from the myriad police and rescue vehicles that converged like a giant vortex of sand falling through the funnel of a gridlike hourglass epicentered at Washington Square Park. Traffic thickened a bit, and Brent placed the magnetic bubblegum machine on the roof of his unmarked car and added his siren to the cacophony. His driving became more aggressive as he weaved between the cars on Seventh Avenue, and James LeRoy Washington III felt a sense of exhilaration in both being privy to something important and on the verge of possibly dying in yet another car crash with the lieutenant, like that awful day in the park after the explosion, which was exactly what he told Brent he didn't want to do at the moment. Brent drove east along Washington Square North and entered the park by the arch. Honking his horn, he slowly rolled through the sea of people and parked next to some police cars by the monument. He and James jumped out of the car and ran through the herd of spectators, toward the action. The crowd seemed to be accumulating faster than the blue police barricades could keep them at bay.

The people, the park, and the world began to take on a more surreal character to James as he followed the lieutenant to something he suspected was, perhaps, going to upset or even ruin his day.

People grew rock concert–dense as the lieutenant and James

pushed their way toward the eastern end of the park and the statue of Garibaldi. When they ducked under the first police barricade, a microphone appeared from out of nowhere, two inches from Brent's nose, and a newswoman barked, "Lieutenant Kramer, what do you have to say about this wave of mutilations plaguing the—"

"What the hell's a matter with you, lady?" Brent snapped. "Can't you see I just got here?" Brent pushed her hand aside, took two steps, and said, "These people think I'm some kind of walking statement generator...." Then another microphone materialized in his face, hitting him squarely in the cheek. Brent grabbed the offending hand, disconnected the cable from the microphone, and threw the mike into the soft mud, where it stuck, grill element down, with a sloshy plop.

The newsman was beside himself—whisperings of unprofessionalism from a technician, growling threats of a lawsuit. "Did you tape that, Sal?" he yelled back at the truck. With the newsman's hand only inches from salvaging the piece of fallen equipment, James LeRoy Washington III casually stepped on the mike as if it were accidental, jamming it deeper into the mud with an artful twist of his shoe. "Hey, you moron!" news stuff yelled, but James had just ducked under the police flagging tape a few steps behind the lieutenant.

And then he saw the arc of grinder sparks spraying into the air from behind a large tree. Lieutenant Kramer softly said to James, "Alex Hall and Jesus Romero." Both men could not believe what they were seeing. The lieutenant grabbed James's arm and said, "Don't look back toward the news cameras. I don't want to find your face on the news tonight—got that?"

"I got it, Lieutenant."

"Now you take a good look at this ... thing over here; then I want you to quietly duck back into the crowd and become completely anonymous. Keep your eyes on my whereabouts, then meet me back at the car. Okay?"

"*Goddamn!*" James sang. "He went an' made hisself some *Siamese twins* dis time!"

"... And the wave of mutilations in the city continues, this time from Washington Square Park, where two people have been surgically joined together at the arms and legs," the newswoman said, broadcasting live in front of a backdrop of spraying sparks from seventy feet away. "These two unfortunate people were discovered, completely naked, only one hour ago, and already, thousands of onlookers are watching this horrible event unfold before their eyes. The identities of the victims are not yet known. As these dramatic live pictures show, rescue workers are separating the two people from that large tree behind me where they are chained as prisoners. As you can also see, their mouths have been surgically closed just like the other two mutilation victims, and possibly a third, and holes have been cut into the sides of their cheeks. Whoever is responsible for these mutilations is apparently fed up with the crime in society. Brutally burned into the back of one of the naked victims are the words 'I murder legally,' and then what appears to be gibberish." The newswoman then read from the sheet of paper: " 'Now my my lefts gone,' and on the back of the other are branded the words 'I steal cars legally, rights and are all.' Police are *unwilling* to make any statement as of yet, but this is obviously the work of a psychopathic vigilante. Even the Nazis never dreamt of anything this inhuman, this barbaric, this insane, this . . ."

The last chain was severed with an electric carbon arc-slice torch. Both naked victims seemed to be medically stable, dumbfounded as they were. They stared at each other like a pair of spaced-out, lobotomized, tortured animals on drugs—half alive, half zombies— biologically bonded in a permanent patty-cake position—arm and leg bones neatly grafted, kneading themselves together in forced molecular union. Facing each other like reflections in a three-dimensional mirror of horror without glass, they didn't seem all that frightened or uncomfortable, and they didn't seem all that alive, either. But their lack of enthusiasm detracted little from their photogenic appeal to the pixelized world of snippets and sound bites. They had made medical history and would become cult heroes—another small step for mankind.

Their four eyes were open, glazed, and neurologically unresponsive to the preliminary examination that had been performed there on the grass by the tree. Both hearts seemed to be beating in a synchronized pattern, and the blood pressure of this pulmonary blivit* was incomprehensibly low, but things were too new and confusing for the paramedics to intelligently assess the situation. Parts of the skin joining the two humans seemed to be normally healed together, with normal scar tissue, and parts of the skin at the interface zone were ulcerated, especially on the underside of the legs. They simply had to get this thing to a hospital as soon as possible.

And Brent had to leave as soon as possible, too. He had to drop off the 30 cc's of whole blood the paramedic drew from the vein of Alex, which pumped the same blood products as the veins of Jesus. It was a mental challenge to imagine what must have been happening inside this artificially created pulmonary circuit now mutually shared by two formerly autonomous humans whose names, for the moment, Brent chose not to disclose to other cops or newspersons.

Up in the tree was the same type of release mechanism that had been used on Rusty Blake, only this time a somewhat larger blanket had unveiled the two-headed thing. Lieutenant Kramer had one of his detectives begin collecting all the hard evidence; then he disappeared behind the barricades and into the crowd as the happy human couplet was rolled onto a litter and lifted by three EMS workers and a cop. The crowd cheered as they were carried into the back of the waiting ambulance, which drove toward the northeast corner of the park and up University Place for the ride to Roosevelt Hospital.

James LeRoy Washington III met Brent back at the car, and they drove off together. Brent phoned ahead to Riverview Research Labs so their serology lab would be ready to receive the fresh blood sample for analysis.

"Did you see those eyes on dem dudes?" James said to Brent.

"Yes. And it looks like it's gonna be happening to more people, too."

"Yeah, these people who it's happenin' to . . . they're all murderers."

"Not *all* of them. Did you see the Hispanic dude?"

"Yeah," James barked, "how many did *he* kill?"

"None. He was a professional car thief."

"Looks like he ain't gonna be stealing too many cars *now,*" James said, laughing.

---

* Engineering slang. A kluge; a mess; 20 pounds of shit in a 10-pound bag.

"Yeah," Brent said. "He just happened to be at the wrong place at the wrong time, when our man was stalking Alex Hall—the man he was attached to."

"So what's your point, Lieutenant?"

"Well, James LeRoy Washington the Third, also known as Handy Hands, the Nigger—that's what they used to call you, wasn't it? Well, philosophically speaking, there's quite a difference between murder and car theft, but, you know, I don't see all that much of a difference between car theft and pickpocketing, do you?"

"Oh come on, *maaaaaan!* Don't be pullin' that kinna shit on me! 'Cause it ain't gonna work. As I *told* you before, I got me a new life on the *right* side of the tracks. You helped set me straight, too. I ain't goin' back to that world, though." There was a long period of silence, and then James said, "So you gettin' anywhere with the case?"

"It's hard to say in a case like this. It's hard to say what evidence could lead you somewhere, and what evidence won't. You never really know till the fat lady sings."

"Till what? . . ."

The car phone rang, and Brent raised his finger to James as he placed the phone to his ear. "Kramer here. . . . Hello, Mr. Mayor." Brent raised his eyebrows, looking at James as if he was in hot water now. ". . . I know, I just came from the park. . . . We're doing everything we can. . . . It's *got* to break eventually. I have some new ideas, Dave," Brent said as he looked at his curious and slightly amazed passenger. "Look. I'll keep *you personally* up-to-date, but I don't fuel any artificial hoopla by talking to the press until the case is concluded. You know how I like to work. . . . No, Mr. Mayor, not hooper. Hoopla. Bad choice of words. . . . Yes, thank you very much, and good luck. . . . Okay. I'll talk to you." Brent hung up the phone. "I ought to get an answering machine for this phone."

James looked at Brent and said, "That was the mayor?"

"Yes."

"Of New York?"

"No, Cleveland. Of course of New York! And he's really pissed, too. His political opponents are using this against him."

"You told the man you had some new ideas."

"I do. I told you, James, you look an awful lot like Clayton George."

"Yeah, we do look alike, don't we?" He and Brent looked intensely at each other for half the duration of a red light. "You ain' gonna quit till I agree to do dis shit, are ya?"

"It's all up to you, James. The entire police force will be behind you."

"That's what I'm afraid of."

"So whadda ya say?" Brent said with puppy-dog eyes.

"After what I just seen, you gotta be *outta yo' fuckin' mind!*"

38   Press Conference

"Oh God! What the fuck *is* that thing?" one emergency room nurse said to another nurse.

"I don't know, but it's more interesting than the last two . . . *things* that came through here."

"Last three, I thought."

"I know, but the first one came through at night. I work the blood room days."

Dr. Spellman approached the two surgically joined humans. "I can't believe this," he said, while shaking his head.

A confused nurse with a blood pressure cuff in her hand looked at him and said, "Where should I . . . how should I do this, Doctor?"

"Good question. Let's try it the normal way first and see what we get. Put it right there." Dr. Spellman pointed at the upper left arm of Alex Hall. "Then try to get a reading on the other one's right arm over there. I think you should get the same reading if the veins and arteries of both arms were cross-connected like the others. But who knows? This one's pulmonary pressure could be higher than that one's, for all I know. This is all new to *me.*"

Dr. Spellman examined the two men. Their eyes were dilated, and they were both spaced-out. He placed his stethoscope on Alex Hall's chest, then on Jesus' chest. Then the doctor concentrated his attention on each of the joined limbs. He examined the oozing ulcers on the legs, and he said to Dr. Aboonda, "I think they're rejecting each other. Erratic heartbeats . . . they don't look well. Find Dr. Leiderman, Dr. Wu, Dr. Cohen—"

"Solomon?" Dr. Aboonda said.

"Sol's a neurosurgeon. I want Henry Cohen, the cardiologist, not Sol, and find me Dr. Christy also. I want full blood chemistry, EKGs on both of them, chest X rays, if that's even possible; I don't know if you can get the angles right. Call that new guy—Dr. Charles Rothenberg; he's the best radiologist here. I want all those graft sites X-rayed, too."

The security in the hospital was tight, and all unnecessary people were kept far away from the medical machinery associated with the new 'IT' on the block. Lieutenant Kramer finished briefing his men; then one more thing occurred to him. "There is a pest that floats around here from time to time, and I have a strong feeling this pest is going to mysteriously appear sometime in the very near future. This pest is about six feet tall; he has curly light brown hair; he's slim, but not skinny—without his ego, about one seventy-five, I would say. His name is Marshall Stanley. He got to previous patients posing as a doctor, then as a cop. You stop any unauthorized medical person trying to enter the perimeter unless Dr. Spellman knows him or her personally. Any security person you don't know is *not* authorized to be here and you stop them. I don't care if they have a walletful of credentials and they say they're with the FBI, or the CIA, or the mayor's office, or CID, the President of the United States, or the Pope himself—dressed in drag, singing 'The Good Ship Lollipop.' If Marshall Stanley even shows his face in the hospital or on the sidewalk surrounding the hospital, arrest him on the spot, no questions asked, read him his rights, and charge him with obstruction of justice; then I'll detain him for forty-eight hours. Lunch is on me for the man or men who arrests him."

These were the type of orders the officers loved even more than sex.

The multiheaded patient was moved to intensive care, where it/they were hooked up to a battery of monitors. The total preop workup was under way, and they would go to surgery to be separated as soon as possible. And they would receive total transfusions to eliminate each other's blood products once separated. Then Dr. Spellman prepared to join Lt. Brent Kramer for the news conference, outside the hospital.

A determined crowd of reporters was gathered outside Roosevelt Hospital, waiting for the first scheduled press conference on the subject of medical mutilations. Lieutenant Kramer had conspicuously avoided making any public statements, but the Siamese twins had finally pushed the story's newsworthiness over the top. Up till now, nobody had told anybody anything about the case, so the news industry had been forced to invent the details by asking the opinions of doctors, surgeons, law professors, ex-cops, private detectives, and criminologists who had nothing to do with the actual case, and they wove scenario after scenario in their televised roundtable discussions among themselves. They eagerly awaited the first public disclosure by the man allegedly heading the investigation.

And then that man walked out the hospital doors and up to a podium filled with a million erect little microphones, all focused down the center of his throat. He adjusted the lapel of his suit and looked at the wall of cameras, all pointed at him. And then Dr. Spellman joined the lieutenant and stood next to him. "Hello, Wally," Brent said. "Well, here goes. . . ."

"Lieutenant Kramer," a reporter barked, "why is your department so unwilling to cooperate with the media about this case?"

"Because we obviously have something to hide." The gaggle of reporters gasped.

"What is it that you're hiding?" one yelled, speaking for many.

"Information." A rumble of human talk from the media biomass.

"What information? Could you be more specific?"

"No."

"Could you tell us the names of the two men who were . . . who were—"

"No."

"Do you have any comment about the strange messages branded onto their backs?"

"Yes. The message isn't strange if you know how to read it.

You have to read it from one man's back to the other. It says, 'Now my rights and my lefts are all gone.' Very profound. You can put that on page one."

"Do you think the message will give you a clue to finding the person or persons—"

"No comment."

"Would you say that this recent wave of mutilations is all being committed by the same individual?"

"No comment."

"Do you have any suspects in the case?"

"No comment."

"Are any of those suspects members of the medical profession?"

"No comment."

"What *branch* of the medical profession are your suspects from?"

"No comment."

"Do you have any comment about the fact that Jerome Lewis and Rusty Blake both committed murder?"

"That's not entirely true, but no anyway."

"What are your thoughts about Jerome Lewis and Rusty Blake taking financial advantage of the situation?"

"They're not taking advantage of *any* situation. The situation is taking advantage of *them.*"

"Do you have any comment on the allegations that the mayor is dragging his tail on this investigation?"

Brent's face grew mean. "I consider that a *very* racist statement."

"Oh, come on, Lieutenant, you know what—"

"Whoever made those pusillanimous allegations is a liar and doesn't have the *guts* to face me or the mayor of this city. The mayor is doing *everything* that can be done, and more. Some people can work their miracles without wasting time screaming into a microphone. If no one's ever told you that, then I'm telling it to you for the very first time, because there really are so many more important things to do."

"Lieutenant, why did you throw the reporter's microphone on the ground in Washington Square Park earlier today?"

"Because he banged me in the cheek with it. That could be construed as battery, assaulting a police officer, and hindering a police investigation, not to mention *violation* of *my* civil rights. It's all right there on tape, kids. The reporter in question should consider himself lucky he wasn't arrested and charged with a felony and a misdemeanor."

"Do *you* mind telling us exactly *how* that incident in the park was a civil rights violation, Lieutenant?"

"I believe that the particular reporter . . . who assaulted me . . . is gay. I, on the other hand, am a heterosexual." Brent then, more quietly and introspectively, continued: "I've never disclosed this publicly before, but it's all true. Every word of it. I admit it. And I felt he was discriminating against me because I'm both a . . . member of the law-enforcement community and . . . and a practicing member of the American heterosexual community. In fact, I think I'm going to temporarily postpone the entire investigation, find a good therapist, and have the ACLU intervene on that one. I *felt* like my rights were violated, and that's all that really matters." Brent smiled warmly at the reporter.

"Are *you* being facetious?"

"No comment."

"Lieutenant," several notepad-wielding reporters yelled in blurry unison to the droning tune of camera shutters madly fluttering like mechanical insects on amphetamines.

"I'm sorry, boys and girls," Brent said with a smile, "I *did* have another statement to make before I was so rudely interrupted, but I think I've just about exceeded my quota of fun for a summer day. I hope you've enlightened yourselves. Now, if you'll excuse me, I have real work to do, and so does the mayor. Dr. Spellman will answer all your medically related questions. They're all yours, Wally."

And with that, Brent walked through the crowd, toward a waiting car, while all kinds of goofy questions were fired at him, and he repeated over and over again the same two words, "No comment."

As his car headed off into traffic, one reporter turned to another and quietly said, "Hey, Phil, what *does* pusillanimous mean, anyway? . . ."

"How *does* he get away with it?" The mayor beamed at one of his aides as he muted the sound on the television in his office. "I *love* that man. If I spoke like that in public, they'd have my head on a stick."

The aide said, "Maybe you should make Mr. Kramer your campaign manager, sir. That's the first unambiguously affirmative public statement anyone has said about you in the past six months."

"Yeah . . . more affirmative action . . ."

39   Quid Pro Quo

"Oh, come on, James!" Brent practically choked on his words. "I *really* don't think the mayor of the city of New York is gonna wanna come to your wedding. I think he'll have much more important things to do than be your guest of honor."

"Not the day I get married he won't."

"You don't even know the mayor."

"That's 'cause we ain' been properly introduced."

"What difference does it make whether the mayor comes to your wedding or not?"

"It makes a *big* difference. It make *allllll* the difference in the world." James yawned and leaned back on Brent's couch, grabbing the backrest with both arms outstretched.

"How come it makes *all* the difference in the world?"

"It's a thing called prestige. You see, if the mayor's at my wedding, it means I'm a *real* important guy aroun' this town. And it means Sharon's a *real* important lawyer. It means money, Kramer. It means *money*. It means *power*. It's good for my business. And it means I got a direct line to important people, like if I ever need a little favor or somethin'."

"Jesus Christ! I can't believe you. You're living in some kind of imaginary world. And you got *some* set a balls."

"I sure do, don' I? An' I got to tell you, some a that shit I learned from you, ma man. So you should be flattered. What's that they say—imitation is the best form a flattery?"

"Yeah? I never thought you'd be pullin' that shit on me, though."

"Look, it's what you call a quid pro quo, right? I'll *be* this Clayton George dude, and risk havin' my arms and legs cut off and pasted onto some other dude, and all you gotta do is guarantee me that the mayor comes to my wedding. That's simple enough. It'd make my fiancée real proud to say the mayor came to her wedding. She's a big fan a his, ya know. And the way I see it, the boy owes you a favor anyway, after all those nice things you went ahead and said about him, defendin' him an' all."

"I was saving it up, though."

"Saving it up fo yo' *olllll'* friend Handy Hands, *the Nigger,* retired, at yo' service!"

"... Live from Roosevelt Hospital. The two men who were found surgically joined were separated earlier today in a three-and-one-half-hour operation. Both men, whose names are being withheld, are in critical condition but are expected to live. Stay tuned for a live news conference at the top of the hour with the team of surgeons that separated the two men in the first operation of its kind ever. ...."

"So, Lieutenant, it's business as usual here?" James LeRoy Washington III asked with a smile.

"Yeah. Business as usual. I get all the wacky cases. . . ."

"That's 'cause you the best."

"Don't patronize me," Brent sighed, then waved him off and typed another sentence into his computer. Then he shook his head and muttered, "This thing keeps mangling my local E-mail—"

"I ain't patronizing you. I hear people talk. I hear what they say. An' I seen you in action, firsthand, my man."

Brent said, "Ninety percent of anything requiring organization and teamwork is surrounding yourself with the right people, along with hard work and, hopefully, clever use of computers, screwed up as this network is, and clever use of databases—especially in a case such as this. Police work is changing nowadays. Anyway, nobody assigned me this case because they thought it was going to be difficult or high visibility. It just fell into my lap accidently."

"Well, it fell into the right lap. The whole world is lookin' at your lap now."

"That reminds me, I have to call Tammy."

"How's she doin', by the way?" James asked.

"Fine. She's got twelve credits left to go; then she graduates this Christmas. She's working part-time at an ad agency, which will become full-time. The more serious she gets about wage slaving, the longer the hemline drops. Pretty soon, she'll dress like Sharon." Brent looked up from his terminal, then said, "I'm sorry. I shouldn't have said that."

"It's okay. I'm taking *goooood* care of your ex-girlfriend. I like her just the way she is, whatever she wears. Anyway, it matters more to me what she wears in the *bedroom* than in the *boardroom*— know what I mean? Only thing about her I don't like is her politics. I think it's that guilt trip she lived with growin' up. She's too damn liberal. Hell, every time I wanna piss her off, I go turn on conservative talk TV." Brent laughed. "That gets her goat real good. An' her mother? I ain' too crazy 'bout her none too much. She thinks it bad enough I'z black, but she want me to convert an' become a person of the Jewish persuasion, like Sammy Davis the Second. That way, maybe them little brown babies we plannin' on havin' be mo' like Mo'zuz than Mo'hamud Ali. Hell, Sammy Davis looked pretty stupid in that little hat, anyway. Don't you think?"

"Never gave it much thought. By the way, James, I need your medical and dental records."

"How come?"

"Just routine."

"Wadda you mean 'just routine'? I don't like the sound a that routine. . . ."

Suddenly, there was a tremendous commotion entering the detective area. "Oh, joy of joys," Lieutenant Kramer said with a face-breaking smile while clasping his hands. "Look what we have here!" Brent walked to the wall of his office and looked through a crack in the tinted glass. "Looks like I owe somebody lunch."

"Mr. Stanley," Brent Kramer sang, "so nice of you to stop by and visit our facility. I hope it's up to your fine standards. I see we're a hospital

orderly today. My, my ... you change professions faster than the Rockettes change their stockings."

"This is bullshit," Marshall Stanley huffed. "Obstruction of justice! The only one obstructing justice around here is you!"

Brent smiled and said, "Fifty years ago, back in the days when cops were cops and men were men, I'd a punched you silly for saying that." Brent leaned close enough to heat Marshall Stanley's face with his breath. "But times have certainly changed, Marshall, m' boy. And we're *all* civilized, politically correct persons of the people persuasion now, right?"

"I don't need a history lesson from *you*, Kramer. Lemme call my lawyer."

"Lieutenant," the arresting officer said, with his smiling partner standing next to him, "we found him in the halls, wheeling a cart of food around and checking the rooms. Here are his personal effects, sir." The officer handed Brent a small cardboard box.

James watched with great amusement as the lieutenant went through all Mr. Stanley's stuff. "Let's see now," Brent said, "we have a wallet. *Hmmmmm.* American Express Gold card, Visa card, a second Visa card, a *third* Visa card, MasterCard, Diners Club, driver's license—*hmmmm,* expired last month—PBA card—that throws a *lot* of weight around here, Stan, m' boy. There's got to be a plastic shield in here somewhere, maybe even a Dick Tracy two-way wrist radio. A condom ... You don't strike me as the safe-sex type, Stanley. We have some keys. A phone book. We have a *badge,* a *security* badge. How *interesting!* Roosevelt Hospital. Manuel Perez. You don't look Hispanic to me. Look! It's *even* got his picture on it. Now how did *that* get there? Oh, look. And we have *two* contracts. Expecting a little business transaction, *are we?"* Then Brent said to the two cops, "By the way, here's a copy of Zagat's restaurant guide. You men tell me *anywhere* you want to eat." Brent handed the book to the closest cop.

"I want to call my lawyer," Marshall said.

"I'm also charging you with trespassing. I'm also charging you with possession of falsified documents. I just love the law. Do you know how many laws there are to break? I'm gonna find every obscure statute from the turn of the century on and ... God I love minuscule details. Here's the phone. Don't press the wrong buttons. One call is all you get."

"Why are you busting my balls?" Stanley said with sorrowful eyes and a voice to match.

"I always bust the balls of people I don't like, and I don't like *you.*"

"What would it take to get you to like me? You know, I'm really not such a bad guy, once you get to know me." Marshall smiled, almost winking at Brent, as if he had a little extra something to say.

"Maybe you're right, Marshall. I *have* been in a bad mood lately. Perhaps maybe we should continue this conversation in private." Lieutenant Kramer loosely held Marshall by the arm and coaxed him to a standing position, then gently walked him into his office and closed the door. "Now what did ya have in mind, Marshall?"

"Well . . . you know, we're making a pile a money, me and the hoopers."

"So, what of it?" Brent seemed mildly curious.

"Well, the way I see it, having a cop, such as yourself, to appear on some of the talk shows and speaking tours . . . well, it would sure help round out the performance. *'And here's Lieutenant Kramer, the man who's tracking down the lunatic who did these dastardly deeds to these poor young men.'* Then they show a close-up of their long faces. They'd love it! We'd make a fortune. You'd make more in one month than you could make in the next ten years as a cop. I promise it. And I can fix it so . . . well, put it this way—I know some very skilled accountants who are committed to putting as much money in *your* pocket, rather than the coffers of the government. You wouldn't have to give too much of it away."

"I don't know. Sounds interesting. But is it worth anything . . . up front?"

"I really wish you'd take these bracelets off me," Marshall said warmly.

"If I take off the bracelets, what will you do for *me,* Marshall?"

"If you'd make a promise to appear on as many shows as I have booked in the immediate future, I could give you . . . oh, say . . . ten grand up front, and we'd negotiate something on an appearance-by-appearance basis, say, something in the range of five to ten percent."

Brent smiled. "Ten grand up front, if I let you walk, then ten or fifteen percent of the door take."

"Well . . . something like that."

"And what if I were a greedy cop, and I wanted fifteen up front; I got some debts, and the interest is slaughtering me."

"I . . . *think* that might be arranged. But I need a commitment. . . ."

"Good. Excellent. Marshall Stanley, I'm charging you with attempting to bribe a police officer. That's a Class C felony." Brent then removed the tape recorder from his breast pocket, rewound it a bit, then hit the play button:

"*. . . got some debts, and the interest is slaughtering me.*"

"*I . . . think that could be arranged. But I need a commitment. . . .*"

"*Good. Excellent. Marshall Stanley, I'm charging you with attempting to bribe a police officer. That's a Class C felony.*"

Click.

"This is entrapment, plain and simple," Marshall choked out. "You won't get away with this."

"Oh yes I will . . . you fungus. You human parasite. Now back outside, before you make me throw up. Christ, you disgust me."

James LeRoy Washington III quickly moved away from the outside of the door, not wanting Brent to know that he'd heard everything.

Brent said, "Make your phone call. And they haven't called 'em bracelets since cops were cops. You're like a caricature of stupidity, you're so stupid. I ought to punch you in the nose, just on general principle. . . . 'I need you to make a commitment. . . .' Fuckin' defective brain . . ."

". . . The mayor's rating has just jumped four percentage points in a recent poll. . . ."

As Nigel stormed into Brent's office, he said, "You were great on the *teeeeee veeeeee,* Brent. The next time you rib me about having an attitude problem, I'll just send you over *another* copy of the tape. You were *magggggg-nificent!*"

"We can critique my style later. What did you find in the blood?"

"The results are preliminary, but we found some Versed and Thorazine, just like with the others, a trace of Valium, a pinch of curare, we think, and we found some other interesting goodies I've never seen before. Then again, we never looked for immunosuppressants before, either. This is a little outside my field. Dr. Solderwick is the real serology expert, and he was all giggles and smiles at the mass spec when we tagged these drugs. We found cyclosporine A, and we found this FK506, and prednisolone."

"Who manufactures them?"

"I don't know. I didn't have time to check with the *PDR,* but Solderwick can tell you more about it than I ever could. He'll be back shortly."

"Lieutenant?" A voice over the phone intercom interrupted. "That psychic is here from downtown."

"Jesus Christ, Joan, they were *really* serious about that hocuspocus, weren't they?"

"Apparently so, Lieutenant."

Nigel smirked at Brent and mouthed the words, *"A psychic?"*

"Don't start with me," Brent barked.

"Excuse me, Lieutenant?" the voice on the intercom said.

"I wasn't talking to you, Joan. Send the psycho up."

"Psychic!" the psychic said, having heard the lieutenant over the speaker phone.

"A . . . yes. Have someone bring Madam Zoloft up, Joan. And thanks."

Nigel looked at Brent, "Have *you* gone off the deep end? A psychic?"

"Look, it wasn't *my* idea. We're just gonna patronize the woman, then send her back to the ozone and tarot cards, okay?"

Nigel said, "If I'd known she was coming, I'd have dressed for the occasion. Perhaps I could have brought some feathers and a grass skirt, and maybe a little war paint—maybe some beads and a chicken head . . ."

"Please."

"On a different subject, how are you coming with Mr. Washington the Three? Is he gonna do it?"

Brent smiled. "You owe me one hundred bucks, smart-ass."

"You're kidding!"

"No. He's studying the Clayton George file in four B right now, as a matter of fact."

"No shit! What did you have to give him?"

"Funny you should ask." Brent grew sarcastic. "All he wanted was for the mayor to attend his wedding."

"Oh, that's all—not the President, too? So you managed to get him the mayor—just like that? Pick up the phone. How'd you like to go to my friend's wedding?"

"Yes . . ." Then there was a knock on the lieutenant's door. "Come in," Brent said. When the door opened, Nigel quietly laughed.

The psychic said, "I am Mrs. Merdesphere, the psychic, and I heard your remarks over the intercom. It wasn't funny. I'll have you know that my success has been significantly above average in my work with police departments. Now, what would you like to ask of me?"

Brent pointed at Nigel with his thumb and said, "When is *his* dick gonna fall off?"

"In late November," the psychic answered.

The news conference was ready to begin, and a battery of doctors stood in a line, preparing to explain what had just happened in an operating room.

Dr. Spellman spoke first. "The patients were facing each other, connected at the femurs in the legs and at the radial and ulna bones in the arms. Without going into too much unnecessary detail, all the arteries and veins were cross-connected, so that the veins of one man connected to the arteries of the other, and vice versa. It was . . . a very complex operation performed by whoever did this. In any event, when they were brought here, they were both in shock, and were rejecting each other. Each patient was seen by the other as an incompatible graft which they were trying to reject.

"Apparently, and this is just speculative for the moment, pending further analysis, but apparently they had been given immunosuppressant drugs throughout the healing period to suppress this natural rejection reaction, while at the same time the bones were knitting together as well as they could, and the muscle tissue and skin, too, so a balance had to be maintained to promote enough immunity suppression to prevent rejection, while at the same time enabling healing at the graft sites. That's the simple explanation." A ripple of laughter was evoked by the way Dr. Spellman said this. "Dr. Wu is the transplant specialist, and he'll explain it in as much detail as you care to hear, later, after we explain the basics.

"I think I have to say at this time, and I speak for all of us, that we were revolted by this mad, unbelievably monstrous thing that has been done to these people. Clinically, we did our jobs, when we separated them, but I know what was going through each of our minds. Whoever did this is a very disturbed individual, and we are working closely with the police to help them apprehend this person or persons as soon as possible.

"Having said that . . . having said that, I would like to introduce the cardiologist of the team, Dr. Henry Cohen."

Henry Cohen was a stout man in his mid-fifties, gray curly hair, and he wore half-moon glasses. He stepped over to the podium, and Dr. Spellman stood next to him. Dr. Cohen said, "At first, we couldn't get an accurate EKG reading of the two patients because there was too much electrical interference between the two separate heartbeats. So we did a *bundle of his* on each man. That's a procedure where a probe is inserted into the esophagus—in this case, both esophagi—so the probes are closer to the heart muscles, both physically and electrically.

"From a fluid-dynamic point of view, what was happening here was extremely complicated. You have two hearts pumping blood in a complex flow circuit, and you have many parallel and series paths for the blood to flow. As Dr. Spellman said, the blood would flow from one man's arteries into another man's vein, while simultaneously, blood has to be pumped everywhere else in the body. So, from one patient's point of view, a portion of the blood goes to his own body, and a percentage of blood goes, with fairly low pulmonary resistance, over to the other patient's, in a parallel circuit. So effectively, each patient is in a parallel circuit with the other. You superimpose both systems on top of one another, and the net result is a lower-than-average blood pressure. Then you have mismatched phasing between the two independent hearts. Although, at times, both heart muscles naturally synchronized. It was fascinating, academically speaking, that is. But when one patient was stimulated, his heart rate fell out of sync with the other, and the total system developed slight instabilities. One patient had a tendency to go into tachycardia, which complicated the picture, because any stabilizing drugs you give to one patient, you automatically give to the other. This, of course, made the monitoring more complicated, anesthesiologically speaking. Never having dealt with anything like this before, a lot of it was, to a certain extent, guesswork. We were lucky. Dr. Leiderman was the anesthesiologist on the team, and he'll tell you a little bit about that aspect of the problem." Dr. Cohen looked over to Dr. Leiderman, who stepped sideways, over to the podium.

"Since we were going to separate the patients from each other anyway, we decided the sooner we isolated the patients from each other, the better. This also enabled us to establish individually valid readings. We constricted the limbs—all four limbs—using tourniquets, in essence, so the patients were isolated from each other. This way, we were able to monitor the status of each individual. Once the tourniquets were on, the blood flow to the extremities of each patient was limited, so the IVs had to be started in the subclavian veins, located over here." Dr. Leiderman raised his hand and pointed to the location on his own neck. "Apparently, there had already been some recent activity there, because there was clear evidence of puncture wounds on both patients. Normally, you can monitor the oxygenated hemoglobin and the deoxygenated hemoglobin using the pulse oxymeter, which is connected to one of the digits of the hand. Since this could not be done, we adapted it to the carotid artery, which gave us adequate readings to proceed. We couldn't use a standard face mask on the ventilator of the Drager, and we didn't have frontal access to the trachea, so it took a little creative adaptation to ventilate the patients through the stoma in the cheek—we rigged up a few makeshift clamps. Once we overcame these problems, the rest was pretty much standard, with the added complexity that everything was multiplied by two, so I had to keep on top of twice as many parameters throughout the course of the procedure. I'll turn you over to Dr. Christy, the orthopedic surgeon, who did most of the cutting."

Dr. Christy stood about five foot two, and he could barely be seen behind the podium. His nervous Tourette's-like mannerisms challenged the powers of concentration for all who stood in his presence, even those who were used to him. His sudden unprovoked hand, arm, and body twitches provided an endless source of distraction from his mouth, which was where most of the sound from this unusual man actually radiated. On the other side of the distraction equation, however, his Chaplinesque mustache drew attention back to his mouth, but on the whole, watching Dr. Christy was like watching a cat agitate a tank full of tropical fish.

"By the time my talents actually came to bear, most of the *hard* work had actually been done by these talented men. The limbs were separated much the same way as an amputation would be performed—in this case, eight amputations. The bones, as we found them, were fused together with the aid of a series of steel plates which were bolted to the bone tissue of each host. I simply removed the four connective slugs of each of the allografts to ensure that each patient would possess no foreign tissue after the procedure. I separated the arms first, and when both patients could be lowered flat on their backs, Dr. Spellman began the process of opening their mouths to gain postoperative frontal access to their oral cavities. Our primary goal was quick separation, not cosmetics, because the patients were in critical condition, and near shock . . . as I think all of *us* were. Once they were separated, we transfused 'em up to snuff, and they're off kickin'. We expect them both to pull through.

"Probably the most complicated part of the operation involved something more theoretical than practical procedure itself, and that's the immunological aspect of what happened today, and must have been happening for the past . . . oh, say, five or six weeks for these unfortunate people. Dr. Wu will give you a short explanation."

Dr. Wu said, "Short?" which caused the doctors to laugh, knowing how complicated the subject was. Dr. Wu stepped to the podium and spoke with a commanding, charismatic, deep voice and a distinguished British accent from his native Singapore. "As Dr. Spellman already said, each patient, or host, saw the other patient, or graft, as an invading body. Not only was each host trying to reject its graft, but each graft was trying to reject the host—which is almost always the case in any transplant. This was a particularly poignant example of the phenomena. There was a microscopic war being waged at the thirty-eighth parallel, so to speak, in this profound border conflict being waged on four separate fronts in a very closed system from which neither patient could escape, and were both doomed to lose eventually without intervention. . . ."

Samples of the 316LVD stainless steel plates removed from the graft zone of the two recently separated people had been rushed over to Riverview Research Labs, where Nigel Atkerson was at that moment examining the metal carefully through a microscope, in search of some residual evidence of the serial numbers or part numbers which had been deliberately filed away. Later the samples would be Fed-Exed to a metallurgical laboratory for further analysis and lot assay.

". . . So it is the normal function of the body to identify and eliminate foreign substances, or what we call modified histocompatibility antigens, as in a cancer cell which is modified from normal cells within the body, or foreign histocompatibility antigens, which is the case in any transplant from a genetically dissimilar donor, which was the case we dealt with today. In a nutshell, for the allograft to be rejected, you must have a difference between the donor and the host at specific molecular sites, which are the Class One or Class Two loci of the major histocompatibility complex cells. The lymphocytes of each donor attack the nearby cells, and an inflammatory response is observed, such as the lesions we observed more on the legs than on the arms. There are many drugs that can interfere with the body's natural rejection response, and each drug employs a specific strategy for frustrating everything from the immediate response to the recognition of foreign tissue, to the actual attack on foreign tissue. Some therapies have short-term action, and others are for longer-term courses. There is still so much we have to learn about allograft rejection and immunosuppression. . . . I seem to be drifting into a general discussion of transplant rejection, which is not what I wanted to do. As far as the problem before us today, though, we seemed to have intervened just in time. In my opinion, their survival without intervention could have been measured in hours, not days. I guess now is when we open the floor to questions."

A frantic wave of camera shutters and human voices were directed at the line of doctors, and the loudest voice said, "Dr. Wu, could you comment on the morality of procedures such as the one you and your team performed today?"

Dr. Wu's face went momentarily blank with disbelief. In the

preconference briefing, the doctors were told they might be asked some antagonistic or stupid questions to provoke some kind of unprofessional response to televise. He took a deep breath and said, "I was expecting a medical question, to be perfectly candid, but if morality is what is on your mind, my response would have to be: In the name of God, man, it is perfectly clear to *me* that the morality of disconnecting these two people superceded the morality of connecting them together in the first place, unless I'm missing some obscure theological point. . . ."

"WHAT!!!!????!!!!!????" Brent exploded.

"You heard me," James LeRoy Washington III said.

"The governor, too!!!"

40   Asswipe

Lt. Brent Kramer had quietly slipped out of the precinct shortly after the arrival of Marshall Stanley's lawyer. Brent's instructions to Sergeant Perato were to follow procedure strictly to the letter, delay as long as possible, and make things as difficult as he could.

Jerome Lewis and Rusty Blake sat on a couch in Marshall's apartment, watching television, unaware that their zookeeper had been arrested in Roosevelt Hospital in an unsuccessful attempt to increase the herd by one, or two, depending on how one looked at it.

A hooper loop is a very limited appendage when it comes to doing anything much more complicated than the dexterity required for public display, and the boys had been completely dependent on Mr. Stanley to feed them, just as cats and dogs are dependent on the punctual return of the master after a hard day at the office. And with Jerome, Mr. Stanley had quickly discovered that the needs of a hooper went beyond the simple duties of lifting a fork from the aluminum tray of a TV dinner. What enters the head must eventually exit someplace else, and Selma was promptly hired. Selma was a professional ass-wiper.

Rusty was the designated operator of the remote control, because he liked television more than Jerome, and he could push the buttons of the remote with the eraser end of a pencil Marshall had taped to his loop. Improvised adaptations such as the pencil thing were a daily reminder to Marshall that he was a creative genius, perhaps something between J. P. Barnum and Marconi.

Throughout the day, the boys were constantly bombarded with images from Washington Square Park, and they were keenly aware that more of them were being manufactured in that very same spawning nursery of which they were both products. They switched from channel to channel, soaking up the same details, in different combinations of words, spoken by different anchorpeople, all expressing the same look of surprise as they disclosed the story as if they were the first and only people privy to the discovery.

But Jerome and Rusty had a slightly different slant on the problem than most of the viewers at home. Blurry as it was, they had lived the experience firsthand, and many fond memories were rekindled.

"Turn up the volume," Jerome told Rusty as the familiar computer graphics appeared on the screen.

"...I'm Ted Koppel, and this is *Nightline*. The amazing story of New York City mutilations continues to unfold, and the story has now taken a bizarre new twist which might just as easily have come straight from the mind of Edgar Allan Poe. Two more human beings were found today—this time, surgically attached to each other, barely alive, chained to a tree in Washington Square Park, here in New York City. The pair of joined men were rushed to Roosevelt Hospital, where emergency surgery separated them from each other. If they survive, which they are expected to do, they will both live out the rest of their lives without hands or feet. To help explain this strange incident, we have with us today Dr. Eric Kimmelman, from the Sloan-Kettering Institute, and, at our Boston bureau, Dr. Milton Rothenberg, from the Harvard Medical School and Transplantation Unit, Department of Surgery, at Massachusetts General Hospital. Both these doctors are transplant specialists, and the thrust of our program tonight will focus more on the scientific and medical aspects of this story, than on the specific problem the law-enforcement community faces in its attempts to capture the party or parties responsible for this madness.

"Dr. Kimmelman, we'll start with you. Tell me, Doctor, how *was* such a thing possible? . . ."

Lieutenant Kramer had just picked up a search warrant for Marshall Stanley's apartment fom his friend Judge Levy. Armed with the keys he'd borrowed from Marshall's personal effects, he hopped a cab over to the East Side, where he knew two very special people would be waiting.

". . . So finding a compatible donor is much more complicated than simply matching blood types. There are more than fifteen major histocompatibility factors to be considered, perhaps as many as forty. Let's say, hypothetically speaking, that the odds are fifty percent that a particular histocompatibility factor is positive, and fifty percent that the factor is negative. If you're trying to match fifteen different factors, the odds of finding a compatible donor is one in thirty-two thousand, seven hundred and sixty-eight. And most of the factors in the general population occur in some distribution other than fifty-fifty. Sometimes it's seventy-eight twenty-two. This is why it's so difficult to find a compatible donor, and why patients have to wait around so long until the right donor happens to come along. . . ."

Jerome and Rusty watched the television, mildly bored by the technical details, realizing that they were the product of an evolving medical science. They were the early experiments for things to come. They were merely the first few prototypes to roll off a modernistic assembly line. As far as they were concerned, this immunology stuff they were making such a big deal about on the TV was all bullshit, anyway.

Jerome looked over to Rusty, wondering what it would have been like to be surgically connected to him. He couldn't imagine actually being Siamese twins with Rusty. Having a loop was bad enough. Having a whole other person attached would have been intolerable.

Throughout the month and a half they'd been together, friction had already begun to develop. When Rusty had first arrived, Jerome was as jealous as any older brother would be after the baby brother is born—half the attention, half the affection, and half the money, which was what this whole thing was really about, anyway. Jerome had been doing reasonably well before Rusty came along. He was getting his 50 percent, and he was happy. He was doing appearances, and things were pretty good. T-shirts, posters, dolls, TV commercials, product endorsements, and Mr. Stanley had even proposed a cartoon series as a sales gimmick to promote an entire line of toys —Hoopers! Yes, the future looked very bright. And then Rusty had to come along and spoil it.

With the appearance of Rusty, 50 percent had instantly been reduced to 25 percent, and it wasn't as if they were doing that many more appearances and Rusty was earning his keep. Rusty was simply cutting into profits—plain and simple. Jerome had never fully accepted Rusty in any way other than that he was medically similar— and to Jerome, that simply wasn't enough. But Rusty was white, Marshall kept telling Jerome, and therefore Rusty added the necessary racial balance to the gig. It was good for business for there to be white *and* black hoopers, because it promoted brotherhood in the newly emerging equal-opportunity world of the twenty-first century.

Back on *Nightline,* the doctors continued the discussion of short-term rejection versus long-term rejection. It was a tedious topic, and Rusty's mind wandered.

"Jerome," Rusty said, "what do you miss the most about not havin' no hands no more?"

"What kinna *dumb* question that?!" Jerome snapped back. "I miss not bein' able to do nothin' f' myself. I miss everythin'."

"What do you think you're gonna do . . . when it's all over? I mean—"

"I know what chu mean."

"I guess wit da money I make . . . if dare any left, dat is . . . I guess I find me someone like Selma, only maybe she do a little mo 'n juss . . . wipe ma ass. Know what I mean?"

And then both boys heard the clicking sound of keys tingling in the locks to the front door, and this evoked a Pavlovian response in the form of the usual question: What new business has Marshall brought home today? But it was not Marshall Stanley who entered the front door. It was Lt. Brent Kramer, armed with the search warrant he was able to keep in his pocket.

Brent entered the living room and looked at the pathetic pair of zoo specimens sitting there on the couch in the tube's dancing glow. "I see we're watching a little television, boys. Anything interesting on?"

"Nothin' essep dat thing dat turn up in da park," Jerome said.

"Same way we turned up," Rusty added.

"Who's askin' you?" Jerome challenged. "Turn down the sound on dat thing."

"Hmmm," Brent said as he assessed something other than brotherly love between the two soul mates of the knife and needle. He watched Rusty Blake awkwardly press the button with the stupid pencil taped to his arm thing. The wad of tape looked to be about ten times larger than it needed to be, twisted and knotted, like the product of a five-year-old gone wild with a tape dispenser. "That's very clever. Did Marshall make that up for you, Rusty?"

"Yeah," he said. "Works like *shit,* too."

Brent saw the tape dispenser on the coffee table and said, "Say, do you mind if I fix it for you? I can make it so it won't bend out the way it does when you press the button."

"Anything you can do would help," Rusty said.

Brent carefully peeled all the tape from Rusty's loop, then retaped the pencil, using more mechanically sound principles. "There ya go. Can I sit down next to you guys for a minute?"

"Be our guest," Jerome said. As Brent sat on the couch, Jerome continued: "We seen you on the TV this afternoon."

"Yeah"—Brent sighed—"how'd I look?"

"I like the way you put that faggot reporter down. You pretty funny, Lieutenant."

Brent began to suspect that if the ACLU decided to involve themselves in the case, it would be on the side of the reporter, not his.

"Hey," Rusty said, "this thing works much better than it used to. Thanks a lot, man."

"You're welcome. Say, as far as the case is concerned, have you guys thought of any new details you might have remembered since the last time we spoke?"

Both shook their heads no. And then Brent heard a noise from the kitchen. "Is there someone else in the apartment?"

"Yeah, dat's jus' Selma. Her nickname's *Asswipe*."

Then Rusty said, "It's getting late. I wonder where Mr. Stanley is?"

"Oh, I didn't tell you," Brent said. "He won't be coming home to you boys tonight because he'll be spending the night in jail, possibly tomorrow night, too."

"How come?" Jerome asked.

And Rusty asked, "Whad he do to get locked up?"

"He got himself arrested posing as an orderly in the hospital —you know, phony ID and everything."

Thank God, Jerome thought, grateful that there would be no extra competition in the hooper stable. One was bad enough. In spite of the fact that Marshall hadn't shared his plans with either of them, they both knew what Marshall was doing at the hospital, and why.

"You know," Brent said, "Marshall even offered *me* ten percent to join your show. Naturally, I turned him down, but whose percentage do you think that offer would come from, his or yours? I know both of you know what Marshall was trying to do in that hospital. And if he'd been successful this afternoon and two more people joined your little circus here, whose percentage do you think he would have split it with, his or yours? By the way, I have a little tape recording I made this afternoon, and I want to play it for you."

Brent switched on the tape recorder and played the exchange between himself and Marshall Stanley. "What do you think of Marshall? He's quite an entrepreneur, isn't he?"

"Ten more percent!" Jerome belched. "Without checkin' wit us firss?!"

Then Brent said, "Look, all that's between you and Mr. Stanley. Now, I'm not telling you boys what to do, and I'm not saying that you shouldn't be milking this for all it's worth, considering what your prospects are, but I know for a fact that at least you, Jerome, are experiencing chest pains sometimes, and that medically you're *both* in questionable health. Both your lives are in—let's say higher-risk categories, and the longer you continue to do this in your present condition, the greater the odds of some kind of medical emergency. Marshall doesn't give a *damn* about either of you. It doesn't matter to him whether either of you live or die. To him you're just commodities—hoopers—a source of income. You're not people to him. You're like machines, or tools to be used up, then thrown out. He'd sell you out in a *minute,* and I think you know it, too. Has either of you had a lawyer look at the contract between you and Mr. Stanley?"

Both men shook their heads no.

"Did it ever *occur* to either of you to have a lawyer look at your contracts?"

Both men shook their heads no.

"Do *either* of you have independent access to *your* bank accounts?"

Both men shook their heads no.

"Do *either* of you have accountants, your own accountants, to keep track of *your* finances and to see that everything you have coming to you you're actually getting?"

Both men shook their heads no.

"It seems to me like you boys have a lot to discuss with Mr. Stanley when he gets out of jail, because personally, I'd be a little bit worried if I had someone like Mr. Stanley looking after *my* best interests.

"Damn," Brent went on to say, "we missed Jay Leno's monologue."

Rusty leaned over and pressed the down channel button three times, just in time to hear the band playing after an intermission. And Jay Leno said, "You've all heard the news today about that *thing* they found in the park in New York today...." The audience exploded into applause, catcalls, booing, hissing, and laughter. "Arright, arright, simmer down. Simmer down, people.... Well, they were rejecting each other, so the doctors separated them. In any normal marriage, all you need are an army of lawyers to separate you. Nowadays, you need an army of doctors, too. *Ehhhh,* what's the world coming to? Well, the way we figure it here on *The Tonight Show,* you're gonna be seeing a lot more a this kinda thing, so we came up with a few ideas of our own—you know, people who we thought would make a perfect joining. Imagine this one. Imagine Iraqi president Saddam Hussein surgically connected to ex-President George Bush." Jay held up a cartoon drawing of both men—facing each other, joined arm-to-arm and leg-to-leg, both wearing red polka-dot boxer trunks, with full-face photographs looking directly into the camera, pasted above each man's neck. The audience went wild. "Arright, imagine this one: the Reverend Al Sharpton and ex-Grand Wizard of the Ku Klux Klan, David Duke." Jay held up a picture of that combination, and the audience exploded. "And how about liberal lawyer William Kunstler, and ex-President Richard M. Nixon? ... And how about famous author of *The Satanic Verses*, Salman Rushdie, and the Iranian leader who put a million-dollar price tag on his head, the Ayatollah Khomeini? They'll be fine as long as they stay at arm's length from each other." Boos and hisses. "What about movie critics Siskel and Ebert?" The picture showed them both wearing one sweater covering the two of them from their waists to their necks. "That's designer Siamese twinwear, I'll have you know." Hisses. "Arright arright. How about feminist movement leader and head of the National Organization for Women, Patricia Ireland, and conservative talk-show host Rush Limbaugh?" The audience broke into wild applause. "What do you think of newsman Sam Donaldson and cartoon megacelebrity Homer Simpson? ... And how about industrialist and third-party presidential candidate H. Ross Perot and TV evangelist Jimmy Swaggart? ... How about Nation of Islam outspoken spokesperson Louis Farrakhan and Jewish actor/writer/director Woody Allen? They'd sure have plenty to discuss over a matzoh and Manischewitz.... How about rock and music-video superstar Michael Jackson and the famous TV celebrity wonder horse Trigger?" All four of Michael's limbs were joined to the corresponding four limbs of the horse.... "We were really torn with this one, folks. So suppose we grafted Michael Jackson and the famous TV celebrity fish, Flipper." Flipper sounds were mixed with a clip of the song "Beat It," which accompanied a picture showing them joined at the waists, wherever Flipper's waist was. The audience roared as they went to break.

"Pretty funny stuff," Brent said.

Rusty Blake suddenly stood up, realizing that *that* time had come, and walked over the bathroom as he loudly called out, "Selma?"

Nigel stood at the blackboard in Brent's office with a piece of chalk in his hand. Sally Chu sat at Brent's desk, quickly tapping away at the keys of the computer as she played a video game. Brent was straddled around a wooden chair facing backward, with his chin on the backrest looking at the blackboard, and Sergeants Perato and Bassett sat on the couch. On the blackboard was a series of labeled intersecting circles, as if someone had taken a snapshot of a pond one second after throwing a handful of pebbles at the surface of the water. "Every few miles, you have a repeater," Nigel said, pointing to the circle labeled "D" on his drawing. "Now let's say you're driving in your car, and you pass from cell D over here, to cell E over here. The computer senses that the power level in the D cell drops, and the power level in the E cell rises, and when the new power exceeds the old power by a certain amount, a control signal is sent to the mobile unit to switch to a new available channel in the target cell, and in this manner the mobile unit is handed off from cell to cell. Now the thought actually occurred to Brent over here, that this might be an interesting way to track a person over a large area." Brent smiled as the two sergeants began to clap. "All right, so he comes up with *one* good idea! You don't have to give him a fat head." Brent threw a pink rubber eraser at Nigel, who caught it in his left hand and in turn threw it at the monitor Sally was staring into.

"Come on, stop that," Sally scolded, without lifting her eyes from the screen. "You're gonna break the equipment."

Nigel continued: "There are about 560 cells in the network covering the northeast. Out in the suburbs and the country, the cells can have anywhere between a five- and fifteen-mile radius, and in Manhattan they can be as close as a few blocks, given the placement of all the buildings and the interference patterns. So the final search perimeter depends on which cell our transmitter comes to rest in, but at least we can define that fuzzy perimeter.

"The cellular phone channels operate on a thirty-kilohertz spacing between the center frequencies. You have your uplink frequencies and your downlink frequencies. A typical conversation on a mobile phone requires one uplink channel and one downlink channel, and you have 1023 channel pairs. For instance, uplink channel number one is 825.030 megahertz; channel two is 825.060; channel three is 825.090, etc. And way over here is channel 355, which is 835.650 megahertz. That's the channel that Herb Gunner, over at NYNEX mobile communications headquarters, gave us to play with. Now we're only interested in the uplink frequency, and that's exactly what this transmitter sends." Nigel held up a very flat transmitter with wires leading to a flat lithium battery pack via a small two-lead connector. "This will be sewn into the clothing of Handy Hands, when he's out of the—"

Brent threw another eraser at Nigel, beaning him on the head this time. "Don't call him Handy Hands anymore! He's James, or Mr. Washington. Give the guy a break already...." Sally looked up at Nigel with a smirk and shook her finger at him.

"... Oh, yes. This will be sewn into the clothing of Mr. James LeRoy Washington the Third, and in theory, they should have no problem tracking the open transmitter on the mobile communications network. Sally and I ran some tests with this transmitter, and they successfully tracked us from Westchester, to New Jersey, to Manhattan, to Queens, to Brooklyn, and back to Manhattan. It works. And then there's this other transmitter over here, for localizing his position still further. There are two buttons on it, a test button, and the emergency trigger button. Once triggered, it stays on permanently until the battery runs out." Nigel walked toward the couch sergeants, and said, "Tracking is more of an art than a science, and since you guys are the ones who'll be working stakeout, I've arranged for my friend and resident RF expert, Kempy Bork, to walk you through the ABC's of radio location. I'll explain the basics to you now, but in a few days, you boys are gonna be thinking loops and nulls in your sleep."

At that moment, Brent stood up, stretched a bit, cracked his back, and then said, "I'm gonna check on James now...."

"You mean Mr. Hands?"

Brent threw the remaining handful of erasers at Nigel, then left his office, shaking his head.

For several weeks, James had been studying the transcript of Clayton George's trial, where he was convicted and sent to prison. Many of the trial details and the crime itself disgusted James. Clayton George was not a nice guy, in spite of the fact that his prison record was not terrible. But it would be this prison record that James would have to defend, and demonstrate to the three parole commissioners that Clayton George, the reformed man, was fit to be returned to society. Only in this way could James LeRoy Washington III, acting as Clayton George, pass through the system like food passing through the great legal intestinal tract, only to emerge as more raw sewage to catch the watchful eye of Dr. Sigma without raising undo suspicion. Toward that goal, Gerrard Singer, an experienced field parole officer from the New York Metro 1 region (mid-Manhattan), and also a good friend of Brent Kramer, was coaching James on his future parole-hearing etiquette.

"... Mr. George, could you clear something up for me, please?" Gerrard Singer said, role-playing one of the commissioners.

"Yes. What would you like to know?" James replied.

"Could you tell me about the Carlos incident?"

"What's there to tell? These two slimy Puerto Ricans jumped me in the laundry room and tried to rape me. So I busted Carlos's nose and Guillermo's arm." James watched Gerrard taking copious notes as he answered the question, and it didn't look good.

"They said you were trying to cop some drugs, and when they told you they couldn't get any for you, you attacked them."

"They're lying. They just wanted a little free black meat, and so I defended myself."

At that moment, Brent Kramer entered the room, sat down, and opened a file folder. Gerrard finished writing on his pad, then shut off the tape recorder. He rewound the tape and hit the play button.

"Mr. George, could you clear something up for me, please?"

"Yes. What would you like to know?"

Gerrard stopped the tape and said, "What you said here is very good. Your voice is calm and nonthreatening, and you are cooperative and confident. Good." Gerrard hit the play button.

"Could you tell me about the Carlos incident?"

"What's there to tell? These two slimy Puerto Ricans jumped me in the laundry room and tried to rape me. So I busted Carlos's nose and Guillermo's arm."

"Very bad," Gerrard said. "Your first reply, 'What's there to tell?'—it's confrontational. Your tone of voice—flippant, as if it was a small incident—like, So I busted up these two guys who tried to butt-fuck me. Your response demeans and devalues not only the question but the person asking the question. You must behave as if this was a traumatic experience, worth great introspection, and no matter how much you needed to defend yourself, your overall tone and attitude must be that this was unfortunate and horrible but unavoidable, and you still must demonstrate a certain amount of remorse. Number two: You use the word *slimy*. Let's keep the adjectives to a minimum—especially the negative ones. Number three: Puerto Ricans are not Puerto Ricans anymore, even though they are, in fact, from the island nation of Puerto Rico. These people who attacked you were Hispanics, or Hispanic men. And don't get sarcastic, either, and call them Hispanic-American persons. Don't call them Puerto Ricans. It will weigh against you. Next, "—Gerrard sighed — "you said they 'jumped' you. The use of the word *jump* might be more carefully chosen—perhaps *attacked,* or *unprovoked attack. Jump* is a street word. *Unprovoked attack* evokes more sympathy in the listener, without getting overly theatrical, which they will be assessing at every minute, so watch your choice of words. *Busted* is simply bad English. I *broke* his nose is better than I *busted* his nose; however, to *bust* or to *break* is demonstrative of an act of aggression. I *protected* myself, or I *defended* myself is a better way to say it, because people naturally side with a *defender* or a *protector* rather than an *offender,* even if we're talking about an act of defensive aggression in response to an act of offensive aggression. The U.S. military is a perfect example of this. The military is in the business of war, and in fact, during World War Two, it called itself the War Department. But shortly after the war, they changed their name to the Department of Defense. *Defense* evokes a more humane image than *War,* even though defense is still war. Psychology! Always imagine what subtle effect your choice of words will have on the listener." Gerrard switched on the tape recorder.

"*They said you were trying to cop some drugs, and when they told you they couldn't get any for you, you attacked them.*"

"*They're lying. They just wanted a little free black meat, and so I defended myself.*"

Gerrard said, "As hypocritical as it seems, the word *lying* is a bad word to use. Respectable people never *lie,* no matter how much they *lie* through their teeth. They simply *do not tell the truth*. President Nixon never *lied*. He *misspoke* the truth. They said you tried to cop drugs. . . . They are *not telling the truth*. The response: *They're lying,* is a defensive response. A more considered response, coming from a position of self-confident strength is, They are *not telling the truth*. This next one, well, *'I defended myself,'* is good. But they just wanted *a little free black meat*—very bad phraseology! Street talk—low-life street talk! They wanted to *violate* me, or they tried to *rape* me. Or you can even react more traumatized, and you can find the words hard to come by, the way many actual rape victims react. Perhaps, They tried to *sodomize* me, but please—no *free black meat!*"

Then Brent said without warning, "Clayton, tell me about your sister, Yvette."

"My sister's name was Tomika. Tomika Lois George. Very unfortunate. I loved her very much. She was born on October fifth, 1965. She started hooking when she was sixteen, shortly after her daughter Suzanne was born. She died of AIDS in 1991, while I was in . . . in prison. Suzanne died of spinal meningitis when she was a year old, on Christmas day, one week before I killed Lawrence Lent."

"Tell me about your mother."

"Mom was a drunk, and a hooker for most of her adult life, but I loved her very much."

"What happened to her?"

"She started hanging with the wrong people, and she died of a drug overdose in 1975."

"Your father?"

"I never knew my father. George is my mother's maiden name."

"What's your birthday?"

"August 19, 1960."

"What day of the week was it?"

"How the fuck should I know what day it was?" Brent and Gerrard stared at James, and then the three of them burst out laughing.

Nigel was now alone with Sally, and he sat down next to her. "I thought you said you were going horseback riding." Nigel told her more than asked.

"I was. But I called the stable and canceled the appointment."

Nigel looked at Sally as if he were attempting to break the secret military encryption ciphers of a foreign government. "So, just to recap, and . . . it's not you, mind you, and it's not even me; it's my brain's fault . . . but . . . my brain needs to know if the following is correct: First, you said you didn't want to go to dinner because you were going to see a movie with a friend possessing an undisclosed name. Then, second, you canceled *that* plan, so that you *could* . . . go to dinner with me. Then you called me to tell me that dinner was canceled so that you could go to the theater with another friend with a different undisclosed name. *Then* you canceled that plan so you could go to dinner with me. That's third and fourth, if I'm not mistaken. Then, fifth, you canceled dinner with me so that you could go horseback riding—in Central Park. Which brings us to six, if the earth is still down and the sky is still up: you cancel your horseback-riding plan so that you can—let me see if I've got this perfectly clear —so that you can go to dinner with me again? Are we following each other, Sally—or, what I mean to say is, am I following you?!"

"Yes. So you want to go to dinner?"

Nigel slapped his head with his hand. "You're not gonna make plans to go skydiving or hang gliding, are you?"

"No. Why would I do a thing like that? That is dangerous stuff."

"You're not gonna schedule a hot-air balloon ride or take a French cooking class?"

"No. Why are you being so strange?"

"You're right. It's me. I get that way sometimes. Please forgive me." Nigel looked at her, then whispered, "You're not going bungee jumping at sundown, are ya?"

"You gonna stop foolin' around and go to dinner with me, or am I gonna have to shoot you in the foot?"

Nigel squinted at her and asked, "Are you hungry?"

"I'm starving. I'm so hungry, I could eat the computer."

At that moment, Nigel could almost feel the pitchfork of Satan jab him in the side. He hesitated to regain his composure, then said, "Where would you like to . . . eat?"

"Well, I figure we could see a movie first, then we could have dinner somewhere near the theater."

"I thought you were ready to eat the computer."

"Ohhhh, that could wait."

"Sharon Weiner!" Brent said with a big smile. "You're looking *very* well." And she was—even better than when she and Brent had been an item, all those years ago. Her hair was blond and full-bodied even though it was dyed, and her skin tone was great. She looked as if she'd reversed the aging process almost ten years. "How are you doing?"

"Stop buttering me up, Brent! I don't like what you're making James do one bit."

"Sharon, it's not going to be all *that* dangerous."

"You call putting my future husband behind bars in a state penitentiary not dangerous?! And then letting him be a target for some psychopathic mutilator is not *that* dangerous?!! Who are we kidding, Lieutenant?!!!"

"Sharon, I—"

"Don't Sharon me!!! Like a fool, I wrote that goddamn letter of recommendation. I handled all the details on my end with the PD's office. But you know what really got to me, and set me straight? It was when James had to give you his dental records! That's what got me. Because it was then that I realized just how dangerous this assignment really is. This is real hard-core undercover work. This is *way* outside his league, and *you* know it. You're using him! He's not trained to do this kind of work. This crash course is just giving him the illusion of confidence. Brent, who are we trying to kid here?"

"Sharon, the dental records are just—"

"Don't Sharon me!!! I know there's a lot of political pressure on the police department to solve this case, and I know they'd do *anything* to draw the flack off the administration. Anything!!! Including sacrifice my future husband!!"

"Sharon, we're employing—"

"Don't Sharon me!!! James is a stubborn man, and once he's made up his mind to do something, he does it. It's one of the things I love about him. But it's also one of the things I hate about him. You can stop this madness right now if you wanted to. I want you to call this whole thing off. It's too dangerous. You hear me! It's too dangerous!!!"

Then, as Sharon Weiner stormed out of Brent's office, he said, "I'm glad we had this talk, Sharon," and the door slammed.

Sharon Weiner looked at her fiancé sitting before all his paperwork and notes and said, "Jamesy, you know you *don't* have to do this. You don't owe these people *shit!*"

"Maybe yes, and maybe no. Maybe I *want* to do this, though. Anyway, Lieutenant Kramer has been mighty good to me, helping me get back on my feet, putting in a good word wherever he could, making phone calls, and even helping me start my consulting business. Don't forget, he got me my first three or four speaking engagements, so don't tell me I don't owe a little—"

"He's *using* you, James!"

"I don't think so, Sharon. I have this opportunity to help them—"

"At no personal risk to yourself?!"

"Of *course* there's *some* personal risk. There's personal risk to everything. Suppose some dude don't like the way you defended him in court, and he gets out a prison and comes back to blow your head off. That shit happens, ya know."

"That's a *hell* of a lot different than deliberately sticking your head in the lion's mouth! James, you don't have to prove anything, *especially* to me, darling." Sharon petted the back of James's head. "Sweetheart, if anything were to happen to you . . . I really wish you'd reconsider this."

"I've made up my mind, Sharon. I'm going through with it. Anyway, it's not as if I didn't get something in return."

"Yeah, *what* did you get in return?"

"I'm not telling you—until the wedding day. . . ."

It was night, and Clayton George sat on a wooden chair in Warden Ellison's office, watching the warden's unoccupied desk. An unarmed guard stood next to him, and another guard stood at the door, at attention, armed with a Taser stun gun. Clayton George raised his hands a half a foot, looked at the shiny steel handcuffs on his hands, then placed his hands back into his lap. "I wonder if this got somethin' to do wit ma upcomin' parole?" he asked the guard next to him. The guard did not answer him, not because he had anything against speaking with the prisoner, but he didn't want the warden to catch him speaking with the prisoner. Conversations between prisoners and guards were strongly discouraged at Sing Sing. "Oh, the silent treatment again, right, Andy?" Clayton said to his escort. The guard looked down at Clay, as if to say with his eyes, Sorry, just can't talk this minute. And then Warden Ellison entered his office with Lt. Brent Kramer, who wore a suit. The warden sat at his desk, and Brent sat on a chair to the right of his desk.

"Hello, Mr. George, how ya doing?"

"Just fine, Warden. How a you?"

"I'm doing well, thank you." Warden Ellison looked up to the guard, Andy, and said, "Could you please remove the handcuffs from Mr. George, and then please leave us alone for a moment?"

"Yes, sir," Andy said, then removed the cuffs.

When the two guards had left his office, Warden Ellison said, "Mr. George, this is Mr. Metzenbaum, and he works in the governor's office. We have something we want to discuss with you."

"Does dis got somethin' ta do wit ma upcomin' parole hearin'?"

"Yes. We have a proposition for you."

"Shouldn't I have a . . . a lawyer present?"

"You could, but then we wouldn't make you the offer, and if you were left completely on your own, you would most probably spend closer to full term here, minus time for good behavior, of course. We could never take that from you."

"What about ma parole? Don't that decide ma disposition?"

"Yes. You're absolutely right; it does. But tell me, Mr.

George, how many of your fellow inmates do you recall offhand having been released from Sing Sing on the basis of their first hearing?" Clayton began the computation in his memory. "Think hard, Clay. Think real hard. Can you recall even *one* who was ever paroled the first time at bat?"

"I got to give the matter some thought. Wait! Yeah—Tito Perez! Didn't he make first parole?"

"Yes. But he wasn't convicted of manslaughter, as you were, and he'd also grown a little closer to God than you've managed to grow, not that that's any criterion, but it did figure into his overall picture, and he had not *one* ticket or institutional infraction. Clay, if you were not to be paroled this time around, you would *not* be up for parole for another twenty-four months, and I can assure you that the odds are against it. I'm just talking the odds as frankly as I can with you. And, statistically speaking, the odds would be against you on your second parole hearing also, which would bring us two more years up on the calendar."

Clayton was listening carefully. "You said you had a . . . proposition?"

"Yes. We—that is to say, myself, and the governor of the state of New York, and Mr. Metzenbaum here—we will unconditionally release you from prison in one year from your upcoming scheduled hearing, if, you agree to be transferred from this facility and skip your parole hearing this time around. If you decide not to, then you're on your own with the system. This way, you're guaranteed to be out in one year, come hell or high water. Of course, you will be out on probation, same as if you were released on parole, but you'll be out, and that's the important thing."

"Why?"

Brent Kramer, in the roll of Mr. Metzenbaum, decided to field this one. "It's part of a new experimental program to circumvent the normal parole process, but the people we consider have all conformed to certain guidelines, such as yourself, Mr. George, and we believe this will empty the prisons of people we believe to show promise. You're a very lucky man, Mr. George."

"If you wanna empty da prison a people like me who show promise, why don't you juss lemme out right now? I've been here long enough."

"The program doesn't work like that, Mr. George," Brent

210

said with a smile. "Now, we've worked long and hard on this project. Do you think you would be interested?"

"Yes, I would. You offer da same deal ta Lasker?"

Michael Lasker, Clayton's cell mate for the past year, had been transferred the previous week to another facility without explanation. Lasker was not given any special deal. He had simply been transferred as part of routine *bus therapy* to *defuse prison tension,* or so the interprison paperwork read, and this would raise no flags of impropriety or breech of procedure.

"No," Warden Ellison said. "Lasker was just transferred, but he is not getting this deal, and he knows nothing about our arrangements with you."

Brent almost felt a little like Marshall Stanley as he popped open his briefcase and removed the order signed by the governor for Clayton George to sign. He placed the paper down for Mr. George to review. Brent felt it was amazing just how much Clayton George looked like James LeRoy Washington III, even up close.

"Now, there *is* one thing you have to promise us *not* to do," Brent said. "You can't talk to anyone about this arrangement, because if word should get out, we would be swamped with all kinds of unsolicited requests, and the program could die before it ever takes root. This is a *very* important point. You will be the *only* one in this program at the facility we're sending you to, so if other inmates there should suddenly start requesting permission to be chosen for this, or if we find you've been flapping your mouth, you come *right* back here and all bets are off, and it says that *rrrrrright* over here...." Brent leaned over and pointed to the part of the contract where it legally said that. "Oh, by the way, I need to take some Polaroids of you." Brent removed the camera from the briefcase and began shooting away at Clay from many different angles as Clay read the contract out loud.

Exactly one hour after the escort car with Clayton George left the Sing Sing State Correctional Facility in Ossining, New York, another car passed through the security entrance off Spring Street and entered through the double-gated sally port with a well-studied James LeRoy Washington III. James listened one last time to the tape recording of Clayton George that Brent had made earlier, and he rubbed the freshly shaven left side of his scalp, which had been groomed in the car so that he would look like Clayton George from the photographs Brent had taken. The bright spotlights within the walls of the prison illuminated the car, and the grounds were well lit. There was barbed wire everywhere, and James was a bit nervous. This place was the real thing. He was going to real prison. It was ironic that after all the time he'd avoided prison in his past, now he was going to prison working for the law. All the humor of the situation was suddenly replaced by a very real fear, especially when the handcuff ratchets crunched around James's wrists, and he, Brent Kramer, and two rather large guards marched to Warden Ellison's office sometime past midnight. Twenty minutes later, Brent and James hugged, and Brent said, "Good luck tomorrow, Clayton George."

James could not sleep. As the pillow of Clayton George compressed around his ears, he listened to his steady heartbeat. Daylight was taking forever to come, and James watched the ceiling, completely awake, listening to the sounds, the echoes off in the distance, the lights and shadows from outside his cage, the cage where they keep the animals, and he thought about how fortunate he was to be exactly where he was.

43   October First

The information officer at the Division of Parole nervously said, "Lieutenant, I have a Dr. Sal Millstone on the line right now, and he's inquiring about the status of Clayton George. He's on the list, so I called you immediately. If your recorder is still working down there in the basement, then you have it on tape, so far."

"Excellent, keep him on as long as you can, Mark. We're having it traced this minute. . . ."

Brent immediately called the phone company.

The phone had already burned a hole in Sergeant Perato's right ear, so in desperation he quickly shifted the receiver to his left. "How long have you been retired from medicine, Dr. Robbins?" he said while drearily glancing through another ten-page single-spaced list of names. This was the most telephone-intensive investigation he'd ever participated in, and if the computers were doing anything to lighten the load through the magic of all this database cross-referencing Brent kept raving about, it wasn't apparent yet. It seemed to the sergeant that not only were they doing things the same old-fashioned way, but they had to drag the computers along for the ride. "So you've been retired for one year," Sergeant Perato said. "I presume there's a doorman in your building? . . . Twenty-four hours?" Al shook his head. "Is there a garage with a service entrance? . . ."

Al saw the lieutenant and his sense of urgency approaching, and Brent interrupted. "We've got a call being traced this minute requesting information on Clayton George. I need you *right* now. . . ."

Sergeant Perato monitored the status of the trace with another line directly to the Office of Public Information. Brent burst into Captain Percella's office, told him the news, then told him to collect every available man and unit in preparation for a potential insurrection. Perato looked up from the receiver of the phone and yelled across the room to Brent. "The Time Life Building! Couldn't ask for closer to home!" Then he punched his hand with his fist and grabbed his jacket.

Perato handed the traced phone number to Brent, who handed it the captain and said, "Phone in the exact location of this extension to us. We're on our way." And within minutes, police cars were screeching across town to block all entrances and exits to the Time Life Building.

All was pandemonium at the Time Life Building. In the lobby, nobody was being allowed into or out of the building. But all this blitzkrieg of activity was buffered from the point of origin of that which had caused all the commotion—the ninth floor, and Warner Books. As Brent entered the lobby, he had the sign-in book impounded, then he rode the elevator with a crowd of police officers. "I don't want anyone on or off this floor," Brent said. "That means I want every *elevator, service* elevator, and *staircase* covered. You see anything that even moves wrong, arrest it. The only way anyone gets off this floor is jumping out the window. Let's not fuck this up, men!" And the doors opened to a perfectly normal-looking lobby. The uniforms went where they had to go, and the remaining three officers followed Brent and Al into the reception area.

Brent dropped his badge before the receptionist could open her mouth, and he said, "Take me to this extension, please."

"I can't leave the—"

Brent shook both his index fingers at her without saying a word, pointed at her, then pointed for her to get out from behind her desk. She exited the enclosed area, took the piece of paper from Brent, then said, "This is Mrs. Jenks's line. Oh God, she's the new editor here. I hope she's not in any trouble. . . ."

They rounded a few corners, passed several partitioned offices, and then stopped in front of Mrs. Jenks's office. Brent and Al walked in and saw a man sitting at a desk, by himself, taking notes. He looked up and was surprised to see the two plainclothes detectives staring into his face. "Trick or treat," Brent said. "Who are you?"

The man looked straight into Brent's burning eyes and said, "My name is Dr. Sal Millstone. . . ."

"Doctor of what?"

"Doctor of sociology. What's this all about?"

"Meet your new editors, Doctor. Now, I'd like to avoid placing you under arrest, for the moment, so I'll ask you to answer some questions for us. . . ."

And when Mrs. Jenks returned with emptied bowels and two cups of freshly brewed coffee in her hands, she was not permitted to enter her office for forty-five minutes, while her author told the police all about the book he was in the process of writing—on the subject of justice in America. He was simply in the wrong place at the wrong time, and trying to make a few extra long-distance calls at his publisher's expense.

And everything about him demonstrated that he was, in fact, exactly who he said he was.

The microwave dishes were uplinking and the news cameras were already taking footage of the growing midtown blood clot. The police really did know nothing, and when the doors to the Time Life Building once again opened for commerce, the mystery continued. Policeman after policeman exited with a "No comment" for the news. But a ray of hope emerged along with the emergence of Lieutenant Kramer and Sergeant Perato.

"Lieutenant Kramer, have there been any developments in—"

"No comment at this time and life."

"Lieutenant Kramer, was your presence here—"

"No comment at this time either."

"Lieutenant Kramer . . ."

"Lieutenant Kramer . . ."

The car door slammed, and all human noise slowly blended into the sounds of traffic.

Brent walked into Sally's office, and she said, "I hear the news from the captain. Just a false alarm. Maybe we will have better luck next time."

"Let's hope so, Sally." Brent was clearly depressed. "Say, I need to do a download from one of the field recorders. I want to hear that conversation."

"Okay, just let me save my status. . . ." Sally typed away, and Brent could hear the hard-drive head sputtering across the surface of the five-hundred-megabyte medium."

"I want to learn this procedure," Brent said as he pulled up a chair and gazed at the screen.

"Okay," Sally said. "First thing you do is get back to DOS prompt. Then you go to G drive. Then you type *tapednld*." The disk banged around a bit then the screen displayed a set of data fields. "Now you fill in all the fields with the parameters you want; otherwise, it defaults to what is there already." Brent watched Sally set the audio-sampling rate and amplitude-quantization resolution, the baud rate, and the error-correction options, paying particular attention to the way she zeroed in on the specific conversation on the on-site tape recorder to be downloaded. Then she said, "Now the cursor controls will act just like the normal controls on a tape recorder to either rewind, fast-forward, play, or stop, and you name the file in this data field over here."

"That seems simple enough," Brent said.

"Nigel wrote the program so it is pretty smart."

"Don't ever make the mistake of telling him that. His head is fat enough without any encouragement."

Sally looked at Brent with a long face and said, "I already made that mistake." Brent frowned as the modem buzzed like bottled insects from the speaker. Then the digitization and download process was complete, and the following conversation came from the speaker when she hit the up arrow:

"Hello, Department of Corrections, Public Information, Loretta speaking. How can I help you?"

"Can I speak with Mr. Silverman, please?"

"Hold on one minute. Let me see if he's available."

About thirty seconds passed; then Mr. Silverman came on the line. "Hello, how can I help you?"

"I would like some information on Clayton George, who, I believe, is scheduled to be paroled shortly. Just exactly when is his parole hearing scheduled?" Dr. Sal Millstone asked.

"Uh . . . uh . . . what . . . sir, what is your—I mean, with whom am I speaking?"

"This is Sal Millstone. Dr. Sal Millstone. You remember me—I've called several times in the past."

Yes . . . Dr. Millstone, for what purpose do you require the information?"

"I'm doing some more research for the same book I'm writing, and Clayton George is one of several prisoners meeting a unique set of profiles."

"All right, Dr. Millstone. I'll need a few minutes to pull the file. We're all manual up here at the moment."

"All right," Dr. Millstone said as Mr. Silverman went off to call Lieutenant Kramer and then retrieve the file.

And after about two minutes, after the sergeant from New York had told him that they had successfully performed the trace, Mr. Silverman said, "October first; today is Mr. George's parole hearing, at the Sing Sing State Correctional Facility. . . ."

James LeRoy Washington III entered the wood-paneled room, with the hairy hand of a large, glazy-eyed prison guard firmly squeezing his left shoulder. This guard seemed to exude a certain measure of pleasure in squeezing his shoulder harder than it needed to be squeezed to get the job done. James wondered how a man's neck could be larger than his head. His head seemed way out of proportion, too little for the other anatomical dimensions of this human bull-robot in a uniform. It was alarming that such a small head could be capable of generating the correct control signals for such a large-framed thing, but then James remembered that the brontosaurus had a brain the size of a walnut, and ants didn't seem to be doing all that poorly as a race of creatures, either, and look how small their brains are. It all made sense now, in a funny sort of way.

The only words he had heard from this man's monotonic mouth were *stop* and *go,* accentuated with a forceful twist to the shoulder, as if James were something between a horse and a machine tool. Granted, one might assemble an infinite variety of life's experiences cryptographically encoded into permutations and combinations of these two powerful words, but it would not likely be in the cards today. Their usage was single-mindedly direct, and always spoken a second or two after that vice grip hand compressed on his shoulder. James was not comfortable with the handcuffs around his wrists, either, but these were necessary for all inmates outside the double-gated cell block. At times, this whole exercise seemed nutty, but this is how Lieutenant Kramer wanted it handled.

James looked, without staring, at the three men seated at a long table at the front of the room. A stenographer was seated at a separate table over to the right. The seats were arranged like a small Las Vegas marriage chapel, and James was led up the center aisle by the gorilla. They sat at a small table in the front of the room, about ten feet from the table with the three commissioners.

Gerrard Singer was one of the two parole officers in the room, which was a rare event, because field parole officers usually don't attend an actual parole hearing. Officer Merryl Oberlin, also from the New York Metro 1 region, was the other parole officer, and an apprentice to Gerrard Singer, but he was not aware of this elaborate plan. Unbeknownst to the parole commissioners, Gerrard Singer's presence gave James LeRoy Washington III an added boost of confidence.

These were the people in the room, along with Clayton George, the center of attention. And James knew that Clayton was no paragon of virtue. He knew that Clayton had murdered a man in cold blood, an innocent man who sat in his car waiting for a red light on a Manhattan street corner. James now had to convince the commissioners that he, Clayton George, was an upstanding member of society and ready to be released back into society. But more to the point, his primary goal was to convince the commissioners that he, Clayton George, posed no threat to society. James almost wanted to throw the parole hearing, like a fighter throwing a match. James did not like Clayton George, not only because Clayton George was a murderer, but because Clayton George looked like *him!* But James realized that this was irrational, because Clayton George's fate had already been determined, no matter what James did.

The handcuffs came off, and James sat erect, with a sense of purpose in his eyes. The three men seated in the front stopped talking among themselves; then in unison they opened their file folders on Clayton George.

"Mr. George, I'm Commissioner Timpkin, and with me today are Commissioner Beal, to my right, and Commissioner Pressman, to my far right. We're here to consider the possibly of your release on parole. How are you today?"

"I'm very well, thank you," James said confidently but with no component of cockiness. James caught a glimpse of Gerrard Singer in his peripheral vision.

Commissioner Timpkin continued: "You have been sentenced to a term of twelve to twenty years, and that sentence was imposed as a result of your being found guilty of a charge of involuntary manslaughter on 207th Street in Washington Heights on the morning of January first, 1981. It was quite a New Year's party, I understand. You were also charged with criminal possession of a firearm in the second degree, criminal possession of a firearm in the third degree, and robbery one, but those charges were dropped, if I remember correctly."

"This is all true," James said.

"You were also charged with possession of a controlled substance, possession of paraphernalia, and public intoxication, and those charges were dropped, if I remember correctly."

"Yes. That is also correct."

"Because you were found guilty by a verdict, Mr. George, I have to ask you the following questions. Did you appeal your verdict to the Appellate Division?"

"Yes, I did."

"And the conviction was affirmed, is that correct?"

"Yes, it was."

"Did you make any further appeals, either to the New York Court of Appeals or to the Federal District Court?"

"Yes, to the New York Court of Appeals."

"And what happened, Mr. George? They affirmed the conviction?"

"Yes, they affirmed it."

"Did you make any further appeals?"

"No, I did not."

Commissioner Pressman then said, "Shortly before the time of your arrest, you had just gotten high on cocaine, and it was confirmed that there was cocaine in your system from a blood test administered by the police after you were in custody."

"Yes, I had just given myself an injection of cocaine. It's no excuse for what I did. It *was* a factor, though. But I take full responsibility for my actions."

"That's not what you said at your trial."

"I said a lot of irresponsible things back then, and I thought a lot a stupid, immature things back then that simply weren't true. At one time in my life, I had a great capacity for self-delusion . . . and self-destruction."

"Excuse me, Mr. George?" Commissioner Beal said. "I didn't hear that last thing you said."

James grew introspective and quiet, and he hesitated before he spoke again. He said, "I said that at one time in my life, I had a great capacity for self-delusion, and self-destruction."

Commissioner Timpkin said, "And you feel you've changed in the twelve years you've been here?"

"Commissioner Timpkin, in twelve years a person can enter undergraduate school, graduate, enter medical school, graduate, complete his residency, and be off in private practice. The same holds true for a degree in law, science, or even the school of hard knocks. Twelve years is an awful lot of time to reinvent a philosophy, and a way of living. Thirteen years ago, I had an angry child's mind trapped inside the body of a twenty-year-old adult. Pretty damn pathetic. I . . . I've done a lot a growin' up in here. Have I changed in thirteen years? When I came here, I was a street punk. It's a wonder I lived long enough to commit the crime in the first place. Today, I'm a man. And I'm not talkin' about no macho man who can go aroun' an' kick some butt. I'm talkin' about a man who is smart enough and wise enough to find creative ways *not* to. Yes, I've changed."

With skepticism, Commissioner Pressman said, "Can you give me some examples—say the Carlos incident?"

"Yes. First of all, that happened six or seven years ago, and it's true—perhaps I overreacted. But let's examine the *actual* facts of that incident. The man *was* trying to rape me."

"That's not what *they* said. They said you wanted *them* to get you drugs, and when they refused, you became enraged and attacked them like a wild animal."

"They are *not* telling the truth. I could use stronger, more streetwise words to describe the character of those two sorry boys, but I would not want to demean the standards of decency we are trying to uphold. I repeat, both of them *were* trying to rape me. . . . Commissioner Pressman, have you ever had two muscle builder-type, sweaty, racially proud Hispanics with a nine-word vocabulary who hate your guts with a passion because you're racially different, pin you against a wall and try to sodomize you in the dark aisles of a . . . a laundry room? I'll bet the answer to that question almost certainly has to be no. These are experiences way outside the realm of the gainfully employed person living in the normal flow of commuting traffic, living the middle-class existence, surrounded by the trappings of suburbia. Please understand what I'm trying to say. I'm *not* making excuses for me being *here*, rather than *there* . . . but . . ." James LeRoy Washington III chuckled in a very calculating manner. "I don't mean to laugh. I know its no laughing matter, but this *is* a prison, and I *am* surrounded by a group of individuals that are somewhat . . . less than savory, so to speak. The man *was* trying to forcibly insert his penis . . . into my . . . well, inside of me, so . . . I guess I defended myself to the full extent of my abilities. Yes, I broke Carlos's nose, and I broke Guillermo's arm, too. But it was two-on-one, so by any standard, at least it was a fair fight. Put it this way: I was not going just to stand there and . . . turn the other cheek —no pun intended, sir."

"I understand that you are living here under less-than-ideal circumstances, and I give you credit for that," Commissioner Timpkin said.

James said, "You have to understand something about the psychology of life behind bars from the inmate's point of view, which unfortunately runs diametrically opposed to the philosophy of rehabilitation by any ideal academic analysis, and that is, that if it becomes known that you are an easy mark, then they'll continue to take advantage of you—a precedent would be set that you're a willing punk, and it could ultimately lead to your death, or at least your continued violation at the capricious whim of any wolf with a little muscle behind him. I've seen it happen firsthand, with my own eyes, and it's a very ugly scene. You've got to keep your space secure— maintain your perimeter, so to speak. And that's simply the way it is in here. I would never have just walked up to some people and start a fight, or even finish one, unless there was absolutely no alternative left to me, given what my judgment and self-control is today, or even then. I don't like physical confrontation."

Commissioner Pressman said, "When you first came to prison, you went through ASAT*, and then you suddenly left the program."

"Yes, I did. The next logical question: How come? I had no desire to get high anymore. I grew up. I think back, and it's like another life ago. But my plan when I get out—if I get out—is that I will enter Narcotics Anonymous *voluntarily*—and no one *put* that thought in my head. I'll enter NA until I have successfully made the transition. I have a pretty strong will, but I *am* in one environment here, and I imagine I'll be in a different environment, with different influences, on the outside. I would like to test my willpower, and I also want the support structure and the positive reinforcement of NA

---

* Alcohol- and Substance-Abuse Treatment.

—till I have proven to myself that I can really handle it. I have every expectation that I will," James said with a proud smile. "I have too much to live for."

Commissioner Beal had been relatively quite and observant throughout the procedure. Then, quite unexpectedly, his glasses dropped to his nose, and he said, "Mr. George, there are some inconsistencies that bother me about the trial—things about this transcript that I am still confused about. In fact, I am surprised that the matter was never pursued in more detail during the trial, and perhaps you can shed a little light on it for me."

"I'll help in any way that I can."

"When you ran up to the car and ordered Lawrence Lent to get out, one eyewitness stated that you appeared to be running from some people, in a state of panic, and that he thought he heard shots being fired on one of the side streets prior to when you ran out into traffic and killed Mr. Lent. Were you running from someone?"

James hesitated for a moment. "I was running from myself. All that happened a real long time ago, but . . . well, that's one of the scary things about coke—you see things; you hear things—you got spirits livin' inside your head you don't have *any* control of—voices tell you ta do things you don't even know you did later. Put it this way: I don't believe there were any *humans* chasing me."

"You don't *believe* there were any humans chasing you, or there *weren't* any humans chasing you. Which is it?"

"I don't *believe* there was anyone chasing me. I do not completely remember the situation. My memory of it is in fragments—bits and pieces—images. It's not like a movie that I can just play back—like to frame two hundred and six—to stop and analyze under a microscope."

"So then, you are saying that you don't know, for sure, if there was anyone chasing you?"

"That is correct. There are states of mind, and I don't want to get mystical with you, but there are states of mind where you just can't tell the difference anymore, between what you actually see with your eyes and what you hallucinate inside your head. It fuses into a sort of mixture. I was probably hallucinating in some paranoid panic. Coke'll do that to you."

"But surely the witness could not have been hallucinating the same people *you* were hallucinating?"

"Did he actually see these alleged people?" James asked, sensing he was entering dangerous waters.

"It says here—wait, let me find it. It say here, 'I thought I seen some men. They was running toward Broadway before I seen him shoot out that car window. Then he got in that car and drive away, and them wheels was burning rubber like them tires was on fire.' Quote unquote."

"I don't even remember anyone saying that in court, but then again, I don't remember too much of anything. But, from what you said, he said he *thought* he saw, not that *he did* see."

"I care less about what he said than what actually happened."

"Well, I can't say, with one hundred percent certainty what actually *did* and *did not* happen on the night of January first, 1981. To the best of my knowledge, I don't *think* there was anyone chasing me . . . period."

There was a silent pause in the room, when all that could be heard was the sounds of the pipes and heating system. James hoped he hadn't blown it, and then Commissioner Timpkin picked up the ball.

"We received many letters on your behalf—one from Sharon Weiner, a public defender from Manhattan. She seems to have taken quite an interest in you. She's arranged a job for you in a New York law firm starting in the spring, if you are released, and in the meantime you would be working at a McDonald's restaurant in Inwood.

"You got your high school equivalency, and you have plans to go to law school. We have other letters of support on your behalf from Cardinal O'Connor, Rabbi Tannenbaum, Benjamin Ward, Lee Brown, Ed Koch, Mario Cuomo, Jimmy Carter, Gerald Ford—quite an impressive list of people. There is one person conspicuously missing in this list of people, though, and he doesn't write anyone any letters. That is Lawrence Lent, the man you killed when you were twenty years and four months old. He was twenty-seven, only seven years older than yourself. He would be thirty-nine—no, he would have just turned forty years old. No. He's not writing any letters for you, or himself, because he has been dead for the past thirteen years.

"We face a difficult job here. It is our job to determine whether you are fit to return to society—to a society you damaged beyond repair. But you are a different man now than you were thirteen years ago. Lawrence Lent would have been a different man, too.

"Up until about a century ago, and for thousands of years before, all over the world, if you killed someone, and it wasn't an accident, or even if it was, society would kill you—plain and simple. If you killed someone, you had to forfeit your own life. It was the law. And then it was decided that maybe this wasn't, maybe . . . such a good idea—that maybe it wasn't right for society to be in the business of killing, too. Many statesmen, greater men than you and I, they spoke eloquently on the subject of what the state should and should not be in the business of doing. And things changed. They called it progress. But things have gotten bad. Some say out of control. Some say we must reevaluate things all over again. Murder is an epidemic in this country. But how much time is enough time? When is enough killing enough? How much time is worth another person's life? And what if those people are really young, or really old? Or what if you kill only one, or two or three or fifty? I don't have the answer to these questions. I don't have the answer to such philosophical and metaphysical questions. It would make our job so much easier if God would simply tell us the right answer. But God doesn't speak to us when we have to make such an important decision—to determine . . . when enough is really enough. But this is our job. And in a few minutes, we are going to make our decision. You understand that."

"Yes, sir."

"I am trying to talk to you as frankly and openly as I can, and you do understand the dilemma we face with you."

"Yes, I understand."

"You *have* taken steps to improve yourself. You had some trouble at first. Often when a young inmate, such as yourself, first enters the system, he realizes the enormity of the task ahead of him, the enormity of the time before him, until he can return to the world. Then inmates often settle down and get with the program. This, Clayton George, you did, for the most part, and we will weigh this in your favor. You received some tickets in your early years here—tickets for misconduct. You received two tickets for fighting—like the one issued for the Carlos affair. And you received three tickets for arguing with the guards. It's not great, but it's not terrible, either. And you have *not* been in trouble here for a long time. You are an intelligent man. You have written letters to many people, and you have decided to do something with your life, and this is very good.

"On the other hand, Lawrence Lent does not have such an opportunity. He is dead. You are alive. This is very complicated, but we have a job to do here, and we are going to do it. You understand that, Mr. George."

"Yes, I understand."

Commissioner Timpkin turned to the other commissioners and said, "Gentlemen, anything further?"

Both said, "No."

"Mr. George, is there anything you would like to ask us, or say before this hearing concludes?"

"Nothing, except that I appreciate the opportunity for you to speak with me, and I would like you to know that I will not disappoint you, whatever you decide for my disposition to be."

"I want to thank you very much, Mr. George. Good-bye and good luck."

"Thank you," James LeRoy Washington III said as the gorilla placed the handcuffs back on him, and marched him down the aisle and out the door, with a strong grip on his shoulder.

45 Joey

Dr. Becker Instlokrownctjz was growing more obsessed with the case as the days rolled by, and much of this was due to the influence of Nigel. Every telephone call Becker made, every E-mail he received or sent, every news broadcast he heard only pulled him further into a consuming obsession which blasted the subject of botany and his research light-years from his brain. He was now in search of a human —the very same human the police searched for.

Becker had spent an entire day going through the old class records of every student he'd ever taught at Columbia University, and the following day he examined all his Rutgers and City College records. He knew in his heart, though, that there was only one pupil who'd possessed both the obsessive qualities and the strangeness index necessary to perform truly brilliant work, and he felt compelled—no, drawn—to avoid this individual, to spend his time moving tangent to the force he obstinately resisted, like a stubborn planet in orbit around a more powerful gravitational sun—the force relentlessly converging him on the only logical conclusion.

"Joseph Barton!" Becker Instlokrownctjz proudly articulated on the telephone after hearing the word *hello,* which he instantly recognized as being produced by the mouth of Nigel Atkerson.

Nigel waited a few seconds longer for extra clarifying words to follow, but none did. At times, Becker's anagram and rebus thought modalities and communication patterns seemed to be a deliberate attempt to waste time while waving the annoying flag of some compulsive intellectual cuteness he'd never outgrown. Conversations with Becker usually began on the exact same note they'd left off, literally, to the word, and if one did not remember the precise point at which the last session had ended, the next one was likely to start with some initial confusion. Nigel, who was in the midst of calculating the product yield of a chemical reaction, squinted while shaking his head. "Becker, that sentence is missing a few key parts of speech. Please do elaborate."

"Oh. Right. I was a little bit preoccupied. Joseph Barton is the name of that student whose name I was looking for—you know, the strange one I told you about?"

"Excellent," Nigel said as he pulled a yellow lined notepad out from a ten-inch pile of crap on the side of his desk and placed it on top of a four-inch pile of crap directly in front of him so he could take notes.

"I had to go through all my old class records to find him. I'm terrible with names, you know."

"Tell me about this Joseph Barton. What makes him so special?"

"Well, this par-tic-u-lar student showed great interest in grafting techniques and the art of bonsai trees. I remember him sitting for four or five hours once, staring at *Holding Hands. . . .*"

"Oh, that pair of plants you spliced together?"

Becker was mildly insulted by the denigrating way Nigel referred to his cytoplasmic creation as a simple "pair of plants." Becker found Nigel to be refreshingly brilliant most of the time, but in some ways he was a pagan. "Yes," Becker sighed—"that pair of plants, as you call it. It mesmerized him."

"Why did that strike you as being odd? I would think any curious and intelligent person would find it interesting, if he had the time on his hands—no pun intended."

"No pun taken." This was not true. Becker always looked for a pun, even when there was no pun to be found. "No. Most people glance at it for a minute or two at the most, even people at the botanical shows; then they lose interest and move on to the roses and the pretty stuff. But not this individual. Not Joseph. He couldn't take his eyes off it. Nobody had ever taken such a keen interest in this type of plant grafting before. At least nobody ever took that kind of interest in any of *my* work."

"Maybe he just appreciated the artistry that went into such a creation."

"Yes, and no. I got a clear sense that with him, there was something more, something deeper. Something was troubling him. At times, he even gave me the creeps. But he also helped me finish up some of the work here in the lab—you know, hauling dirt and rocks. You know how I am when it comes to volunteer labor. One can never get enough. And he was a real good worker. Tremen-dous concentration span. Self-motivated. He was a strange one, though. Didn't talk much. But he always kept his appoint-ments. Many of the students who helped me would never show for future appointments, or they would come late, or they were unreliable, or they simply lost interest. But not Joseph. He was like clockwork. The Joseph Barton I knew was a working machine. He wasted no time between finishing one task and beginning another. He had everything outlined in his mind. He was very orga-nized. And he was fascinated by both the biological work going on here, and the excavation for my extra space, so to speak. I gave him an *A*. . . ."

"What about his class work?" Nigel spit.

"The *A* was *for* his class work. You're bad! *And,* he had some in-ter-es-ting physical attributes, one might say. This is probably the most striking thing about him. . . ."

"Well?" Nigel was attempting to short out two or three sentences of preamble before Becker actually got to this most striking thing about Joey Barton.

"He had some in-ter-es-ting facial scars," Becker said, "on his chin and around his nose. And one more thing. His voice was a bit on the high side. In fact, if you weren't looking directly at him, you might almost have thought he were another gender. And there was something else that I never resolved, and I never asked him about, but it always bothered me, though. A few years before I first met Joseph, a young high school student, a girl, came to visit Columbia from someplace in Pennsylvania, I think. She was visiting prospective colleges, and Columbia was on her list. And she had a harelip and a cleft palate. I remember it being the first time I'd ever seen such a facial deformity. I only saw her briefly, and she specifically inquired about the subject of botany, so I was one of the professors she came to see. And then I remembered thinking about her when I met Joseph Barton as a student. As I said, I never raised the subject with him, and he never mentioned it to me, so that was that. But I can't help but think that, perhaps, they might *even* have been the same person."

"Well, well, well. That could *still* make him difficult to track down. Do you remember what the girl's name was?"

"No."

"Do you think there would be any records of such a visit to Columbia?"

"I doubt it. If there is a record, I'm sure it would take some digging."

"Becker, when I think of digging, I think of one person."

"I'll make some calls," Becker volunteered.

"Good. And do you know where Joseph Barton is, and how we can contact him? Did you guys keep in touch?"

"He used to call every so often, for a few years after he left my classes and went to Cornell, but then I never heard from him again. We'll have to go to the school records. Maybe *they* can shed some light on him, and where he might be."

"A call to Cornell might be in order, too. When was the last time you spoke to him?"

"About fifteen or eighteen years ago, I should say."

"*Hmmmm,*" Nigel hummed. "An awful lot can happen in fifteen years...."

After Becker got off the phone with Nigel, he decided to call his old friend Dr. Mell Fisher and approach the problem from an entirely different angle. Nigel told Becker that while people move from place to place, they rarely change their interests or hobbies, and the corresponding publications and magazine subscriptions tend to follow them around wherever they go. And Dr. Fisher possessed the circulation lists for a number of publications, and Nigel wanted Becker to get the lists for analysis.

Dr. Fisher was also a research botanist, and his specialty was population genetics. He wrote his obligatory 1.8 papers per year to keep his office and lab at Rockefeller University, and, not being independently wealthy like his friend Becker, his was a far more structured existence. He and Becker had known each other since they were both grad students at Cornell, and since Mell had come to New York, the two of them would get together for dinner and an evening of shoptalk about as often as Mell churned out his papers.

"Mell, Becker here."

"How the hell are ya?" Dr. Fisher said.

"I'm doing . . . well, actually, I'm not . . . but I might have been, if I weren't doing what I happen to be doing at the moment."

"That's ah . . . perfectly clear to me, Becker. Are you eating any of your mutated vegetables, by any chance? That might explain this exchange of information so far."

"Yes to one. No to two. Let me explain. I need copies of those circulation lists you keep—you know, the *Botanical Quarterly,* the *Bonsai Club Newsletter* . . . oh, and the *American Bonsai Society Abstracts.* I know you have that stuff on disk for the past several years."

"I also have the *Bonsai Clubs International.* You want that, too?"

"Yes."

"So you want the current subscription lists?"

"Well, yes. I also want the lists for as long as the records have been computerized."

"Well, this will take some time for me to put together. Do you mind telling me what this is all about?"

"I will, eventually, but first I have to visit a horticultural club in New Jersey. I'm late."

"Becker, sometimes you sincerely worry me. . . ."

With a large suitcase in his right hand, James LeRoy Washington III walked north along Seaman Avenue, bound for his brand-new home during his temporary absorption into the unwanted life and personality of Clayton George, the newly released parolee on the block. And that block was no middle-class haven, either. This was lowlife city at the northernmost end of Manhattan Island. The dregs. He glanced left, over to the trees of Inwood Park on the west, then over to that drug-land pharmacopoeia known as Isham Park, to the east. He deliberately stepped on his third crack vial, this one with a green cap. This neighborhood gave James the shivers just thinking about how quietly a person could be plucked from the street here—or anywhere else, for that matter, but here in particular. This place screamed abduction from every wide-open space and dark little crevice of brick and mortar. Seaman Avenue, James thought, I'm gonna get good and fucked over on Seaman Avenue. Kramer sure knows how to pick 'em. This place got TAKE ME 'N' CUT MY ARMS OFF written all over it!

James's hand slowly crept into his left pants pocket, where he felt the flattened shape of the tiny transmitter box sewn into a pouch dangling in the vicinity of his balls, with the flat foil wire antenna sewn into the seams of his pants. Knowing it was there gave him a certain measure of security, but not a whole lot. As he approached the apartment building, he wondered what it would feel like to be hit by the silent whiz of a tranquilizer dart from out of nowhere, when he least expected it, and how much time he would have to press the emergency beacon, which was a separate transmitter sewn into his shirt. He knew that emergency transmitter would be radiating the most important two hundred milliwatts of his life—a burst of power every two seconds. The experts told him the tranquilizer induction time could be anywhere between thirty seconds and five minutes. They told him he would have plenty of time to press the button, provided he had the presence of mind to do so. He didn't believe a word of it. He envisioned himself collapsing instantly, just like in the movies, in spite of what the experts told him.

He inserted the key into the front door, then pushed, realizing that the key had no effect on the lock. The door just swung open. He pulled the key from the lock and looked at it as if it were the key's fault that the door was unlockable. *That's one less thing I got to carry around with me.* James looked at the cracked hexagonal tiles in the hallway, then walked to the stairs. He could hear a man and woman arguing in Spanish upstairs somewhere, and in the background he heard a baby crying—no, two babies crying. He trudged up the third flight of stairs in the crumbly tenement which was to be his home for who knew how long. He rattled the banister, which was broken off its supports at both landings. "Place looks like *shit,*" he muttered to himself. The humid hallway sweat faint streamlines of urine from the crumbling grout between the tiles. James shook his head in disgust. *Even the first place he was able to afford on his own was better than this shithole.* His own transformation from being a homeless pickpocket to a self-employed consultant with his very own Social Security number had somehow leapfrogged over *this* level of depravity.

Apartment thirteen. *Great! James* thought. *Kramer must have picked this one for good luck. Let's see if this key works now.* Salsa music blasted from apartment fourteen next door. He placed the suitcase down and pushed on the door. It wiggled a bit, but it was locked. He turned the key and entered the musty living room just as the phone rang.

James watched the phone as it rang three more times. He picked up the receiver, smelled it, then put it to the side of his face. "Yo!" he said.

"Yo," replied the voice in the telephone.

James's face lit up. "Hey! Sergeant Perato, how you doin', man?"

"Great. Except for these four flights a steps in paradise palace here. God, I got to lose some weight before this job kills me. I saw you enter the building from up here in number seventeen, so I gave you a minute before I decided to call and see if all systems are go."

"Thanks a lot, man. I appreciate it. Yeah, all systems are go. We're gettin' ready to blast off and go to the moon. I ain't no damn hooper yet, an' I still got lips on my face. So I guess all systems are go."

"Well, you're under constant surveillance. We've got two cars cruising the neighborhood. Bassett is joining me soon, and one of us will always be on, with overlapping shifts, and I'm picking up your signal loud and clear."

"Oh, big deal, Tracy! You're only ten feet above my head. A Tonka truck got more range than that!"

"Let's assume if I'm getting any signal at all, that it's working at full range."

"That's easy for *you* to assume. They ain't gonna turn your ass into no damn hooper if your signal isn't working at *full damn range.*"

"*Alllllll right,* James," the sergeant patronized, "let's not let our imaginations get the better of us. I checked with the contact person at NYNEX, and they've tracked your cellular phone transmitter all the way from Sing Sing. Now, I want you to test the emergency transmitter with the test button."

"Okay. Here goes." James reached his finger over to the test button on the emergency beacon, which was in an awkward position so it could not inadvertently be confused with the main trigger button, which was easy to press. Once pressed, would automatically remain on for the full seventy-two-hour duration, until the lithium battery died. Nobody spoke about it, but if a full seventy-two hours were necessary, something would probably have gone very wrong.

Sergeant Perato heard the beep in his headphones, saw the needle deflect on the receiver box, and heard the raucous trigger alarm go off, which was so loud, it could bring a dead man back to life if he happened to temporarily die during the stakeout. "I got you," the sergeant said to James as he disabled and reset the emergency receiver. "Okay now. You know the procedure, right?"

"Yeah. Every two days, at nine o'clock at night, I put on a different pair a pants, an' I leave the old pair in front a your door so you can change the battery in the cellular phone."

"You got it, James. You got the number here?"

"Five-five-five-four-six-nine-nine," James said from memory.

"Good. Did you check in with the Thirty-fourth?"

"Yep. And Gerrard Singer comes to visit me mañana. It's good to know in this day and age that you can suck down a few beers with your parole officer. Tomorrow, I report for my first day of work flippin' burgers for my McMinimum wage, an' after work, I report to my first Narcotics Anonymous meeting at Abernesia House. Sergeant, come tomorrow, your gonna be talkin' to one happy, drug-free, gainfully employed nigga on parole, with a steady routine like so much clockwork a moron could pick me off like a lame cow. Sho' nuf, Clayton George. Sho' nuf done 'n get yo' black ass outta jail."

"Gerrard says you put on one hell of a performance up there."

"Yes, I did, didn't I?" James beamed. "This whole thing was one hell of a character-building experience—to see the inside of a place I managed to stay out of all those years."

"Well, congratulations, James. Now anything strange or out of the ordinary happens, you let us know immediately. We're not taking any chances."

"That's so good to hear. 'Cause if you fuck up, you 'n the missus gonna be wearin' me around your necks like jewelry for the rest a your natural life, man."

James and Sergeant Perato said their good-byes and hung up. Then James removed a roll of masking tape from his suitcase. He ran down the stairs and placed a large strip of tape on the mailbox and a piece over the nameplate by the useless buzzer of apartment thirteen. Then he conspicuously wrote the name Clayton George at both locations. After unpacking some of his clothes and tidying up the semifurnished apartment, he reviewed the file on Clayton George one more time. James believed he knew who most of Clayton's remaining friends were—the ones still alive—and where the last remaining hot spots were where he used to hang. He studied the videos of Clayton, and he studied his mannerisms. Now it was time to get a bit conspicuous in the neighborhood. But that would have to wait till tomorrow.

James had just spent four real weeks in the big house—the time between his parole hearing and his release. He felt as if he had almost really been in prison, which, in fact, he had been, except that, unlike the rest of the prison population at Sing Sing, he could pull the cork on the experience anytime he wanted. At times, the realism of this operation was spooky. At times, he almost felt that he had actually transformed into Clayton George. In prison, he'd had to behave like the model prisoner, but now that he was out on the street, it was time to revert back to Clayton, the street punk.

But that would all have to wait till tomorrow, because today James LeRoy Washington III was expecting a guest—a special guest. And it would be his first conjugal visit since entering prison. Tonight,

Sharon Weiner, his fiancée in real life, would be visiting him with a full bag of Chinese food, a bottle of wine, and a body full of hot libido, because it had been three weeks for her also.

Luckily, the sergeant's radio didn't receive audio. If the boys upstairs wanted to get their thrills, they would have to put their ears to the floor, the same way everyone else does.

Then the buzzer rang. Home sweet home.

47   Equal Split

It was during the taping of the *Geraldo* show that Jerome Lewis collapsed in his chair and was ambulanced away. The cameras caught everything, and the footage made the usual distribution circuit. Perhaps it was the extra exercise that Jerome had been doing lately, or perhaps it was the heat of the lights, or all that rich food at the buffet that he was hand-fed like an emperor. No one really knew why he'd fainted, except that his heart rate was on the high side; he was stabilized, and the free publicity was unbelievable. Hooper paraphernalia sales had jumped, and Marshall Stanley had his hands full managing his turnover. The last thing he wanted to do was go back to that awful Midtown North police precinct to see Lt. Brent Kramer, but that was exactly what Brent *told* him to do, and *without* his lawyer.

Marshall Stanley paced back and forth in Brent's office while waiting for Brent to get off the phone. As soon as Brent hung up the receiver, Marshall said, "I'm so worried about Jerome. I *hope* he'll be okay. Can I call the hospital, Lieutenant?"

"You're *so* full of shit, Stanley," Brent said while shaking his head. "You have no greater interest in his health than a person would have about the family car at the shop. But in the spirit of truce, you can use the phone—after you hear my offer."

"Thank you." Stanley then squinted at Brent. *"Eeeee,* what offer did you have in mind? I'm a little uncomfortable talking without my lawyer."

"This is a business proposition, so to speak. Consider me your friendly business consultant."

"Lieutenant, I've seen the result of your friendliness."

"Look, Marshall, I'm willing to drop the bribery charge. You realize that bribing a police officer is a Class C felony, and I played my tape for a judge friend of mine, and he says the case is open and shut. And let's not forget impersonating a police officer! You know we have a whole unit dedicated to police impersonators; you're in deep shit, Marsh! You could be fined, *and* you could go to prison. You could waste a fortune's worth of time and money in a courtroom fighting this, even if there were some chance in hell that you could get off. But I'm willing to make a deal with you, and save us all a lot of trouble."

"What deal?"

"I want you to split equally all monies you make from the hooper tours and all spin-off business—with Jerome Lewis, Rusty Blake, and a reserve fund for other victims—you know, to cover their medical expenses and to help get them started. So basically, everyone gets a fourth—you, Jerome, Rusty, and the reserve."

"Lieutenant! This is—"

"Fair! This is fair, Marshall. These people are going to have medical expenses. These people are going to have trouble getting started again. After this is all over, you'll move on to greener pastures. But these people are all fucked up—fucked up for life. I think what you're doing is morally wrong, but it's not my place to tell other people what they can and what they can't do, unless they're breaking the law. And don't forget, you *did* break the law—several times. But let's face facts. It's a market economy out there. And if people didn't want what it is you're selling, they wouldn't be paying good money for it. Equal split. So that's my proposal. What you *can* do with your lawyer is have him draw up a new contract for Jerome and Rusty, and it better be a true equal split in good faith—not that bullshit I read in their contracts, where all the marketing expenses come out of their share. You make it fair, as if *you* were a hooper."

"This isn't right—what you're asking me to do."

"If you do this, I'll erase the original copy of the tape, and I'll give you the three copies I made."

"Why can't I have the original, too?"

"Because I have other incriminating evidence against other

fine, upstanding citizens. Look at it this way, Stanley, by setting up the reserve publicly, say in a news conference, you'll be such a hero in the eyes of the public, I wouldn't be a bit surprised if you actually got donations for the Save the Hooper fund. You'd get a lot of free publicity out of it."

The wheels were turning in Marshall Stanley's head, and he began to smile. "You know, Lieutenant, I like the way you think. You could have a big future in advertising and marketing—*if* you ever decided to change careers."

"Don't count on it. By the way, I think I can get the hospital to drop the other charges against you, but only if you do *this* for the hoopers you love so much."

"Equal split, you say?"

"Equal split."

"Equal split as of the time I draw up the new—"

"Retroactive! That's my offer. Now you can call the hospital on any phone that's free. Just dial nine to get an outside line."

"By the way, Lieutenant, you wouldn't know where we could find the Mr. Lopez who Dr. Spellman accidentally—"

"Run along now, Marshall. I have work to do."

48   The Puerto Rican Vacuum Technique

A tranquilizer dart was placed into the breach of a rifle and the bolt was slammed into position while simultaneously clicking the mechanical safety. The rifle carrying case was zipped closed, and a handful of extra darts were grabbed from the refrigerator and nonchalantly tossed into a fanny pack as if they were a handful of tampons ensuring the integrity of a summer picnic. And in some sense, they were.

Today was stalking day, and Doctor Sigma was dressed for the occasion—all bundled up, covered, and unrecognizable. It was a chilly night in late October, and it was so dark. Ideal conditions for hunting a human. The car was fully gassed. The egg room had been empty too long, and all the tools were sharp and steamy clean. Shiny tools on ready trays. Tools and clamps and saws and needles. Sutures by the scores. Drugs in bottles keeping cool. A place for everything, and everything in its place. And the boards with the restraining straps were ready, like an amusement-park ride.

Adrenaline pumped through the doctor's veins as the ignition key to the Nova was turned, and the mouth went dry with cold anticipation, as always, before taking the act on the road, but it was an increasingly familiar routine. It was all very necessary.

Julio Rodriquez was partial to tequila. Unfortunately, he was more partial to it than his liver was. His liver had been acting up again lately, but the constraints of mortality, his or anybody else's, never did seem to have any influence on Julio, except that the shakes seemed to be coming on a bit more violently and a bit more frequently, and this only amplified the difficulty of raising a shot glass to his mouth. But Julio was not without personality. Even in prison, everyone said he had personality. Without alcohol most of the time, personality had to suffice. But throughout most of his stay in the slammer, he'd dreamed of the day when he would be unconditionally reunited with the bottle. In prison, on occasion, a bottle managed to find its way here and there—for a price. A few cartons of cigarettes and the casual services of his mouth or his anus saw to that.

Julio was a man aged beyond his years, and while on the scale of desirability he was no Miss America, word had gotten around that he was not half-bad, and that the man liked his ethanol and was willing to negotiate services for spirits. And negotiate he did—up until six months ago, when he'd served out fourteen of his seventeen years and had to be moved out to make room for the freshman class —in a New Jersey prison.

The liver is considered a regenerative organ, but the liver still has a memory of past abuses. When Julio first visited the big house for murder, car theft, resisting arrest, and the unlawful discharging of a firearm in the direction of oncoming police officers, about 10 percent of his liver remained intact, even after the bullets hit him. When he returned to the streets, he had some serious catching up to do. Within six months, he'd managed to reliquify his brain and undo all the deleterious mental effects of sobriety, separated by those periodic sex-for-hydrocarbon binges.

In the bars of Newark, he was as much the storyteller as he was behind the bars of Rahway State Prison. His favorite story was one he told over and over again, called "De Puerto Rican Bacume Technee-ca" (The Puerto Rican Vacuum Technique). No one ever knew precisely what the hell he was talking about, but it maybe had something to do with men or women, suction, and Puerto Ricans.

Alcohol poured into Julio's head, and ridiculous combinations of words and phrases regurgitated back out. The more alcohol entered the head, the more ridiculous the combinations of words it belched up. Until it was time to leave, when his wobbling mental gyroscope commanded his feet to do the spastic shuffle to keep himself vertical against the unpredictable forces of static gravity, which, after mental reconfiguration, more resembled a never-ending earthquake measuring off the alcoholic Richter scale.

Pfffft.

Nobody ever missed him.

49 Kappy's Bar

Chantel reclipped her left stocking before strutting her shapely fat ass into Kappy's dingy basement bar on Broadway just off Dyckman Street. The lighting was low and the drunks were all regulars. Their faces lit up whenever they saw her, because she'd blown every one of them countless times, usually after the welfare checks got cashed in a three-way split between OTB, the bar, and her big black mouth, which was almost as big as her big black ass. She watered herself at Kappy's not to shag clients so much as to keep herself pickled with 40 percent alcoholic mouthwash between the trick runs out on the street. Her clinic-give-away condoms littered the adjoining parks and alleyways, reservoir tips filled with frustrated droplets of intoxicated neighborhood semen, and when the taste of latex exceeded sobriety, or when it was snowflake cold like it was tonight, a few good belts of Scotch whiskey could really set the record straight before returning to the field.

Clayton George, or at least the man who appeared to be Clayton George, ordered another whiskey as Chantel clicked her shiny heels up to the empty bar stool next to him. She thrust her imitation fur jacket open, exposing enough cleavage to stuff a Scarsdale mortgage down, then folded her right leg over her left. James held his whiskey glass tightly in his fist, knowing she was checking him out as she rubbed her legs together, producing that unmistakable nylon-on-nylon noise. She ain't no grasshopper, he thought. From the corner of his right eye, he could see her tight white dress hiked up far enough to expose that little triangular patch of panties and other underthings. "Oh, come now, *honey,* you don't got to be so coy wit me," she sang in Momma-speak as a shot glass appeared before her without her so much as looking at the bartender. "You can look *right 'n proper* if you want. That's what it's here for."

James LeRoy Washington III knew she was a regular around this place, along with the rest of the drunks, even though he hadn't yet seen her since he'd hit the Inwood scene. He turned with an effort to be mildly intimidating. "You talkin' 'n me, girl?"

"Come on, sugar, who you think I'z talkin' to, that glass in yo' hand? I ain' seen yo' face aroun' here befo'." She poured the brown liquid down her throat with one professional swallow, then delicately placed her glass on the counter like a lady, pinky pointed to the rafters.

At that moment, Kappy, the white-haired bartender, intervened with the refill bottle in his hand. "Clay, this here's Chantel, an' Chantel, this here's Clay . . . Clayton George. We go quite a ways back." He leaned across the bar an extra foot and continued confidentially, "He juss got back in *town* lass week."

"Doin' big time?" Chantel said, turning to James with twinkling, knowledgeable eyes.

"What's it to ya?" James challenged.

"Don' be gettin' so defensive, honey; I just spent ten days in jail myself."

"Ten days a lot different than twelve years," James said as he downed his shot and snapped the shot glass back on the bar. Kappy smiled and kept the glass full.

"Well, well, well," she seductively said while turning to give Clay a better view, "Mr. Clayton George . . . you must be missin' the fine company of a sister with *talent,* then." She smiled warmly and placed her hand on James's leg while making suggestive gestures with her tongue.

"Maybe I am, 'n maybe I ain't." James remained aloof, thinking about his white Jewish fiancée downtown. His left hand casually drifted up to the emergency transmitter in his shirt pocket. It gave him security knowing it was still there.

"Well, if you ain' lookin' for no pussy, you didn't by any chance . . . swing with them boys, *did you?"*

He looked at her as if he'd been insulted and said, "I don' *doooo* that kin' a shit."

"Well then what kin' a shit *do* you do, Clay?"

"Don' you think we gettin' to know each other awfully fast?" Some of the men within earshot of this titillating conversation laughed at that point, and James turned to stare them down.

"You readin' yo' Bible too often, boy." She swallowed another shot of the cheap stuff, and grew more flamboyant as her beverage continued diffusing into her blood. Chantel loved a good challenge. Most dudes just out of jail wanted their dicks tamed before their feet hit the pavement on this side of the big gate. This one was either gay, religious, crazy, or just a little confused. She slowly slid her hand up his leg.

James grabbed her hand before it touched anything too naughty and looked at her with a half-proud, half-evil smirk. "Last time I looked at a Bible was when I put my hand on one an' promised to tell the truth, the whole truth, and nothin' but the truth."

"What happened, Clay?"

"They didn' believe me!"

Chantel burst out laughing. She put her hand on James's shoulder. "You a funny guy." So he wasn't gay or religious, and he didn't seem all that crazy. This narrowed Clay's problem down to confusion. She downed another shot. "So what's you so uptight for? You don't seem like the shy type. Why don' you 'n me go to a hotel 'n . . . have a little fun? Don't you want no pussy? You want me to make you a special introductory offer?" She pulled her panties to the side, exposing the dense Brillo pad between her legs and the pink lips of her other working hole, which she spread centerfold-style for him to peruse, with the two of them seated right there on a pair of adjacent bar stools. Then she said almost in a whisper, "You done kill someone, did'n you? You know that kind a shit turns me on big-time." Then she pushed her finger up inside herself and wiggled it for his eyes only. James remained disinterested as he sipped his shot, but not so disinterested that he didn't peek here and there to see if it was still happening. "You got some kind a medical problem, honey? 'Cause if ya do . . . You know I understan', an I'll work wit cha."

James smiled at her. "You don' give up, do you?" He shook his head. "Juss 'cause a man don' wanna go jumpin' inta bed . . . with a—"

"Say it, Clay . . . big proud man . . . say it, Mr. *Jailbird!* A whore! Juss 'cause a man don' wanna be jumpin' in bed with no whore, it don' mean it don' make him a man? Dat what you tryin' to say, big man?"

"*Shhhhh,*" James said, all embarrassed. "Not so loud."

Chantel had just turned into a shrew. She angrily gulped another shot. "You be thinkin' you too good fo a woman like me. Like maybe you be lookin' fo a proper woman? Either way, you pay, or don' they teach you that in shop class? Maybe you like some *white* pussy?" James's eyebrows raised a millimeter. "I *seeeeee,*" she said with clinical certainty.

A bitch like Chantel was the last thing James expected. The way she came on to him took him completely by surprise. This street woman was a lot like him, though. It hadn't been too long since he was a street man, reading people's body language like she did. This assignment, or volunteer field work, was James's first return to the street. He despised Chantel, and he simultaneously felt sympathy for her. Despising her, though, was like despising himself. But he felt he was better than she was. He knew he was better than she was. He had pulled himself out of the gutter. He was respectable. But deep in his heart, he knew he wasn't respectable, and he was no better than she. He was a fake. In fact, the reason he was busy being Clayton George in the first place was because he was not respectable. If it weren't for Lieutenant Kramer, he would still be out on the street. He would still be *Handy Hands, the Nigger,* picking pockets in Times Square and the Port Authority. This was a moral dilemma for James. So magically and efficiently, he had left all this behind, and was now traveling the high road, with all them white folk and their white-folk ways. Now he was right back here in Niggaland. Maybe all Chantel needed was a guardian angel, too.

Chantel looked at James LeRoy Washington III as if she were the soul of all black women on earth. "You done got yourself a white woman, don' you?"

"I juss spent the past twelve years in prison, an' I been out less 'n two weeks. Now how you figure I got myself some white pussy stashed somewhere, like maybe on the bottom a dis here glass?" But James knew the answer. He'd screamed it through a megaphone.

"Oh, juss a feelin', Clayton George, juss a feelin'. Maybe you got one, 'n' maybe you don't—*yet!* But I know my men. Dat's one thing I know, 'n you want one, honey. *Ooooooo yeah!* I seen 'em come, 'n I seen 'em go. 'N dis nigga got da Jones for them nice light honky lips." Chantel placed a ten on the counter and confidently tipped her head back and poured the last fluid ounce down her throat. "If you change your mind, though, 'n you get lonely, I'll be in and out...if ya *know* what I mean." She then placed a packaged condom on the rim of James's shot glass and said, "Here's my business card, Clay." And with that, Chantel strutted her shapely fat ass out the broken-down hole-in-the-wall bar the same way she'd entered, just after conspicuously adjusting the front clip holding up her left stocking.

50   The Entropy

$$\oint \frac{dQ}{T} \le 0$$

Becker rarely drove, because he rarely left his house. But he did own a '48 Chrysler Windsor, which was the very car that had belonged to his parents, and the thought never crossed his mind that somehow the vortex of automotive entropy had avoided his ancient machine.

Actually, none of Becker's appliances seemed to age very much, including Becker himself, and the plight of the chaotic world, obsessed with the process of growing old, presented yet another curious anomaly to him; his universe was highly ordered, with everything in its proper place, properly maintained, and always operating within spec. In seclusion, the caustic effects of the world could be carefully dispensed with stoichiometric precision, but occasionally he did have to venture out into the sea of chaos, and therefore, the utmost care had to be taken with the old Chrysler.

When Becker operated his machine, he methodically went through a mental checklist, similar to a pilot's preflight check. First, he threw the big switch on the garage wall, and six powerful floodlights bathed the car in brilliant white light. He opened the hood and checked the oil, the wires, the fan belt, the fan, the distributor, the oil filter, and the radiator-fluid level. He measured the battery voltage with the meter he kept in the small glove compartment. He popped the top off the brake-fluid reservoir and touched the fluid with his index finger to examine both color and viscosity. He checked the tire pressure of each tire, including the spares; he kept two. He felt the rigidity of the steering linkages. He pressed his weight onto the car over each tire, assessing all four suspension responses. He visually inspected the exterior and the interior of the car, and he opened the toolbox in the trunk and inspected all the tools he might need in the event of a breakdown—out there in the world. Only when his static check was complete would he dare seat himself in front of the steering wheel and belt himself down with the seat belt he'd installed some years back.

He pulled the choke out and took one last look around the interior panel work. Then he pushed the starter button on the wooden front panel, and the engine turned over. A plume of gray smoke filled the garage interior, and as he carefully shifted into gear and began to roll, his electric garage door seemed to know all by itself that the car was now in gear and backing up. Once outside, in the driveway, the car passed the external group of IR photo detectors, and the door automatically closed and the floodlights went out. Next stop: the Whitestone Bridge, and Long Island. His destination today: the Cedarhurst Horticultural Club.

The Cedarhurst Horticultural Club met on the third Monday of every month in the basement of the Peninsula Public Library, and it was another one of several botanical clubs in the New York metropolitan area that Becker was investigating on his own. It seemed to Becker that bonsai clubs were sprouting up all over the place these days. In the past two weeks, he'd visited one up in West-chester, two in New Jersey, two out in Suffolk County, one in Hart-ford, Connecticut, and now this one. He was determined to attend at least one meeting of each and every club, to see the people for himself, firsthand. And what he saw was very disappointing—botanically speaking. Back in the old days, Becker even ran one of these clubs himself, over at the Bronx Botanical Gardens. Class size ranged from three all the way up to eleven one year. And with all those people, there were still too many. But back in those days, the enthusiasts were all quite serious about bonsai. These new clubs seemed to consist mostly of a bunch of middle-aged women on Valium, with too much time on their hands, strangling *Ficus benjaminas* with galvanized steel wire. Like all things nowadays, it was an ancient Eastern technology of restraint and patience gone wild with modernistic Western overin-dulgence and accelerated expectations. Nature can't be rushed, Becker sadly thought. But Becker's purpose was not to educate these people with self-proclaimed green thumbs, as much as it pained him to witness their inept butchery. When he saw all he needed to see, he quietly disappeared as mysteriously as he had arrived, without even so much as a glimmer of recognition from anyone in attendance that he was, perhaps, the foremost authority in the field.

Becker drove unlike most people. If, for instance, he were approaching a red light, he would impart only as much kinetic energy to his rolling mass as needed so that he would not have to apply the brakes and create heat, thus unnecessarily raising the entropy of the universe. He would also rate each of his driving maneuvers based upon how much rolling energy he was able to retain after the light changed or the cars moved, constantly weighing in his playful brain the multitude of probabilities that events external to the vehicle either would or would not occur before he had to apply the dreaded en-tropy-raising force of acceleration or deceleration. And he usually hummed a tone in his throat that would glissando up or down depending on what the car did, as if to simulate the sound of some giant acoustic generator or geared machinery directly coupled to the axles.

While Becker's method of driving on the urban road was

kind to all the moving parts in his car, and his throat, it was an insane form of harassment to all the surrounding stop-and-go jockeys, who only know to burn rubber to the last possible second, then screech to a halt within inches of a blocking obstruction.

As Becker drove south on the Van Wyck Expressway, he reminisced about his own horticultural classes, back in those good old days, and how far he'd come in all this time. And then his thoughts were interrupted by a carload of Puerto Ricans yelling at either him or his car; it was difficult to tell. "Yo mothafucka dude," one kid in the front seat yelled out the window, and Becker swerved a bit to keep his distance from the adolescent disturbance passing him. "Like yo' fuckin' tool, *mannnnnn*. Fuck you, you cocksucka *asshoooo....*" The young man's voice Doppler shifted away as he threw an empty Budweiser can at the rolling antique, but the wind caught it and it blew over the roof, just missing the top of the Chrysler's windshield. Becker slowed to 45 from the 52.5 he'd been cruising at, and then the carload of screaming hoodlums turned off onto the entrance ramp of the Long Island Expressway, heading west toward the city. Becker breathed a sigh of relief as he resumed cruising speed, but he knew the car would now require another full inspection.

At Kennedy Airport, the rush-hour traffic grew denser, and Becker worried about all the entropy and over exercising the clutch and brake of his machine, but it had gotten him this far, he reasoned; it would probably get him the rest of the way. And it did.

Becker pulled into the parking lot of the Peninsula Public Library, placed the transmission in neutral, and rolled between two parallel white lines with just enough momentum for his front wheels to touch the edge of the pavement. He set the emergency brake, and then ran to the front and popped the hood. He watched all the moving parts with the same fascination and wonder of those who first witnessed internal combustion, and he attentively listened to the music of the valves. He took a deep breath of the vapors. He behaved as if the car had suffered the same emotional trauma as he had at the hands of the Puerto Ricans. But it hadn't, because it was a machine, which Becker sometimes forgot, treating it more like a horse than a car. For the next five minutes, he communed with the rattle of the idling forty-five-year-old Chrysler engine, and from behind the raised hood he watched other cars fill the cramped lot. Based on the psychological profile he'd constructed from his attendance at the other horticultural clubs, he felt he could tell who was coming for the meeting and who was simply visiting the library. Of course, the ladies with the flowerpots tucked under their arms were dead giveaways.

And then a Mercedes pulled into the lot and took the last available space. He could see through the tinted windows that the driver was a woman. She removed a pair of poles, and then she removed twelve potted plants from the floors and the seats, one at a time. She hung six flowerpots from the evenly spaced hooks on one pole, and six on the other. Becker watched the fog from her breath in the cool air as she methodically attached the strings. Then she stood, with a pole over each shoulder, and walked up the stairs to the back door of the library.

She suddenly turned and looked straight at the antique car in the back of the lot, as if she knew it had been there all along, and, like a tortoise, Becker retracted his head behind the open hood of his car, and he hoped she hadn't seen his face.

He contemplated what he'd just seen for another minute, dropped the hood, shut off the engine, and locked the door. Then he briskly entered the library and walked up to the front desk. He asked a woman gazing into a computer screen where the Cedarhurst Horticultural Club met, and he was directed to the stairs, which led to the basement.

Becker slowly walked to the basement, and he was distracted by the student artwork that was Scotch-taped to the blue-painted cinderblock walls. He walked down a hallway, and stood outside the only door that he heard talking from the other side of. He listened, with his hand on the doorknob, waiting. And then the door flew open, startling him, and he was standing there face-to-face with the woman who had carried in all the plants. "I presume you're here for the Horticultural Club. Please come in and take a seat," she said, or, more accurately, ordered, so it seemed to Becker, who was psychologically thrown off balance by having the control of his entry so prematurely and efficiently stripped from him, as if this woman knew he was standing outside the door.

"Yes," Becker said, glancing at the eight women and one man seated at the long wooden table with their botanical projects before them, "I think . . . I will do that." He entered the room, and the woman closed the door behind him.

"My name is Dr. Frieda Marx, and I run the Cedarhurst Horticultural Club." She looked into Becker's eyes, and as Becker was about to introduce himself, she leaned closer to him and almost inaudibly said, "Dr. Instlokrownctjz, so good of you to join our quaint effort here. We have much to discuss—but after class." And with that, Dr. Marx took her place at the head of the table.

Becker watched this Frieda Marx conduct her class, and he could not believe what he was seeing. His mind was swirling with bizarre thoughts—thoughts of the past colliding with the future, like matter and antimatter, to produce an incomprehensible transformation of a human being. Could the Joseph Barton he'd known as a student so many years ago possibly be the Frieda Marx who stood before him now? The voice seemed similar, but Frieda Marx was so much more assertive as a female than Joseph Barton had ever been as a male. Becker had heard of these operations to change men into women, and even women into men—one of the weirder effects of modern society, he mused. He was less concerned with the stranger applications of plastic surgery than the arts of plant grafting, but protoplasm was not interchangeable with cytoplasm. Plants are not people, and plants have no emotions. Could it be that his former pupil Joseph Barton had been a woman pretending to be a man all along; or worse, could she have been a man surgically altered to become a woman?

Bursting with curiosity, Becker watched Frieda Marx cut a little wedge of branch from one ficus and graft it onto another ficus with a similar cut of shape and size, and her pupils observed what they would soon imitate. She buzzed from person to person, like a happy little bee, confident, affectionately nurturing and guiding each student, and always aware of Becker's presence, as if the principal were sitting in back of the class grading the teacher. And in some sense, he was, because this was the best horticultural class he'd visited yet. This Dr. Marx really knew her stuff. And she knew him, too— by name! She pronounced it correctly, and not too many people were capable of such a linguistic feat even after several introductions. If she were not Becker's former pupil, then she must have met him at one of the botanical conferences. Becker knew there were circles in which he was well known. He'd met so many people, though, and he couldn't begin to remember all their names or faces. The more

Becker pondered Frieda Marx, the more he realized that this was the only logical explanation. More comfortable within this perspective, his anxiety subsided slightly. She had met him sometime in the past and had simply remembered him. No more to it than that. But Becker watched Dr. Marx's upper lip. There was just a hint of pulled skin. Very strange. Very coincidental.

And the two hours passed, very slowly.

But all good things come to those who wait, and when the last of Dr. Marx's students departed, she turned to face Becker Instlokrownctjz. Each waited for the other to speak, but only the hum from the fluorescent fixtures on the ceiling serenaded the silence. They stared apprehensively, almost challengingly, at each other. And then Frieda finally said, "What brought you here, Doctor?"

The muscles in Becker's face relaxed, and he calmly said, "You are Joseph Barton, aren't you?"

"Do I look like this individual?" Frieda teased.

"You sound more like the way he used to sound than you presently look the way he used to look, but in essence, I believe you to be one and the same . . . I think. . . ."

Becker's face was all lit up, with his head tilted to the right, and Frieda watched that nervous left eye of his wiggling about in its socket, doing most of the work. "So much has happened . . . since you last knew me, Becker. I have a very interesting . . . and difficult story to tell you. In fact, as much as I awaited this moment, I dreaded it, knowing you might come . . . especially now, because . . . I have a completely different life, a successful life, and, now *you* are the only connection between what I was . . . and what I am. Do you understand what I am trying to tell you?"

Becker dipped his head with respect and said, "I presume that I should call you Frieda?"

"You presume correctly. I am Frieda Marx now. What you remember about who I was in the past is history. What I am now, is what I am. Why have you come?"

Becker hesitated, because he'd never thought about how he might answer such a direct question, and he couldn't very well come out and say, I think you are manufacturing hoopers, and the police think you are a raving lunatic, if it is you who is doing what we

248

think you might be doing. Instead, he awkwardly said, "I was looking through some old school records, and I wondered what had happened to my gifted young student Joseph." Frieda smiled curtly, and Becker continued: "My last record of you ended when you went off to Cornell. I think you called a couple of times since then. You were studying botany. And then we fell out of touch with each other. I decided to check some of the botanical clubs . . . thinking you could not have lost interest in . . . well, you know. What kind of doctor are you?"

"I'm a veterinarian."

"So you switched majors at Cornell?"

"Precisely. I got bored with . . . well, you know. But I never lost interest. Why have you really come, Dr. Instlokrownctjz?"

Becker was *really* not prepared for this direct a grilling, and he had come to find Joseph Barton anyway, not Dr. Frieda Marx. He felt a sudden panic-fueled urge to run out the door. "I just came looking for you. I have become very sen-ti-men-tal lately."

"Speaking of sentimental, I see you still have your '48 Chrysler Windsor. How's the old beast running?"

"It's running very well. It's like I always say . . ."

And Frieda joined in, and they both chanted in unison, "A little bit of preventive maintenance keeps *the en-tro-py* away." Then they both laughed. "The library closes soon," Frieda said as she began to string up the plants so she could take them back to the car. "And there is much to talk about. How would you like to come by the house?"

"Sounds like fun," Becker said, and helped his former pupil straighten up the place.

"We could get some Chinese food, and you'll meet . . . Julia." Frieda pursed her lips, slightly embarrassed.

"Who's Julia?"

"Julia . . . is the mother of Arthur, the man I almost married, and she has no knowledge of the existence of Joseph Barton, and that is just the way I would like to keep it. That's all I ask of you. She knows that I attended Cornell, but she does not know that I also attended Columbia, and who I was at the time."

"I will respect your wishes . . . Frieda."

"Thank you," Frieda said as she turned off the lights.

As Becker Instlokrownctjz drove from the library parking lot, he could not wait to tell Nigel that he'd found his former pupil from Columbia, Joseph Barton, who had undergone this remarkable transformation to become Frieda Marx, and that she was a veterinarian. Becker followed behind the Mercedes, and he now had no thoughts of Joseph Barton being Dr. Sigma, and certainly no thoughts of Frieda Marx being Dr. Sigma. Never having had firsthand knowledge of any transsexual, he was merely trying to acclimate himself to the concept of Frieda Marx being Joseph Barton, or vice versa. With the thought of Chinese food now firmly planted in his mind, his stomach growled—his focus on caloric consumption displacing even his fear of the entropy dissolving his car out from under him. Not paying much attention to the streets, or anything in particular, he followed Frieda past the golf course, where the woods grew thicker and the sky darker. He made a left, and then another left onto a narrow, overgrown driveway, and Becker followed the taillights all the way up to the house. The garage door automatically opened, and Frieda hopped out of her car and ran to Becker and said, "You park in the garage. It'll be better for your car." Becker looked at her, a bit confused, and she further prompted him with a smile and those magic words, "The en-tro-py; I remember." They both smiled, and Becker pulled into the garage.

As Becker executed the automotive shutdown procedure, Frieda said, "Remember, no mention of Joseph Barton or our past."

"I'll say that we met at Cornell. How's that?"

"Good. We met at Cornell . . . at an alumni reunion, with a common interest in . . . botany, which is true. Now Mama will probably try to marry us, so be prepared for endless suggestions and little innuendos."

This thought seemed mildly revolting to Becker, having only logged two hours with Joseph Barton as a woman, and as the garage door closed, locking them both inside, they entered the house from the basement steps. Frieda marched straight to the kitchen and yanked a Chinese menu out from under a '64 World's Fair magnet on the refrigerator, and then handed it to Becker as she put her hand on the telephone. "What would you like?" she asked. He studied the menu, then called off his MSG-free selections to Frieda, who combined it with hers and what she knew would be Julia's regular order. The moment Frieda hung up the phone, it rang, and she reflexively picked up—some kind of medical problem with a large dog. Becker instinctively wandered out of the kitchen, to leave her alone with her patient's technical details.

He drifted into the living room and saw a wheelchair at the base of the ornate spiral staircase. He looked up the stairs at the guiding track of the automatic lift mechanism. He'd heard about these lifts, but he'd never actually seen one up close, and his first instinct was to run upstairs and ride the machine around. Instead, he looked at all the things in the living room, seeing if he could determine where the influence of Joseph had affected this household. And when he saw the two glass doors and the greenhouse beyond, he had his answer. His face lit up as his pace quickened to see the goodies his former pupil was cultivating. He entered, and completely filled his lungs with the air.

Every greenhouse had its own characteristic smell to Becker —almost like a fingerprint. This one had an almost antiseptic component to it. He'd never smelled anything like it before. He pulled a string on a seventy-five-watt bare bulb and looked to the right, where the aisles were wide, then looked to the left, where the aisles were thin and more like trails. His natural instincts drew him in toward the less commercial section.

Becker was one of the few who could appreciate the botanical anomalies protruding from the soil in Frieda's greenhouse. He pulled the string on another bare bulb at the far end, and the plants became distinguishable. To Becker, every leaf had a name, and every cell belonged to a phylum, with its origins extending back to the first amino acids on the cooling planet. He strolled up and down the aisles, observing the plants and then the table with all the tools.

Then Becker heard a ruffling in the leaves, and Frieda said, "Food's ordered, and Mom is dressing." With a nod of her head toward the plants she continued, "Well, whadda ya think?"

"Quite . . . im-press-ive, I must say. Very in-ter-es-ting. I'm glad to see that you maintained our in-ter-est in . . . in-ter-es-ting plants."

"To this day, your influence is still felt."

"Thank you," Becker said with a smile, then glanced at a large area of the same species of plant. "I see that you have a rather large garden of *Chondodendron tomentosum.**"

"Yes. I do."

"Any par-tic-u-lar reason?"

Frieda looked at Becker, more at all of him than at any specific feature of his face. With a detached coldness, she instinctively knew what she might have to do, and when she might have to do it. But Becker was waiting patiently for an answer, which finally came. "I discovered something interesting about the molecule. It appears that the replacement of one of the hydroxyls with another methyl group makes a tremendous difference."

"Which one, if you don't mind me asking—the one up by the salt-binding nitrogen, or the one . . . with the ox-y-gen bond?"

"You never cease to amaze me, Dr. Instlokrownctjz." Becker smiled. "The ring with the oxygen bond."

"Very in-ter-es-ting," Becker looked up to the ceiling and smiled. "That must be very . . . relaxing," Becker sensed that this was one of his funnier remarks for the day, which it was, because his former pupil had serendipitously stumbled on a way to modify the chemical structure of the extract from this native plant.

---

* Curare.

"I have never sampled it myself," Frieda casually said, "but it seems to have less side effect, based on my clinical studies . . . on animals."

"On animals? Have you written up the work? It sounds like it might be useful."

"I haven't really had the time, but I'm sure I'll get around to it, eventually."

"I have so many questions," Becker said, mildly over-whelmed with the life of his former pupil. In his mind, he could not directly think of the person before him as Frieda Marx. Joseph Barton was the first thought that always popped into his head; then he had to consciously make the substitution, the same way novice language students can't immediately compose sentences in a new language, needing first to express a thought in the native tongue, then do the translation. "I wish you'd have kept in touch. Tell me what happened when . . . well, how it came to be that . . . you are who you are?"

"It's a *very* long story, and I'll answer *all* your questions, but I just remembered the plants out in the car, and . . . there are a few other things I have to . . . take care of. I'll be right—"

"I'll help you," Becker said, preparing to leave with her.

"No, no. Why don't you amuse yourself here for a moment. I'll be *right* back." And with that said, Frieda left the solarium and disappeared back across the living room and down the stairs. But she did not go to the car for the plants.

In the greenhouse, Becker lost himself in the craftsmanship of the bonsai trees and the wealth of semitropical plants. About five minutes passed, and Becker began to think about food again, and about this person Julia who Frieda called Mom. He wanted to know how it was that Frieda happened to be living in the house of the man she almost married, as she put it. Where was he? Did he live there, too? Becker felt that Frieda was certainly piquing his interest, whether deliberate or not. The next time Frieda appeared, he was not going to let her go until she told him all about herself.

And then she came and grabbed his hand. "Come, I have something to show you." She led him to the basement. "When I helped you build your underground room, I knew that someday . . . I would build one of my own. I have something . . . *wonderful* to show you, Professor."

Becker eagerly followed, propelled by a seductive, overpowering curiosity he could not explain, and Frieda guided him to the big sliding door with the *Threepenny Opera* poster on it. She unlatched the door and slid it halfway open. At first, Becker hesitated. She tugged on his hand, and he followed—down the steep slope, into the egg room, and the source of the antiseptic smell.

52 Becker's Ring

Becker Instlokrownctjz entered Frieda's egg room, and his first thought was that this was a dangerous place. But it was also a fascinating underground place, and he was hypnotically drawn in by its strangeness, regularity, and seductive shape. As he neared the base of the incline, he saw what appeared to be a wooden structure on wheels, and it was filled with wine bottles on racks. "You built this place?" Becker asked with great admiration.

"Yes. I built it with my own two hands."

"Very im-pres-sive."

"Very impressive? It's beautiful!" Frieda bellowed with pride. "It took me eight years to build. What do you *really* think, Professor?"

While Becker could appreciate the dedication and drive of this woman, or whatever he'd turned into, he felt a definite pull to walk right out exactly the way he'd walked in. But he also felt a compulsion to stay and see more. "I . . . I think . . . eight years it took?"

"Yes. Eight years."

Becker looked around the perimeter of the room. He could see what appeared to be lots of medical equipment mounted on rolling racks. There was black cloth around some of the objects in the room, and a pair of black curtains blocked off both ends of the room.

"Look at it, Doctor! Look around you. One point eight three million pounds of dirt, with *no* student help—all by myself."

"Unbelievable. I presume the walls are ferro-cement."

"Precisely. Just like yours. I learned well, *Professor*."

This Frieda Marx was making Becker feel increasingly uncomfortable, and thoughts were beginning to percolate in his mind that perhaps he should go check on his car. "Why did you build it? I mean, it's not as if you're exactly at a loss for space out here in the suburbs."

"You disappoint me, Dr. Instlokrownctjz. I thought you, of *all* the people in the world, would know the answer to that."

"I built *my* rooms because I needed the space. I'd simply run out of room, and I had that wonderful granite and gneiss mountain next to me. . . ."

"Well, I needed the *privacy*, for . . . *my work*."

Becker looked at the door, then at her, slightly perplexed, and said, "Exactly what *is* your work?"

Frieda slinked over to a tall rectangular box, and she threw open a curtain, exposing a bright light from within, and there appeared to be something botanical inside. "Look, Becker. Look at what I have made, from *your* very blueprint." Becker cautiously walked toward the bright light in the box against the far wall. Frieda had a huge grin on her face. "Come," she said, beckoning him forward like a game-show mistress with her luring hands. She suddenly seemed very feminine, very soft, *and* very crazy.

Becker looked in the box, and he saw the ring. "You made one," he said with joy. "You actually made one!"

He gazed at Becker's Ring—the very plant *he* had proposed so many years ago! Becker leaned over the clay pot that this marvelous creation drew nutrients from. It was a five-inch-diameter ring of well-groomed little bonsai trees—thirty-two of them—a little ring of trees, and they had all grown together to form one single cytoplasmic entity. All their cambium layers had fused together as the diameters of each tree grew, but their center-to-center spacing remained fixed, and finally, in time, they had all bumped up against one another, and the magic began, aided, of course, by some skillful incisions. Becker had only proposed such a creation, but now someone had actually gone ahead and made one. Becker had even proposed a full-scale version—one using full-sized trees to create a ring large enough to live in. But on any scale, it was a thing of beauty —this icon that lay before him. "It's beautiful," he said. "Simply beautiful."

"I knew you would come back, eventually," Frieda said with gleaming eyes. "How philosophically appropriate that, of all the people in the world, you have returned to be part of this great work, as if you knew instinctively that it was now time to return home to the nest, your nest, like the inescapable drive of the salmon returning to that one spawning nursery. *Oh,* this was somehow all meant to be."

Crazy talk, Becker thought. He had come of his own free will. And then he heard what he thought was the groan of a person. "Is there someone in here with us?" Becker said, looking around with a growing sense of alarm.

"Professor, I have taken your work to . . . *new levels.*"

Becker walked to the curtain, turned to face Frieda, and said, "It *is* you, isn't it?!" Then he flung the curtain aside and saw a blindfolded Hispanic man lying on a horizontal board, with an intravenous line feeding into the subclavian vein of his neck.

"Joseph . . . I mean Frieda, you call this 'new levels'? I taught you science. This is not science. This is wrong."

"NO, Professor!! This is right. It is *society* that is wrong!" Frieda pointed to the man on the board. "What *they* do is wrong. What *I* do is right. I right the wrong that society is incapable of righting! Doctor, recall your basic chemistry. An oxygen atom is highly reactive, and corrosive to its environment. Bind one oxygen atom with another, and you have the much more stable and less reactive oxygen molecule. But I have transcended molecular chemistry. I am now a social chemist. I am binding up the free radicals, so to speak, so they are less reactive. And clearly I cannot trust you."

Becker alternated glances between the man on the slab and Frieda Marx, temporarily suspending his disbelief as she removed a pistol and pointed it at him.

Then a bell rang from a speaker on the wall, and Frieda said with a sudden jerk of her head, "Food's here . . . but I'm afraid you won't be dining with us as originally planned."

Pfffft.

Pfffft.

Two darts flew into Becker's body from twelve feet away, and he stared at her in disbelief. His former pupil said, "I'm sorry I had to do this, Professor. We'll chat later. I mustn't keep Julia waiting."

Becker watched her calmly walk up the ramp. Then he heard

the sliding door slam shut, followed by a stout latching noise like the kind he'd heard in large walk-in refrigerators. He pulled one of the tranquilizer darts from his gut, just below his rib cage on the left side, and he pulled the other from just above his belly button. He dropped them on the floor as he jogged up the ramp to test the door to see if he could get out. He was definitely locked in, and it would only be a matter of time, he reasoned, before he would collapse like the tranquilized large African cats he'd seen on *Wild Kingdom* on the television.

Frieda paid the delivery man as Julia rode the lift all the way to the bottom. She wore a white blouse and a gray skirt, and her favorite pearl necklace draped over her breastbone. She wiggled herself off the lift and into the wheelchair, and she rolled herself into the dining room as Frieda set the table and spread out the containers of food. Julia patted her blue hair with both hands, then said, "I thought you said there was company."

"There was. But he had to leave in a hurry—some kind of emergency."

"Oh, that's *too* bad. Who is he?" Julia said with the matchmaker's gleam in her eye.

"An old friend." Then Frieda smiled, shook her finger at Julia, and said, "And I know exactly what you're thinking, Mother, so stop it."

Becker shook the man strapped to the restraint board, but he was nonresponsive—bordering on unconsciousness. This man had both an antiseptic and alcoholic smell about him. Becker delicately removed the catheter from the man's neck in the hopes that he would eventually come to. He then removed all the man's restraint straps. It was a long shot, and Becker expected to be unconscious shortly, but perhaps this man, who ever he was, would spring to consciousness, and save him by clobbering Frieda Marx over the head with a tool. He slapped the man's face to try to coax him to consciousness, but he was too groggy and out of it.

Becker could feel himself growing light-headed in waves. It all began to seem rather funny. Then Becker wondered whether there was a telephone in this wacky room. At least *he* had the decency to keep the natural rock walls in *his* underground rooms and tunnels. This thing was so geometrically perfect. It must have been the combination of that stupid Long Island sand, and the woman hidden inside the Joseph Barton he never knew.

Becker studied the shape of the room, and began estimating the cubic footage, but he became lost in the calculation of multiplying π times the major diameter of the room times the minor diameter of the room, if the room was, in fact, an ellipse at all. Now where would one keep a telephone in here? he thought. Against the wall, silly . . . but the wall is everywhere. It was all becoming very funny—especially if Joseph Barton decided to connect me and this Spanish gentleman together . . . just like that plant over there . . . the ring is the key to his—her madness! Becker thought in his delirium. The ring is the key!. . .

After scooping out several liberal portions of food, Frieda said to Julia, "I have to check something. I'll be right back." Frieda walked to the basement and removed the dart pistol from a shelf where she'd left it. She unlocked the door to the egg room and slid it open with caution. Then she discovered the handiwork of her old professor. She looked at Becker's unconscious body and said aloud with a smile, "Nice try, Dr. Instlokrownctjz." She methodically reattached the restraints to Julio Rodriquez and replaced the IV catheter entering his neck. She filled a hypo with fluid from a bottle she removed from the refrigerator. "It's good to know that, after all these years, you can still impress me." And then she gave Becker the injection, and said, "Sleep well, Professor. We have so much to discuss."

. . . God does not know accidents.
—MARY BAKER EDDY,
FOUNDER OF CHRISTIAN SCIENCE

Becker knew he was drugged as he lay there, on his back, staring into the blankness of the egg room. Becker was unfamiliar with profoundly altered states of consciousness. He liked having total command of his intellectual faculties, and for him an occasional cup of coffee or an even less occasional peppermint schnapps was more than enough. His head felt clogged, and periodically he had the sensation that his entire body was suddenly jolting one or two feet to the right or the left. It was disorienting and nauseating in one sense, but almost pleasant in another. He found it difficult to remember exactly what he was thinking from one second to the next. He then remembered what he had to do, and he attempted to lift his arms and legs to test the restraints which held him flat on his back and completely immobile.

Frieda Marx slid open the door with the *Threepenny Opera* poster on it and entered the wine room. She grabbed a piece of rope from a shelf and hooked the loop end over an eyelet screwed into the far wall. She pulled the rope tightly and wrapped it several times around another hook attached to the wall outside, and held to rope firmly. Then she knelt down and pressed a lever near the floor to the right, under the lowest shelf, and then she pressed a similar lever on the left. The floor moved slightly, then she backed out, while holding the rope.

    The entire closet was mounted on wheels, like a wagon. Frieda payed out line and lowered this wine-room facade down the cement incline, all the way into the egg room. Then she entered and walked directly to Julio Rodriquez, who was mumbling nonsense again with a half grin. She wanted him unconscious, so she turned the stopcock to one of his bottles clockwise and the other counter clockwise. Within a minute, his heart rate and respiration dropped.

"There," she said, and went to the refrigerator to get Becker's new IV solution. It was time for her little chat with her old professor. She changed his bottle while smiling sympathetically, as if he were a naughty child who needed some detention therapy to effect the desired attitude change. "How *are* we this morning, Dr. Instlokrownctjz?"

Becker had heard the·sound of the wine bottles rattling around as the closet was being lowered into this space, but he didn't know exactly what it was he was hearing. He did think he recognized his name, and he groaned as he processed and reprocessed the words he thought he heard. "Frieda?" he said.

"Yes. I am here. Please hold on a moment, Doctor. I am going to tilt the board up so you can stand. You may become a bit light-headed." Frieda removed a stout metal pin and then rotated Becker to the vertical position. She locked him into position, and his weight shifted to his feet while remaining strapped to the board. "There. You'll feel better in a minute or two."

Becker needed answers, and he fought the drugs. "Why are you doing this?"

"I told you why. It is necessary."

"Why is it . . . necessary?"

"Because society is misguided at this time in history, and society needs a little guidance," Frieda said with a touch of mysticism in her voice. "I can provide that guidance, and now is the time. This is the moment we have *all* been waiting for."

"What moment is that?"

"The ring, Doctor, the ring is complete, so now it is time to bind up all the naughty free radicals."

Becker felt the return of some mental clarity, perhaps, he thought, at the expense of Frieda's. "You mean . . . the men on parole?"

"Exactly! *Seeeeee,* I knew why you came here all along. But then again, I knew you would come eventually, *anyway.*"

"How?"

"Because we are similar, you and I . . . except that your blood is B positive."

This is not what Becker wanted to be hearing. This conversation had started out all wrong to begin with, and it was now leaning in an even less desirable direction. "I think I'm beginning to under-stand."

"NO!" she snapped. "You don't understand anything! You do *not* understand the first thing about me, or Arthur! You don't understand who I was before you met me, Dr. Instlokrownctjz. You knew me only as . . . Joseph Barton—one slice in a continuum of transformations. Before that, I was Emily, Emily Gordon. Professor, just how much do you know about Christian Science?"

"Christian Science? Next to nothing."

"Let me tell you a little bit about Christian Science, Doctor. Christian Science is not like *real* science. In fact, Christian Science, like many other products of the human psychosis throughout history, is not very far from exactly the opposite of real science. One particular attribute peculiar to the Christian Science brand of miracles and madness is their rejection of medicine, and any medical procedure, no matter how large or small, no matter how necessary or frivolous. When you get sick, if it is God's will for you to get better, then you get better. Hallelujah! If it is God's will that you should die, then you should die. Amen! Except for prayer, no intervention by man is permissible, because no mere mortal can or should interfere with the handiwork of the omnipotent Lord, who dispenses all good medicine, spiritually and naturally, in that pharmaceutical-free waiting room for the cemetery that embraces us all, sooner or later.

"And it was in the spirit of this belief system, that *one little girl* came into the world with a congenital birth defect, a birth defect for which Western medicine has a common name: a cleft palate and harelip, tragically obvious from the moment *little Emily* exited her mother's birth canal and breathed her first breath of unassisted life through her deformed little nostrils and mouth. That little girl was *me*, Professor. That little girl was *ME!*"

In Becker's mind, details from the past were now beginning to fall into place, but he sensed it was far more complicated than he had originally imagined. He looked at Frieda, who was wide-eyed and manic, and he said, "Then it was you who came to visit Columbia."

"Yes. I met you two years before I first attended classes there."

"I always wanted to ask you that."

"Yes, Dr. Instlokrownctjz, I'm sure you did. But you were always so polite—a regular old-fashioned gentleman. It was so good of you to drop by so I could finally tell you my life's story. Arthur was the only one who knew the complete truth about me. Dear Arthur. Do you know how lonely it gets . . . when you live a secret life? Yes, I first met you when I was a senior in Accident, Pennsylvania. Accident, Pennsylvania. What a joke. Accident, Pennsylvania—the town that fell with the buttered side down! Accident. I WAS THE ACCIDENT!!!" Frieda screamed, practically in tears now. "How I *hate* Accident, Pennsylvania, with all its . . . *stupid* people living *stupid* lives in a *stupid* town in a *stupid* state full of *stupid* people!"

Frieda was now speaking with a scathingly sarcastic edge. "In the *normal* wing of the Western world, problems like mine are corrected shortly after birth. But in the *Christian Science* world, these things stay with you for *life,* indelibly *marking* you, *permanently,* because it is all part of *God's* plan, not the fault of some complex chemistry of *replication.* And with the mark of deformity comes all the social responsibility as well. No child with such a physical deformity could ever be expected to survive the *public school system* without absorbing every scorn, humiliation, and the *limitless* cruelty of the *stupid* children you're surrounded by, and so it was for *me,* Professor. Do you have any idea what it must have been like for me to grow up in . . . Accident, Pennsylvania, where two plus two does not equal four?"

"No," Becker quietly replied, not wanting to further rile Frieda. All she would have to do is turn a little knob, and he would wake up six weeks later joined to the unconscious man on the other side of the room.

"Of course you don't know what it was like to grow up in Accident, Pennsylvania, my old professor. *Nobody* knows what it was like, because the carbon atom left me with a little *extra* gift, compliments of *Mommy* and *Daddy* and *Christian Science.* Would you believe me if I told you that I had a little *extra* piece of skin on me as well as my facial deformity? Yes Professor, now we're getting a little closer to home. I had a penis. I was a little girl, *and* I was a little boy. Now what exactly do you suppose the odds of *that* were, Professor? I estimate somewhere between a billion, and . . . a trillion to one. Luckily, I was able to hide *that* one a little better than my face. In gym, I would always turn away from the other girls when I dressed, and I always wore baggy underwear so it hid the other . . . stranger half of my gender.

"I don't know how you *men* manage to live with a penis." Frieda's face grimaced, as if she were about to vomit. "It's so . . . *disgustingly* male. You know, it's really a disgraceful organ—one you'd all be better off without. It gets in the way, and it sticks out—just like an electrode of some kind." Frieda smiled sardonically. "Yes, just like an electrode.

"Did you know, I used to urinate from both orifices? Yes, it's true. Usually the penis is nonfunctional in these types of cases. *Ahhhhh,* but not *mine.* I had a bifurcated urinary tract. Yes, I could pee from the penis *and* my urethra simultaneously—my Urethra Franklin; that's what I used to call it. At first, when I was little, if I sat, I could make urine come out of my urethra by pinching the penis closed with my fingers, and I could almost make it work the other way around, but I never had one hundred percent control over the parallel circuit. I was always working on my muscular control—to perfect it to go out of one or the other. One day, I would practice being a boy; the next day, I would practice being a girl. Boy, then girl, then boy, then girl. Sometimes, to amuse myself, I would make it come from one, then the other, then back again, and see how many alternations I could do before my bladder was empty. Nine times, if you're interested. Once, I can remember, when I was Joseph, I embarrassed myself at the urinal, because I leaked a little into my underpants . . . from below. I knew I was taking a risk, but I wanted to try being a boy back then. How many people have *that* opportunity? And that was the period of time when you knew me, Doctor.

"Christian Science!" Frieda growled.

Becker could not believe what he was hearing. He could not believe what he was seeing. He could not believe that he was strapped up by a raving lunatic who had typed his blood with a purpose in mind. And the mind of the Joseph Barton he had known was logical and methodical and would not waste time doing anything unnecessary, no matter what its hormone composition might have been.

And that voice continued: "Ever since I was a little girl, I knew the operation to fix my face existed. I did my research, as always. I did my homework. I always did my homework, because I was such a good little child. I begged Daddy for permission to see

263

the doctor and get the operation. Daddy explained it to me, over and over, about God and all. But it never seemed to make any sense. After all, I'd seen all the medical pictures—you know, the before and after pictures, and it was God's will that *they* should all be cured. Why not me? It just didn't make any sense." Frieda continued speaking as if she were talking to a toddler. "But Daddy told me I would understand someday. Mommy told me I would understand someday. All the people down at the *reading room* told me I would understand someday. They all said I would *thank* them someday. They told me I would know God's love. They told me I was loved by Jesus. Mary Baker Eddy says in her books that God does not know accidents—accidents like me? They read me testimony after testimony of people healed by only the power of loving thoughts and prayer. Janey Beth was walking down the street and then she sprained her little ankle. *'Janey Beth prayed reeeeeeeal hard, and by the time she walked her good little ass up to the front door, she was aaaaaaaaaalllll better. Seeeeeee! Look at the power God has to heal.'* Love and goodness fills space, and evil is nothingness. *Fuck* them all!!! You have *no* idea how much I *hate* those people. You have no idea how much I *hated* my parents. Yeah, I would understand someday.

"Well, I graduated from high school early, when I was sixteen, and I left home for good, and I came to New York. But my freshman year at Columbia would have to be delayed, because I needed to get the operation on my face already, so I could get on with my life, with no connection to the past. Do you know I legally changed my name to Joseph Barton from Emily Gordon?"

"No," Becker squeaked. "I had no idea. How could I?—"

"You couldn't, because I never told you. I had to escape that place, and everything associated with that place—even my gender. Yeah. I outgrew *Christian Science* all right. And I studied *real* science for a change.

"You can't imagine how it felt when the bandages finally came off. For the first time, I could look into a mirror and see the face *I* wanted to see, not that accidental mask the God of my parents intended for me to pass through life wearing. My parents were furious with me for such defiant behavior. I never spoke to them again. It was no great loss, either. The older they got, the crazier they got. Mommy was spending almost all her time down at the reading room.

And Daddy—dear Daddy—I remember one day he came into the bathroom when I was peeing. I wanted to show him how I was almost able to control my wee-wee from either hole. I called it my 'water tricks.' I wanted to show Daddy my water tricks. He beat me ... and made me cry ... and told me never to do that again. He said God would punish me if I did that. *Christian* Science, and *real* science; *Christian* scientists, and *real* scientists. If you ever want a good laugh, you should try reading some of their literature. I never heard so much self-referential circular reasoning—tautological sequential disconnected thoughts ... strung together like long run-on sentences with no beginning, no middle, no end—truly torturous reading for the scientific mind, but not the Christian Scientific mind. Christian Science is about as close to real science as an amoeba is to an ape!

"Professor, you don't understand why I'm doing what I'm doing? Society is like Christian Science. Society has gone Christian Science on murderers! I have gone real science. They do nothing. I do something. Nothing. Something. Christian Science. Real science. Get it! GET IT!!!

"Dr. Instlokrownctjz, do you remember when I switched from engineering to biology?"

"Yes, I do."

"Well, the following winter, Daddy got sick and died—some kind of respiratory failure; nobody really ever knew for sure. I heard the news, and the symptoms, from the Honorable Judge Ernest Richardson; he was the probate court judge who allowed me to legally change my name to Joseph Barton.

"And less than a year after Daddy *dropped dead,* Mommy cracked the car into a phone pole, and five days later it was God's will that the doors to heaven open, to admit one, as a result of excessive blood loss, infection, and high fever, although the blasphemous bulb of a thermometer never touched her faithful lips.

"Then I met Arthur...."

At 4:30 in the morning a '48 Chrysler Windsor turned left into the sand lot off 25A in the town of Mattituck. Frieda hopped out and removed the license plates from the bumpers. Then she shifted Becker's car into first gear and drove up the overgrown dirt road—the same road she had driven along the day she abducted Rusty Blake. She drove the old car up the path and into the woods by one of the many swamps. The car came to rest, with the front wheels sinking into the muddy water, inside a giant mass of sticker bushes. Such a shame, she thought as she removed her bicycle from the backseat.

Frieda didn't want to be out here in the first place. She'd been visiting the neighborhood of Clayton George for the past two weeks. And she'd sighted him, too—several times. It's amazing how little some people change in twelve years. And Becker had changed very little, too, but his appearance had complicated things, and had disrupted the timetable. But a scientist must be adaptable. A true scientist must boldly seize opportunity. A true scientist must always have a backup plan. The appearance of Becker would have to be transformed into an opportunity. Yes, everything was becoming so clear.

"Sorry about the entropy, Doctor," Frieda said as she tossed the keys and plates into the swamp, then removed her leather gloves, "but you should have stayed in the Bronx, tinkering with your toys and projects."

She carried her bike through the woods, back up to the trail. She straddled the seat, and figured she had more than enough time to pedal to the more populated town of Riverhead to catch the 6:07 back to civilization. Such a shame.

The little girl was asleep once again, with tears in her eyes, reviewing her childhood memories, categorizing in exactly how many ways her father had damaged her beyond repair. A cesspool of anger raged behind her reddened eyeballs. He'd been dead for so many years, and while he was still alive, she'd never told him how much she hated what he'd done to her, making her go through life as a circus freak. And he got off easily—by dropping dead. He never suffered nearly as much as he should have, considering what he'd done.

Emily, the child, prayed for the existence of a hell, so that her parents should go there. She wanted to torture them the same way they passively tortured her, to deform them—for God. This would be the thanks she would give to them all. She would thank them all someday! *WHEN HELL FREEZES OVER!!!* she always thought.

But Frieda, the methodical and scientific shell around Emily, knew that there was no heaven and hell, no God and no Satan. Too bad. She pitied what their faith had done to the little girl she once was, and faith can *never* be understood or explained; it can only be sympathized with, like any untreatable mental disorder.

But her religion had influenced her life in more ways than she ever cared to admit to herself. She hated the people who had imprisoned her inside a deformed body, a body easily correctable with a sharp knife and a skilled hand. And the hatred created the guilt, which created false repentance, which created still deeper hatred, which created more guilt, and it grew, and it grew, like swirling particles accelerating in the cyclotron of her overactive mind.

As she lay half-awake, she remembered the children putting chewing gum on her seat when she'd gotten up to go to the bathroom. She remembered the children imitating the way that she spoke with her lisp. "Thuffering Thuckatath (Suffering Succotash)," they would say to tease her. "Thuffering Thuckatath. Here comes Thuffering Thuckatath."

She remembered coming home all bloody from the fights she always got into in the schoolyard and on the school bus, and on the streets, and everywhere she ever went. "MONSTER FACE," they called her. They mocked her. "Here comes Monster Face!" She remembered the time when she'd been hit on the head with the volleyball in the schoolyard. It was deliberate. And the teachers made *her* apologize to the girl who had hit *her*, telling *her* it was an accident, when she knew that it was deliberate. All the girls knew it was deliberate, but they pretended it was an accident to make *her* look bad when she fought back. They all knew that it was deliberate, even the teachers. *Especially* the teachers. It was like some grand crazy plot against her. Everyone played their part in the play.

And it was all her father's fault when all the fluff was boiled away. It was always her father's fault. Dear sweet Daddy, always there to pick up the pieces, and he created those pieces in the first place. Tears rolled down her face in the morning light. *I HATE YOU, DADDY!!!* she screamed in her mind. *I HATE YOU!!! I HATE YOU!!! I HATE YOU!!! I hope you died miserably! . . .*

"Next stop, Jamaica," the voice of the conductor said, "Next stop, Jamaica."

Frieda wiped the tears from her eyes, grabbed the fold-up bicycle, and exited the train.

Frieda returned to the house, took a quick shower, and returned to the egg room to check on Becker and Julio Rodriquez. She changed Becker's solution and tipped his board up. *"Professor,"* she sang, "how are we?"

Becker was groggy, and he had no idea how much time had elapsed since his last conversation with his former pupil. He flexed his hands and toes to see if they were still attached to the rest of him. The last thing he remembered was Frieda mumbling something about Arthur being a urologist and performing a penectomy on her to make her a complete woman—and that Frieda and Arthur fell in love shortly afterward. Becker then remembered her doing something to the mixture. And now he heard her voice again, and he opened his eyes.

For the time being, Frieda refrained from telling Becker that she had just returned from disposing of his car. *"Professor?"*

"Frieda?"

"Yes, I am here."

"How long was I out for?"

"You were asleep all night. It's morning."

"Why are you doing this to *me?*"

"You speak as if I we are doing something bad. Dr. Instlokrownctjz, you are to be witness to a great experiment—not only a great biological experiment, but an even *greater* social experiment." Frieda was beaming with manic energy. "The world has regressed, and it has developed new methods and ludicrous techniques to handle the murderers and the troublemakers that ruin life for the rest of us. But the world is stupid, and getting stupider by the minute, and therefore any method devised by a defective, politically based, fundamentally stupid culture could not possibly work. You wouldn't let a child design a bridge, would you? You wouldn't let a child perform an operation. You wouldn't let a child run an aircraft carrier. But we let children run the country. We let silly children determine the future direction the world is headed. These *poor children* are ill equipped to deal with real problems, because they are stupid, and they cannot see. But *I* can see. I have developed my own methods for solving the problem. You must admit, Professor, my methods are far more effective, far more creative, far more . . . permanent? Have you turned on your TV lately?"

"Yes, I have. And I think you are doing magnificent work. I would like very much to help. . . ."

"You cannot help us. We must continue the work alone."

"By us, you mean . . . me and you?"

"No, Doctor," Frieda sadly said. "Arthur and I. You see, this is *our* project."

"I thought you said that Arthur . . . had passed on."

"Arthur's *body* is dead, but *he* is right here with me, in here. Through the power of our minds, he now lives with me."

"You mean . . . the memory of Arthur?"

"No. Him. His mind. Who he is. He's in here, with me," she said, holding her bosom. With a twinkle in her eyes, Frieda tapped her head with her finger. "I absorbed him. . . ."

This conversation was beginning to depress Becker, and he was beginning to realize that he might never find any combination of words to influence his former pupil to release him, because his former pupil was psychotic.

But Frieda didn't have time for Becker or his bad moods. There was much to do today, and it was time to make preparations. She turned the valves.

56   Two Dark Shadows

James LeRoy Washington III had been checking out the bars of northern Manhattan, the hookers, the drug hangouts, and the numbers scene. He knew Inwood Park intimately. He knew every entrance to the park. He'd hiked all the trails. He knew where all the holes in the fences were, the location of the rock shelter caves, the drainage culverts, and all the retaining walls. He knew the entire shoreline, and just how rotted away all the rivets on the Henry Hudson Bridge were. He'd walked the old abandoned tracks of the West Side Rail Line as far south as the train tunnel where homeless people lived.

James had managed to become a regular fixture in the neighborhood at a greatly accelerated rate, and he'd met many of the same people Clayton George used to know before Clayton visited the big house for a dozen years. Many of Clay's old buddies were either dead or in prison. Still others, James knew from the police file on Clayton. Many of the regular neighborhood characters, even if they had nothing on record to do with Clayton George, he knew from the conveniently provided police records on the neighborhood fauna. James had committed over a hundred of them to memory. If one walked up to him on the street, and knew him, he knew who they were and pretended he'd known them forever, with the warm greeting, prison stories, and the full nine yards. And still others James had to subtly pry the past out of with cross-referenced leading questions. It seemed that James often knew more about what he was supposed to have done than the people who supposedly experienced that shared history firsthand. People's lack of memory never ceased to amaze James, and this he attributed to innate stupidity, synergistically multiplied by drugs and alcohol. In any event, it worked to his advantage, and

James was beginning to like the thrill of undercover work and the sense of control and power one feels from possessing information and a secret life.

Through this one random walk in this slice of neighborhood life from the perspective of a man named Clayton George, James was able to keep his finger on the pulse of enough seedy activity that it was surprising, if not astonishing to him, that the police were doing as poor a job as they actually were. It seemed to James that a single blindfolded cop could accidentally produce more anticrime results than the entire police force combined could deliberately produce. And James kept meticulous records of all the people he met and the activities they were involved in. Lieutenant Kramer spoke to James at least once a day, and while incidental crime was not an objective, it was noted for future reference. James still had much to learn about such things as accountability, correct police procedure, and the law. But his heart was in the right place, which, for the moment, was safely beating inside his chest.

At times, it seemed that this whole decoy exercise was one big crazy wild-goose chase which was eating up tremendous police resources. But Brent was committed to every aspect of the investigation, and he kept the political dogs at bay as best as he could. Brent periodically briefed the mayor directly, and the police commissioner and Captain Percella were the best help when it came to smoke-screening the press.

What James LeRoy Washington III saw from his myopic perspective was only the tip of an investigative iceberg which, by now, also involved the FBI. At least it started out with the bureau's computers and databases, but increasing personnel demands were drawing manpower from less publicized police work. And there are still only so many hours in a day. The world and its tabloids had their hungry eye on this case, though, and the administration wanted Dr. Sigma found and permanently separated from his scalpel.

Until one cold Wednesday, on the night of the freak snowstorm, when James LeRoy Washington III sat at his table in Kappy's Bar, drinking his Wild Turkey on the rocks. Two black men entered the doorway. The time was about one o'clock in the morning, which technically made it Thursday. They both wore leather jackets and pointy black shoes. The taller of the two wore aviation shades, and he had a perfectly groomed mustache and goatee. The shorter wore a slick dress hat with a small red feather, and red leather gloves. Slight bulges protruded from the left side of both men, which to James meant they were both right-handed professionals. He instinctively knew these dudes were bad people. It didn't take a genius to figure out. The moment the pair of silhouettes appeared in the doorway, all talking hushed, the same way the forest creatures grow silent when the hawks fly overhead. These men were the hawks. Bad hawks.

The smaller hawk brushed the snow from his jacket and scanned the bar, registering all the personnel. And then they saw James, although the man with the shades didn't move his head a millionth of a degree. They began to walk, slowly and cautiously, arms to their sides, fingers spread wide apart. James felt the emergency directional transmitter in his shirt and the cellular phone transmitter in his pants. The men were approaching him. No mistake about it. Outwardly, James seemed casual and disinterested, but inside he was scared. Burning, excited fear—like liquid nitrogen pouring down the nerves of his spinal cord. These men kept walking toward him. They could blow him away at any second if they wanted. James considered pressing that button right below his shirt pocket. But he waited. Everyone in the bar saw the men approaching Clayton George. Both men stopped in unison, in front of James's table, and watched him drink without saying a word. James deliberately moved the glass to his lips extra slowly. Extra cool. And he still hadn't acknowledged the presence of the two dark shadows, except by his slow and purposely nonthreatening motions.

The shorter of the two gentlemen allowed his jacket to swing open, revealing to James the modified shoulder holster and the nine-millimeter semiautomatic pistol, which caught the dim light of the bar, reflecting speckles off the knurled handle and magazine where all those bullets sat in a spring-loaded chorus line, just waiting for any excuse to hop into the firing chamber and make the straight line through space.

It was clear to James that these men were here for Clay. It was clear to everyone that they were here for Clay. They knew who he was, but he did not know them. Police intelligence was a little shabby, and of course this was to be expected, because this is where

272

it counted. James knew everyone in the whole damn world, from Three Finger Louie, the numbers man, to Fly Bones, the child molester, but these two dudes drew a total blank. Either Clayton George was supposed to know who they were or he wasn't. In any event, James could no longer simply sit there. He smiled at the two gentlemen, took another sip of his whiskey, then said, "What took you boys so long to find me?"

The shorter of the two said, "Clay, The Doc wants to see you. Right now."

57 Doc

"The Doc?" James LeRoy Washington III squeaked in a barely audible voice. He felt sudden pains in his wrists and ankles, wondering how long he might be keeping them.

"Don' look so surprised, man. You knew we would catch up wit you, sooner or later." The shorter man adjusted his hat as James thought about his choice of the word *we*. "Now get up *reeeeeeeeeal slow,* Clay. *Reeeeeeeeeal* slow, 'n keep both them hands in plain view for me." He readjusted his hat, then placed his hand on the edge of his holster.

James touched his glass, almost as if he were petting the rim good-bye. He contemplated taking another sip, but figured he might need every ounce of sobriety in the minutes to come, which he hoped would be more minutes than less. He stood, as slowly and deliberately as he drank when these muscle men had first arrived. Looking around, he tried to summon assistance from the regulars in the bar, but it seemed no one wanted to know him now. They stared straight ahead, drinking quietly. No one wanted to see him. No one wanted to see what was happening. No one wanted to be a witness. James made brief eye contact with a sorry-eyed Kappy behind the counter, but then the old man looked away, too. James had a very bad feeling.

"That's it, Clay. You just put your coat on, like *nice and slow.* No sudden movements."

James slowly did what the man said. He put his right arm through the sleeve. Then he put his left arm through the sleeve, and as his hand popped out the cuff, his right hand firmly pressed the button of the emergency transmitter. He compressed the button one more time for good measure, then straightened the lapel of his jacket with confidence. "Well, gentlemen," James said with a smile, "shall we see . . . The Doc?"

"Come," Mr. Hat said, half-annoyed, then he adjusted his hat and frisked James for heavy metal.

James walked toward the door, with his friends right behind him. The trio exited Kappy's, leaving their quarter-inch-deep footprints in the fresh snow on their way to the black Fleetwood. The white dust blew in waves across the streets, speckling past the streetlamps as they piled into the front seat, with James sandwiched in the middle.

James LeRoy Washington III was still trying to figure out who the hell these people were. Mr. Hat, the more talkative of the two, seemed to be in his mid- to late thirties, which would have put him in his early to mid-twenties twelve years earlier, when Clayton George might have known him. The Shades 'n Goatee seemed to be in his early forties, but it was difficult to tell; he had one of those faces that would never age too dramatically. He was probably born looking that way, and would probably die looking that way, too. As Mr. Hat pulled away from Kappy's and made a slow U-turn, James saw the lights of the familiar van with the directional antenna, and smiled.

But the smile disappeared the moment he heard the sound of a distant collision. Shades 'n Goatee smiled as Mr. Hat looked out the rearview and said, "Some dude juss slid *clear* across the road into a green van. Folks juss don't know how ta operate a motorized vehicle in the snow. . . ."

". . . Lieutenant, we had a little collision here," Sergeant Perato said into his cellular phone.

"What about Washington?!" Kramer snapped, already suspecting the worst.

"Well, ah . . . that's just it; we lost him going east on Dyckman in a black Fleetwood, plate number Y E X eight seven eight, I think. He was escorted by two black men. We didn't get a good look at them, but one was wearing a hat, and they both appeared to be well dressed."

"Christ! I'll get some extra cars on it, and I'm gonna activate the cellular net right now. How bad is the truck?"

"We think we can get it back on the road as soon as I shoot this asshole. . . ."

Toggling between great disbelief and even greater disappointment, James looked back and could see that the van was pinned between a lamppost and the car that hit it. All his confidence had squashed to nothing in the epicenter of that collision, and he was now practically shitting in his pants. He didn't know for sure whether his beacon was actually transmitting, and even if it was, there was no one there to localize his position now. If the cellular phone network was activated in time, his position could only be tracked from cell to cell, and that didn't seem nearly good enough anymore. James didn't know whether any of this bullshit technology was working. Only now did it occur to him that Sharon had been right: and he'd been a fool to trust the cops and their electronic gizmos. And he certainly didn't want to see this Doc. He wondered why he was being abducted this way. Things didn't seem to be adding up quite right. All the others had been tranquilized. Whenever he walked along the streets, he expected to feel a dart smack him in the ribs or in his back at any time. And if a dart didn't hit him, perhaps a real bullet would. It was the right neighborhood for that shit. But James had the distinct impression that *The Doc* was someone Clayton George had known, and with one last fleeting glance, James hoped to God the radio van wasn't permanently out of commission.

"Nervous, Clay? Maybe *you* learn to drive . . . in the back of a garbage truck," Mr. Hat teased. "Say, how long you been out, anyway? Doc estimates it must be goin' on three weeks already."

"Yeah," James sighed, now staring despondently through the front windshield. "Been about three weeks." A moment passed, and James looked over to Mr. Hat behind the wheel and said, "How long you been wit Doc?"

"Long enough, ma man. Long enough to know *what* to do . . . 'n *what not* to do. Yo' ass is in *deep* shit, mothafucka. I'm glad I ain' in yo' shoes, nigga. He might just cut you up real good if he's in the mood."

Cut me up? James thought as he swallowed. He turned to Mr. Shades 'n Goatee. "You know, I don't remember you. The mind grows a little foggy after all dem years. What's your name?" The mystery man slowly turned his head toward James and lifted his shades to his forehead, revealing a pair of eerie white eyeballs with no irises, no pupils, no nothing to see out of. "Oh! Sorry I asked. You muss be *Stevie Wonder!*"

Like a steel-jaw trap slamming shut, the blind man's right hand swung around and grabbed James by the throat. As the car rolled down Dyckman Street, the sightless man's expression remained changeless while his vise-grip animal paw sealed James's trachea completely shut, slowly squeezing the life out of him. James squirmed in his seat, trying to free himself.

Mr. Hat was enjoying the entertainment while gently guiding the motions of the flailing pair of feet to keep them away from the control pedals on the floor. Grinning from ear to ear, he said, "You shouldn't a said that to 'im. He don't see too well, but he can hear *real* good. And I don' think he like what he heard come outta yo' mouth."

James's eyes were bursting out of his head as he struggled. He couldn't believe what was happening. It felt as if his head were exploding. This blind animal with glazy Ping-Pong ball eyes was killing him in the front seat of a goddamn Caddy while it was snowing outside in November. Where were the rest of the cops. James wondered. *Where the fuck are they? Kramer! Perato! They're gonna leave me here to die! HELP!!! HELP!!!* ... James felt his strength leaving his body, and so did the blind man connected to those tool steel fingers. He'd strangled many people. He was a career professional, though, just like an anesthesiologist, and experience had taught him the precise moment to release a man's neck before he slips into unconsciousness and death. Very calmly, the hand opened and retracted.

James wheezed and coughed and spit. Mucus dribbled from his mouth and nostrils. He coughed every time he filled his lungs to about half capacity. He regained his composure and said, "All right ... all right ... bad joke ... bad joke, man. ..." What the hell's a blind man doin' with a gun? he thought. Then he reached for his only lifeline to safety, and pressed the flat transmitter button one more time. He looked around, hoping to see a police car, but he saw nothing.

Back at the precinct, Brent Kramer dialed the direct line to the mobile switching unit at New York NYNEX in Westchester County. The phone rang six times, and then the nasal voice on the line said, "Lou Drayer here."

"Lou, I'm Lieutenant Brent Kramer, of Midtown North. I don't believe we've spoken before, but we need to run that emergency internal cell trace on 835.650 megahertz; that's channel 355."

"Yes, I can figure out what channel it is. Lieutenant, you know you need a court order for me to authorize a—"

"Lou, Herb Gunner authorized this more than a month ago, and this *is* an emergency."

"Lieutenant, I don't care *who* authorized it. The procedure is quite clear on these matters. If I were to—"

"Authorize this, we *might* save a man's life? We're losing valuable time as we speak. This is not a random call we're tracing. We're not eavesdropping on some drug deal. 835.650 was specifically set aside for an ongoing stakeout to specifically provide directional tracking information. It's an open channel."

"An open channel?"

"Yes. Not full duplex. It's a transmit only. You *must* have a record of this in your assignment tables."

"I've never heard of such a thing."

"Well, now you have. Surely Herb left a record of this somewhere."

"Herb is on vacation."

"SHIT!!!" Lieutenant Kramer barked. "Shit, shit, SHIT!!! Wouldn't you know it? Look, isn't there a record anywhere? A posting? A slip of paper? An asterisk in a comment field? Something? Anything?"

"Hold on," Lou said with a full measure of annoyance. While the academic nature of an RF trace exercise intrigued the last feeble vestiges of the communications engineer still lurking in a foggy cobweb-infested shell of the former younger man with an otherwise-bright future, the alcoholic senior operator and graveyard-shift supervisor approaching retirement and pension had full respect for following strict procedure, to cover his ass, first, and in the name of protecting people's civil liberties, second. Kramer knew these types well, and he hated the thought that people like Lou chose the worst possible moments to exercise their flimsy politics. Lieutenant Kramer heard the tapping of keystrokes on a computer terminal and hoped that Herb hadn't let him down, but Lou returned with the words: "Sorry, Lieutenant. There's no record of this on the system anywhere."

Brent could not believe it. Herb had assured him that all the "internal paperwork" would be handled. "Lou, could you check Herb's office? He assured me I would have *no problem*. He assured me that all the supervisors would be notified—including you. Lou, this is a life-or-death situation. You've got to find that documentation somewhere. I *know* Herb wouldn't let me down." This was a lie. Brent didn't know that Herb wouldn't let him down. According to Nigel, Herb's marriage was going down the tubes, and he might have had much more important things on his mind. It was entirely possible that the channel was technically allocated, but there was no follow-up documentation to make it useful as an actual tool.

"Okay, Lieutenant," Lou sighed, "I'll check his office."

"Thanks, Lou. Please hurry. Time is of the essence." Brent waited for what felt like an infinity of time. He needed the cellular location net activated, and this Lou guy was going to be a pain in the ass.

And true to predicted form, Lou returned to the phone and said, "I'm sorry, Lieutenant, his office is locked. We don't have any record of this transmit only channel, and Herb's office is locked. You're gonna need a court order for me to proceed with this."

"Lou, surely the records show that 835.650 has been deactivated from the pass-off call-frequency assignment table. This is *one* dedicated frequency being passed off from cell to cell. If you don't actively capture the pass-off power levels for 835.65, the data will be lost forever. . . ."

"Well, not exactly. Statistical records are periodically generated for stochastic—"

"Please don't feed me Schrödinger's cat for lunch. I need certainties—not probabilities. Can you put me through to Herb?"

"Lieutenant! He's on vacation in Hawaii with his wife."

With his mistress, Brent figured. "What hotel is he staying at? I must speak with him."

"How should I know where he's staying?"

"Didn't he leave an itinerary? Isn't there *anything* at all?"

"He went on vacation like everyone else goes on vacation. I'm sure the man wants to be left alone. It's one fifteen in the morning. Personnel is closed. How am I gonna get such information? I'm here with a small technical skeleton crew. All I do is keep the computers running. And as far as I know, you could be anyone. You're just a voice on the phone."

Brent chose to ignore for the moment just what nastiness this voice on the phone was capable of. "How about this? Can you do the internal trace, and I'll have a court order inside of two hours?" Brent knew where he could find Judge Levy at 1:15 in the morning and get the order to NYNEX by chopper. "Would that be acceptable?"

"Lieutenant, if that's who you really are, you know as well as I that you need the court order *before* I begin the analysis, not after. People have a right to their privacy, you know. We hold a very special public trust. Do you know how big a lawsuit we could be slapped with, on top of the FCC fines we'd be hit with? We could lose our operating license."

Brent rubbed his gun, and he began to harbor thoughts of killing Lou—killing him slowly with his bare hands. "Lou, I want you to listen to me very carefully. Just between you and me, I've got a man in the field with a cellular phone sewn into his pants, and that man is about to have his arms and legs amputated and transformed into the next great MEDIA EVENT!!! And it's all going to be your fault—your fault personally. Lou, if that comes to pass, I'm gonna be forced to hurt you very badly."

"Are you physically threatening me?" Lou said, with growing anger in his voice.

"No, Lou. That's a professional threat. I know *everyone* in your industry. You are obstructing justice—not promoting it. And by the time I get through with you, you'll lose your clearance because you'll be a convicted felon. You won't even be able to get a job emptying coin boxes. I can do all that I say. And more! And I will. I swear on my mother's grave. And as far as the *physical* threat goes, I don't have to stoop so low, because at Rikers, . . . well, I'll bet you never wondered just exactly *how much* blood can pour out of a man's asshole. I mean literally. Did ya ever wonder how much blood can flow from hemorrhaging rectal tissue? Ya know what those boys would do to a little honky white-collar sugarplum like you? You wanna be known as Tampon Suzy? Now look, I'm willing to meet you halfway, so to speak. Obviously, there's been a major fuckup on *your* end. So what I want you to do is to perform a routine cell handoff power-level diagnostic, specifically on 835.650 megahertz— that's channel 355—and I'm going to get you your court order. Otherwise, my options are limited. I'll arrest you for obstruction of justice within one hour, and that skeleton crew a yours will watch you hauled off in irons. Now when I *wake* Judge Levy up out of a nice sound sleep, he's gonna have my ass, but that's so I can save yours. Now I can still keep you out of trouble, but don't push me. Let's keep this relationship clean, now. Don't force me to go ballistic on you."

For a moment, there was silence, and then Lou spoke. "I suppose I could perform a routine cell handoff power-level diagnostic on 835.650 megahertz, but I need that court order, Lieutenant. . . ."

"Attaboy, Lou, I'm glad you're with the program again. The court order is on the way."

Lieutenant Kramer hung up the phone with the assurance that the trace was a happening thing, and then he proceeded to call the judge, who he knew was at that very moment not sleeping, but in the midst of a heated poker game, and probably losing as usual.

The black Fleetwood turned left on Nagel Avenue and drove past the Dyckman Houses. A few blocks more, and they intersected Tenth Avenue. A block or two farther, they turned right, heading up a dead-end street terminating at the Harlem River. They pulled up to the curb in front of a closed warehouse, just one in a series of unoccupied ground-floor gated-up entrances compressed under a row of sooty brick factory buildings. Time seemed to compress for James, too. He looked around at the parked cars on the street. He looked at the placement of the structure across the street—some kind of a garbage-recycling plant. There were several holes in the fence leading to the river. He thought about running for it when they got out of the car. He thought about diving into the murky dark water and swimming to the Bronx. He was on his own—all alone. The cops were nowhere to be seen. Mr. Hat straightened his hat and removed the key from the ignition. It was snowing harder now, and the windshield was pelted with accumulating flakes which instantly turned to slush upon impact. Both front doors simultaneously flung open and the boys exited, with James's shoulder firmly guided by the blind-eyed choker's machine grip.

Mr. Hat pushed open the metal door to the building, and Clayton George was marched in. The dimly lit hallway to the musty building had two staircases, one in the front, which led to the warehouse somewhere to the left in the building, and one in the back. The back staircase was the one they climbed, and at the top of the first landing, they entered a door to the right, single file. James looked around this small, sparsely decorated room, which resembled a waiting room of sorts. The hat man adjusted his hat, then knocked three times on the only other door. James felt panic in his gut—a panic that grew less manageable as the dilated seconds ticked.

And then the hat man looked up at the blind strangler, and James was coaxed through the door.

James half-expected to walk into an anesthesia mask in an operating room, but what he found was an eighty-foot-long room, with a few couches and tables and a desk with a computer at the far south end, which was back toward the front of the building. And at that desk, a bald black man was seated, a bald black man wearing a black eye patch over his right eye. The blind strangler then released James, and for the first time since he'd been in the car, he was able to stand unassisted. He pushed his transmitter button one more time as he straightened his jacket and thought, These two dudes don't got but one good eye between 'em.

Then the man with the eye patch said in a deep baritone voice, "Thank you, Orion." The blind man nodded his head.

James assumed that One-eye was the man they called The Doc, so he took the gamble and said, "Hello, Doc. Been a long time."

The Doc stood, squinted his one good eye, and said, "Commere, an' let me take a better look at cha." James walked closer to The Doc, figuring that he was the same Doc they spoke of. As he walked closer to the desk, he noticed that there was another man inconspicuously standing like a fixture in the room, farther back, behind the door where he'd entered the room. Four men. Five eyes. One hat. And one James LeRoy Washington III, who everyone thought was named Clayton George.

The blind man walked in lockstep with James, matching speed and course exactly. James watched this blind enigma, Orion, as The Doc called him. James stopped for a moment, and Orion stopped, too. James wondered how this blind monster with a goatee named Orion could navigate his way around the place without any visual aids. He had managed to walk in and out of Kappy's. He had managed to walk in and out of the car, straight through the front door to the building, up the stairs, into the damn waiting room, and through the door. He never bumped into things. James watched him and walked forward as quietly as he could, and Orion walked forward, too. James stopped, and so did Orion.

"He's really quite talented, Clay," The Doc said.

"He sho' is, like a infrared sensor," James replied. As The Doc stood there, James studied him and his eye patch carefully. He looked to be about fifty, six feet tall, muscular, and 260 pounds at least. He hoped to God this one-eyed man wasn't the man who was going to slice him up and turn him into a hooper, or worse. The Doc walked out from behind the desk and approached James. The two men approached each other until they stood about a foot apart. As The Doc began to smile, James began to smile, maintaining parity with The Doc's increasingly friendly expression.

Then The Doc said, "You could have stopped by to see us, ya know. Why you make us come get you like this, you asshole?" Then The Doc threw his arms open and hugged Clayton George. James hugged him back.

"It's good to see you, man," James said. "It's real good to see you again." It was a strange welcome, but James breathed a sigh of relief. And in his relief, he'd temporarily forgotten that the Orion had almost choked him to death. But then he remembered. "Say, Doc, on the ride over, Orion here almost choked me to death. Why do ya suppose he'd go 'n do a thing like that?"

"Well, Clay . . . ya know you like a brother ta me. But there's still that little matter of the hundred grand . . . and that's if I'm good and forget the interest—sort a like a welcome-home gift." James and The Doc separated to arm's distance as they continued to hold each other on the waist. "Clay, if we don't settle up proper, though, I'm afraid I'm gonna have ta kill ya."

James LeRoy Washington III was suddenly overcome by that sinking feeling that inevitably accompanies all hopeless situations bridging the chasm between asphyxiation and amputation. He looked around the room at the odd number of eyeballs focused intensely upon him. Even the damn blind man was watching him. James concluded that these people had brought him here either to scare the shit out of him or to kill him—to kill Clayton George. And he was less concerned with what relationship Clayton and this Doc had an eighth of a century ago than he was with the practical reality of the present. He considered hurling himself out the window. The survival odds of a second-story free fall might be better than in Orion's entertaining grip.

None of this $100,000 business was so much as hinted at in any of Clayton's files, though. The cops were such fuckups, but at that moment, James would have kissed the ground a cop would spit on; police intelligence, as they called it—it sucked the big one this time. This hundred grand bullshit completely took him by surprise. Intelligence! And these transmitters were less useful than a scrotumload of shit! James looked at The Doc and tried to calculate a next move.

"Look, man, that was a long time ago. I was all fucked up then. What are my options right now?"

"*Welllllll*..." The Doc slowly walked around James as if he were a planet in orbit around the sun. "What are you *really* worth to me, Clay, in your present condition? At McDonald's, you *might* be able to work off your debt in *saaaaay*...a hundred years? Dat's no good. Not fo me. An not fo you, either. And how do I know you'd stick around to make good? You see my problem here? You seem to a...lost a little weight up in Sing Sing there. They feed ya there?"

"Just barely. Food is *shit!* But I done ma time, 'n I kept my wits about me."

"Now you could eat all the hamburger you could cram down yo' little throat. Regain your strength. You be as good as new. How often them boys lube yo' asshole, son? I hear hemorrhoids a real occupational hazard up there."

"They tried. But nobody messed wit me 'n didn't find it ta be mo' trouble than it worth. Even them big muscle dudes. I kept ma virginity the whole time, though," James said with a smile. Doc began to laugh; then Mr. Hat chuckled, followed by a smile from the fixture in the back of the room. Orion's expression remained changeless over there by the window.

"You hear that, boys?" Doc said. "Clayton here kept his virginity. Well, if that ain't righteous." The Doc hesitated, occasionally laughing in short nerve-racking bursts. "That's real good. But things has changed since you went away, Clay. Virginity ain't politically correct no more. Maybe you get fucked right now. Ya see, I don't know what ta do wit cha, Clay. It might be worth a hundred grand juss ta rip ya heart out right there where you stand. And the river's only fifty feet away. It ain't too clean, but it gets the job done, same as it *always* did. On the other hand, maybe we can come to some kind a arrangement. I don't know, Clay. This a real difficult decision I gotta make here. Personally, I don't think you *worth* a hundred grand. . . ."

Orion tilted his head over by the window, and this alerted everyone in the room. He then quickly said in a low Caribbean-sounding monotone, "Company. One car." James was relieved. One car, and most likely the police—finally. He now had to take back all the bad things he'd thought about the cops. They were just being real cool about the whole thing, except that if the blind man had killed him back in the car, he'd be dead now, and they'd be dragging a net through the Harlem River to find his body. James was relieved, though. That car was his salvation.

The Hat walked over to the window to confirm what Orion had heard. It was a car, traveling slowly up the street, headed toward the dead end. He nodded his head toward The Doc. Then, The Doc said, "Dim the lights, Damean. We got ourselves a visitor." Then he grabbed James by the arm and said, "Clay, you stay with me." The Doc guided James to the back of the room and they hid behind a couch against a five-foot-high partition that jutted out from the east wall of the long space. "He's got some set a ears, that boy."

James looked at The Doc's eye patch and said, "I never thought I'd see a blind lookout man."

"Some people see better without any eyes than most do with

two good ones. And don't be lookin' at my eye patch. I *hate* it when people do dat shit ta me. You look me in the eye, will ya?"

So the fixture in the back went by the name of Damean; Orion was the blind lookout man; The Doc was in charge; and James still had to learn the name of The Hat Man, who at that moment adjusted his hat as he peeked out the window to see if he could recognize who their visitors were.

"It ain't one of Ortega's cars," The Hat said. "I don't recognize it."

James looked over the back of the room carefully. There was a door which looked like it led to the bathroom, and it was on the same side of the room as the entrance to the big room. There was also another door, open a crack, and it was in the opposite wall, opposite the bathroom. The back window had bars on it like the ones in prison. James had this eerie feeling that things were about to get noisy when the cops finally came to rescue him. Orion quietly entered the bathroom in the back, with Damean and The Hat in the front.

The approaching car parked in front of the DEAD END sign, as close to the rotting cyclone fence and the water as it could get. The driver shut his lights. The Hat and Damean watched attentively; then they began to smile as they saw the passenger lean over the driver. No mistake about it. The passenger was a woman, and the driver was a man, and her head was bobbing around over his lap.

"False alarm. Juss John Boy gettin' his little dick sucked."

James's heart sank. Doc smiled, and so did Orion, a little. James pressed the transmitter button one more time, just in case it decided to work this time.

"Wait a minute," The Hat said. "We got us anotha car comin' up the street. An' this one don't got no lights on."

Once again, James was filled with hope. The cops were now on their way to save him. It was about time, too. The bastards had really made him sweat, and he had plenty to tell Kramer.

The car slowly drove toward the building. It stopped about a hundred feet from the front door and parked on the snow-blanketed road. Damean had his face pressed up tightly against the darkened glass to see out the locked second-story double-insulated window. Five men got out the driver's side. "We got trouble!" Damean said.

And then four people slipped out the passenger side of the

blow job car. The Hat caught a glimpse of them running toward the building to join the five men from the other car. "It's Crazy Santos 'n that psycho chick a his. Nine of 'em total. We in deep shit, Doc."

"Goddamn Colombians," The Doc muttered to James. "They've taken over the whole fuckin' place."

"What can I do ta help ya?" James said to Doc.

"Get me a egg-a-muffin to go . . . 'n some fries."

James grabbed Doc aggressively and yelled only an inch or two from his face, "Don't treat me like no *fuckin'* child, man! We outnumbered. This one's blind, 'n you a fuckin' cyclops! I can help. I ain't gonna juss lay down 'n die wit chu dudes cause the spics comin' to blow all yo' asses ta hell!"

Damean locked the front door with the dead bolt and looked into the security monitor. "They're entering the building."

Doc ran to the closet door, which was opened a crack, and pulled a wood panel out from the back. Then he collected an armful of Uzi submachine guns. Damean grabbed two and tossed one across the room to The Hat. Then Doc threw Damean a pair of pump shotguns, and he threw one over to The Hat. Extra ammo clips flew across the room as they all took up their defensive positions behind steel-impregnated furniture. Doc slammed the bolt back and forth and handed an Uzi to James and said, "Here's your big chance to blow yo' parole ta hell, Burger Boy! Just point, and pull the trigger." James looked a little confused as he delicately took the machine gun from Doc and they took up defensive positions behind the couch at the back of the room. Orion stood just inside the bathroom, his body in line with the plane of the wall, and he squeezed spongy earplugs into his super-sensitive ears. James curiously watched him remove his nine-millimeter from his holster and hold it tightly against his chest. The Doc handed James a spare clip and said, "Here's thirty more rounds. You ever use one a these?"

"They didn't exactly take us out to the range every day ta practice."

"Okay. Listen carefully. They come out real fast, so don't blow your whole wad like Rambo. Pace yourself, three or four at a time. It tends ta pull up as ya shoot, so don' be wastin' 'em on ma ceiling. These dudes are gonna be crazy. I seen the kind a work they do, so don' be losin' ya head." The Doc then slid a pair of shotguns out from under the couch. He pumped them both and slid one over to James. "Pump it after every shot. You got seven in each."

James grabbed the shotgun and caressed its metallic form. The barrel was so big. He'd never fired a shotgun before, or a machine gun. In fact, he'd never fired a weapon in his life—except for the BB rifle at Coney Island. A half hour ago, he'd been drinking whiskey in Kappy's, and now he was at the Manhattan equivalent of the O.K. Corral. He glanced over to The Doc and said, "If we get outta this alive, far as I'm concerned, we all square, Doc."

The Doc looked at him and laughed. "Clay, I must say you got some set a balls when it come to negotiatin'." The Doc laughed again. "Okay, Clay. We get outta this alive, we all square, but you workin' for me! An' you ever pull any shit like that again, I am personally gonna—"

Machine-gun fire blasted through the front door until it literally disintegrated off its hinges and fell in, collapsing over the dead bolt and falling flat onto the floor. Then two objects were lobbed into the room. "GRENADES!!!" someone yelled from within. James and The Doc ducked behind the couch as a pair of explosions rocked the room, sending shrapnel and debris everywhere. Then two men in black burst in through the open door, and the muzzle flashes of a machine-gun duet stroboscopically lit the room like a downtown discotheque. Bullets punctured the plaster walls everywhere. Orion's hand emerged from the bathroom, and he rapidly fired three rounds.

Orion had downed one of the gunners; then machine-gun fire crackled from the other side of the room, and the other gunner was nearly cut in half at the waist while his finger emptied his remaining rounds into the ceiling, raining plaster onto the floor. Then there was silence. James couldn't believe what had just gone down. "How the fuck did he do that?!!" he blurted to Doc while looking at Orion in the doorway to the bathroom. James held the Uzi in one hand and the shotgun in the other, not knowing which one was worth more points.

One of Santos's men was wounded. He moaned from where he lay on the floor in the middle of the room. Then the rotating beacons from the street could be seen through the smoke and airborne dust in the room. This time, the cavalry had arrived. James felt he could sit tight and wait it out. He saw reflections of light in the two lenses covering Orion's eyes. People began arguing in Spanish from the hallway. Then another object was tossed into the room. "GRENADES!!!"

And another explosion. One more gunner dove into the room while spraying the place with copper-jacketed lead. Machine-gun fire was returned from the other side of the room. Then shotguns blasted from the hallway. Fire was being returned from the top of the stairs. Orion stuck his blind hand in the direction of the invading muzzle noise, and he fired many times. It seemed to James that he kept shooting forever. Doc rose and began shooting over the top of the couch. Then another person ran into the room. James saw it all from the floor, peeking out from behind the couch. It was Crazy Santos's chick, and she held a .45 in each hand. As Orion emptied his gun in the direction of the machine-gun fire, the chick rushed toward him, staying low and keeping close to the wall. She fired both pistols at the same time, and Orion was thrown backward. She then pointed her pistols at the flames strobing from the muzzle of Doc's Uzi. James was flat against the floor. He wasn't sure how it came to pass that the shotgun was the only weapon he now held in a lover's embrace, but he pointed it in the direction of the flashes of light, and pulled the trigger. It felt like a tremendous explosion going off in his arms. The chick flew backward weightlessly, slamming into the wall. Then she seemed to bounce off the wall like a rubber ball, and fall toward James. He pumped the shotgun and fired again. The body fell flat on its back, only five or six feet from him. What he saw was unbelievable. The body had no head. Just a bloody stump of a neck. He'd blown her head completely off her neck. Obliterated! James stared at the headless lump of flesh on the floor, only touching distance away. The cause and effect was impossible to comprehend. It was incomprehensible to imagine that such a small muscular twitch of the finger could make a human head completely disappear into spray. Time was slow, but not slow enough to savor reality too closely. Death was everywhere in this room.

Another source of light entered the room and machine-gun fire was continuous. James fired the shotgun twice. It had one hell of a kick. His brain was now off. He was now operating on impulse and instinct and automatic. This was real war. It didn't sound like TV. Everything was so much louder, and the vibrations were so much closer. A tear-gas canister went off in the hallway, and another person burst into the room. James pulled the trigger and the dark form flew into the air. Another person entered, and James pulled the trigger once more. This pellet cannon could stop anything, he thought, and suddenly he remembered his purpose, which was to get the hell out of there.

There was a moment of silence, and James noticed that The Doc had been hit. In the dim light, his arm and shoulder glistened with wetness. James crawled over to The Doc and looked at him, and The Doc looked up at James. "You done pretty good, man," Doc said. "A deal is a deal. We even."

James held Doc's head and said, "I hate to hit 'n run, ma man, but I got ta get ma ass outta here while I still in one piece. See you around." And James crawled into the bathroom as another dude entered the room from the tear-gassed hallway. Santos and his men were now caught in a cross fire between The Doc's men and the cops below. Bullhorns were sounding over the machine-gun fire, but James couldn't understand a word they said. He crawled over the body of Orion, who was good and dead. Both bullets of the chick's .45s had blown out both his blind eyeballs. James stared at the two sockets of blood. His face was a mess. As James turned to stand and face the bathroom window, he moved Orion's head, and the remains of a brain fell out the giant hole in the back of his skull. James looked clinically at the lumpy organ, then remembered that it was that organ that commanded a hand to strangle him. He leaned over to the bloody face of the corpse and compassionately said, "Maybe next time round, you come back with a pair of eyes that work. I paid the bitch back, though."

Then James crawled out the tiny window without bars. He hung from his hands and dropped to the ground, onto a greasy tire fifteen feet below his legs. The ground was soft and slimy, but the snow felt so good on his face. He walked along the inside of a barbed-wire fence, through greasy, oily boxes and garbage. The black water of the Harlem River was less than twenty feet away, to his right, and lights from the Bronx reflected in wiggly dancing patterns. He walked along the back of the building, where the shooting was still happening. James squeezed between the wall and the cyclone fence. A large rat ran over his foot and he yelped. It was funny, but this rodent was more real than the three people he'd killed in that horrible room upstairs. The reality was trying to sink in as he pulled himself along, compressed against the wall by this rusting fence. He popped out and walked through some tall weeds and soggy ground. Finally, he stepped onto the street north of Doc's old place. He heard the explosion of another hand grenade. While still physically close, it might just as well have been a million miles away. James felt he was safe. He heard police sirens, but he wanted to get as far away from the shooting as he could. His brain was numb. He'd actually killed human beings with a shotgun, and his brain wanted to forget the last half hour had ever happened.

He walked west along the street, mildly detached, and buzzing. He opened his mouth and caught snowflakes on his tongue, the way he used to do as a child. His ears were ringing from all the noise. It was like a steady high-pitched hissing in his head. Somehow it didn't matter anymore whether Doc or The Hat or Damean were alive or dead. James knew that Orion had returned to the stars, but that didn't seem all too real, either. In a certain sense, none of it seemed very real. James decided that what he really needed was to return to Kappy's and get a drink. Yes, a drink was in order—a celebration drink. In his mind, he had became Clayton George again, and he was returning to the bar of Clayton George. His pace quickened as he headed west. In spite of all the activity on the other block, the streets were deserted and white. He still heard gunfire off in the distance.

James approached the Pathmark parking lot as a wave of police cars raced east, followed by ambulances and a bomb truck and some other emergency vehicles. Desolation returned to the street.

Pfffffffft.

Astonishment! A sudden sensation in his back. James reached for the cylinder of plastic and stainless steel and pulled it from his skin. Oh God, he thought. Oh shit!!! He ran frantically eastward. No. Gotta get to the cops. Induction time. Gotta beat the induction time. Oh God, I almost forgot about this. This shit couldn't wait till tomorrow! James ran through the parking lot of the Pathmark, back in the direction of the battle. He pressed the button to the emergency transmitter as he'd rehearsed a hundred times in his mind, then realized that he'd been pushing that damn button all night long. Things grew slower and fuzzier in waves. And the throbbing became louder in his body, clogging his mind. He continued to walk in the direction of the shooting. He put one rubbery leg in front of the other and continued to move in the direction he thought the shooting was coming from. He could sense a funny taste in his mouth, sort of sweet. Then he became confused. He was not sure which direction he was supposed to go. The lights grew more distant through the speckles of snow, almost as if he were looking through a telescope pointed backward. Everything was small and far away. He continued to wobble in a direction that seemed correct. He had to get to the cops. They were where all the shooting was. He just had to get to the shooting. But he could no longer hear the shooting. Sirens were coming from somewhere. And he thought he was walking, too, but then he realized that he wasn't. He was on his knees, or was he? Maybe he just thought he was on his knees, but he was really walking. He really wasn't quite sure. He didn't remember what he was supposed to be doing. The layers of denial's denial were infinite. He wasn't really sure of anything, and he had to get to Kappy's for some reason. . . .

A Chevy Nova backed up to James LeRoy Washington III, who finally collapsed and lay unconscious on the snow-covered pavement in the parking lot of a Pathmark supermarket. A person got out of the car, and a hypo was unrolled from a paper towel. After the injection, the car trunk was popped open. The body was propped over the edge, then dumped inside. The trunk was slammed shut, and the Nova drove off, turning left onto Tenth Avenue, leaving a pair of tire imprints in the snow as far as the eye could see.

```
receive m:subscrip.1st
```

Nigel Atkerson hit the enter key and his computer was now ready to receive the entire subscription list for the *Botanical Quarterly* for the past twenty-one years, which was ever since the list had been computerized. "Dr. Fisher, I'm ready to receive."

"Okay, here it comes," Dr. Fisher replied. He did not have a dedicated phone line on his modem, so he had to hang up the phone to allow his computer to send the file.

Nigel waited patiently for the fourth of four subscription lists to trickle over the phone line into the M drive of his computer. He glanced over to Sally Chu, who sat next to him over by the computer. Sally was becoming increasingly absorbed in Nigel's computer setup, which more resembled the control center of a war room in a small country than a simple personal computer, or several of them all interconnected in ways unfamiliar to her conventional network-minded brain. Sally played with Nigel's satellite-tracking program, and she could not believe that the orbital data of so many artificial skyborne objects and other space debris were publicly available from NASA. Sally wanted a copy of the program so she could add it to the collection of junk software she was quickly cluttering the disks of her computer system at the precinct with.

Then the prompt appeared on one of Nigel's monitors:

```
C: Thur 11-18-1993 1:02:46.13 C:\sat>
```

"I've got the file," Nigel told Dr. Fisher as Sally looked up from a screenload of azimuth and elevation data.

Nigel thanked Dr. Fisher for parting with his proprietary lists, then began examining them, looking for anything interesting or unusual. Nigel shook his head and rolled his eyes.

"What?" Sally said. "What is wrong this time?"

"Nothing," Nigel said with an arrogant smile of superiority. "Fixed fields. It's a stupid way to store records. This program was probably written by some college asshole that was overcome with his alleged mastery of machine language."

"Nigel, you know," Sally said, having transformed from sweet and seductive to sour and combative in one breath's worth of time, "you think you know everything all the time. It is really annoying. No wonder your ex-wife leave you. Maybe they have good reason for making fix field. I do that myself sometimes."

Nigel looked at the outline of Sally's undergarments, wondering whether a few thousand bytes of data were worth having another technical argument over. These confrontations were happening more often with Sally. It seemed to Nigel as if she was deliberately testing him to see how far she could push him, and he felt that her cheap crack about his ex-wife was completely uncalled for. But Nigel also reasoned that such a statement revealed that she might possibly imagine herself in the role of his ex-wife, before his ex-wife became his ex-wife, and the thought of having sex with Sally might still yield more pleasure than guilt, but she was slowly closing the gap, Nigel thought. If the probability of guilt exceeded the probability of pleasure, he would simply have to tell her to go to hell; then he looked at the outline of her undergarments again, and realized that it *was* after one o'clock in the morning, seven hours after work had officially ended for her, and she was probably in his loft for something more than professional interest. "Rather then belabor the countless merits of fixed field databases, let's do a little police work, why don't we?"

"Yeah. Police work! Countless merits, huh! Why don't we clean this place up already? It looks like a pigsty. Yeah! Let's look at the data." Then she unfolded her legs and leaned into Nigel's shoulder to get a little closer to the screen.

"Let's see if we can find our friend Joseph Barton. . . ." Nigel typed some characters onto the keyboard, and like magic, Joey and all his information appeared on the screen. "Bingo! Well, what do you know?! Joseph Barton. Age twenty, back in 1972. *Hmmm* . . . He was in Ithaca, New York, back in '74, but in 1973 . . . he was in . . . Brooklyn Heights? Occupation—student. Doesn't surprise me. I'll bet he was a student at Cornell, too."

It seemed to Nigel that the quicker his fingers produced results on the screen, the more affectionate Sally became. *"Hmmmmm.* Look at this." Nigel typed another burst of keystrokes on the keyboard, and all Becker's information appeared on the monitor.

Sally's left hand took hold of Nigel's left arm, pulling their shoulders closer together, and the thought occurred to him more than once that he should turn his head and kiss her lips. She slipped her right shoulder behind Nigel's left shoulder, rubbing her breast against him. He turned his head to face her, and their noses touched. Then their lips touched, ever so softly, and Sally jerked away and said, "What do you got on the screen now?"

Nigel was really beginning to suspect that Sally's mind was unhinging, and he thought that perhaps the time had come to throw her out before she did the same to his mind. This woman seemed to be in too many places at once, like a heated Ping-Pong game between several competing components of her personality. Then he looked down at her stockings and said, "See, they listed Becker as a college professor. . . ."

"I never liked that man," Sally said, and her face soured again. "I think he is a *very* strange man. In fact, I think he is our Dr. Sigma."

Nigel immediately removed Becker's information from the screen. Actually, Nigel was getting a little worried about Becker, because he hadn't answered his telephone in three days. "I don't think he's Dr. Smegma."

"Sigma, not Smegma. Are *you* trying to make me sick?"

"No. I'm trying to make you laugh."

"Well, you are making me *sick* instead. Sometimes you say the weirdest things. So how come you do not think Becka In-stlo-clown-a-witz is Dr. Sigma?" Nigel burst out laughing. Sally pounded him on the shoulder and said, "What so funny, you?"

"His name is Instlokrownctjz."

"That's what I said. How come you don't . . ."

"Just a hunch. I'll bet Joey studied botany at Cornell."

"Why do you think that?" Sally softly said, then smiled and tilted her head, looking into Nigel's eyes.

"Because, my dear . . ." Nigel put his hand on Sally's leg and decided not to mention Becker's name again, or how he'd probably had a major influence on this particular student. "Just a hunch."

Sally's red hair draped over the left half of the keyboard as she said, "You got so many hunches. How come you never joined the police department?"

"The salary sucks, and I just do this as a hobby. *Hmmmm,* it seems that Joseph Barton let his subscription lapse in 1973." Nigel hit the print screen key, then said, "How come you never went into physics?"

"The salary sucks, and now I only do physics as hobby." Then Sally's face lit up. "Let's play wit your espresso machine."

"My espresso machine?" Nigel said. "Wouldn't you rather play with—"

"We got plenty a time for that later. I want you to show me how to make espresso." She bounced up, grabbed Nigel's hand, and led him to the other side of the loft, into the kitchen area. "Now, how does this crazy thing work?"

The machine or you? Nigel thought, then took out the bag of espresso beans from the refrigerator and tossed them in the grinder. Sally held out her arms and took an exaggerated breath of the pulverizing beans, as if she were on the mountaintop, singing in *The Sound of Music.* Nigel poured the water into the canister, wondering if he belonged in the very same rubber room that he believed Sally belonged in.

Sally pressed her waist against the counter and watched the hissing appliance, and she then heard Nigel approach her from behind, and she felt his hands firmly take hold of both her shoulders and begin massaging them. *"Oooo,* that feels *soooo* good," she said, submissively relaxing her muscles to encourage him. "It been so long since I get a good . . . *ooooo, yeah* . . . that's a good spot."

Then Sally suddenly turned, looked at Nigel with wild eyes, grabbed his hand, and led him back across the loft toward the computers, only she kept walking, all the way to the bedroom.

"What about the espresso?" Nigel said.

"We drink espresso later." Then she climbed onto the bed in a near panic, faced away from Nigel, unbuttoned her blouse, and pulled it out from the waistband of her skirt. Nigel could not believe the rapid transformations inside the brain inside the body he'd longed to see for all this time, finally in his bed, and he was bombarded with thoughts that there was something very wrong about this. Sally flung her blouse at the backrest, then she unclipped her bra, and without removing it, she tipped like a board, pivoted at the knees, and fell flat, with her face in a pillow, and said with a muffled voice, "Rub!"

Nigel slowly climbed onto the bed, looked at her legs spread suggestively wide, then looked at her long red hair over her bare back, thought yet another time about his reserved hot plate in hell, and said, "Where?!"

"Don't be smart!" she ordered while turning just enough to completely expose a breast for him to see. "Now rub!" She plopped her head back to the pillow.

Nigel peeked under her skirt, and could see an exposed hour-glass-shaped piece of her white lace panties. So that's ground zero, he thought as he climbed over her and sat on her ass. She moaned as his weight pressed down on her hips; then his hands began their massaging expedition across the naked contour of her back. She appeared to be in ecstasy as he applied forceful pressure to the muscles of her back. Nigel's mind wandered, and he heard the sound of the hissing espresso machine back there in the kitchen. This was the first woman he'd touched the flesh of since his ex-wife had left him, and it made him feel both happy and sad. Why can't anything be simple? he thought, feeling almost like crying.

Sally moaned rhythmically in time to the strokes of his powerful fingers. Her pelvis was in flames under the weight of this man. She could feel herself growing wet, and she knew the time was approaching. Her hands worked their way to her side, as if she were at attention on her stomach. She tugged at the edge of her skirt and began to wiggle it down over her hips and garter belt. Nigel lifted his weight to help; then she rotated to face him. He looked at her face, her eyes, her breasts, and her form. She ran her hands up his side, then took his hands and placed them on her breasts, speaking softly to him in Cantonese. She pulled him down to her and pressed his face to hers, and they kissed and rolled to their sides while continuing to kiss.

Their tongues darted about in each other's mouths. Nigel had been looking forward to this since the day they'd first met, but now he felt as if he were going through the motions, and his mind was really back on the computer screen with Joseph Barton, or with his ex-wife and her nutty crystals from Atlantis. He actively tried to shut off his brain, because her hands were all over the end of his urinary tract, which was turning into a penis for the fist time in more than a year.

His hand massaged her hip, then slid over the garter strap and across the waistband of her panties, and his fingers felt her pubic bone. Through the lace fabric, he could feel the well-defined outline of her swollen clitoris. Sally gasped as his fingers rubbed her, and her teeth nibbled on his tongue. His fingers slid inside her, which poured slippery wetness like an oozing faucet. His hand more forcefully pressed against her, and she kicked her skirt from her ankles. Sally licked Nigel's lips, then the end of his nose, all the way down to his Adam's apple. She bounced up on all fours and slid his pants off. Then she straddled him and undulated her pelvis up and down, rubbing against his penis. She took hold of it, pulled her panties aside, and touched it to her, nearly inserting it, rubbing it back and forth between her legs like a wet crayon coloring the edge of her warm interior. She teased herself with it, pressing it in ever so slightly, then taking it out, then in, then out. Then, in a much heavier Cantonese accent, she said, "You got da condom?"

"The condom? Oh yeah, the condom. God, I . . . haven't used one in years."

"You mean you don't got da condom?"

"No, I don't got da condom," Nigel said, imitating her accent.

"What you mean, you don't got da condom? I thought all men got da condom."

"Not this one. I've been out of action for quite—"

"I can't *believe* you don't got da condom."

"Sally, I didn't know this was gonna happen. Why don't *you* have one?"

"What you think I do, walk around all day long wit da condom in my bag?!"

"Well *that's* a double standard if I ever heard one. Maybe we should improvise."

"What you mean 'improvise'? You build one in shop like Mr. Fix-it?"

"Maybe I have some aluminum foil out there—right next to the espresso machine."

"You crazy!" Sally bounced to her feet and grabbed the

handle of a random drawer. "There *got* to be a condom in here somewhere!" She pulled Nigel's ex-wife's diaphragm out of the drawer and threw it at Nigel in disgust. "What this?!"

"Evidence of a past life—Exhibit A."

She ran into the bathroom and opened the medicine cabinet. "I can't *believe* you don't got no condom. . . ."

Nigel sat up on the side of the bed and looked at his penis, now at half-mast, and said in a Humphrey Bogart accent, "It's just you and me, kid." Then Nigel held the end of his penis and wiggled it like a little puppet and said in a high-pitched Mickey Mouse voice, "You fucked up again, you big dummy! You did a *baaaaaaad* thing. You always keep getting me in trouble, and now I gotta find another place to throw up. . . ."

"WHAT?!!" Sally screamed from the bathroom as she continued foraging for latex.

"Nothing, dear, just talking to myself."

"Crazy people talk to themselve!"

"Don't I know it!"

"What?! Oh, there *got* to be one in here. . . ."

Nigel walked into the bathroom, put his hands on Sally's shoulders, pulled her close to him, and said, "I could go out to a store and pick up a gross or two."

She looked in the mirror and at him and said, "It nearly *two o'clock* in da morning. What kind a store be open at . . . ?"

"There are lots of all-night delis, and the shelves are full of—"

"Now I not in da mood no more, damn you!" Sally broke free from Nigel's embrace and marched back to the bed and crawled under the covers.

Nigel looked at the prenatal lump under the covers as he walked out of the bedroom and into the main area of the loft. He wondered whether he should run out to an all-night deli, just in case, or whether he should just forget the whole thing. He wandered over to the espresso machine and shut it off. He poured himself a small cup of the black liquid and wandered over to the psychology section of his bookcases. He touched his copy of the *Diagnostic and Statistical Manual,* third revision, as if to derive strength from it; then he glanced at the bedroom door. "She behaves a lot like a borderline personality," he said quietly. "Ping-Pong personality. She's got a

Ping-Pong personality. *P* cubed. Meet *P* Cubed, my next ex-girlfriend —a real Asian with red hair."

Nigel chuckled, then walked to the computer. He pulled the sheet of paper from the laser printer and looked at the 1973 data for Joseph Barton. Nigel sat at the terminal and called Becker one more time. Still no answer.

He said to himself, "Now let's see what new subscriptions were opened in 1973 . . . and 1974, too." Nigel searched for all the new subscriptions and methodically transferred each of the eighteen new subscriptions from 1973, and the twenty-one new subscriptions from 1974, and the fourteen new subscriptions from 1975 and placed them in a separate file. "Now, let's take a look at *Bonsai Clubs International,* and the *Bonsai Club Newsletter,* and the *American Bonsai Society Abstracts.*"

Joseph Barton had also received the *Bonsai Club Newsletter.* He had listed the same Ithaca address, the same phone number, same student occupation, same everything, including the same year of subscription lapse—1973. But these were far more esoteric publications than the *Botanical Quarterly.* In 1973, there were four new subscriptions to the *Bonsai Club International,* and there were six new subscriptions in 1974, and five in 1975, which Nigel then printed:

	1973 New Subscriptions	1974 New Subscriptions	1975 New Subscriptions
Botanical Quarterly	18	21	14
Bonsai Clubs International	4	6	5
Bonsai Club Newsletter	8	7	6
American Bonsai Society Abstracts	4	12	10

Sally walked out of the bedroom and watched Nigel sitting naked at the computer. She played the long face, and said, "Why don't you come back to me?"

Nigel clinically examined her symmetrical breasts, then said, "Com'mere, Officer Chu. Check this out." Sally sat down next to Nigel, and before she could place her head on his shoulder, he held the most recent printout of the new subscribers to the four publications in her face, and then he double-checked the old Brooklyn Heights address, when Joseph Barton used to live on Carroll Street. "This is very weird, Sally. Check the '74 and '75 addresses and tell me what you see."

Sally looked at Nigel and said, "In 1975, there was Jo Barton, who subscribed to *Bonsai Clubs International* at the same Ithaca address as Joseph Barton for the *Botanical Quarterly* two years earlier. And now this Frieda Marx lives at the same address as Joseph Barton in Brooklyn?"

"I've got a strange feeling about this one," Nigel said.

"Me, too," Sally said. "You thinkin' what I'm thinkin'?"

"It's hard for me to know *what* you think, Sal, because by the time I respond to anything you say or do, you've already changed your mind—possibly more than once."

Sally shook her fist at Nigel and said, "One day, I'm gonna punch you in the nose."

Nigel laughed. "Okay, *P* Cubed."

"Who are you callin' *P* Cubed?"

"You're *P* Cubed."

"You mean like *P* to the third power? *P* cubed?"

"Yes."

"Why are you callin' me that?"

"I'll tell you later," Nigel teased. "I think all these people are the same person."

"That's what I think, too," Sally said. "This is the same person who got a little bit sloppy in covering his tracks. They do this kinna thing all the time. They get a whole new identity, new Social Security number, new driver's license, birth certificate, credit cards, passport, everything. Then they leave one little piece of data that links the past with the present."

"And note the age of Frieda Marx."

"Twenty-two years old in 1974," Sally said. "Joseph Barton was twenty in 1972. That would be just about right. That name Frieda Marx sounds familiar. I think I remember Brent mentioned that name for some reason. We have got to access the computer at the precinct."

"No problem," Nigel said, cracking his knuckles.

"So why are you callin' me *P* Cubed?"

"I'll tell you later."

Nigel hacked his way into Lt. Brent Kramer's computer to poke through his files and see what he could see. He downloaded the latest map of the greater metropolitan area, the same map he'd helped Sally construct from the airplane acoustic data. Overlaid on top of the map were the subscription lists for various medical and surgical journals, as well as locations of the osteopathic surgeons, doctors, and dentists. And then Nigel downloaded the names of relatives and friends of car-jacking victims. And on that list was the name Frieda Marx, veterinarian, age forty-one, living on Pond X'ing in Lawrence, Long Island.

"I wonder if Cornell has a veterinary program?" Nigel said. He smiled when he saw the address overlaid on the map. It was what they called "Zone One" residence, which meant that the house was almost directly under the approach or takeoff pattern for an airport —in this case, Kennedy Airport. Nigel also knew the neighborhood reasonably well, because he grew up only one town away, in Cedarhurst—the very town where Frieda Marx's animal hospital was.

"Sally, I'll bet this bitch is the dude we're looking for."

"Another hunch of yours?"

"Exactly. You said you wanted to do a little field work, right?"

"Right. I'm getting sick of working at the computer terminal all day long. That's all they had me do back in San Diego."

"Good," Nigel said as he sent the following E-mail to Brent:

```
Hacked some of your files. I believe Jo-
seph Barton=Jo Barton=Frieda Marx as
per my appended compilation sublst05.zip.
Pls review and comment. How is JLW III
doing? Handy Hands has some set of
balls. Visiting the vet and breaking in
one of the NY's finest. While in area
might visit my mother too—N
```

Nigel then leaned over and kissed Sally on the lips, and she responded favorably. Her hand dropped to his crotch; then Nigel bounced up and said, "P Cubed, get dressed. You're gonna do a little police work."

"You mean, outside? In the snow? Now? What about the espresso?"

Fire trucks raced up the street as flames and thickening smoke engulfed the warehouse. Sergeant Perato and Sergeant Bassett grew increasingly nervous as The Doc's men were removed one at a time from the burning building. There was no sign of James LeRoy Washington III anywhere.

Footprints of police from the Thirty-fourth were everywhere, and the building complex was now surrounded. Once the shooting had stopped, firefighters began unloading the hoses and connecting up their plumbing. The sounds of radios crackled and hissed nonstop, and sirens screamed from off in the distance as emergency vehicles of every nature approached from the west.

Sergeant Bassett approached The Hat as Sergeant Perato approached Damean, who was being packaged for travel by the paramedics. "Clayton George!" Perato nervously barked at the bleeding man. "Where is he?"

Damean looked up at the man in plain clothes, knowing he was a cop. He knew how to handle nosy cops. He'd been doing it his whole life. "Who?" he squeaked with choirboy innocence. And he pretended to be in more pain than he actually was.

Perato grabbed Damean's jacket by the shoulders and raised him up two feet off the stretcher with the clenched fists of a madman. He held the injured man to within inches of his face and violently shook him with wild-eyed indifference to life. "DON'T FUCK WITH ME, PAL!!! Now where's Clayton George?"

"I don't know what chu talkin' 'bout," Damean cried.

Sergeant Bassett wasn't able to penetrate the halo of innocence orbiting above The Hat either, but he and Perato continued their questioning.

The Doc was in great pain over on the next stretcher, but he was coherent enough to hear the cops screaming at his men. They were good soldiers, and Doc knew they would withstand any beating the cops could dish out. Doc's mind was still working, in spite of all the blood leaking from him, and he was beginning to see the picture, at least some picture. He reasoned that Clay had either deliberately brought the cops with him or they'd been following Clay without his knowledge. Clay couldn't possibly have known that he'd soon be visiting The Doc when the boys picked him up. But even if Clay *had* brought the cops for some reason, he hadn't brought Crazy Santos, and Clay blew that chick away real professional, and who knows how many others during that brief little firefight. He'd earned his keep. Clay was okay, and a deal was a deal.

"Yo," Doc said with the voice of a beach's worth of sand grinding in his gurgling throat.

Sergeant Perato glanced at the bloody man with the wet black eye patch. "You talkin' to me?" Perato said.

"Yeah," Doc groaned in a hoarse, viscous voice. He motioned feebly with his good arm for the cop to join him, imparting the sense that he might expire any second.

The sergeant dropped Damean like a sack of potatoes as he overheard one of the detectives from the Thirty-fourth say to another, "That's Doc Slater, ain't it?"

Sergeant Perato leaned over Doc as light flakes of snow melted into his superficial head wound. "Where's Clayton George? You know where he is?"

"What you want him for?" Doc struggled to get out, then turned his head to spit some bloody phlegm from his mouth.

"Just answer the question. We need to find him immediately! His life's in danger."

"No," Doc said with a pained smile, wondering why the cops thought *his* life was in danger. "His life *was* in danger twenty minutes ago. At the moment, his life's over."

"What?!" Perato belched as Bassett joined him to share the unbelievable news.

"You heard me the first time, man. Clay's in there. Santos's boys got 'im. Boy deserves a hero's funeral. Too bad for Clay, him juss gettin' out 'n all...." Doc deliberately grew detached while thinking, In the land of the blind, the one-eyed man is king. Doc waited until he thought the moment was right, then continued. "...I juss love when it snows in New York...." He began coughing uncontrollably as he was placed in the back of the ambulance.

"Jesus fucking Christ!" Perato yelled in disbelief. "I can't *believe* we fucked up this bad...."

The fire was under control, and draperies and mounds of frozen water clung to almost every vertical and horizontal surface at the site of Doc's warehouse. The fire hoses behaved like snow-making machinery, and the exterior of the building looked like a winter wonderland even though it had stopped snowing, with stalactites of ice competing with the residual heat of the blaze, melting, recrystalizing, melting, and recrystalizing to produce a strange and beautiful counterpoint to the burned-out horror within those walls.

And within those walls, Lt. Brent Kramer crawled on his stomach along the unstable second-story ledge of the floor that used to be the Doc's place of business—whatever that was. Sergeant Bassett and Sergeant Perato had unsuccessfully tried to talk Brent out of entering the building after he'd arrived at the scene. Brent insisted on finding the body himself, which also meant as soon as possible. The stairs leading to the second floor had been burned away and had collapsed, so the lieutenant gained access to the space through a window the fire truck's ladder had raised him to. The center of the floor was burned away and gone—the places where the grenades had started the smoldering ball rolling. The inside of the building reminded Brent of the caves he and Nigel had mapped deep within the limestone mountains of central Mexico. Except that it was much cooler in the caves, and the caves were natural formations and stable. This building was hot, smoky, man-made, and unstable. Any move could bring the building down on top of him.

The Scott pack air tank on his back was heavy and uncomfortable. The regulator was acting up, and the air was stale and metallic-tasting; but it was breathable. The electric headlamp could not be focused to a tight beam because the unit was defective, and the face shield was almost too scratched and opaque to see through. And his body was hurting, perhaps because it was humid out, but mostly because he hadn't exercised in more than a week. Of course, the one time he hadn't exercised for the longest he'd ever gone was the one time he had to go crawling through the rubble of a fire. But Brent was determined to sift through every burned-out cubic foot of wreckage to find James's corpse if it was in there. Brent could not explain to himself exactly why he felt James's body was not in the building. He was always so coldly scientific about the world, data, and information. But an unexplainable faith overpowered the grim news which he resisted believing; all his information came from

Sergeant Perato, whose only information came from Doc Slater. The more he thought about it, the less he believed James was dead.

Water rained from the ceiling and dripped down the walls from the continuous hosing from outside. Brent continued crawling along the west wall ledge of the space—when he heard Sergeant Perato's words through the earpiece of the radio: "Are you okay, Lieutenant?"

"Yes, Al. I'm fine . . ." Brent knew that in spite of the fact that he was not in 100 percent top physical condition, he, by virtue of his caving experience, was probably one of the most qualified people to be doing what he was doing, except maybe for Nigel, wherever the hell he was. Unaware of Nigel's recent E-mail to him, Brent thought about not having heard from him in several days. He thought this curious, because Nigel had taken such a keen interest both in the case and in Sally. Nigel checked in even if there was no damn reason to—usually to see if he could figure out what undergarments she was wearing and what style numbers they represented in the Frederick's catalog. Nigel was incorrigible, and it was unlike him to not check in—pervert that he was. Brent suspected Nigel would be pretty upset when he learned the news about James LeRoy Washington III.

"I think I have something here, Al. . . ."

Burned human flesh has a unique smell all its own. Mix that with the pungent additives of burned plastic, burned upholstery, burned wood, burned solvents, burned fabric and clothing, burned foam rubber, and burned plaster and you get the smell that permeated the nostrils of Brent Kramer as he climbed over the mutilated lump of semihuman form.

Brent pried open the cooked, steaming mouth and examined the teeth as charred skin peeled off the skull like old cracked paint from a hundred-year-old wall. And very matter-of-factly he said into the mouthpiece, "Nope. This one isn't James, either."

He crawled a few feet further, and his hand sunk into the sloshy, hot abdominal cavity of a partially cremated human being, sinking all the way to the warm vertebrae. Brent removed his hand, instantly knowing in what part of the human anatomy it was. A length of small intestine and the pancreas followed his hand out, along with several shotgun pellets; no doubt about which way this one went. Brent wiped his gooey hand on the charred floor beneath him. He knew the temperature of the body had been elevated above 140°F, so he felt reasonably certain that he had not inadvertently contracted HIV, which was his first concern. His second concern was to find the mouth of this thing. But there was no mouth. There was no mouth because there was no head. A dilemma. But not for long. This one seemed to have greater-than-average mammary development for a male. Brent temporarily became something between an archaeologist and a gynecologist, because he found what was clearly a very well done vagina. "There'll be no sexual harassment charges today," he said into his radio.

"Excuse me, Lieutenant?"

"Kitty burger—well done."

"What?"

"Another body, female—not James."

The lieutenant continued his expedition through the smoky rubble of northern Manhattan. And then he found another body near the bathroom. The occlusal pattern and fillings were not right, which was good, because the back of this one's skull was missing, and it was medium well done, anyway. Brent surmised that he was not hit with a shotgun, but the coroner would have to reverse-engineer this one's cause of death.

All this crawling around was making Brent a bit punchy. He said, "Worst case of ingrown toenails I ever saw."

"Excuse me, Lieutenant?"

"You bring the steak sauce, Al?"

"Jesus Christ, Brent! I think you've been in there breathing fumes too long."

"All right, all right. No James in this dead boy, either." Brent crawled over the body of Orion and into the bathroom. He noticed that the window was open. He looked out the window and was filled with more unexplainable hope, because what he saw was a bunch of footprints under the window. He knew in every fiber of his guts that James was out there somewhere, and that he had not been transformed into stew meat.

The floor collapsed underneath Lieutenant Kramer as he straddled the window. He climbed onto the metal extension ladder as Sergeant Perato nervously watched from the street, his radio still creating an imprint in the side of his face. "You were nuts to go in there, you know," the sergeant scolded the lieutenant.

Brent climbed off the fire truck and said, "Yeah, but if I didn't do it, it wouldn't get done. Anyway, I found some footprints in the snow below the bathroom window I wanna check out. Help me off with this shit. . . ."

Brent took off through the hole in the fence and climbed through the garbage along the edge of the Harlem River as a shortcut to gain him closer access to the side of the building. He climbed back over the fence and around the back of the building. Sergeant Perato was too fat to follow the lieutenant, and Sergeant Bassett could barely keep up with him. Brent examined the footprints under the bathroom window as Bassett approached. "What kind of sneakers was he wearing?" Brent asked Bassett.

"How the hell should I know? I didn't see him."

Brent took off after the footprints till they disappeared into the flattened snow of the street north of the warehouse, where more cops and firemen were mulling about doing their thing. Brent walked west, toward the Pathmark, but there was too much activity to pick up a trail. The commotion had brought hundreds of bystanders. The only virgin footprints were under that window.

Brent rejoined Bassett and Perato at the front of the burned-out warehouse and leaned against the radio location van, quietly observing the commotion. His attentions then drifted to the dented body and fender the vehicle had suffered during the collision. He ran his hand over the metal, then inadvertently noticed the loop antenna on the roof. He took a step back, and realized that something was not quite right. If James had met his demise in the burning building, along with the radio transmitters in his clothing, the angle of the receiving loop would have been nulled for the warehouse, not some direction almost perpendicular to where the RF source should have been, and terminated. Lieutenant Kramer entered the truck and examined the mode of the homing receiver. The autonull was still on, which meant the receiver was trying to track the direction of the transmitting source even after the fire had started.

"Gentlemen," he said to the pair of sergeants, his head tilted with the realization of having made a potentially useful discovery, "were you tracking James in autonull mode until the moment he . . . disappeared in the building?"

"Yes," Sergeant Bassett said. "Actually, he was already in the building when we drove up, and the autonull pointed to the building during the shootout."

"But you never turned it off."

"No."

"Were you watching your receiver here, after the shooting began?"

"Christ, I think we were a little bit distracted at the time."

"Well, power to the system is still on. Look at the loop, now."

"Hmmmm," Sergeant Bassett said. "That's very interesting. I wonder how *that* happened."

61   Nigel's Wheels

Nigel and Sally hopped into Nigel's VW bus and kicked the snow off their feet. Sally's first observation was that the dense entanglement of wires oozing out from under the dashboard resembled the canopy of an Amazon rain forest. Nigel reached under the dashboard and closed a series of dangling switches.

"What are you doing under there?" Sally asked.

"I'm enabling the engine, and disabling the Tasers under the seats. If I didn't disable them, we'd both be electrocuted thirty seconds after the engine starts." Sally jumped off the seat, molding her body into the dash and roof. Nigel laughed out loud and said, "Don't worry. It's perfectly safe now."

"What voltage is that thing?"

"Twenty thousand volts DC at twenty-three milliamps. It runs off a pair of rectified oil burner ignition transformers wired in series powered by an inverter running off a hidden battery. Why?"

"You expect me to sit on that thing after what you just said to me?"

"Well, yeah. It's much more comfortable than the position you're in at the moment."

Sally was nervous, and there was discernible fear in her voice.

"Is there any chance that thing could accidentally go off while we are ... driving on the streets?"

"It's never done it before." Sally began to lower her ass to the seat, and Nigel added, "But I could never say it was absolutely impossible."

"Oh shit!" Sally pressed herself back into the dashboard of the bus.

Sally watched Nigel start the vehicle by twisting a pair of twelve-gauge stranded, bare copper wires together. She looked at the back of the van, thinking that she might seek refuge there instead of on the seat.

The voluminous shit pile in the back of the van had a character all its own. A nonhomogeneous mixture of strange tools, hard hats, and helmet-mounted electric lamps, alkaline, nicad, and gel-cell battery packs, other caving gear, and rotting clothes permanently lived inside this VW van. An entire spare engine was bolted to a greasy piece of three-quarter-inch plywood. There was a three-foot-diameter collection of topographic maps stuffed into an array of bungee cord–bound cardboard cylinders. There were all kinds of clamps, metal stock, wood, plastic, and electrical supplies, a BernzO-matic torch, automotive supplies such as oil, transmission lubricant, half-filled gas cans, extra parts—like the carburetor rebuilding kit, an oil pump, a water pump, gaskets of every size and shape, a starter motor, and a pair of different-sized generators, used and new air filters, hose clamps, extra hoses, dried-up tubes of silicone rubber and caulking compound, a spare radiator, an extra muffler and connecting pipes, spark plugs and connecting wires, and all that seemed to be only the top layer. Sally snarled and said, "This place looks like your apartment."

"Yeah, don't flatter me." Sally began to climb over the engine compartment, and Nigel said, "Please don't go back there."

"Why not? I'd rather sit there than on this ... electrified seat a yours."

"If you want to sit back there, I have to disarm the crossbows, and it's a real pain in the ass to do that at the moment." Nigel reached behind him and tossed the curtain aside, and there was a crossbow, fully cocked and loaded, with a ten-inch bolt equipped with a razor hunting tip. "And there's another one just like it, behind you," he casually added.

Sally decided to take the hot seat, and said in Cantonese,

唔怪得之你老婆離開你．

[No wonder your wife leave you]

"What?"

Sally said sourly, "You crazy. This thing completely illegal. You could be arrested an' thrown in jail. I think you are mad!"

"Don't think it. I *am* mad. Mad enough to believe my right to own this vehicle and everything in it exceeds the right of anyone stupid enough to try to take it away." Nigel smiled as he drove the van out of the parking lot, then skidded off onto the street.

"You be careful," Sally scolded.

"Don't worry. I know what I'm doing."

"I don' think you know what you doing. Look, over there!" Sally pointed across the street.

"What?!"

"Fruit store. I bet you could get da condom there."

"Later. We have to go to Long Island."

On Delancey Street, Nigel stopped at a light, deliberately leaving twenty feet between himself and the car in front of him in anticipation of what might approach from the sidewalk. And sure enough, a man with his squeegee mop strutted toward his car, and Nigel pulled up five feet to avoid having his windshield slimed on. But this man was determined to extort some money, and he was antagonized by the fact that the driver of the beat-up VW van had pulled away before he had had a chance to infect the windshield with the mop. Nigel was determined not to be a victim, and said, "Get your badge, Officer Chu. Maybe he'll go away if he knows you're a cop."

"Oh, damn," Sally said as she popped open her purse and began feeling around for it. "I know I got the badge in here some-where." She grew increasingly nervous because she saw the rage welling up in Nigel. She wanted to avoid a psycho confrontation.

But some confrontations are written in the stone of destiny. The squeegee man walked toward the front of the van, and Nigel pulled up still farther to avoid becoming a customer, then turned his windshield wipers on to punctuate his desires. By now, the man would not take no for an answer. He slammed the squeegee mop onto Nigel's window for spite. Nigel reached under the seat and removed an old typewriter cylinder as he cranked down the window to pay the man for services rendered.

"There ya go, assho'," the man said. "Wadda ya gonna do, now?"

"I can't hear you," Nigel said in a cracked, timid voice. "Come closer."

The man smiled triumphantly, knowing he had shown this asshole a thing or two, and stuck his head into the window to repeat his message. With reptilian striking speed, Nigel whacked him on the side of the head with the rubberized cylinder, sending him to the street without a muscle's twitch of resistance. "There ya go, guy. Don't *spend* it all in one place," Nigel yelled, then rolled up the window and drove to the Williamsburg Bridge.

Sally looked at Nigel in amazement, only half-believing she'd actually seen Nigel clobber the offending life-form. "Why did you do that?"

"Well, I *had* to pay the man for snotting up my window. Look at that mess." The windshield wipers swept back and forth, and an arc of frozen oily slime streaked across the glass. "Turn on the defroster, Sally. Maybe we can melt it off."

"Where is the switch?"

"You see those two blue wires taped together?" Nigel reached to the ceiling and threw a three-inch copper knife switch, turning on the overhead light for Sally to see. Sally found the blue pair of wires in the rat's nest of electrical confusion.

She looked at Nigel for his next instruction. "What should I do with the wires?"

"Wadda ya think? Jesus Christ. A degree in physics from MIT and . . . Twist 'em together, damn it."

"Well, I don't know. I might electrocute myself in this death trap you driving here." Sally twisted the wires together, and warm air instantly blew along the base of the window.

"It's only a death trap to someone who doesn't belong in it. . . ."

Nigel and Sally sat quietly as they rattled across the Williamsburg Bridge. The bridge was almost beautiful in the silent snow of the night. From over the water, the lights from Brooklyn and Manhattan were soft and hazy. But then there was the agglutinating traffic jam on the Brooklyn Queens Expressway, and anything aesthetic instantly transformed into slushy stop-and-go frustration.

62   The Invisible Man

At the Thirty-fourth Precinct, in northern Manhattan, the desk sergeant put a call through to one of his detectives who'd just returned from an extended vacation; actually, the detective sergeant had just returned to duty after a four-month medical leave to recover from a gunshot wound. The telephone rang, and he snatched it up on the first ring. "Detective Sergeant Samuels here."

Chantel hesitated at first, not knowing whether she should just hang the phone up and forget the whole thing or tell the detective what she'd seen out there in the snow. She had no great love affair with the police, and Samuels had busted her at least twice within the past three years. "Hello?" he said. "Anybody there?"

"Yeah," Chantel sighed. "Dare someone here."

"Is there something you want to say, ma'am?"

"Yes . . . there is. I juss collectin' ma thoughts."

"Okay, ma'am, take your time . . . collect those thoughts. . . ." The detective heard street noises and the sound of an elevated train in the background and could tell this call was coming from a pay phone—probably over on Broadway. "Try to collect them all before you have to drop more money in the phone, though."

"Oright. Here it is. I seen somethin' out dare by da Pathmark. I seen somethin' bad."

"Wait, *you* sound familiar. Who *is* this?"

"What difference dat make to you? I juss tellin' you what I seen down by the Pathmark, in 'n parkin' lot."

"What did you see, when you were . . . working, *sweetheart?!!*"

"You wan' me hang up right now," Chantel snapped, "or you gonna stop bein' a wiseass?!!"

"All right, ma'am, we'll play it your way. What did you see ...after you got out of the supermarket, in the parking lot ...after shopping, ma'am?"

"I seen dis man throw another man in the trunk of a car. Den he close da trunk 'n drive away. Man's name was Clay. Clayton George."

"Wait...." The detective began taking notes as fast as he could write. "Was this Clayton George the man who threw this other man in the trunk, or was—"

"Clay was the man dat got hissef throwed in 'n trunk ...ya dig?"

"I take it you knew Clayton George."

"No, I psychic! I juss guess people's names outta da air! Course I know 'im. Don' know 'im well, but I seen 'im aroun' town a bit."

"Was he dead?"

"I think he been shot. He walkin' real funny, like he drunk or somthin'. Then he fall ta his knees, crawlin' aroun' like he hurt *real* bad ...or maybe he *dyin'*. Then he drop, 'n he don' move no more. That car back up, 'n dat man get outta da car 'n throwed Clay inna trunk 'n drive away."

"Can you describe the man who shot him?"

"He all bundle up. He had a scarf all rap aroun' his head. He white. Only skin I seen on his face was aroun' his eyes. I know he's white."

"How tall was this man?"

"He not short, but he not tall, either. Oh, I say he about five seven, five eight, five nine—somethin' aroun' there."

"What else was he wearing?"

"Oh, he wearin' dark pants, an' a dark coat. I mos'ly just lookin' at his head—all covered up 'n shit, almos' like a Arab dude."

"How many shots were fired?"

"I didn't hear no shots fired. He muss a used one a dem silencers ...on 'n gun."

"Approximately what time did this occur?"

"I don' know, azac'ly. I don' *got* no watch. But it was 'roun 'n time all dem fire trucks start headin' up da street, 'n all dem sirens 'n shit. There's some heavy shit goin' down tonight. . . ."

"Did you get a good look at the car. Could you describe it for me?"

"I could do a lot mo' 'n dat." Chantel looked at the piece of paper that had almost dissolved into her hand. "Da license on 'n car was H U Z fifteen K."

"You really have an eye for your cars, ma'am. . . ."

A New York City police helicopter slowly approached the front lawn of the NYNEX building in Westchester County. The security guard watched the snow swirl off the grass in the prop wash as the craft touched the ground. A police officer climbed out of the helicopter and ran to the front door, with a large yellow envelope in his hand. The guard opened the front door, and the two men walked down a long corridor, turned right, ran up a flight of stairs, then jogged to the end of the hallway. They entered a room full of computers, and a middle-aged man with a red nose and a potbelly turned to see who had entered the room. He saw the officer with the guard, and he approached while still holding a fresh computer printout in his hand.

"Are you Louis Drayer?" the officer asked in a monotone.

"Yes. Gee, you got here awfully fast." Lou looked at the large yellow envelope. "Is that—"

"The court order, sir," the officer said, completing Lou's sentence for him. "Could you please sign here for me, and then call Lieutenant Kramer at *this* number immediately."

The time was 3:28 A.M., and only moments later the police helicopter became airborne, on its way back to a heliport in New York City.

At the Thirty-fourth Precinct, Detective Sergeant Samuels ran the plates through the computer and came up with the information: FRIEDA MARX / 77 CHEVR / SEDAN / VEHICLE IDENTIFICATION NUMBER 1X27D7T141949 / CLASS 1B0011 / ADDRESS 11 POND X'ING RD. LAWRENCE NY 11559

Because it was his first night back, Detective Samuels didn't know the significance of the name Clayton George and that all information pertaining to him should be forwarded to Lt. Brent Kramer at Midtown North. And any of the other detectives from the Thirty-fourth who might have known this were all still over at The Doc's warehouse, where charred bodies were being pulled from the wreckage.

Detective Samuels called the Fifth Precinct in Nassau County.

"... One a the local hookers here made positive ID on a vehicle she claims she saw somebody throw a body into the trunk of. She claims the plate number is H U Z fifteen K. I ran the plate through and came up with someone in your neck of the woods...."

Sergeant Samuels gave the Nassau County police all the relevant information.

Up in Westchester County, Lou Drayer was diligently examining all the adjacent phone cells for any received energy at 835.650 megahertz. Northern Manhattan showed a normal power level within the cell, but the seven adjacent and overlapping cells showed none of the characteristic power increase which would constitute a handoff criteria. In the course of his analysis, he discovered that the intimidating police lieutenant was correct, and that 835.650 had been removed from the active-frequency assignment table. But Herb had left no notes to that effect. He determined this by dynamically examining the repeater reserve-frequency assignments available and comparing them to the total system capacity number of channels. Lou was rather pleased with himself for figuring this out, in spite of the fact that there were easier ways to deduce this, had he been more familiar with his system software.

Then he decided to expand the search radius to all cells within a hundred miles. It could be possible, he reasoned all by himself, for the dedicated transmitter to have been shut off, only to reappear in a nonadjacent cell. Tunneling was rare, but it had been known to happen from time to time. Usually, it resulted in a signal disconnect or an unexplained receiver-sensitivity change. In any event, this would all have to be done by hand, because the system designers had never anticipated such a misapplication.

This was going to be one of those nights.

The wheels of a Nassau County police car slowly crushed the three-inch-deep snow next to the bushes along the property line on the far left side of the road. "This is crazy," P.O. Stucky said to his more experienced partner and driver of the unit.

P.O. Pinhoe stopped the car momentarily and said, "Look at the tire tracks leading up the driveway." If fifteen years in law enforcement had taught him one thing, it was how to spot signs of recent activity. "I should be a goddamn detective." He drove up the driveway, stopping about fifty feet from the house. He shut the engine and left the rotating beacon on.

"It's three-forty-six in the morning," Stucky said. "There's no *body* in this house. These people are asleep."

"We have to check it out, anyway. You never know." What Pinhoe was really thinking, was that it would make a *great* story at the Christmas party if they *did* find a body in a trunk, even though he felt he would probably never top Marlington's story about the human head found stuffed in that bowling bag at the Green Acres Shopping Center.

The two officers walked toward the house, looking for the best route to the front door through the freshly fallen snow. "Ten to one they're gonna be mad as hell when we ring that bell," Stucky said. "They're gonna love hearing this is all because a *prostitute* said she saw some guy in this house dump a body in the trunk of a car!"

"The car owner lives here, if the car was ID'd correctly. Hell, the car or the plates might turn up stolen, for all we know. Well, here goes." P.O. Pinhoe rang the doorbell, then waited as P.O. Stucky unclipped the leather strap to his holster and placed his hand firmly on his service revolver—just in case.

Frieda Marx looked up the moment the sound of the doorbell came through the speaker. She looked at her watch and wondered who could be visiting the house at this late hour. She checked the straps on her recent arrival, then on Julio Rodriquez, to make sure they were both secured tightly. She angrily glanced at Becker, wondering whether he'd lied to her about not having told anyone that he was visiting the Cedarhurst Horticultural Club. She removed her surgical gown and walked to the entrance ramp. She pushed up on both trip levers and gently lowered the wine closet to the floor. Then she walked around the closet, hooked the rope on the eye hook, and pulled the closet back into position till she heard both latches snap into place. The doorbell rang again as she walked to the laundry room to change. She rapidly stripped naked, then put on a pink terry-cloth robe. She let her hair down, disheveled it a bit, then hopped into her pair of Ronald and Nancy Reagan slippers. Then she shut off the lights and ran up the stairs, just as the lights went on from above. Julia was awake.

Frieda could see the flashing lights through the distorted glass to the left of the front door as she approached, and she felt as if her whole world had just come crashing to an end. She composed herself, then asked in her most befuddled, helpless, and feminine voice, "Who *is* it?"

"Nassau County Police. Can you open the door, please?"

This guy sounded like he meant business. Somehow, she'd been discovered. She thought she'd either been spotted that evening or that somehow Becker was responsible. She had never considered the possibility that the double life she'd been living for the past two decades could so abruptly end. And end at the hands of all people— the damn police! Wasn't *she* the one doing *their* work for them?

"Frieda!" called the feeble voice from above. "Frieda?"

"I've got it, Mother."

Frieda cracked the door and peeked out at the two officers. She observed that there was only one police car in the driveway. "Yes?" she said, "What can I do for you?"

"Frieda! Who is it? Who is there?"

"You've woken my mother. She's very sick."

"We're very sorry about that, ma'am, but we have to check something out."

"Frieda!" came the insistent voice from the landing at the top of the stairs.

Frieda turned her head and yelled up the stairs, "Mother, please go back to bed. I'll tell you all about it later." Then she turned to the officers. "Come in."

The two cops stepped into the house, and Officer Pinhoe removed his notebook from his back pocket and said, "Do you own a car with the license plate number H U Z fifteen K?"

"Yes I do," Frieda said with a perplexed look. "Was my car stolen?" She grew agitated, as if she were worried about her car.

"Ma'am, can we go to your garage and—"

Frieda had already taken off, like the worried car owner that she was, and the policemen followed her down the stairs.

Julia had rolled her wheelchair to the bathroom and saw the police car in the driveway. She rolled to the stair lift and began to position herself so she could shift her weight from the wheelchair onto the lift seat.

In the cellar, Frieda opened the door to the garage and appeared relieved to find both the Mercedes and the Nova there, and intact. The officers walked down the steps and onto the floor of the garage. Pinhoe circled the car to the left while Stucky circled to the right. "Thank God they're both here," Frieda said with relief.

"Could you please open the trunk, ma'am?"

"Why, yes. How come?" Frieda said, as if this was the most peculiar request in the world.

"We had a report that there was . . . something inside that we should know about."

"Well, what exactly did you hear was inside—a body?" she said with a ridiculing smile.

Stucky exploded in a short one-syllable laugh. Pinhoe looked at him with the mean *shut-da-fuck-up* look, then turned to Frieda and said, "Exactly, ma'am. No foolin'. We heard there was a body in the trunk. Please let us have a little peek inside; then we'll be on our way."

"I have to get the keys upstairs. I'll be *right back*," she sang, as if this were truly ridiculous. Then she continued under her breath, "Mother will be so pleased to learn we keep bodies in the trunk of the car. . . ."

"I told you this was crazy," Stucky said, popping the safety back on his revolver and snapping the leather strap in place. "These are decent people. You gonna tell her a *whore* sent us here?"

"Please," Pinhoe said. He was really hoping a body would mysteriously appear in that trunk when the lady appeared with the keys.

Frieda Marx said, "Now if there's a body in there, I'm going to be *really* surprised." Then she opened the trunk and said, "There's your body. Allow me introduce you to the invisible man. Hey, wake up in there and show some respect, Freddy." By this time, both officers were smiling, and Frieda had allowed just enough of her robe to open so that the tops of her breasts were amply revealing themselves.

Pinhoe then said, "How many people live in this house?"

"I live here with my mother. Just the two of us."

"There are no men living in the house?"

"No, there aren't."

Pinhoe continued: "I noticed that there are tracks leading up to the garage in the snow. Do you mind telling me where you and your mother were this evening?"

"Not at all. My mother is an invalid, and she almost never leaves the house. Actually, I take her to the beauty parlor every Wednesday. That's her, sort of, special day out. And I'm a veterinarian in town. I took the car out earlier. You see, I performed a spleenectomy on a dog this afternoon, and I decided to check up on her, because I had a feeling there was some possibility of complications. It's a good thing I stopped by the hospital when I did. She was running a fever, and I gave her some antibiotics. We'll see how she is by morning. Does that answer your question?"

"Yes, it does. Sorry to have bothered you, ma'am. Does this thing open from in here?" Pinhoe asked, pointing at the garage door.

"Yes, it does." Frieda pressed the button, and the cold air whooshed in the garage as the door curled up into its track.

"Have a nice evening, ma'am," Stucky said, to get in the last word. And the two policemen ducked under the ascending garage door.

Frieda closed the door, and when the motor slammed the door into the pavement, she breathed a sigh of relief. Someone must have seen me, she thought. I must be more careful in the future. Then she walked up the stairs, to find Julia rolling around in her chair. "Mother, what are you doing down here? I told you I would take care of everything."

"Why were the police here?"

"Something about the car. It was nothing, though. Just something routine they were checking. They're gone now." Frieda then grabbed the handles of the wheelchair and turned Julia around, back toward the base of the stairs. "Now it's back to bed with you."

Nigel took the right turn onto Rockaway Boulevard, and the slushy road became noticeably bumpier—even bumpier than it had been the last time he'd driven on it during the obligatory semiannual parental visit to keep his guilt in check. It was still snowing east of the great thermal influence of New York City, and Nigel continued his eastward trek with Sally Chu, who was silently watching the planes land on Runway 331 Right at Kennedy Airport. Then she said apprehensively, "Nigel, are you sure we are doing the right thing? If this Frieda Marx turns out to be our . . . Dr. Sigma, we could be entering a dangerous situation."

"Driving on this road is dangerous," Nigel barked philosophically.

"Driving in this stupid *bus* is dangerous," Sally added, "and you are purposely avoiding the question. Don't you think we should call for some backup?"

"No. At least not yet."

"We propose to be on the property of a suspect, and if things should get *ugly*—"

"Things are *already* ugly."

Sally was half scared and half annoyed. "Well, couldn't we be in danger?"

"*Danger* is a relative term. Danger greets the division of every cell in your body—every microsecond of your existence. Think how dangerous it is . . . just to be alive, sweetheart."

"I am *not* your sweetheart," Sally angrily barked. "If I was your sweetheart, you would not forget the condom."

"Again, with the goddamn condom! I'm gonna buy enough condoms to make you ride sidesaddle the rest of your life!"

Sally almost cracked a smile, because this was the first confirmation since the blow up in the bedroom that he wanted to make love with her. She looked at him and perked up. "Why did you call me *P* Cubed? Boltzman distribution is *T* to the fourth. What is *P* Cubed? Is that pressure, or momentum, or power? What?"

"I'll tell you later."

"Nigel, it's approaching four in the morning! You're going

to walk up to someone's door like . . . like a Jehovah's Witness in the middle of the afternoon, and then ask, 'Are you by any chance . . . cutting up people and splicing them together to make hooper people? Because if you are, we find it a very artistic creation—medically speaking, that is—and by the way, you are under arrest.' "

"Well, *now* who's being sarcastic? In actuality, though, that's not too far off the money. Of course we won't be carrying our Bibles, but we'll have our trusty can of Mace, and you have your service revolver, Officer Chu. Come to think of it, I never saw you carry a gun—ever." There was no response from Sally, and after the dwell became monotonous, Nigel continued, "You do have a gun, don't you?"

"Yes, I have a gun . . . in my purse," she said to shut him up.

"Right there next to the condom you never carry around?" Sally nervously watched the road as the vehicle skidded a bit. "Tell me," he said with a hint of challenge in his voice, "when was the last time you fired it?"

"I dunno. Oh, about two years ago."

"You're a cop," Nigel said, squinting at her, "and you haven't fired your gun in two years?"

"*Ehhhh* . . . the type a police work I do, I do not use a gun. I'm a computer jockey, remember? Most of the time, I never even carry it, let alone shoot it."

"But you say you want to get back in the field. You can't go walking around without your gun."

"You do."

"I'm not a cop, remember? But I still go shooting once a week with friends. Anyway, I have this." Nigel removed a can of Cap-Stun II from under the seat next to the typewriter cylinder, and he tossed it onto Sally's lap.

She examined the Mace-like 5% pepper-extract substance, which, in theory, was only available to law-enforcement officials. "Where did you get this? This is *illegal* for you to have."

"So arrest me, Officer Chu."

"You push me, I might just do that. Might do you some good to spend some time in the clink. Or maybe I'll just handcuff you to the bed, interrogate the prisoner, see what comes up."

"Sounds like police harassment to me."

"Yeah, I show you harassment—thirty-eight-caliber harassment. Anyway, it's a good thing you have the Mace, because I got no bullets in the gun, anyway."

Nigel turned his head and looked at Sally. "You have no bullets in your gun? Are you crazy!"

"If you keep the bullets in the gun, it might accidently go off. So to be on the safe side, I take all the bullets out."

"I can't believe I'm hearing this—and from a cop! Sally, what good is having a gun if you don't have bullets in it?"

"It's safer to take the bullets out."

"So you put the goddamn safety on. That's what it's there for, right?"

"But sometimes the little button could get pushed an—"

"Sally, millions of people carry loaded guns each and every day, and not one of 'em ever accidently goes off. I can't believe you carry around an unloaded . . . paperweight! A paperweight she carries around. It's more dangerous to have an *unloaded* gun than a loaded one. Someone sees you with that, they'd blow your head off. At least if it's loaded . . . Could you do me a favor and load it, please?" Sally was silently brooding, and Nigel began to feel bad. He glanced over to her and softly said, "Sally, I'm sorry I raised my voice. Now, could you please load your piece?"

She looked up at Nigel and said, "I can't."

"Why not?"

"I left all the bullets at home."

Nigel smacked his forehead with his hand. "A hundred forty-five IQ she has, and she forgot the bullets in her gun, but she carries it around in her purse. A hundred forty-five IQ, but she's an idiot. God help her, she's an idiot! Even someone with a ninety IQ would remember to put bullets in the gun, but *P* Cubed—"

"How do you know my IQ?"

"I read your file."

"Lieutenant Kramer let you read my file?! How could he—"

"He didn't *let* me read it. I . . . read it when he left the room."

"That's all personal stuff. You snoop around where you don't belong."

"And you don't! I thought you were gonna lose your marbles there for a minute, the way you were going through all the drawers

322

in my bedroom and my bathroom. Then you threw my ex-wife's diaphragm at me. Who are *you* kidding?"

"Ahhhh . . ." Sally threw her hands at Nigel in disgust. "I see why you wife divorced you. You just a big bully. Are we getting close to Frieda Marx's house already? I'm getting anxious, an' I don't think I wanna see you no more."

"I never saw anybody change subjects as fast as you, *P* Cubed. Has anyone ever made that observation about you before?"

"No! An why do you keep callin' me *P* Cubed? I only change subjects with *you* because you are such a bully, an' you always try to keep intimidating me like the typical stereotype male. What's your IQ?"

"Seventy-two, I'm dull normal on the dumb bell curve."

"You dull normal on the dumb bell curve, all right. We don't know where the *hell* we're going. This could be *very* dangerous. What if *this* person has a loaded gun? What if we're walking into a deathtrap with only a can of Cap-Stun? We got to call in for backup."

"Calm down, Sally." Nigel reached over and took Sally's hand. She feebly tried to pull away; then she let it stay in her lap, and her fingers began to squeeze his hand to make sure it would stay where she could keep an eye on it. "We're not gonna make a big stink about being here. We're just going to quietly check out the place to find some evidence to support this little hypothesis we have."

"How are we gonna do that? We got two issues here. One: Is this Frieda Marx equal to Joseph Barton, and also this Jo Barton? Two—an'—this is where I got the big problem with your dull normal brain—why should this person be the Dr. Sigma we are looking for? And if she is Dr. Sigma, you think we're going to get this Frieda Marx to give us a guided tour of some . . . some underground operating room?"

"Very in-ter-es-ting prospect."

"I *told* you to stop talking like that horrible man!" Sally exploded. "I don't *like* that horrible man!"

They were just crossing West Broadway, and they didn't have very far to go. "Well, in any event, we're probably dealing with an egomaniac. . . ."

"What does that got to do with it? I think *you're* a egomaniac! That don't make you Dr. Sigma. Maybe you are. You are pretty weird."

"You think just because I'm never wrong that *that* makes me an egomaniac?"

"No wonder you got a ex-wife instead of a wife. Let's do the worst-case analysis. Let's assume that this *is* Dr. Sigma. This is a *very* dangerous person. How do you suppose this person managed to abduct all the people he turned into hoopers—he lures them with candy? He, or she, shoot them all with darts."

"They didn't know they were being abducted. There was the element of surprise on the side of the abductor. We, on the other hand, have the *distinct* advantage, because we suspect who we're dealing with. Dr. *Sigma* doesn't."

"Nigel, I think you are crazy. Do you think that anyone who is mutilating half the paroled population is going to have . . . not a shred of paranoia when two grown adults come knockin' at the door . . . at this hour of the night?"

"Well," Nigel said, "I hadn't planned on just walking up to the front door and introducing ourselves. We're going to have a little look around the premises."

Sally conspicuously registered discomfort when Nigel made a left turn onto the Causeway. The road was not heavily traveled enough to show the surface of the road through the patted-down snow. The Lawrence Golf Course was beautiful and white, and this area was much more rural, and this disturbed Sally. "What then? What is the first thing you plan to do to . . . check out the place?"

"Park the van a couple of hundred feet past the house."

"You know what I mean! After that!

唔怪得之你老婆離開你。

[No wonder your wife leave you]

"Will you speak English, damn it?!"

"Of course I was jealous when I found the diaphragm!"

P cubed, Nigel thought, then smiled. "Of course you were. I understand completely," he said, then made a left turn onto Pond X'ing.

"After we look around premises and see all the bushes and the outside of the house in the snow, what then?"

324

Nigel knew his next statement was going to irritate Sally thoroughly. "We're probably going to break in, so as to acquire a little background data, so to speak."

"That *illegal!*" she exploded.

"Not if ya don't get *caught,*" Nigel sang.

"Yeah, what do we *do* if we *get* caught?!! I'm a police officer. I could lose my badge. I could lose my job. This a breech a procedure. We don't got no search warrant. This is wrong. We could blow the case on a technicality . . ."

"Hopefully more than just the case. . . ."

"Oh *you* gonna get it," Sally said, shaking her fist at Nigel. "I have seen cases get lost in court all the time. If we get caught—"

"The odds are against it. Once again, we have the advantage. In any event . . . you'll be right there with me."

"What?!!"

"Oh, lighten up, Sally. Anyway, we're here. Welcome to field work." Nigel pulled over to the far left and disconnected the wires, which, in a normal vehicle, constituted turning the ignition key to the off position. He observed two pairs—no, three pairs—of tire tracks leading up the driveway to a house, the house in which Brent's computer said Frieda Marx lived. In the accent of Elmer Fudd, Nigel said, "Be perfectwee quiet, now. We're hunting wabbits!"

Sally thought Nigel was out of his mind, and she saw visions of herself in handcuffs, marching off to the Women's Correctional Facility in West Virginia, wearing a long number on gray coveralls.

Nigel reached behind him and confirmed that the crossbow trigger mechanism was armed. Then he leaned over behind Sally and checked the other crossbow. Sally instinctively got out of the car and Nigel quietly closed the passenger door. He then reached under the dashboard and disabled the vehicle and armed the time-delayed electrified seats. He placed the shoulder strap of a small Gore-Tex bag around his neck, then tightened the waist strap from the same bag, securing it tightly against his body. From the bag, he removed a Maglite flashlight and Minox camera tied to a leather thong and placed it around his neck. He grabbed the can of Cap-Stun, then locked the driver's side door.

Sally could not believe she'd been talked into coming to this place in the first place. Second, she could not believe that Nigel was readying himself as if he were a spy preparing for a covert mission.

She watched Nigel fixing himself up with all kinds of fancy doodads, and when she saw the set of lock picks, she knew Nigel was not only serious about breaking into the house, but he was determined to do so. Then Nigel slipped his hands into a pair of latex gloves. He handed Sally a pair of gloves and said, "Here, put these on," then walked toward the driveway and the tire treads that disappeared into the white-laced darkness.

64 B & E

Nigel approached the pair of parallel two-inch-deep tire treads which snaked their way up the driveway toward the house at the top of the hill. It was clear that one of the cars that had produced one set of these tracks had skidded several times on its way to the other side of the closed garage door. Nigel slinked like a cat up the right tire tread, and Sally delicately followed about fifty feet behind. A single low-wattage amber night-light dimly burned above the front door of the house, but under the present conditions, no extra light was necessary. The moon, the low cloud cover, and the light pollution from the Five Towns and Atlantic Beach provided all the diffuse light necessary to reflect off the blanket of virgin snow surrounding this house and the grounds. Clumps of snow clung to the drooping foliage. Nigel contemplated his next move while waiting for Sally to join him.

Sally's heart was pounding not only because she had climbed up a hill in the snow in the dead of night, but also because this type of activity was way out of her league. She was a data cop, not a spy. She watched Nigel with a certain admiration, because he was not afraid. He was not afraid of anything, or anyone. And at the moment, Sally's biggest fear was encountering people. This place was clearly inhabited. The tire treads were proof of that, and from the look of these marks, they had been formed recently. And if it was so important for Nigel not to leave footprints, Sally wondered, then what was he planning to do when he got up to the house—fly? And there were already footprints leading to the house, and from the garage.

Sally pondered the meaning of the word *covert*. Nigel was making decisions faster than she could agree or disagree with. Brent had warned her about Nigel and his uncanny ability to talk people into doing things they would never dream of doing on their own. It was as if Nigel were a kind of psychotic magnet pulling all things in. But to where? Sally had no idea. She simply followed.

Nigel stood before the pair of tire imprints leading up to the metal garage door. It was an automatic garage door, and there was no way to enter the house without the aid of an oxyacetylene torch. Instinct told Nigel to circle the house in the direction of maximum darkness, to the right. Darkness was familiar to Nigel. It was his ally —the darkness of the caves he liked to play in with his friends. To sit in total darkness, surrounded by the rocks. To be surrounded by tons of limestone, deep under the ground. The darkness, whether below ground or above, was always the way to go.

He ran back down the tire imprint toward Sally Chu, motioning for her to stop where she was. Nigel did not want to climb the retaining wall to the right of the driveway, preferring instead to walk around it. Sally was about to speak as Nigel raised his finger to his mouth, requesting silence, then he walked past her and leaped to the edge of the driveway. He walked along the edge of the wall and approached the house. Sally reluctantly followed.

Just as Sally got close enough to say something to Nigel, he took off again, continuing along the perimeter of the house. Nigel stopped at the eastern solarium and waited for Sally to join him. "We should not be here!" were the first sounds from Sally's mouth since Nigel had disconnected his ignition wires.

"Will you think like a detective for one minute?" Nigel said.

"Okay. You want me to tell you how many statutes we are breaking by being here without a search warrant?"

"I said think like a detective, not a lawyer."

"Okay. I play your game for a minute. We have a little greenhouse, here. Look at all the lovely plants. Now let's get the *hell* outta here."

"Doesn't something strike you odd about this, Sally?"

They both looked at the longest face of this plastic-paneled extension to the side of the house. And then their eyes slowly dropped to the lawn, which was not covered with snow. A patch of bare lawn in the shape of a fuzzy-edged fifteen-foot-long half ellipse intersected the side of the greenhouse. "That's pretty strange," Sally whispered. "Do you think it was the direction of the snow?"

"No. I don't think so," Nigel said, shaking his head as he looked at the rest of the eastern face of the house. "The pattern is all wrong."

Sally's curiosity was piqued slightly, and she knelt down and felt for warm air leakage through the walls of the greenhouse—the warm air she suspected might melt the newly fallen snow near the house. Nigel shook his head, no, more for himself than for her, and he awaited her thermal report. Sally waved her hands all along the base of the greenhouse. "I think it is sealed pretty good," she said.

Nigel felt the ground in the center of the green patch. Then he stepped back and raised the Minox camera to his eye. He took two photographs of the bare patch on the lawn and said, "I've seen these shapes in snow before. . . ."

"You think there's something down there?" Sally said.

"Yes. I've seen this on top of heated underground bunkers," Nigel added, then walked up to the greenhouse. It was dark inside, and Nigel listened carefully for the sounds of any human activity. Thirty seconds passed; then he shined his flashlight through the panels of the greenhouse, observing the floor plan and any indication of an alarm system. Nigel could see all the way through to the living room, which was as far as his beam could reach.

Sally grabbed Nigel's arm and said, "Anything interesting in there?"

"I don't know yet, but I really want to know what's directly under where we're standing. Let's go." And Nigel took off, around to the back of the house, to find a proper point of entry. Then they discovered the western solarium on the other side of this large house. Nigel and Sally peeked inside, then continued their counterclockwise stroll around the house.

The side door. Nigel removed a compass from his bag. He swept the instrument across the top of the door frame, and the needle deflected about four inches from the left edge. Definitely the magnet of a magnetic door switch. The door was alarmed. Whether it was armed or not was unknowable. Nigel did not want to find out the hard way. He continued to work his way around the house. There was a magnetic switch on the front door also. And one on the door to the left of the garage. Sally could not believe that this same Nigel she'd been programming the computer with at the precinct was also a professional second-story man. She was now curious to know if Nigel had a criminal record; he seemed to behave with the MO of a jewel thief. He looked up to the windows on the higher floors, knowing that they don't often put switches on hard to access windows. For Nigel, though, it was not hard to access windows—any windows. He had all the tools he needed for scaling walls back in the bus. It was simply a matter of finding the easiest point of entry. Then he got an idea. He backtracked back around the house. Sally caught up to him at the western solarium, which had glass windows. "Sally, wasn't the other greenhouse made of plastic?"

"Yes. Why?"

"Follow me." Nigel returned to the eastern solarium and felt the plastic.

Sally, the physicist, authoritatively said, "It's a special acrylic that doesn't filter the UV below—"

"I don't give a damn what its spectral response is. I'm only interested in its melting point. Wait right here. I'll be *right back*."

"Wait!" she whispered, then stood there on the patch of bare lawn, looking into the darkened greenhouse. It suddenly hit her, once again, exactly how crazy this whole thing was. She awaited Nigel's return, wondering what he would do next. Melting point? Sally thought. Then Nigel returned with the BernzOmatic torch and a tire iron.

"My feet are freezing!" Sally said.

"This will only take a minute, sweetheart."

"I told you before, you are *not* my sweetheart!"

Nigel removed a lighter from his pouch and lit the torch with a muffled *pop*. He adjusted the flame to burn a deep blue then he began heating one of the lowest plastic panels. When the plastic in the immediate vicinity of the flame began to sag, Nigel poked it at its softest spot with the tire iron, swirling out a hole.

Sally held her face with her hands, shaking her head, and said, *"Ohhhhh,* this is all wrong. We should not be doing this." Nigel smiled up at her, then continued advancing the torch, not burning the plastic, just melting it enough to push out the rectangular perimeter of a slot large enough to crawl through. And when the melted plastic panel was pulled clear, Nigel crawled into the solarium. When he was completely inside, he turned and looked out at Sally, who was on her hands and knees, peeking back through the hole at Nigel.

"You actually expect me to follow you into there . . . through *this?*" she whispered.

"Yes. Why?"

"I'll never fit through there!"

"Of course you will. I fit through, and so will you. Put both your hands through first; then the rest of you will follow."

"But that means I got to lie down flat on the wet grass."

"So? Your knees are already wet, and take that stupid coat off." He waved for her to come, and she got down on her stomach and passed her coat through the hole. She put her hands and head through the rectangular hole and struggled at first, because she was not used to squirming around on her belly. "I'm never going to make it."

"Of course you will. You're doing fine. Just keep going."

Sally couldn't believe that she was actually half in and half out of somebody's home in the middle of the night. Nigel moved some planters out of the way so she wouldn't inadvertently knock them over. She was not moving elegantly, at least not nearly as elegantly as she'd moved back at the loft, Nigel mused. Then he grabbed her arms and slid her the rest of the way in. Nigel leaned the panel he'd melted back up against the hole while Sally caught her breath.

They quietly walked between the dense rows of plants, until they could see into the living room. Nigel entered first, slowly. He looked around the room for any signs of an LED mounted on an electronic box stuck to a wall somewhere. There didn't seem to be any high-tech security devices anywhere. He waved for them to proceed. They walked across the living room, then approached the area near the front door.

Nigel periodically rubbed his can of Cap-Stun Mace. Knowing it was there gave him a sense of security. Then he walked toward the kitchen. He found the door to the cellar, and he proceeded down the steps. The light was on down there; in fact, several lights were on. Nigel reached the bottom step, and he looked up to Sally, who gingerly followed.

Nigel opened the door to the garage, and saw the car that had produced some of the tire treads in the snow. There was melted water under the tires, and the body of the car still had beads of water on it. It was an old Chevy Nova. Looked like the late seventies—'77 or '78, Nigel guessed. And the trunk was open. How odd. Nigel quietly walked down the steps and walked around the car. He grabbed his Minox and photographed the Nova and the open trunk, and the Mercedes in the next slot. Then Nigel left the garage and entered the bathroom with Sally. They silently observed that the tub was still wet. They entered the main area of the cellar, wandered around a bit, and both ultimately gravitated toward the table saw and the tools.

While both Nigel and Sally were quite familiar with passive infrared sensors, they could not have been aware of the fact that an emergency light had just lit inside the elliptical egg room, only a few feet from where they were standing at that very moment, and that while most of the Eastern Seaboard was asleep in their beds, someone was very much alert, and armed with a battery of chemical weapons, one of which had already been used once that evening.

Then Nigel whispered, "I think what we're looking for is against *that* wall." And he pointed at the *Threepenny Opera* poster tacked to the big wooden sliding door.

65   Interesting Possibility

Nigel held his can of Cap-Stun Mace firmly in his right hand as he and Sally cautiously approached the door. It was the only spot against the east wall of the building substructure that could possibly lead farther to the east, which was where they had to go to be under the solarium and that anomalous hot spot on the lawn. Nigel took hold of the big wooden door and slid it to the right as quietly as he could. He shone his light inside, and they looked at all the rows of bottles in the wine room. They both took a step forward onto the wooden floor, which sagged slightly from their combined weight. Nigel looked straight ahead at the hook in the far wall, and Sally examined a curious length of rope on the shelf to her right, a length of rope with a loop tied at the end.

This place didn't look right. It didn't feel right. And it didn't smell right, either. "Recently poured concrete," Nigel whispered. "It smells like recently poured concrete." He leaned against one of the side rails supporting a row of bottles to the left, then pushed his weight into it. The whole wooden structure rattled slightly.

Frieda stood just on the other side of the back wall to the closet. She heard the cage rattle. More people! More people in the closet. The cops brought more people, she thought.

She ran silently to the light-control panel and immediately shut the main lights. She ran to the area of the refrigerator and dimmed the light by the workstation. She removed five little bottles of tranquilizer mix from the refrigerator, unscrewed the caps, and swiftly placed them into the custom loading fixture she'd built. She dropped the control bar, and five hypodermic needles simultaneously punctured the latex drip caps of the five bottles, penetrating deep into the fluid of each bottle. She pulled the bar up, and all the hypos simultaneously filled to the 3-cc mark. With a flick of the wrist, five fresh darts mechanically took the place of the five bottles, and she simultaneously injected the tip of each hypo into the larger-gauge dart points and filled all five darts. She smeared Vaseline over the tips of the darts to seal them so fluid would not leak out when the dart assumed the horizontal position. Then Frieda loaded the darts into the magazine of the pistol. She turned a screw, and the CO_2 cartridge was punctured with a hiss; the pistol was now ready to fire.

She ran to the ramp, and looked helplessly, at first, at the back of the closet, listening to the shifting weight inside, and Frieda held the dart pistol tightly in both hands, pointed directly in front of her.

Inside the wine closet, Nigel knelt toward the wooden floor and shone his light under the lowest shelf on the left. He saw the curious latching lever, and instinctively reached his hand out to touch it. He pushed the handle end, and with little resistance, the hooking end popped out. "Very strange," he said.

Sally knelt down and whispered, "What are you doing down there?"

"You see that lever to your right over there?" Nigel whispered as he shone his light on the other lever under the bottom shelf to the right. Sally looked, and she saw the lever Nigel was pointing to. "Push it in."

Sally pushed on the lever. "It's stuck."

"Push it harder."

Sally grunted. "This is a awkward position. . . ."

"Change places with me," Nigel whispered.

Nigel slithered around Sally as she duck-walked out of his way. Nigel shone his light at the lever, and, with a single thrust, jammed the heal of his boot into the lever. . . .

"AHHHHHHHHH!!!" both screamed as the entire wine closet took off down the cement ramp, picking up speed with every inch it rolled. And the next thing they knew, when the wooden structure hit the level floor, they were both still rolling backward, into the darkness, with wine bottles dropping from shelves and rolling all around them.

Nigel's first action was to try to find the can of Cap-Stun he'd dropped and lost somewhere within all the wine bottles that had come crashing down on them. But instinct told him to kill his flashlight immediately, which he did. He looked across the dark room but could see only panel display lights of various colors from lots of electronic equipment, none of which he could make out. There was no indication as to the shape of the room or that there was anyone inside. He held his breath and listened for about ten seconds, but all he could hear was the sixty-cycle hum of AC transformer laminates somewhere from within this acoustical reflection chamber.

Then Sally moved, and knocked a pair of bottles together. "Shhhhhh!" Nigel whispered.

Nigel stood and slowly walked out into the open, attempting to avoid stepping on the wine bottles, which were everywhere on the floor. He was listening for anything he could hear, anything to break the regularity of the droning hum, as his night vision acclimated to the darkness of the room. He hoped that the panel LEDs could guide his cave-sensitized retinas to the conclusion that he and Sally were really all alone.

Nigel focused on what appeared to be a light in a rectangular form which was covered with a thick cloth of some kind. He could definitely see tiny speckles of light through fabric. He approached the source, listening, listening carefully for any change in the background noise, moving closer to the source, which he now stood in front of. He reached out and pulled the curtain aside, and intense light escaped.

Nigel caught a glimpse of a person wearing a light blue surgical gown and a surgical face mask about fifteen feet away. There appeared to be something wired to the head of this person, but he could not make out what it was; then he saw a puff of gas from the center of the form. . . .

Pfffft.

"FUCK!!!" Nigel screamed as he dropped the curtain and scampered back to the wine closet and Sally. He kicked several bottles as he felt his way inside the wooden structure. Then he yanked the dart from the meaty portion of his left thigh and stuffed it into his fanny pack.

Nigel said to Sally, "We have to run for it while we still have time." And Nigel bolted from behind the wine closet and toward the exit. A bright flashlight shined at him in the dark, the same way he used to hunt frogs at night with his .22, only now he was the frog . . .

Pfffft.

Nigel was hit in his right hiking boot, just above his heel. He continued to run—out the egg room corridor and up the stairs.

The doctor walked with urgency to the entrance. Sally was frozen by the side of the wine closet, squinting into the bright light. The doctor looked at Sally and said into the harmonizer, **"A woman!"**

Then, like a robot, the blue figure raised the pistol and pointed it directly at Sally Chu, who watched in terror, trying to see around the blinding corona of light, and could barely produce the words, "Don't shoot."

Pfffft.

And then, very methodically, the doctor walked out after Nigel, hoping he wouldn't make too much of a scene before he was apprehended.

334

Sally watched this person with the flashlight walk up the ramp and slam the door, locking her inside. Now she was alone in the darkness, frightened, and stinging in the place where the dart had punctured her skin above her right breast. She twisted the dart from her flesh and probed its shape with her fingers. She felt defeated, and part of her wanted to cry. But part of her wanted to be strong and take control of the situation if at all possible. She fondled the dart as she walked into the darkness of the egg room, kicking the wine bottles away from her feet. She felt her way up the ramp and prodded the area of the door to find a way out. She pulled and wiggled a lever with no success, and she heard it rattling on the other side of the door, but she heard no signs of human activity.

At that moment, Nigel was clawing his way through the hole in the plastic panel of the eastern solarium. The surgically gowned doctor ran up the steps two at a time, with the tranquilizer pistol raised vertically in the air.

Commotion in the solarium. The doctor swiftly and silently strutted across the living room and into the solarium, following the noises she heard. Whatever happened, she did not want to wake Julia, who was probably dead to the world anyway, but Frieda didn't want to take any chances with Julia, especially after she'd been awakened once already. Julia knew nothing about the double life of Frieda Marx, and Frieda wasn't going to take time out to explain it.

In the solarium, Frieda was startled to see the man she'd shot twice suddenly stand on the other side of the clear panels, look back to make fleeting eye contact, then take off into the yard. She felt cold air blowing on her feet, and she instantly knelt down and saw the hole in the plastic. Without hesitating, she dropped to her stomach and crawled out the hole, never losing sight of her target, who had about a hundred-foot lead on her. But she knew that it would be only a matter of time for this one. She'd stalked humans before, and this one wouldn't be any chemically different from all the rest— including the one she'd locked in the egg room. It was unfortunate that that one happened to be a woman.

—————

Back in the egg room, Sally needed to find the lights, or whatever light Nigel had found before the sound of the dart. She wandered back down the ramp and approached the panel lights on some electronic equipment. Then she was distracted by those same bright speckles of light through the fabric.

She touched the rectangular box and pulled the curtain aside, instantly bathing the middle section of the room in light from this one source. She saw the ring plant inside but was unimpressed. To her, this box was one thing and one thing only—a source of light. She threw the curtains on top of this display case, then looked at the shape of the egg room and the things inside.

She gasped when she saw the three men strapped to boards and horizontally restrained. She instantly recognized Becker Instlokrownctjz and James LeRoy Washington III. The other man was a stranger. Sally now knew that she and Nigel had found Dr. Sigma, and she knew these would be the next people to be mutilated. And then the eerie thought occurred to her that if James LeRoy Washington III had somehow managed to get here without the police having followed with all the tracking receivers, something had gone very wrong sometime that night, and her fear level jumped a notch.

Sally shook Becker, but he was semiconscious. Then she walked over to James and shook him, too. She glanced at the man she did not recognize. All three had IV tubes leading to their necks and Foley catheters leading out from under their gowns. Suddenly, she felt tremendous anger toward Nigel.

Nigel was running through the woods, attempting to make his way toward the road. At first, he was putting good distance between himself and Frieda Marx. Time passed, though, and his gazellelike motions were, quite suddenly, more resembling those of a beached walrus.

His plan was simple enough. He would lure his nemesis into the back of the van, and the crossbows would do the rest. The trusty crossbows. He could hear the sounds of his pursuer in the woods, and the tangle of foliage grew denser as he struggled through the slippery snow. Less gain for more effort. Must find a better route, he thought. He knew he was growing clumsier as the seconds ticked away. He removed his flashlight and Minox camera from around his neck and stuffed them into his pack. He grabbed his wallet and attempted to stuff it into the pack, too. Then he unclipped the fanny pack and lobbed it like a hand grenade into the snow a few feet from where he struggled. He knew someone might find it eventually, and in his mind, he screamed the name Brent.

He was surprised at how rapidly the effects of the drugs accelerated after his first perception of any pharmacological effects. He refused to accept the growing inevitability that he might never make it to his van, where he could kill his assailant. *Kill* was the only word circulating in his mind as he fought the relentless effects of the drug. It had a similar sensation to the effects of CO_2 poisoning—by the time you feel the effects, it's almost too late. And this sensation had one other difference; he could taste a sickening sweetness in his mouth. And his lips felt like they were made of rubber.

Nigel crawled through the snow on hands and knees, because he could no longer stand. He felt he might still be able to crawl to the van and kill. Kill . . . Kill . . . . . . Kill . . . .

Frieda Marx approached her collapsed prey. She slung his snow-covered body over her shoulder and carried him back through the woods, toward the house, and across the lawn. She looked at the ellipse of bare grass for a moment, shook her head, knowing she would have to remedy this revealing situation, then continued walking over to the front door, with Nigel slung over her shoulder.

Frieda set Nigel down next to Sally, who lay unconscious under the electrical panel with the can of Cap-Stun Mace in her limp hand. Frieda placed the can on a table and shook her head. She then removed the remaining two darts from the five-shot magazine of the pistol and emptied them, saving the drugs in the refrigerator.

She filled two hypodermic needles with fluid from a bottle and approached her two unexpected guests to prep them. They would have to be cleaned and sterilized. She injected them both, then gazed at Sally. "A woman," Frieda repeated. "Interesting possibility."

Lieutenant Kramer sat down at his desk back at Midtown North after just returning from the warehouse. He reeked of smoke and he was only now beginning to realize how exhausted he was. He nervously pelted the wall clock with an eraser and wondered if Lou Drayer up at NYNEX had the faintest idea what he was doing on his end. Brent felt guilty that he had not personally spoken with all the mobile communications supervisors, and he believed it now might have cost him valuable time. Ten minutes earlier, back in the car, Lou had told Brent he would have some information compiled within twenty minutes, so Brent touched the mouse of his computer and the screen sprang to life. He clicked up his electronic mail to continue where he had left off before the fire, and he noticed some new messages, one from Nigel, and another from Carl Spatts at the bureau. He clicked on Nigel's first:

```
Hacked some of your files. I believe
Joseph Bar@@@@@@@@@Barton@@@@@@@@@@
@@@@@@@@@@@@@@@@@@@@@@@@@@@@@@@@@@@@
@@@@@@@@@@@@@@@@@@@@@@@@@@and comment.
How is JLW III doing?  Handy Hands has
@@@@@@@@@@@@@@@@@@@@@@@@@@@@@@@@@@@@@@@
breaking in one of NY's finest.
While in area might visit my@@@@@@@@@@@@
@@@@@@@@@@@@@@@@@@@@@@@@@@@@@@@@@@@
@@@@@@@@@@@@@@@@@@@@@@@@@@@@@@@@@@@
@@@@@@@@<<*&&*>>@@@@@@@@@@@@@@@@@@
@@@@@@@@@@@@@@@@@@@@@@@@@@@@@@@@@@@
@@@@@@@@
```

Brent examined the cryptic message which had somehow been mutilated by the computer system in much the same way as other messages had been mutilated before and since Sally had allegedly tampered with the system. Brent muttered, "How many times have I told him not to inject messages directly into the interoffice system from the outside?" He shook his head in disgust, then clicked up on the next message, from Spatts:

```
11/17/93

FROM:   S.A. Carl Spatts
        FBI, Albany Office

TO:     Lt. Brent Kramer

RE:     Call to Div. of Parole

At 3:54PM we unsuccessfully attempted to
trace a telephone call to the informa-
tion officer at the Division of Parole.
The caller requested information for a
Charles Ebel but did not stay on the
line long enough to complete the trace.
We'll get him.—CS

DW/rs
cc: Dep. Dir./EL/DDB/SMB/BT/MM/MHS/NP
```

"Interesting," Brent said. Maybe they couldn't trace the call, but Brent figured at least he could listen to the voice of the caller if the tape recorder had picked it up. He bounced up and shuffled to Sally's office to download the conversation. And the following is what he heard:

"Hello, Department of Corrections, Public Information. How can I help you?"

"I would like some information on the parole status of an inmate."

"Hold on one minute. Let me see if Mr. Silverman is available."

Silence for fifteen seconds; then Mark Silverman came on the line. *"This is Mr. Silverman."*

"I would like to know the parole status of Charles Ebel."

"Hmmm. . . . Charles Ebel?"

"Yes."

"Please hold, while I get his file." Brent knew that this was the time when Mark Silverman would be contacting the FBI, which was the new procedure they'd worked out so the call could be traced

more quickly, but not quickly enough, because no sooner had the wheels been set into motion when the line went dead.

Brent listened to the conversation over and over. It was unclear to him whether the caller was male or female, and there was a fair amount of automobile traffic in the background, so the call was probably made from a pay phone out on the street somewhere. There didn't seem to be any obvious sounds that would indicate a point of origin, like the city, or the country, or the suburbs, or near a train station, or along a bus route, or near a schoolyard, or an airport, or anything except the sound of cars passing at what sounded like less than forty miles per hour; the audio experts would have to analyze this later. Brent consolidated the digital audio data file so he could hear the mystery caller's three utterances concatenated:

"I would like some information on the parole status of an inmate."
"I would like to know the parole status of Charles Ebel."
"Yes."

He listened to his new file several times—still no help. Then went back to his office to call NYNEX.

"Lou, how's my trace coming?" Brent asked.

"Lieutenant, the last power signature we have for 835.650 was in the northern Manhattan cell. There were no handoffs recorded to any adjacent cells, as might be expected for a mobile transmitter."

"Are you absolutely sure?"

"I could run it again, Lieutenant, but I'll come up with exactly the same thing. Your man must have shut off his transmitter, or his batteries failed, or maybe the radio just died. . . ."

Or maybe he just died, Brent morbidly thought.

". . . These things happen, you know," Lou continued. "I even checked all cells within a hundred miles. I checked New York. I checked New Jersey and Pennsylvania. I checked Connecticut, and even southern Massachusetts." Brent drifted off in thought as he watched Perato, Bassett, and several other detectives enter with depressed faces. "Are you there, Lieutenant?"

"Yes, Lou. Still here. Say, were there any anomalous power readings, at all, anywhere, for any duration?"

"Funny you should ask *that* specifically, Lieutenant. There *were* several sporadic glitches that the computers recorded, but they weren't significant."

"What do you mean 'they *weren't* significant'?"

"Exactly what I said, Lieutenant. They weren't significant. The durations were too short to be of any significance."

"How short *were* the durations, and what were the locations?"

"Well, they varied in duration, and they were all over the net —must be about ten or twelve of 'em. You want me to give you *all* of them?"

"Yes."

"Well, we have a half-minute power reading from the Kearny-South Kearny area over in Jersey, and that was logged at 2:16 A.M. We have another half-minute reading from City Island at 1:53. Here's *aaaaa* . . . one-minute-and-twenty-second reading in Teaneck. Here's one that's a minute and a half over in Lynbrook, Long Island. . . ."

"Wait a second, Lou. Let me bring something up on my computer here." Brent waved Perato and Bassett into his office as he brought up the airplane acoustics map with the overlay of the suspects list, color-coded by priority. "Kearny–South Kearny? Interesting. That repeater happens to be on the approach pattern to Runways Twenty-two Left and Right at Newark Airport. . . ."

"Why is *that* significant?" Brent did not answer, and Lou continued pedantically, "You have to realize something, Lieutenant, these were probably faulty phones free-running on the wrong as-signed frequencies until they resynced on the command pulse we send. The phones are manufactured by many companies these days, and some of them are not well made. Occasionally, the internal logic of a mobile unit misaddresses the frequency synthesizer. Then the mobile unit transmits on the wrong frequency for awhile. These things happen, you know. Any phone is capable of transmitting 835.650 megahertz. It's just that the network is presently configured *not* to transmit a command word to any cellular phone on that frequency, which is your dedicated channel—channel 355. The fact that two mobile units transmitted . . . what . . . twenty-three minutes apart in two distant locations from each other is proof that this happens frequently, because it was impossible for *us* to send a command pulse at 835.650. Lieutenant? Are you still there?"

Brent was lost in thought as Lou droned on. When Brent thought about a glitch in the context of electronic systems, somehow the time span of milliseconds or microseconds came to mind. He reasoned that the glitches, as Lou called them, occurred for periods of time more than long enough to drag a body from one electromagnetically shielded area to another electromagnetically shielded area. This could explain why a signal might disappear from one cell and reappear so far away. But how could a signal appear at several distant locations separated by only minutes? Brent hated to admit it, but Lou had to be right—at least about all but one of the signals, possibly all of them. If Lou was right about all the signals, James LeRoy Washington III *might* really be dead, just as The Doc had said.

"A minute and a half, you say?"

"Yes. Actually, about a minute and forty seconds for the glitch in Lynbrook."

"I find it hard to believe that a one-hundred-second carrier signal is called a *glitch*. A hundred milliseconds maybe, but a hundred seconds?"

"Sometimes it takes a while to reestablish sync. The system is *very* complicated, and this type of thing happens all the time. . . ."

"Lou, I'm putting you on the speaker phone. I need you to repeat all those locations, and I need the radius of each cell and the locations of the transmitters in each cell."

Brent printed out his maps, and he and his men began plotting the coordinates of each glitch and suspect probabilities based on his estimation, James LeRoy Washington III's time of abduction and the time each glitch was recorded in the net, and where it was relative to any flight path.

And after Lou downloaded all his glitches, Brent had his men listen to the digital recording he had downloaded, but nobody recognized the mystery voice on the phone.

Frieda Marx returned to the egg room from the shop in the main area of the basement with a makeshift restraint board for the woman. Frieda hadn't counted on acquiring five people so quickly. Julio

Rodriquez and the recent arrival she believed to be Clayton George were peacefully vegetating on their restraint boards. Her old professor was also at peace with the world, at least temporarily, and so was that nasty man who had made her run out into the snow to retrieve him.

She looked with contempt at the beautiful Chinese girl, dressed as she was, lying there on the floor. Frieda hated the pretty ones. While she'd dug out the egg room for eight long years, other girls, the pretty ones, like this one, would be stair stepping and dancing in their colorful, tight exercise leotards, squeezing their wiggling little labial flaps to the four-four beat of mindless technopop. Frieda hated the sexy ones who took all the men—the sexy ones who thought they knew what the meaning of exercise was. But the exercise of building the egg room was complete now, and the future looked bright for less conventional exercise, she thought as she strapped the girl to the board.

As Beethoven's Piano Sonata in F Minor, op. 57, "The Appassionata," concluded, Frieda worked into the unseen night up above. She felt as if she had an unusual amount of energy this morning. She felt as if she had all the time in the world, and as if time didn't exist. The task was all that mattered, just like when she was digging out the egg room, bucket by bucket, and lugging all those tons of earth out to the lumps and mounds she'd created around town.

Frieda cleaned and prepared her tools before her unconscious captive audience of five, strapped to their boards, with IV-drip tubes taped to their necks like life-giving vines feeding a patch of naughty pumpkins. The patients were all behaving so well, now that they were under control, and so cooperatively taking their medication. But the time had now come to type some blood, change some bottles, get some answers, and get down to the business at hand. "Solutions for answers," Frieda said as she waltzed across the room and removed those blue and amber bottles from her refrigerator full of dwindling chemicals. "Let's mix up a batch of solutions for answers."

Drip . . . drip . . . drip . . . drip . . .

More detectives trickled into the station as Brent handed out regional assignments to all available bodies. Within each mobile communications cell they would investigate the highest-priority suspects and work their way to the lowest, and if that failed, who knew where the hell James would turn up in six weeks, and what he would turn up as.

"Gentlemen," Brent announced, "Washington is either alive, or he's dead. Our only indications that he might be alive are some footprints outside a window, a directional antenna that was *not* pointing to where he would have to have been had he and his transmitter burned up in the fire, and I *didn't* find a body—yet—and lastly, we have all these friggin' glitches we're gonna check out. We don't have time for telephone search warrants, so we're bypassing the code of criminal procedures on this. We're acting in good faith, though, so legally there shouldn't be any problem after the dust settles, but I want each and every one of you to use the utmost discretion. Use honey, not vinegar—do what you gotta do, but let's keep the civil and criminal liabilities to a minimum, please. My neck is already out a mile on this one. Let's not make it any worse.

"As far as jurisdiction goes, you'll be met by detectives at the respective rendezvous points outside the boroughs—that goes for New Jersey, Connecticut, and Nassau County. Lieutenant Morales will be centrally coordinating here at the station if there are any communications that don't come directly to one of us. We all have each other's cellular numbers on the printouts I gave you. Good luck. Let's get moving."

And with that, Brent stood, and a roomful of detectives hit the road.

The operating table on which James LeRoy Washington III lay bound and semiconscious was tipped to the horizontal position, and he had a pair of dotted lines inked onto both his arms, five inches above the wrists. Dotted lines were also drawn on his legs to indicate the precise spot where they would be amputated.

Frieda Marx was so pleased that her version of Clayton George pumped type A-negative blood through his vessels. And this was convenient, because stockpiling too many comatose patients with incompatible blood types used lots of precious drugs, and it could eventually set all kinds of unnecessary flags with the pharmaceutical regulatory people up in Albany; but they had their job to do, and Frieda had hers. These things had to be handled properly, however, like everything else in the world. All the rings would have to be properly matched. But once again, fortune had smiled on Frieda Marx, and it was time to forge on ahead with the work that needed to be done—the work that now could proceed ahead of schedule.

Julio's table was tipped to the horizontal, and dotted lines were inked onto his arms and legs, too. His operating table was rolled over to Clayton George's, and the wheels of both tables were locked into position.

With anger, Frieda glanced at the Oriental woman and that awful man who had invited themselves into her egg room. They would require some special custom therapy; after all, they'd deliberately trespassed into the egg room. Trespassing must be punished. All crime must be punished. Without punishment, the free radicals bring anarchy, and will oxidize an otherwise-stable society. Social oxidation is bad. Social stability is good. Crime is bad, and therefore punishment is good, and punishment is necessary. But what punishment is appropriate for these two? Frieda thought. Interrogation would be necessary, and they would soon be recovering from the tranquilizers. Perhaps the girl would be transformed into one link in a chain of hoopers, along with the other incompatible oddballs who would periodically accumulate. Perhaps she would be transformed into a mermaid—a beautiful Oriental mermaid with a blowhole. All the long bones in her legs could be fused, allowing the knees to still flex and the skin could all be sewn together. It would be a fascinating challenge, mechanically and surgically, and the problem would have to be carefully considered, but she would not go to waste, this trespasser. All scientists know that scientific resources must never be wasted. And that other horrible man—why had he come?

Frieda waltzed over to Becker and adjusted his valves, because she wanted him awake enough to observe her skill with the knife firsthand. She placed a surgical mask on him while leaving his blindfold on for the moment, then checked the timer on the autoclave. There were still many preparations to be made.

Lt. Brent Kramer had met Nassau County detective Falcone in the parking lot of the White Castle on Sunrise Highway and Peninsula Boulevard in Lynbrook, Long Island. Falcone was a glib man with absolutely no sense of humor, and he accompanied the hyperactive lieutenant from New York on this miserable night only because he was told to do so by his lieutenant, but otherwise, he thought this Kramer with his weird acoustics maps and computer printouts was out of his mind. They approached the now-underutilized home office of the fourth suspect's house—a third-rate orthopedic surgeon who had recently had his license revoked. There were tire prints in the driveway and footprints leading to the office entrance. Falcone was not impressed, probably because he'd never heard of James LeRoy Washington III, and personally he didn't give a hoot whether he or anyone else became a hooper or not. Brent rang the bell, and they both watched a light go on in the house.

Becker, Nigel, and Sally became less groggy as Rachmaninoff's Piano Concerto no. 3 in D Minor concluded. Frieda tilted all their restraint boards to the vertical position, then switched on the harmonizer and adjusted the pitch offset. **"Hello, Doctor. How are we this morning?"**

Becker Instlokrownctjz was not in the most responsive state of mind, but when he realized he was aware of his own existence, the first thing he did was to try to move his hands to determine that the sensation his brain was perceiving was not a phantom sensation, but the real thing.

"They're still there, Doctor. I don't want to harm *you.*"

"What is it that you want from me, Jos—Frieda?"

"I want you to understand what I am doing, and why. I must tell you, though, that I am *very* disappointed in you, Professor. I thought that you, of all people, would understand what the world needs—what needs to be done, and the purity of my purpose."

"Why must you talk to me . . . through that voice pro-ces-sing machine?

"I *always* talk through the harmonizer during the operation."

"Operation?" Becker said, still unaware that three more people were now present in the egg room.

"Yes. You are going to witness the creation of stability. Clayton George and Julio Rodriquez are about to be made stable. Now it seems that *I* am the professor, and *you* are the student."

Nigel was in a similar state of mind to that of Becker, except that Nigel had had far more firsthand experience with mind-bending drugs. And Nigel could have sworn that he heard the sounds of Becker, and, through the camouflage of a harmonized human monstrosity of a voice, the familiar name Clayton George.

"Becker?" Nigel uttered.

"Nigel?" Becker said.

"Soo*oooo,* you two know each other! What an in-ter-esting coincidence, as you would say, Doctor. You have *both* been *very, very* naughty boys, and you will both have to be punished. . . ."

Sergeants Perato and Bassett approached the house of Drs. Stella and Richard Isman in Montclair, where they were met by New Jersey detective sergeant Garbini, who'd been dispatched from the Newark Major Crimes Unit to assist. Detective Garbini was a bit surprised to find himself now assisting the NYPD on the famous hooper case, and he joined Perato and Bassett in their vehicle, and then the three of them watched the house, which seemed to have only one light on upstairs. And only one car was in the driveway: the Volvo with the license plate BROTHER—and it hadn't been moved. Tire prints from another car, probably SISTER, were visible, but about three-quarters of the cumulative snowfall covered them, placing the imprint time of departure somewhere between 12:00 A.M. and 1:30, they estimated. A possibility. The Ismans were at the top of the suspect list, so the detectives approached the house and circled it with caution. There appeared to be no other activity other than the light on upstairs.

The three detectives silently looked at one another, removed their weapons, and Sergeant Perato rang the doorbell twice. There was no response from inside, but movement was heard upstairs from the second floor, possibly the room where the light was on. Perato rang the bell again, several times. No response, but the detectives convinced themselves that they were really hearing noises from the second floor. Perato knocked loudly on the door five times, then said, "God, I gotta lose some weight." No response. Then Perato and Bassett looked at Garbini, being that he was from New Jersey, who took a step back, planted his left foot firmly on the ground, then kicked the front door open with one quick thrust of his right foot. The detectives cautiously climbed the stairs and approached the door where the light was on.

The door to Stella Isman's bedroom flew open, and the three detectives stood there gazing across the room at Dr. Richard Isman, professor of mathematics, dressed in his sister's panty hose, black pumps, a cute little red pleated skirt with a shiny black vinyl belt, a smart all-occasion blouse, a blond wig—the good professor's left hand was still handcuffed to his sister's bedpost, and he could not quite reach with his outstretched foot the key, which he had nervously dropped just outside his desperate reach during his hasty retreat to ready himself for his unexpected guests in the middle of the night.

"So, your name is *Nigel,*" Frieda Marx said as she shook her head sorrowfully.

"Just . . . a nickname," Nigel lied, hoping to buy some time while the hypo wore off. "So . . . you must be . . . Frieda Marx. Is the woman all right?"

"Why were you trespassing on my property?"

"Is the woman all right?"

"I can see that you are going to be difficult," Frieda said as she removed an electric cattle prod from a stainless steel drawer. **"Why were you trespassing on my property?"**

"Sally!" Nigel called.

"I would advise you to answer my questions, so that I may ascertain what your disposition is to be."

"My disposition?! If I were you, Frieda Marx, aka Joseph Barton, aka Jo Barton, I should start thinking about *your* disposition."

"How *dare* you!" Frieda growled, then jammed the cattle prod under the gown and into the soft tissue beneath Nigel's ribs. She pressed the button, blasting him with a high-voltage shock.

Nigel screamed as his body went into involuntary squirming spasms in reaction to the unexpected shot of voltage.

"Are you all right, Nigel?" Becker asked through his own clearing veil of delirium. "What did she do to you?"

Frieda prodded Nigel with another shot of voltage and said, **"You broke in rather professionally. Do you know what happens to naughty criminals who trespass on other people's property?"**

"Huh?" Nigel moaned. He felt his coherence level jump a notch with the burst of adrenaline released by the current passing through his body.

"Dr. Instlokrownctjz, *why* did you bring him here?"

"I didn't . . . bring him."

"Then how do you two know each other?"

"Just friends."

Unsatisfied, Frieda asked, **"Is *he* a cop?"**

"No."

"Who is the woman who was with him?"

"I . . . am blindfolded. . . . I . . . don't know what . . . woman you mean."

Detective Falcone had followed the New York lieutenant all over Lynbrook and Rockville Centre waking people up out of their sound sleep, so when he received an APB for the oil truck that skidded into a pole near the LIRR overpass, he bid Kramer farewell and went his way. And only moments later, Brent's car phone rang, and it was Lou Drayer at NYNEX.

"It's probably nothing, Lieutenant, but the computers picked up another glitch that we missed earlier. We recorded a power reading from southern Nassau County. This signal was logged at two-fifty A.M., and it only lasted about a minute and a half."

"Where in southern Nassau County?"

"The Reynolds Channel repeater."

Lou fed Brent the latitude and longitude coordinates, and it was instantly clear that the Reynolds Channel repeater was on the approach pattern to Runway 31 at Kennedy. And one more thing was clear: Frieda Marx lived within that zone.

"Nigel?" came the feeble, drugged-out voice of the man impersonating Clayton George.

"James?" Nigel squeaked. "Is that you?"

"She got me," James said. "Didn't feel . . . nothin' like I thought it would. . . ."

"The time has come for you, Clayton George, you naughty boy."

"Frieda, baby," Nigel said, "That's not Clayton George."

"That is Clayton George, and he is a murderer, and he *must* be stabilized."

"Wrong! His name is James LeRoy Washington the Third, and he's a cop, Frieda. We planted him in place of Clayton George. They look quite similar, don't they? Oh, this is all too beautiful. The woman—she's a cop. I'm a cop. Becker is working with the cops. We're all cops! In a few minutes, this place is gonna be full of even more cops," Nigel risked saying with a smile, unaware that his E-mail to Brent was corrupted and useless as a navigational aid. "You're outta business, Frieda, baby."

"Stop . . . antagonizing her," Sally said in delirious disgust from behind her blindfold.

"Sally!" Nigel said. "Didn't I tell you this was the place! I think she's overloaded. . . ."

唔怪得之你老婆離開你。

[No wonder your wife leave you]

"This can't be true. You are a trespasser. He is a murderer. Dr. Instlokrownctjz said you weren't a cop, and if you are, then *he* lied and must be punished. The woman—"

"Did I eva toll you about de Porto Reeka ba-que technee?" [Did I ever tell you about the Puerto Rican Vacuum Technique]?" Julio Rodriquez blurted. Frieda alternated glances between Sally and Julio.

"Why don't you . . . turn off the harmonizer," Nigel said. "We all know who you are."

Frieda thrust the cattle prod into Nigel's mouth and pressed the button. **"You *don't* know who I am!"** she snarled. **"You don't know *what* I am! You don't know *anything* about me—none of you! And I don't *like* you!!"**

Nigel's eyes were tearing under his blindfold. "You're gonna pay for this," Nigel spit through his tightly compressed teeth.

"No, *you're* going to pay, you little *worm!"* Frieda said, then jammed the cattle prod into Nigel's testicles and blasted him with bovine-intended voltage, which instantly caused him to go erect. **"Men!"** Frieda sadly said while shaking her head, examining each of her male captives, then glancing at the woman. **"Simply disgusting! You are a very bad boy, and I think you need to be neutered."**

The chilling thought suddenly occurred to Nigel that this is exactly what that psychic in Brent's office had predicted a few months back.

Frieda looked with pity at the unsightly bulge under Nigel's gown, created by his—thing! She remembered when she still had that extra ugly appendage of skin, back before dear Arthur removed it for her—to transform her into a whole woman—an anatomically correct whole woman. Only Arthur had the real penis, and his penis was for her—for her and her alone. But his body is dead now, she thought remorsefully. Dead because of people like them—dead, but his mind lives within me. All other penises are therefore useless— unnecessary vestigial pimples of skin—simply the end of the urinary tract—a waste of flesh—ugly skin that sticks out, disrupting the contour of the perfect feminine form. The female urethra is the only true method by which a urinary tract should terminate, and must terminate. It is the only clean solution to the problem of emptying the bladder. Everyone knows that this is true—at least every woman knows this.

Brent drove along the slushy asphalt on autopilot, shaking his head to keep from nodding out, and soon he felt as if some of his energy was returning.

Then a thought occurred to him. When he'd first met Frieda Marx, she'd said something about a high-powered police investigator showing up at *his* door. Brent even remembered correcting her, and she'd said she didn't buy into political correctness. Then he thought about the tape recording he'd downloaded from Albany, and how androgynous the voice sounded. Then he thought about Nigel's E-mail again, wondering exactly what Nigel meant by "breaking in one of NY's finest."

Frieda had just finished blood-typing Nigel and Sally, and they both possessed A-negative blood. Frieda now saw clearly what she had to do, and this was more than a stroke of good luck. This was the very definition of destiny itself—four people with the same blood type and the same RH factor.

Four patients with type A blood made things convenient from a philosophical standpoint as well, because numerologically, and scientifically, four is a magic number, and therefore a very good number for the new project. After all, there are four nucleotides defining the entire gene code, and two squared is four, and four squared is sixteen, which is only half of thirty-two, Frieda reasoned as she ran her fingers, with great satisfaction, across the cylindrical contour of fused bark in Becker's Ring, which was created from thirty-two little trees all lovingly joined throughout years of delicate care and precisely controlled growth.

Within Frieda's present capacity to reason, she knew that Nigel and Sally were not murderers, as such, but they were guilty of seeking her out, most probably to disrupt the work that needed to proceed on schedule, according to plan, and for that reason alone they needed to be punished—both of them. They would all be mechanically reconfigured—these two and the murderers—the four of them, such that their blood would mix with one another's, and they would all purge themselves together and know the love of union and stability. And Becker had now lied to her; of this she was convinced. He would watch the operation, which would now involve a ring of four—not simply two. This would be her greatest achievement yet, and her old professor would witness it, and then he would understand the next logical extension of the work he himself began all those years ago.

Oh, the joy! Frieda thought as she took stock of the few remaining drugs she had in the refrigerator, estimating that there would be just about enough to do what needed to be done. Oh, the joy!

Frieda was filled with renewed confidence, and she was now thinking in verse:

> *Were their voices all still sleeping—were they still sedated?*
> *I wonder what the threshold is, that my boys are rated?*
> *The very first in-ci-sion . . . will commence the fun.*
> *In just a few short days from now, my boys will all be one.*
>
> *Yes, my boys will merge and sing.*
> *No arms—no feet—I'll make a ring.*
> *My boys and me.*
> *My boys and I.*
> *My ring of boys,*
> *Will sing and cry—plus that Oriental woman!*

Frieda removed several pounds of sharp tools from the steamy autoclave and placed them on a pair of trays; then she removed the miter box from a large plastic bag. She turned the stopcocks on James and Julio. Then she inserted the catheter into Sally's subclavian vein and began to draw dotted lines on her wrists and ankles.

Brent turned left onto Pond X'ing, and immediately saw Nigel's van. He hit the brakes and skidded twenty feet. He thought for a moment, then pulled up to the driveway of 11 Pond X'ing, blocking it, so that no cars could enter or leave. He walked over to Nigel's van and looked inside. He almost touched the vehicle, then thought better of it. He knew all about Nigel and his vehicle. And he also knew that Sally was with him, because her footprints were all around the passenger side of the van, and this answered the part of Nigel's E-mail riddle: "While in area might visit my . . ." Brent knew Nigel's mother lived in the town of Cedarhurst.

As Frieda slowly inserted the catheter into Nigel's neck, he said, "You know you can't continue this. I personally agree with you, philosophically, and I think you've been doing good work—till now."

"I think you should be quiet and try to get some rest."

"Hear me out, sweetie. The cops are all gonna be here any minute. You better escape while you still can."

"I am only doing what the police should have been doing all along—binding up the free radicals. You, too, are a free radical, and you must be made stable, like the others. . . ."

Brent held off making any calls for the moment, and ran up the driveway. He saw two sets of footprints leading to the front door and a return pair of footprints leading from the garage. Footprints were leading up the side of the house, and these he followed. He walked to the solarium, and saw snow and footprints all around its perimeter. It appeared as if there had been an awful lot of snow shoveling in the yard. Brent noticed the hole in the plastic panel, and how it had been melted out. He looked at the pattern of the snow, which now covered the spot where there had been no snow before, but he could make no sense of it. He saw the footprints leading off into the woods, and he wondered why they were there, and what would possess someone to go in that direction. He followed the prints and found the spot where Nigel had collapsed.

And then he saw the fanny pack—Nigel's fanny pack. Brent lifted the pack and folded back the Velcro flap. Lock picks, screwdrivers, needle-nose pliers, tweezers, dental mirror, voltmeter, some Krazy Glue, small Pomona jumpers, a compass, flashlight, Minox camera—on the eighth picture—a pair of shorted number-six detonators with an electronic timer, sample collection bags, and then there was this curious cylindrical item with some blood on the tip—a tranquilizer dart—a used tranquilizer dart. Brent turned, and there on the snow was a wallet, which he picked up; it was Nigel's wallet. He walked back to the solarium and stood in front of the hole burned into the plastic.

For a moment, he thought he heard an electronic sound from

somewhere. He listened more carefully, and thought he heard
"**... You are a free radical ...**"

"Free radical?" Brent said out loud.

Brent had heard and seen enough. He ran back down the driveway to his car. He called the Nassau County Fifth Precinct and requested a backup unit. Then he returned to the house, walked to the front door, removed his Glock 17 from his holster, *click-click,* and rang the bell.

69   A Leg Up

Frieda Marx looked up when she heard the bell through the speaker. Someone *else* at the door. She did not know what to do. She looked at Nigel with hatred. Could this be the cops he said would come? She thought for a moment, composed herself, and looked at her other brave but naughty boys, who looked like they could be counted on to be quiet. After all, there was not much they could do. But there was plenty that she could do.

She turned the stopcock on Nigel, 1.5 cc's per minute; then she ran to the refrigerator and began the dart pistol loading procedure for the second time that evening.

Julia Belden was remarkably awake, considering that she'd already been awakened once out of a sound sleep that night. The television was on, and she heard the doorbell ring. She called to Frieda but heard no reply. Frieda had been answering her calls less frequently these days; she must have been out on another one of her walks. Julia leaned over to the intercom by the side of her bed and pressed the talk button. "Who is it?"

"Julia, this is Lieutenant Brent Kramer. Remember me?"

"Oh, yes, of course I do, Lieutenant. I'll be right down to let you inside."

Brent waited outside, with his gun pointed straight up in the air. More snow had fallen into his shoes, and the sides of his feet were growing wet and numb yet another time that evening. He watched the fog he created with each breath he exhaled, wondering whether he should wait for the backup squad car or go in alone. He had the feeling that time was of the essence. Thoughts of coffee percolated in his mind while he waited for Julia in her wheelchair.

And then the door opened, and Brent cautiously looked inside. Julia saw the gun and said, "Lieutenant, why is your gun out? This is not a movie."

"It will be when the cameras get here. Julia, where is Frieda?"

"I don't know. She didn't answer me. She must be out for a walk." Brent entered the house and instinctively walked toward the solarium. "Lieutenant Kramer, what is going on here?"

"Did anyone come to the house today?"

"No, except for the police last night."

Brent stopped and turned. "WHAT?!"

Frieda removed the old CO_2 cartridge from the pistol, even though it was not empty, and screwed another one into position. She did not want to be caught without enough compressed gas to propel her solutions into the flesh of yet another naughty boy coming to invade the sanctity of the egg room. She knew that she would be safe with her chemicals inside her egg, as long as she could sit tight, and as long as her boys were quiet.

"It's true," Julia said. "The police were here last night, but Frieda handled it."

"Why were the police here?"

"I don't know. All Frieda told me was that the police came by . . . something about a car, but Frieda assured me that it was nothing serious, though. I saw the police car myself, in the driveway. I was watching from the bathroom window."

That explained the extra pair of tire treads in the driveway, and some of the footprints, maybe. "Did they leave the house through the garage?"

"Why, yes, how did you know?"

"What time were they here?"

"Maybe three o'clock or three-thirty in the morning. Then I went back to bed."

"Julia, I'm going down to the basement. There should be some more police here shortly."

"Lieutenant Kramer, what is going on here?"

"I haven't got time to explain right now." Brent ran down the stairs and stopped at the landing. He lowered his gun to the horizontal position and slowly walked across the floor, checking all the rooms, one at a time. He glanced across the shop area, then walked to the big sliding door and whispered, "I always hated that poster."

The infrared sensor told Frieda Marx that some unwanted intruder was in her basement, in the vicinity of the door to the egg room. She fixed a small halogen intensity lamp to one of the threaded rods sticking out from the wall. She ran the extension cord over to the lighting panel and plugged it into one of the switchable outlets. She turned off the lights, as she had done before, and quietly waited by the wall to see what might appear.

Brent grabbed hold of the door in his left hand and slid it all the way to the right. He looked into the dim wine closet, then entered, his gun still pointed forward. He removed a small penlight and examined the interior of the room closely, without touching anything. And something was odd. The last time he'd visited this room, he observed that all the chardonnays were along the right shelf at eye level and the Côtes du Rhônes were on the shelf directly below. Everything was nice and logical, including an assortment of Australian cabernets he remembered over to the left. Why, then, was everything so haphazardly arranged now? Graves '71, a white zinfandel, next to a Côtes de Bourg '86 next to a merlot—whites and reds and roses, all as integrated as the personnel department of a Fortune 500 corporation after a few field-leveling rounds of affirmative action. It was as if all the bottles had been randomly arranged. Frieda Marx wasn't into busing her wine bottles into different neighborhoods. If anything, she was on the anal-retentive side. Something had happened here.

Brent's examination of the wine closet eventually drew him closer to the floor and that interesting pair of levers. He pushed one, and the entire room jogged slightly. He pushed the other one, but it appeared to be stuck. He sat on the floor and tapped the lever with his foot several times, and he felt the lever moving with each light thrust. He looked up at the rope with the loop in it, then over to the hook in the back, and suddenly it all hit him, but too late for him to do anything about it; the entire closet began moving, then all the bottles came crashing down from all over the place. And the next thing he knew, he was in total darkness, on his back. Instant fear.

And then the intensity light switched on, and he saw the outline of someone with a gun. "DROP IT!" he yelled, pointing his gun at the silhouette in the light.

Pfffffft.

Brent fired his gun with a deafening explosion as he thought he heard his name being called. Then he realized something had hit his shoulder—a dart, not a bullet. A dart! There was a goddamn dart in his shoulder, and it hurt like hell. "Jesus fucking Christ!" he said as he yanked it out of his skin. Then he stood up and looked for the person he'd shot.

"Brent!" Nigel yelled. "Am I glad you're here."

Brent said nothing. He walked over to where he thought his target was, and there on the floor, on her back, was Frieda Marx, bleeding from her side, to the right of her breast. He knelt down and removed the surgical mask from her face and said, "Jig's up, pal." Then he saw Sally strapped to a board, and everyone else. *"Hmmmm, I see we're all here."*

"Brent," Nigel said

Brent placed the tranquilizer pistol in his pocket, then walked over to James LeRoy Washington III, who was unconscious on his board. He placed his fingers on James's neck and felt a strong pulse. "God, am I glad you're—"

"Brent!!" Nigel yelled. "You got the E-mail!"

"What fuckin' E-mail?!! The system's as fucked up as it ever was. . . ." He yanked the blindfold off Nigel and said, "And what the *ffffuck* are you doing here, asshole?! And why did you take *her* here? I oughta smack you. . . ."

"Brent," Nigel pleaded, "did she shoot you with the gun— the tranquilizer gun?"

"Yeah, she shot me with the gun, right in the shoulder here, but I shot her with this!" And he held his gun triumphantly in the air.

"We're not out of the woods yet. Brent, can you still understand me."

"Why sure, buddy."

Bad sign. This was how Brent spoke when he was shit-faced drunk. "Brent, is she dead?"

"No, Nige, she's still alive."

Becker turned his head and said, "Lieutenant Kramer . . ."

"Hmmmm, Dr. Instant-loco-witz . . ." Brent laughed.

"Becker, don't distract him!" Nigel yelled. "Brent. Undo these straps. Undo these straps right now, before you collapse. BRENT!!!"

"Don't yell, Nige. I can hear ya. You know, I should leave you here for a while. It would serve you right."

"Brent, please listen. That stuff comes on like a brick wall. Undo me quick. Pull the needle out of my neck." Brent slowly peeled back the tape and began to withdraw the catheter. "Ahhh! Be careful, you're hurting me!"

"It's okay. It's okay, man. . . ."

"Yeah, it's not your neck. Now take this strap off—this one right here." Nigel wiggled his right arm so Brent would know where to start.

"Okay buddy. Hold your horses." Brent reached for the strap to Nigel's right upper arm and tugged at the Velcro. Most of it came apart, but not all of it. Then Brent tugged at the strap that held his wrist.

Nigel could see Brent's pupils dilating, and he was becoming rubber-legged. It was hitting him, and Nigel wasn't sure if Brent even knew he was being overtaken by the tranquilizer. Nigel didn't want to distract him with the slightest tangent, because every second counted. "Hurry, Brent," Nigel whispered.

"I'm going as fasht . . . azz I can. Jushhht hang on there. I'll . . . I'll get ya loosh . . ."

The strap was looser, but not off. There was not enough elbow mobility to slide his hand out yet.

Then Brent looked down at Nigel's gown and saw that he had an erection. He laughed as he struggled to say, "I didn't know . . . you'd be . . . that glad ta shee me . . ."

"Get this shit off me, or you're gonna wind up like this, too. Brent? Brent . . ."

All wasted words, because Brent's gun dropped off his finger onto the floor; then he collapsed, and the dart pistol fell from his pocket and lay there, on the cement floor, next to his unconscious body.

Nigel twisted and tugged at the strap frantically, trying to free his right arm. He rocked his elbow and his entire body back and forth, and could feel a few fibers of Velcro peel away with every painful thrust of strength. He was still sedated, but at least the drip was out of his neck. And then he saw Frieda stand, holding her bloody side. She lumbered over to the work area, by the refrigerator. She rummaged through a drawer and removed some bandages. The lighting was low over in that part of the room, and it was hard to see exactly what she was doing, but Nigel kept working at the elbow restraint, which was his only chance at freeing himself.

Frieda looked over in his direction. Nigel kept his head low, as if he were unconscious, while he continued struggling with the strap. It was a frustratingly awkward position, and he felt like Houdini trying to free himself from a straitjacket while upside down in a tank of water. He saw the tip of Brent's gun sticking out from the side of his body, and all he could think of doing was reaching for it and blowing out the brains of Frieda Marx—blowing out her brains with the remainder of the clip.

Becker said, "Lieutenant?" Nigel wanted to tell him to keep his mouth shut, but he couldn't risk drawing attention to himself. And all this time, Frieda continued to mend her wound, slowly and methodically. She was naked from the waist up, and Nigel could catch glimpses of the red stuff, lots of red stuff, so much red stuff that he couldn't make out where exactly she'd been shot; it looked like somewhere on the right side of her body, with blood over both her breasts. He tugged frantically but could not free his arm.

Then the doorbell rang again. Frieda turned in slow motion and looked at the speaker that had produced the offending sound. "Oh, will they never stop coming?" she said, without the aid of the harmonizer.

Nigel dropped his head to his side, keeping his eyes open in tiny slits, to keep an eye on her. She stuffed a fist-sized cotton ball into the hole in her side; then she drifted over to the wine closet.

Bottles were everywhere. She got down on her hands and knees and swept the bottles out of the way as if her arms were windshield wipers. She walked up the ramp and closed the big wooden sliding door. She returned to the egg room, then climbed into the wine closet and began returning the bottles to the shelves once again.

The doorbell rang once more.

Frieda seemed disinterested in her captives, as she returned to the workstation area to continue attending the front and back puncture wounds in her body. Apparently, the bullet had passed completely through her chest, about four inches below her armpit. Nigel hoped she'd punctured a lung and that she would bleed to death and drown in her own bloody fluids, but that would be unlikely with only a single lung punctured. He prayed for it to collapse. Nigel wanted to shoot her in the other lung. He wanted to rip her lungs out of her chest cavity and watch her die. He drew strength from his urge to kill her like a beast. He kept banging his elbow into the strap, trying to break loose, Velcro fiber by Velcro fiber.

"Hello, ma'am," P.O. Pinhoe said to Julia Belden at the front door. "We're sorry to bother you again. But is there a Lieutenant Kramer here from NYPD?"

"Yes," Julia said. "He's down in the cellar." She pointed in the direction of the stairs.

"We already know where it is," P.O. Stucky said.

Both men looked at the invalid woman, who apparently was the mother of the woman whom they'd met earlier that morning. Everything appeared to be as the younger woman said. The two officers went to the basement and walked around, checking out all the rooms. "Lieutenant Kramer?" Pinhoe called. "Check the garage," he told Stucky.

"Lieutenant?" Stucky yelled from in the garage. He walked between the cars. "There's no one in here."

"And there's no one in here, either," Pinhoe said to his partner. "Wait. Let's see what's in here," he said, noticing that there might be something on the other side of the sliding door with the *Threepenny Opera* poster on it.

Frieda noticed that the light went on, indicating the presence of more warm bodies outside the egg room. She could feel herself still bleeding, but she had to push the closet back into position, and she had to do it now. She walked behind the wooden structure and slowly and quietly pushed the entire closet up the incline, latching it into place just as the sliding door opened.

"A wine cellar," Officer Pinhoe said to Stucky, "And he ain't in here, either."

Then the two officers walked up the stairs.

"There's no one down there, ma'am," Pinhoe said to Julia Belden.

"He has to be down there, because he never came back up here," she insisted from her wheelchair.

Pinhoe insisted, "There's nobody down there, ma'am. We checked the entire basement, and the garage."

"I spoke with him in the foyer . . . not ten minutes ago, right here in this spot. I saw the lieutenant go down there with my very own eyes."

"Let's check again," Pinhoe said, rolling his eyes, and he and his partner returned downstairs. "There's something very strange going on in this place." Then, while pointing his fingers at his head and twirling them, implying the old woman was mad, he whispered to Stucky, "I think the old lady's bats."

"*Lieutenant?*" Pinhoe sang patronizingly. "*Oh, Lieutenant Kramer? Come out. Come out, wherever you are . . .*"

Nigel continued to struggle, relentlessly working the stubborn strap on his right arm, and he watched Frieda return from the ramp, and he knew he was locked inside once again. They were all locked inside, and the madwoman was walking toward him, so he let his body go limp, pretending to be unconscious. She stopped about five feet from him, naked from the waist up, and shook her head when she saw the IV missing from Nigel's neck. She looked down at Brent, then over to the tranquilizer gun. She knelt down to pick up the gun, and then Nigel opened his eyes long enough to see the exit wound in her back. Blood oozed from the hole, and Nigel thought, Bleed, bleed, bleed to death, my dear.

Then she stood up and walked over to Becker, who lay unconscious against his board. She leaned her head close to him to see if he was still breathing; he was awfully quiet. Suddenly, Becker's right arm ripped up through the straps and grabbed Frieda by the jaw. He jammed his four fingers in her mouth and dug his thumb into the soft spot under the bottom of her jaw.

She struggled as he lifted her off her feet, and she bit down on his machinelike fingers. She kicked her feet frantically and she gurgled and screamed like a wild struggling animal. Every muscle in Becker's face contorted like an Olympic weight lifter as he labored to hold her off her feet in the air and to fight the pain of his fingers being bitten and scored to the bone by her gnawing teeth. He began to rotate and wiggle his hand to try to break her jaw off its hinges.

Pft.

She fired off a dart, and it hit the ferro-cement wall, shattering upon impact, leaving a wet, angular splatter pattern. Becker could not see through the blindfold, but he heard the shot. He continued to rotate her back and forth.

Pft.

Another wild shot from the pistol.

Nigel felt his right elbow strap finally coming loose. He broke his elbow free, then pulled his hand out of the wrist restraint. He reached his free hand over to his arm and ripped off the straps. Both hands free. Using both hands, he removed the chest strap, then the neck strap, then the waist strap, then the thigh straps. Then he knelt, lost his balance with the ankle straps still on, and fell forward.

Pft.

Another shot, which hit the restraint board right where Nigel's head had been before he fell.

Frieda dangled from her jaw, and then she swung her arm around, pressing the tranquilizer pistol straight into Becker's cheek.

Pft.

Becker instantly released her, and she fell to the floor and crawled toward the center of the egg room. Nigel grabbed Brent's gun in his right hand, watching Frieda on her hands and knees. With his left hand, he undid both his ankle straps, and was now completely free. He watched her, with his arm outstretched, pointing the gun at her. She stood, with her back toward Nigel and Becker and the rest of them. Nigel pointed Brent's gun at the center of her spine. He tightened up on the trigger, knowing he could blow her straight to hell.

"Lieutenant!" Pinhoe sang into the empty basement for the sole purpose of appeasing the crazy woman in the wheelchair above. *"Lieutenant Kramer. Yoo-hoo!"*

Nigel thought he heard something, or someone calling. He pointed the gun a foot to the left of Frieda and fired twice in rapid succession to attract attention. Frieda turned and looked at Nigel with the expression of a maniac. Nigel returned the expression, staring straight into her psycho eyes. She raised the tranquilizer gun, and Nigel growled, "Don't . . . you . . . dare!"

She continued to raise the pistol, pointing it at him, and Nigel took aim and snapped off six rounds at her left kneecap, blowing her leg completely off—from the kneecap down—and she was knocked backward and off balance from the impact.

With a German accent, Nigel said, "There you go, *Frieda*. You'd better get yourself a pogo stick now. *Ha-ha-ha!*"

Nigel could not have realized at the time that Frieda was out of ammunition.

"IN HERE!!!" Pinhoe yelled. "The shots came from in here." He and Officer Stucky drew their service revolvers and both entered the wine closet. "IS ANYBODY IN THERE?"

"IN HERE!!!" Nigel yelled. "IN HERE. THERE'S A ROOM IN HERE ON THE OTHER SIDE OF THE WALL."

"WHERE?" Pinhoe yelled.

"THE OTHER SIDE OF THE WINE ROOM. PUSH THE LEVERS ON THE FLOOR."

Pinhoe looked at Stucky. " 'Push the levers on the floor,' I thought he said."

"That's what *I* thought he said, too."

They both looked at each other. "Fuck this."

Both officers kicked out the back of the closet like a pair of storm troopers, then came crashing into the egg room.

"DROP IT!" Stucky yelled to Nigel, and assumed an assault stance.

"Whooo!" Nigel said. "Hold on, cowboy. I'm a police officer." Nigel very, very slowly raised Brent's gun till it was pointed straight up at the ceiling; then he very visibly engaged the safety.

"You Lieutenant Kramer?" Pinhoe asked from over by the bloody body of Frieda Marx.

"Yes," Nigel answered, figuring this was the quickest way not to get shot, for the moment; then he placed the gun down on the floor. He walked over to Becker, who was in pain and completely conscious, and twirled the broken tranquilizer dart from his left cheekbone.

Pinhoe examined Frieda Marx, who lay sobbing on the floor. "This is that same woman from last night," he told his partner.

"Oh yeah," Nigel said. "Look what she was about to do." Then he showed the cops the dotted lines on his wrists, not wanting them to show any unnecessary sympathy. "That *thing* on the floor there," Nigel continued, "is the person who's been mutilating all the people in the city. This little woman over here . . . that's the inventor of that great contribution to modern medicine—the hooper! Don't you feel a little tingle just being in her presence? Of course, not the same tingle I felt in my balls a few minutes ago."

In disgust, Nigel removed all the IV-drip tubes from the captive men on the boards—the men he might have been surgically connected to. Then he removed the feed from Sally, removed the straps, and gently placed her on her back on the floor. Siamese quintuplets! Nigel thought with a smile.

In the meantime, Officer Pinhoe kept applying direct pressure to Frieda Marx's leg, or what was left of it. Nigel released the wine closet, and lowered it to the floor of the egg room. Suddenly, it was as if every cop in Nassau County were in the house. Then, in the confusion and all the commotion of recovering people walking about, Nigel very calmly picked up the bullet-amputated leg of Frieda Marx, carried it over to the workstation area, and said, "Free radical this!!" as he stuffed it in a drawer so no one would find it and try to attach it later. This was Nigel's personal gift to Frieda in exchange for the electrotherapy. Always return a favor, he thought.

Frieda Marx sobbed like a child, she had transformed back to that very same little Emily Gordon she once was in childhood and had always been, perhaps. She repeated over and over, "I wanted to save Ookie. Daddy? Daddy? All I wanted to do was save Ookie. My Ookie. My Ookie. Ookie. Ookie? Where are you, Ookie? . . ."

"Who is Ookie?" one of the policemen asked.

"Rosebud," Becker replied, sitting up against the wall of the egg room, attempting to recover from his former student's postgraduate research project, completely unaware that this was a nickname for a lost part of her anatomy.

Without the aid of her wheelchair, Julia Belden slowly and unsteadily walked into the egg room as more police began to appear in her house. She saw Frieda, being packaged on the gurney on the floor of this strange room which she never knew existed, and she saw the bloody leg stump of the woman who'd been a daughter to her all these years. Blood was everywhere. She could not believe her eyes. She overheard the police saying that her daughter was the very person responsible for all those horrible things she'd seen on the television—all those hooper people! She could not believe that any of it was true. She did not believe that any of it *could* be true. She could not believe that all those horrible things were taking place right here, in this room, in her house.

"How did this room get here?" she repeated over and over. It was so big. How did it manage to get built without her knowing about it? It is all too unbelievable, she kept thinking over and over again as she slowly walked around the perimeter of this space, touching the walls, looking at the restraint boards, and all the electronic monitoring equipment, and the strange fixtures and jigs peculiar to her dead son's fiancé's home-brewed profession—all too unbelievable for words.

"Where the hell is it?" Pinhoe said. "It was just here a few minutes ago, damn it! Did someone already take it to the hospital?"

Nigel smirked and tried to pretend he didn't know what on earth Pinhoe was looking for.

It seemed that Officer Pinhoe would have his story to tell at the Christmas party after all.

An order of magnitude more police were mulling about inside the egg room than was actually necessary. But it was more because they had to see the place with their own eyes than because their law-enforcement prowess was required.

Brent Kramer had recovered from his temporary outage, and he and Nassau County detectives led James LeRoy Washington III and Julio Rodriquez out of this madhouse. Julio wasted no time in telling anyone within earshot about the Puerto Rican Vacuum Technique, while James explained to Brent exactly what had happened over at the warehouse with The Doc and his men, describing the shoot-out and his escape and subsequent abduction.

Sally was walking in befuddled circles, and Nigel and Becker stood at the north end of the egg room, still in their gowns, examining all the chemistry apparatus, trying to deduce what chemical process had taken place in this strange room. Becker had a big, swollen purple cheek and a hole leading straight through to one of his sinus cavities, but his curiosity prevented him from leaving.

Becker told Nigel how it was that he came to visit Frieda Marx, about how she had locked him in the egg room, and some of the things Frieda had told him during his incarceration—who she was as Emily Gordon and Joseph Barton, and how he came to be Frieda Marx, and how she fell in love with Arthur, her urologist and surgeon.

Then Nigel casually said, "You know, she'd have had a problem if she'd made Siamese quadruplets out of us."

"Barring any immunological problems, there doesn't seem to be any theoretical problem," Becker said with certainty. "The pulmonary zone of each element would probably be well defined enough that it would remain stable, at least for a while. The blood-flow pattern would be very in-ter-es-ting nonetheless." Becker was now lost in thought, and Nigel was smirking. This was one thing about Becker he really liked. Becker could immerse himself in virtually any subject under the sun, then become completely lost in it, grinding out the technical details way beyond the point of diminishing return. "I wonder what would happen if one of the elements died. I wonder how long the rest would live. I wonder what the death pattern would be for a ring of four people."

"We could have stuck around to find out, but that's not what I was even thinking. There's a more obvious mechanical problem."

"What me-chan-i-cal—"

"Well, it's kind of like those guys who spend five years of their life building a boat or an airplane in their basement. Then one day they realize they can't get the damn thing out of the house."

Becker looked at Nigel. "You're right. If they were all unconscious, how would she get it out? I mean them." Both men explosively laughed.

Then Nigel said, "They'd have to all be awake. They'd ... sort of have to roll themselves out, like a tractor tread. It would be like leading a large, funny sort a ... class trip. . . ."

Brent Kramer approached the two men in blue gowns. "Why don't the two of you get the hell out of here?" Turning to Becker, he continued, "And you should probably get yourself to a hospital and get that cheek taken care of."

Sally watched Nigel rummaging through the refrigerator, looking at all the different drugs and bottles of interesting chemicals, and she grew more furious with each passing second he ignored her.

Brent sensed her distress and said, "Are you okay? You look like hell."

"I'm okay. I'm beginning to feel a little better now, but I think I'm going to commit a murder soon." With rage that was difficult to contain, she slowly approached Nigel.

". . . There are still some things I don't understand," Becker said, pondering Frieda's belief that she had absorbed Arthur and that they had become one single person.

"What's there to understand?" Nigel said flippantly. "Joey Barton went ahead and got himself a misterectomy. That's when you have your mister removed. A misterectomy—get it?"

"I'm gonna give *you* a misterectomy!" Sally said, with her hands clenched in fists.

Nigel put his hands on Sally's waist and said, "Sweetheart, if she'd have connected the four of us in a ring, we could all go crazy together, every time *you* had a period!"

Sally's face puckered and she growled in disgust.

唔怪得之你老婆離開你.

[No wonder your wife leave you]

Nigel removed the dart-loading fixture from the refrigerator and handed it to Brent, who studied it, trying to figure out how it worked. Then Nigel opened the freezer compartment, and two frozen hands slid out and hit the floor with a pair of dull thuds. Nigel picked them up and dropped them onto a stainless steel work surface. "It was very thoughtful of her," Nigel said, "to leave us some leftovers. I'm getting hungry. I presume we could just nuke 'em and slip 'em between two slices of rye bread."

Brent, Becker, and Sally looked at the frozen severed hands in horror. Nigel removed more hands from the freezer, and deliberately dropped them to the counter surface from high enough so they made a loud rattling noise when they hit. "Will someone lend me a hand here? Hey, look at this. . . . Give someone an inch and they take a foot . . . well, actually . . . four feet, to be exact. . . ." Nigel held out one of the frozen hands and said, "We should send this over to that palm reader . . . Madam what's-her-name . . ."

He dropped four frozen legs on the surface, and Brent, Sally, and Becker watched the growing crazy expression on Nigel's face. "You could decorate the tree with these," Nigel said. "Wait! I have a better idea! It's Christmas season, right? In the spirit of Christmas, let's feed the homeless to the homeless. Helping neighborhoods to help themselves. What a holiday slogan. I'm sure our mayor wouldn't have lost the election if only he'd run with that slogan. Feed the homeless to the homeless! I *really* like it." Then as Nigel dropped the last hand onto the pile, Sally turned, shook her head, and walked out of the egg room, muttering to herself in Cantonese.

Brent looked at the hands and legs, attempting to pair rights with lefts. Then Nigel said, "You might find that the oldest ones have the most frost on them."

"Yeah, yeah. But something else is wrong. . . ."

"Brent, there's so much wrong with this place. . . ."

"We had Freddy Lopez, and Jerome Lewis, and Rusty Blake, and Alex Hall, and Jesus Romero. Right? We have four legs, and we have twelve hands. We should only have ten hands and four legs. There's an extra set of hands. There's an extra hooper somewhere."

"So?"

"And something else is missing, Nigel."

Nigel looked at Brent innocently and said in a southern accent, "Why, whatever could *that* be?"

"Frieda Marx's leg, Nigel. What did *you* do with the leg?"

"Here, give her one of these," Nigel said, then tossed one of the frozen legs at Brent, who let it fall to the floor.

"Nigel!"

"Don't you think Frieda Marx would make a great one-legged flamenco dancer?"

"Nigel, what did you do with the leg?"

"*Ohhhhh* . . . I'm sure . . . when the time comes . . . someone'll smell it. . . ."

Julia Belden walked back up the cellar stairs with an energy she hadn't felt in years, but she was exhausted nonetheless. She stood in the center of the living room, feeling like a stranger in her own house. People seemed to be everywhere, talking, measuring things with tape measures, taking pictures, having conversations, talking on cellular telephones; there was even a man taking the temperature of that room in the basement. It was like some grand surrealistic dream she was sleepwalking through, and none of the characters in this waking nightmare so much as even looked at her or acknowledged her existence, or the fact that they were in *her* house. "Times have certainly changed," she said out loud to herself with detached resignation.

And then the silence of her thought was broken by the sound of a tall, heavy man in a suit, who even looked a little like Arthur, except that Arthur had had a full head of hair. "Excuse me, ma'am," he said. "Are you the owner of this house?"

"Yes, I am," Julia said with a smile, then patted her hair with both hands.

"My name is Lieutenant Nussbaum. I have a few questions I would like to ask you."

"You seem like such a nice young man. Are you married?"

The lieutenant was caught completely off guard by this strange but prophetic question; his divorce had just come through the day before, and his mind was not really on his job. He smiled and said, "No, ma'am. As a matter of fact, I'm not." They looked into each other's eyes for close to half a minute, then the lieutenant said, "I need to ask you some questions, ma'am."

"Please, Lieutenant, call me Julia."

"Julia—"

"Excuse me for one moment. I need to go upstairs. I'll be right back."

Julia walked slowly, but all by herself, over to the stairs. As she walked up, she looked at the groove in the wall which had supported the mechanical chair that had carried her up and down for so many years, except when Frieda carried her like a child in her big strong arms.

Julia Belden crawled into bed and climbed under the covers. Suddenly, she grew very cold. She grabbed the TV remote control and flicked on the television, just in time to see Kaity Tong on her snow-covered front lawn, only a few feet away from where she lay in her bed. The newswoman was speaking into a microphone, live. A tear rolled down Julia's cheek as she muted the sound. She closed her eyes, softly called the name Ben in her mind, and a moment later, she joined him, wherever he was.

71   Epilogue

Nigel Atkerson walked up the path leading to Becker Instlokrownctjz's house and saw all the closed-circuit television cameras track his movements to the front door. Then, as he reached out his hand to ring the bell, the door opened, and the forbidding form of Becker stood there in the shadows, as it had done so many times in the past.

"Here," Nigel said, "I thought you should have this." Nigel

then handed him the plant that Frieda Marx had created and nurtured for so many years—the plant known as Becker's Ring. "Emily, Joseph, Jo, Ookie, and/or Frieda won't be around to take care of it, and it seems such a waste to just let it die of neglect in a big empty house."

"Thank you," Becker said, taking the clay pot from Nigel. "I will give it a good home."

"They might need it as evidence when the trial comes up, but I personally don't think it's gonna make a damn bit of difference whether the prosecution, or the defense, has the plant or they don't. I don't give a rat's ass for all the psychological angles they'll concoct to explain why she did what she did. 'Misterectomy rage,' they'll probably call it. Woman's guilty as sin."

Again, Nigel had referred to a brilliant creation as a "plant," in that condescending tone of voice. Nigel was a heathen. It didn't matter, though. A gift was a gift. Becker rubbed the bandage on his cheek and said, "Well, it's here if they need it. And don't stand there in the cold. Come in."

"I can't. Sally's in the car. I only stopped by to drop the plant off."

"Wait, there is something I need to give you. . . ." Becker carried his brand-new acquisition into his living room, where he delicately put it down on a table. Then a moment later, he returned to his front door and handed Nigel a ring. "This has been in my family for over two hundred years, but I want you to give it to James, for his wedding."

Nigel examined the shape and size of the diamonds, then said, "Becker, this must be worth a fortune."

"It is, but it's not doing me any good. And you have given me something much more valuable than a piece of crystalline carbon. Please, I would like for James to have this, as a gift from me."

"Then so it shall be," Nigel said. "I'll call ya later." Nigel ran down the path to the car as Becker walked over to the clay pot, sat in front of Becker's Ring, turned on a high-intensity lamp, and proceeded to examine every square inch of it with a jeweler's loupe.

Sally drove off, with Nigel next to her, and she still did not want to talk. His hand crept slowly toward her as she drove along. "You know," he said, "I did a little shopping, and picked up a whole box of . . . Well, if you're interested, we could . . ."

唔怪得之你老婆離開你．

[No wonder your wife leave you]

"Can't we have one conversation about *us* for a change, and leave my ex-wife out of this?"

"I told you, I do not *like* that man."

"Who, Becker?"

"Who else—the man in the moon? I'm hungry. I wanna get some coffee, and take your hand off my lap."

"You have to let go of it first."

"Now, why do you call me *P* Cubed? . . ."

Becker's '48 Chrysler Windsor was recovered from the swamp in Mattituck, and while the deleterious effects of the entropy were not entirely reversible, he nursed his machine back to its former mechanical proficiency.

Warden McFarland was slightly pickled again when he received a summons to appear before a special internal review panel. His performance pertaining to a recent criminal investigation was to be examined in great detail. His willful lack of action had directly resulted in the mutilation of the paroled prisoner, Alex Hall, whom he had released despite the communication, in writing, by Lt. Brent Kramer, of the NYPD. The $100 million lawsuit against the Department of Corrections was an extra little thorn, and Brent would be appearing on behalf of the plaintiff.

Mr. McFarland, as his status soon became, would add to his misery by perjuring himself numerous times, denying he'd received anything in writing from the New York City police lieutenant telling him to detain the prisoner. He destroyed the letter and all records of its existence, which added obstruction of justice to the list of charges. The ex-warden even denied at first that the voice on the tape was his, which meant one of two things: either he really was a drunken sot or he was purposely misspeaking the truth. Unfortunately for him, the answer was C: all of the above, and, after numerous delays and appeals, Mr. McFarland's name eventually became 42662938.

One day, after settling into his new home, he received an audiocassette with four songs recorded in the following order:

"It Had to Be You," as sung by Frank Sinatra
"Cocktails for Two," by Spike Jones
"What a Wonderful World," sung by Louis Armstrong
"We'll Meet Again," by Kate Smith

And, for added effect, just so the former prison warden would never again suffer a lapse of memory, there was the tape-recorded conversation he had had with the two-bit cop, and the conversation repeated over and over, until the end of the tape, so he would know whom to thank.

There was nothing recorded on side B of the tape, which was labeled "Your Pension, Sonny Boy."

Julio Rodriquez continued to haunt the bars of downtown Newark, and he continued to tell his most famous story, "The Puerto Rican Vacuum Technique," until the day he died of sclerosis of the liver, proving once again, that some people insist upon killing themselves no matter how many second chances they are given to live a better life.

Andy Belden was the sole survivor of his mother, Julia Belden. The house, the money, the securities, and other assets all fell into his reluctant lap, and the entire fortune funneled its way to the Hare Krishnas, who used the money to increase their numbers.

After the capture of Frieda Marx, the public grew bored with the novelty of Jerome Lewis and Rusty Blake, and when Marshall Stanley's traveling show hit the malls and taco chains of the southwest, Marshall realized it was finally time to call it quits. He even managed to squeeze a few dollars from the presurgical-separation publicity, being that the hoopers were growing anxious and no longer cared to wait for the trial and its anticipated publicity, and eventually, all that remained of Marshall's profit center was a pair of men without hands and the 900 number.

All the money that had accumulated in Marshall Stanley's Save the Hooper fund did help pay for a series of experimental high-tech prosthetic devices designed and installed on the limbs of the mutilation victims by Dr. Alvin Lent, of the Lent Institute.

Marshall Stanley now imports novelty dime-store trash from Hong Kong, and one of his items is the always popular Chinese handcuffs—those little braided straw tubes that join fingers together.

While his mouth reconstruction was not entirely successful, Freddy Lopez, a.k.a. *Zippy,* the first and most forgotten mutilation victim, is now one of the many helpful information operators at AT&T.

It was a beautiful afternoon for a Saturday wedding in early June at the Cathedral of Saint John the Divine in New York City. Bishop Wilson was the presiding servant of the Lord for the matrimonial union of James LeRoy Washington III and Sharon Weiner, Esq. The governor of the state of New York was the presiding servant of the people, followed by the past and present mayors of the city of New York. The present and former chiefs of police were also present, along with more than half the police and detectives of the Midtown North police precinct. Naturally, some of the borough presidents and a handful of councilmen and state senators had to show their faces so they could score points. Then there was the small army of political hacks to fill out the pews a bit, and very few even knew who the hell this interracial couple was that getting married, but it had to be important.

Nigel Atkerson leaned over to Sally Chu and Brent's wife, Tammy, and said, "Did you ever see the movie *Pocketful of Miracles?*"

"No," they said almost in unison.

But Becker *had* seen the movie and began to laugh. Then Becker said to Nigel, "By the way, I started work on the design of your custom tree."

"Which custom tree?" Nigel said, squinting at Becker.

"The one in the shape of a nude, the nude with the fig leaf; remember?"

"Oh, yes," Nigel said, jogging his memory. "You're not really ..."

"You should know me better by now, Nigel. I have worked out most of the technical details."

"You're really serious, aren't you?"

"Dead serious. Consider it ... sort of a textbook exercise in preparation for my next group of experiments. I am going to make ... what I call, piezo trees. They will generate electricity when the wind blows through the leaves. Imagine, forests of trees that make their own electricity when the wind blows."

Nigel said, "Then you'll have to make storage-battery trees to store the power."

"*Hmmmmm ...*" Becker sang. "Storage-battery trees. Now *that's* a thought. . . ."

Sally said to Nigel, "If he makes storage-battery trees, then I could have *my* chance to electrocute *you,* if you touched the wrong tree." Then Sally whispered into Nigel's ear after licking it, "I *told* you I don't like that man. Now, why do you call me *P* Cubed?"

The low-grade chatter was interrupted by the first powerful chord from the pipe organ, and all grew quiet in the pews.

Lt. Brenton Kramer was the best man for James LeRoy Washington III, and in his pocket he fondled the two-hundred-year-old ring Becker had given to James for his wedding.

Sharon Weiner looked magnificent. None of her friends could believe she had such clout, albeit the result of what started out as an irrational fetish attraction for black men. And Sharon's incredibly Jewish mother could not come to the impossible terms that not only was her daughter marrying a black man in a church, but that it was to be televised for all her friends at the temple to watch on the TV.

But it's not every day that a Brooklyn nobody gets to meet the governor and the mayor in the same day. It's a story she would tell for the rest of her life.